A Time to Kill

Stephen Puleston

ABOUT THE AUTHOR

Stephen Puleston was born and educated in Anglesey, North Wales. He graduated in theology before training as a lawyer. A Time to Kill is his fifth novel in the Inspector Drake series

www.stephenpuleston.co.uk
Facebook:stephenpulestoncrimewriter

OTHER NOVELS

Inspector Drake Mysteries

Brass in Pocket
Worse than Dead
Against the Tide
Dead on your Feet
Prequel Novella– Ebook only
Devil's Kitchen

Inspector Marco Novels

Speechless
Another Good Killing
Somebody Told Me
Prequel Novella– Ebook only
Dead Smart

ISBN-13:978-1985720084
ISBN-10:1985720086

In memory of my mother
Gwenno Puleston

Chapter 1

Darkness descended like a thin shroud, smothering the last remnants of daylight.

Harry Jones reached the top of the wooden staircase and stood looking out over the lake letting his breath get back to normal. The last of the evening gloom filtered away and he gazed over at the Quarryman's Hospital. It looked grey and foreboding and the dense trees covering the hillside seemed to press down on it. Another hour and it would be pitch black, Harry thought. Why were they meeting here? He drew the lapels of his coat to his cheeks: at this time of year, he could think of better places.

The fine gravel of the path crunched under the soles of his shoes as he made for the main entrance of the old hospital building. He had been inside many times and each occasion learned something new about the injuries men suffered blasting slate from the nearby quarry.

He glanced to his left towards the small mortuary building where a path led off into the heavy shadows of the trees. He reached the hospital doorway and stood glancing around, hoping he wouldn't have to wait too long. Over to his left a sound like footfall on dry twigs spooked him and he peered into the darkness.

Nothing.

He read the time again, resolving to stay another few minutes before heading home.

He cut across the lawn in front of the hospital and neared the red railings looking out over the lake. Thickening clouds billowed overhead and the lights of the town glowed below him. The sweet smell of pine and conifer filled the air. It made him recall his childhood in the village when the forests and the paths through them had been his playgrounds.

He turned sharply when he heard a sound behind him and he thought he noticed movement, perhaps a figure wearing a long winter coat. He paced over towards the far end of the building, knowing a gravelled road led down to the lake.

No one.

He squinted over, a sense of unease invading his mind.

He looked at his watch again, annoyed now; angry that he was here on a fool's errand. Five more minutes and he'd retrace his steps down the wooden staircase, along the footpath at the edge of the lake and then back home.

Nothing particularly enticed him home. Long ago he had fallen out of love with his wife who had announced that morning she was visiting her mother and that he'd find a ready meal in the freezer. At least there was a decent crime drama on the television.

He wandered back under a Scots pine, tapping out a message on his mobile. The signal was poor so he moved his position hoping it would improve.

An owl hooting and a crowing bird of prey somewhere above him unsettled Harry. The hair on the back of his neck bristled. When he heard movement behind him, he turned sharply, his heart racing. A badger scampered past the hospital. He really didn't like being in this place during the hours of darkness.

Then something more substantial took his attention.

This time he saw the unmistakable shape of

someone moving near the corner of the hospital but it was a fleeting glance and not enough for Harry to recognise who it might be.

His mouth dried. If it wasn't who he was expecting, who could it possibly be?

'Harry.'

He recognised the voice and immediately relaxed.

Harry walked over, puzzled when he saw the figure retreating from view; he picked up his pace and soon reached the bin enclosure behind the building, the smell of stale food prickling his nostrils.

'What the hell are you doing?' Harry said.

'I could ask the same about you.'

'I don't know what you—'

'It's very simple. Some things need to be left unchanged. Enough is enough. I have had more than I can stomach of you.'

Harry stepped forward.

'You're talking in riddles. I know things have been difficult but—'

'Difficult. You bastard, how dare you …'

'Now look …'

A hand dipped into a jacket pocket and in a smooth movement drew out a heavy object. The moon broke through a thinning section of cloud and a brief flash lit up the muzzle of a handgun pointing at Harry's chest. He swallowed hard, his feet rooted to the spot, but a voice in his head shouted at him to run. Instead he froze. A practised eye told him it was an old weapon, so part of his mind wanted to believe it was a museum piece.

'I don't understand. What do you want?' Harry tried to sound reasonable, using a soft tone.

This wasn't happening, simply couldn't be true. He must be dreaming. He'd wake up soon and it would be morning. But his hammering pulse reminded him he was alive and staring down the barrel of a gun.

'Some things are a step too far.'

Harry watched the trigger being pulled.

The sound of the gun shattered the silence.

The last thing Harry thought about was his mother. He even tried forming her name on his lips. He fell to the floor, the gap in the clouds closed, the moon disappeared.

Darkness.

Chapter 2

Detective Inspector Ian Drake drummed the fingers of both hands over the top of the steering wheel of his Ford Mondeo. He had been stationary for no more than five minutes although it felt like much longer. Roadworks were to blame for the traffic chaos on the A55, the major route that stretched along the North Wales coast. Being so early in the morning exacerbated Drake's irritation. He glanced at the clock on the dashboard.

Unless he made progress soon he and Sara would be late for their interview at Caernarfon police station. Articulated lorries streamed past them in the opposite direction: he couldn't even see the red light.

'When are they going to finish all these alterations?' Sara said.

Drake was accustomed to her measured tone. He didn't reply immediately but stared straight ahead hoping he could get through the one-way system when the lights next changed.

'Superintendent Price circulated a memo last month. Apparently the work of removing the roundabouts in Penmaenmawr and Llanfairfechan will take a couple of years.'

'The traffic department can't be too pleased with that.'

Drake nodded.

One accident would be enough to bring the entire A55 to a halt in the middle of summer with its caravans and trailers and families heading for the beaches and holiday camps. Three enormous lorries passed Drake, shedding a fine dust over his car; he sprayed the windscreen and washed away most of the dirt, resolving that he'd have to clean the car again. The inside still smelled fresh and clean after the deep clean the previous weekend – exactly as he liked it.

'Shall we review the interview notes, boss?' Sara said.

More vehicles passed Drake. He read the time again, worrying he might be late for their interview with a serial house-burglar. A homeowner, returning unexpectedly early from visiting his daughter in Lincoln, had caught the man red-handed. The property was a large detached house in the country. One of the local detectives had established that the owner's house cleaner shared details about the valuables that were to be found at the various properties where she worked. In exchange for this information, she received ready cash that made a much-needed dent in her substantial credit card bill.

Drake glanced over at Sara, the file open on her lap.

'Good idea,' Drake said.

Sara started to review the basic format of the interview they had planned the previous afternoon, as the vehicles ahead of Drake moved off. He crunched the car into first gear and slowly followed the van in front of him. He prayed silently that he could negotiate the contraflow system before the light turned red and it was a relief when he passed the traffic lights still on green.

He changed down through the gears and soon he engaged cruise control.

Sara read aloud their draft questions. Drake interjected occasionally, making mental notes of questions to ask the suspect, as he took the junction for Caernarfon and left the A55. After parking they negotiated the security protocols at the police station and headed to the custody suite.

The sergeant in charge was a man in his forties with thinning hair and an enormous paunch. His face looked leathered. 'Detective Inspector Drake. You can have the day off!' He said.

Drake frowned. 'What do you mean?'

'Your man isn't here.'

Traffic delays and a smartarse custody sergeant weren't going to improve Drake's mood.

'He's just been taken to hospital. He complained of chest pains. It must have been the prospect of being interviewed by you.' The sergeant grinned.

Drake didn't find it funny.

'We got the doctor to him this morning. I organised for one of our uniformed lads and a probationer to go with him in the ambulance.'

Drake drew a hand through his hair. He couldn't afford a wasted day; he already had a pile of reports back in headquarters that would require hours of work.

'You can go and have a *paned*,' the sergeant said. The harsh Scouse accent made the Welsh word for a cup of tea sound odd. Drake guessed it was the only Welsh word the officer knew.

In the canteen, Sara volunteered to organise their drinks. Drake sat down and watched her as she reached the counter and spoke to one of the staff. It had been almost six months since her first day on his team. She was fitting in well, becoming accustomed to how he liked things done. When Caren Waits, his previous sergeant, had left for maternity leave he harboured doubts; perhaps having a new partner would make things difficult. But he reassured himself that Sara would have no inkling about the rituals that forced him to order and reorder his paperwork, and keep regimented colour-coordinated lists of Post It notes. A recent documentary about obsessive-compulsive disorder had followed a mother and daughter who couldn't sleep in their own beds because to do so would cause the sheets to crease. At least he wasn't that bad – never had been. And knowing the Wales Police Service's counsellor was at the end of the telephone helped.

Looking at Sara reminded him of the way Sian, his estranged wife, could grab his attention. Sara was slim, like Sian. There was something different about Sara's hair that morning, perhaps she had cut it differently. The auburn colour seemed a shade darker too. He knew her to be unmarried but otherwise he hadn't heard her mention a boyfriend. He quickly smothered any romantic aspirations. There was a protocol about officers being romantically involved; there was a protocol for everything these days. And he had Helen and Megan, his daughters, to think about.

Sara returned carrying a tray with two mugs.

Drake turned up his nose at the mug of weak-looking coffee she placed in front of him.

'Sorry about the coffee, boss. It's cheap instant.'

Drake nodded.

Sara sat down and took a sip of her tea.

Drake reached over for his drink as his mobile rang. He recognised area control.

'Drake.'

'We have a missing persons report for you to

investigate.'

'Missing person?' Drake looked up at Sara; she showed her interest by raising her eyebrows. But it was hardly the stuff for his team.

'The chief inspector in Caernarfon has approved it with Superintendent Price.'

'Is there nobody else?'

For a moment, Drake thought about marching up to the DCI's office and giving him a piece of his mind about allocating a missing persons inquiry to a detective inspector. The woman from area control wouldn't have mentioned Wyndham Price's name unless it were true.

'Send me the details.' Drake finished the call without waiting for a reply.

'Missing person?' Sara said, getting a degree of interest into her voice.

He nodded, reached for his drink and took a mouthful. 'A woman has reported her husband missing.' Drake grimaced at the tasteless liquid. Moments later, his mobile bleeped into life. He studied the message.

'It's in Llanberis,' Drake said, allowing the relief that the village wasn't too much of a detour on his way back to headquarters to filter into his voice.

'I did a couple of missing person inquiries when I started out in Wrexham,' Sara said.

Drake pushed the unfinished coffee to one side. 'A satisfactory outcome to both?'

Sara shook her head. 'The wife who was reported missing had gone to live with an old boyfriend in Inverness. When we traced her, she told us she'd been wanting to leave her husband for years. She begged us not tell him where she was. But in the other case we found a dead body in a lake. It looked like suicide.'

Drake and Sara returned to the car park. It took less than fifteen minutes until the voice on the satnav formally announced they had reached their destination. Drake parked outside the home of Harry and Fiona Jones. It was a detached property with a bay window on the ground floor matching a similar one on the bedroom above it. The slates on the roof were the dark blue variety from the local Dinorwig quarry.

Carefully tended flowerbeds lined the garden, the bark covering their surfaces a disincentive for any weeds. Drake paced up to the front door, Sara following behind. He glanced at his watch. It should be routine: check the details, establish an identity, get a list of friends and a sense of any conflict in the family, before handing the whole case to the sergeant in charge of missing persons at headquarters.

The doorbell rang and a few seconds elapsed before they heard footsteps walking across what sounded like bare tiles. A woman in her mid-fifties, blotchy expression, tired eyes and a face with despair etched into her skin opened the door and stared at Drake and Sara. Drake looked down at her, guessing she was about five foot five. He smiled and gave her a cursory flash of his warrant card.

'I'm Detective Inspector Ian Drake and this is Detective Sergeant Sara Morgan. I understand you reported your husband missing. I've been asked to take some preliminary details from you.'

Fiona Jones stood rooted to the spot looking first at Drake and then at Sara, as though she couldn't quite make out what she should say.

'Have you found him?' Her bottom lip quivered.

'Mrs Jones, may we come in?'

Fiona regained some composure. 'Of course. I'm sorry.'

She led Drake and Sara into the front sitting room filled with well-polished and expensive-looking antiques. Watercolours hung from a picture rail in heavy frames and Drake noticed Sara scanning them carefully. Fiona perched on the edge of a chaise longue, twisting a white handkerchief through her fingers. Drake sat on a sofa, a coffee table in front of him displaying magazines and two hardback books, one with a striking image of a lighthouse perched on a cliff. Sara sat down and gave Drake a brief smile as he turned to face Fiona.

'Can you give us more details about your husband? When did you realise he was missing?'

'Last night.'

'Can you be more precise, please?'

'I was expecting him to be back by the time I arrived home.'

'So when did you arrive home?'

'About ten.'

Drake sighed to himself. 'So, it's about twelve hours since you expected to see him.' There wasn't a minimum time period before the police would investigate a missing person – each case was judged on the individual facts. Drake continued. 'Did you know where Harry was going last night?'

'Some council thing.'

'What council is that?'

'The local parish council. They had some meeting about the development of the quarry.'

'Do you know the name of the council secretary?'

Fiona shook her head. 'John something, maybe …
Harry knew all their names.'

'So, when did you see Harry last?'

'I saw him at lunchtime when I called into the
shop. I told him I was going to visit my mother. She's
just left hospital.'

'What shop does Harry run?' Drake was warming
up to ask Fiona about her marriage.

'The antique shop in the village. But what has that
got to do with anything?'

'I need as much information about Harry as
possible. Does he have any financial problems?'

Fiona Jones frowned at Drake, 'No, of course not.
Don't be stupid. Why are you asking these questions?
You should go out and find him.'

Fiona blinked rapidly.

'We need to build a complete picture of your
husband and his life. It's very likely we shall have to
ask you a lot of questions about Harry.' He paused and
looked over at Fiona but she avoided his eye contact.
'And we'll need a photograph of your husband.'

Fiona nodded. 'I found this.' She handed Drake a
passport-sized image. Drake gave it a cursory glance
before sharing it with Sara.

'And we need to ask you about your relationship
with Harry.'

Fiona moved back a few inches, drawing together
her composure.

'What are you suggesting?'

'I'm not suggesting anything, Mrs Jones. I
appreciate this must be a difficult time for you.' Drake
paused; perhaps handling a missing person inquiry was
something he needed to practise more. 'We have to

consider all eventualities.' Drake smiled as he finished.

Fiona raised her hands in exasperation. 'Just find him, please.'

Drake's mobile vibrated in his pocket. He was tempted to ignore it until he had finished with Fiona Jones, but he reached for the telephone and read the message. *Urgent – please contact area control, murder investigation pending.* Drake stood up abruptly.

'I'm sorry, we need to leave. I'll get another officer to contact you in due course.'

Drake and Sara left a distressed Fiona Jones standing at the front door, her arms folded in front of her.

Drake jogged down to his car thrusting his mobile to his ear.

'Detective Inspector Drake. What are the details about the homicide?'

'A body has been discovered near the old Quarryman's Hospital in Llanberis.'

Drake stopped and stood, scarcely believing what the detached voice from area control had actually said. 'Llanberis?' In the distance Drake made out the chimney pots of the historic building perched on a ledge overlooking the lake.

'Yes, Inspector. I'll send you the details of the officers at the scene.'

Drake glanced towards the house, but Fiona had gone inside. He turned to face Sara. 'I think that photograph of Harry Jones might be useful. There's a report of a body.'

Chapter 3

'A body has been found near the old Quarryman's Hospital.' Drake waved a hand in the air, pointing in the general direction of the densely wooded hillside on the opposite side of the lake.

He yanked open the car door, and it took just seconds to clip their seatbelts in place before Drake floored the accelerator. The Quarryman's Hospital had long since stopped treating patients and was now part of the sprawling slate museum, a popular tourist attraction. He passed the Llanberis Lake Railway terminus on his way to the museum car park.

'Do you think it could be Harry Jones?' Sara said.

Drake made no reply: he had been thinking that exact thought since leaving Fiona Jones. If it was Harry Jones, a routine missing person inquiry would become a murder investigation.

He glanced out of the windscreen at the massive gaping wound in the mountain where slate had been extracted from the Dinorwig quarry and exported all over the world. The various inclines and piles of slate waste and discarded buildings were the only record of activities that once employed thousands of men.

Drake turned left and approached the entrance of the museum. A uniformed officer waved at him and pointed to a place for him to park.

Tourists milled around, coats shrugged onto shoulders, cars locked, rucksacks threaded over arms. Some glanced over at them as Drake and Sara made their way across the car park, the occasional worried frown on their faces. Others stood on the station platform ready for the narrow-gauge train, and others wandered off to the slate museum nearby.

'Chris Bell, sir.' The young officer had pimples and a pallid, frightened look. 'The staff at the hospital found the body. It was dumped behind the building.'

The sound of police sirens filled the air as two more cars arrived.

Two uniformed officers from each car ran over to Drake and Sara.

Drake scanned the various faces. 'I want a full perimeter established. Nobody gets anywhere near the hospital.'

Heads nodded.

Drake raised a hand towards a footpath that led around the side of the lake. 'There's an outcrop over there that leads to a staircase that goes up to the hospital building. One of you go to the top and make certain you stop anybody coming through the forest passing the possible crime scene. Tell them to retrace their steps.'

'A train is due to leave in the next ten minutes,' Bell said, clearly wanting Drake to make a decision.

The likelihood of the killer being on the train taking passengers to the end of the lake and back again was remote. But he had a crime scene to secure, a murderer to catch. He couldn't take chances.

'Get down and tell them to stop the train. Record the names and addresses of everybody, no exceptions. And get more officers down here straightaway.' Drake turned to Sara. 'Come on, let's go.'

They made their way to the track from the car park up to the hospital. Drake grimaced silently as the gravel and dirt covered his recently cleaned black brogues. And the hems of his trousers would be filthy, so he picked up his pace, blanking out worries about his clothes.

They'd been walking for a couple of minutes when Drake's mobile rang.

He recognised the voice of Mike Foulds, the crime scene manager from headquarters.

'Where are you, Mike?'

For the first time in any of his murder inquiries, Drake had been near to the scene when he'd received the initial call. The first twenty-four hours of any case was crucial. But would that make any difference when the crime scene investigators were the key to securing evidence? Even so, it gave Drake a powerful sense of being close to the killer.

'I should be with you in fifteen minutes.'

Drake turned to Sara. 'CSIs are on their way.'

Drake hurried on and soon he saw the gable of the hospital. Three people stood outside, anxious faces, nails being chewed.

A uniformed officer emerged from a small enclosure behind a ground-floor annex that abutted the main building. Behind him, Drake noticed several large wheelie bins.

'Over here, sir.'

Drake strode over towards him. 'Constable Chris Newland, sir. The body's over there in the corner.'

Drake edged his way around two wheelie bins, a wooden pallet propped against a side wall and various flattened cardboard boxes.

He stopped as he reached the end, taking everything in. He blanked out the whispered voices behind him, the murmurings of animals and birds in the forest stretching high above him. He scarcely registered Sara's presence by his side.

The body of a man lay discarded and dumped in a bloody mess. His sweater, stained a deep crimson, suggested he had either been stabbed or shot. The leather jacket looked expensive, the check lining once a delicate buff check now smeared with blood.

'Is it …?' Sara said.

'Give me the photograph.'

Sara passed it over and Drake gave it a long look before stepping nearer the corpse. He held it out and glanced back and forth until he was satisfied.

He stepped back. 'No question, the face matches.'

'So we've got another trip to see Fiona Jones.'

Drake gave Sara a sharp look, uncertain if he sensed any criticism in her voice. Had he been too short with Fiona Jones? Now he was investigating a murder and his questioning of Fiona Jones would be quite different. She had appeared evasive, but was it more than confusion and raw emotion? Was the report of her husband being missing part of an elaborate ploy? They'd be finding out a lot more about Fiona Jones in due course.

He tilted his head back towards Jones. 'There's probably identification on the body. So we'll wait for the CSIs to do a search.'

Sara nodded.

'In the meantime let's go and talk to the person who found him.'

Drake retraced his steps to the gable of the building. The body's location, in the far corner of the bin enclosure, suggested the killer had lured his victim there. But why was Jones in such an isolated spot? Had he met his killer for a prearranged rendezvous? Or had this been a spur-of-the-moment killing? And if so, why? Their second discussion with Fiona Jones would be quite different from the first, Drake concluded.

He walked over with Sara to Constable Newland, the uniformed officer standing with three people who Drake guessed were the staff of the Quarryman's Hospital.

Drake spoke to the officer. 'Who found the body?'

'Lisa Parry, sir.' Newland tilted his head at the older woman at the end of the group. Her short curly hair covered an unruly, disorganised face. She sniffed loudly and blew into a tissue.

Drake felt the chill of the early October air. 'Let's go inside. It'll be more comfortable.' Drake turned to Newland. 'Just make certain nobody gets anywhere near the crime scene and tell me when the CSIs arrive.'

The tepid warmth of the hallway in the Quarryman's Hospital barely took the edge off the autumn temperature. But the worried faces Drake had seen outside relaxed once they were in a familiar environment. He looked at all three in turn. 'Who was the first to arrive this morning?'

'I'm the manager,' the man said. 'I was here first, about 8:30.'

'Did you see anything unusual?'

'No, I don't think so—'

'Did you notice anybody else, anybody at all? Early-morning walkers, people taking a stroll, walking the dog?'

He shook his head. 'I didn't pass anyone. I never do at this time of the year.'

'Have any of the bins been moved?'

'I don't think so.'

He turned again to Lisa. 'Tell me how you found

the body?'

She blinked nervously, shot a glance at the older man and pursed her lips.

'I was taking some rubbish out to one of the bins – it's one of my jobs. We've been cleaning one of the store rooms and there was lots of old paper and cardboard. And every morning we empty the bins from the day before.'

She paused, composing herself.

'I took out some cardboard first and then I took out the black bin bags. I was going to the furthest wheelie bin. That's when I saw his shoe. I couldn't believe it.' She put a hand to her mouth, the horror of the memory still raw.

'Tell me exactly what you remember.'

Lisa stared at Drake. 'There was blood … And he didn't move. I just knew.'

'We'll need to take detailed statements from you in due course.' Drake struck a helpful tone. 'Sergeant Morgan will take down telephone numbers and addresses. If you do remember anything unusual you must contact us.'

Three heads nodded in unison.

'Do you have CCTV?' It was a standard question, but Drake had no realistic expectation the place would have any.

'No,' the manager said. 'We're only a small museum.'

Drake stepped towards a table by the entrance and opened the pages of the visitors' book. He read the last two entries; a husband and wife from Rotherham thought the place 'magical', a woman from Wisconsin had jotted down 'such a valuable historical record'.

'Will we be able to open today?'

Drake glanced at him. 'Of course not, this is a crime scene. We'll need all your fingerprints in order to eliminate you from the inquiry.'

Now he gazed at three frightened faces.

Drake left the building with Sara and stood for a moment checking his messages. Mike Foulds had been caught up in the same traffic they had experienced earlier. It would be another ten minutes before he'd arrive. Drake made his way over to the ancient red railings that topped a wall in front of a lawned area. He and Sara looked out over the lake.

'Why was he killed here?' Sara said.

'He must have been meeting someone he knew.'

'Like his wife?'

'We treat her as a person of interest for sure.'

They both knew that most murders were committed by someone known to the victim.

Drake continued. 'I got the feeling she was hiding something. Something about Harry or their marriage. We'll need to tread carefully when we speak to her again.'

A vehicle approached up the roadway, its engine straining in low gear. Drake and Sara retraced their steps to the officer standing wide-legged before the bin enclosure. The scientific support vehicle parked and Mike Foulds jumped out, followed by another investigator.

'Good morning, Mike.'

'You got here pronto.'

'We were in the area.'

'Really?'

'We were dealing with a missing person report—,'

'And you think this body is that misper?'

Drake shrugged. 'I need you to examine the body for identification.' Drake motioned for Foulds to follow him towards the crime scene.

Once they reached the bin enclosure Foulds climbed into a one-piece white suit and snapped on a pair of latex gloves. Expertly he dug through all of the pockets in the leather jacket before turning to the trousers. He got to his feet holding a wallet that soon produced a driving licence and a bank card.

'Harry Jones,' Foulds announced. 'Is that who you were expecting?'

Chapter 4

Drake sat in his car while Sara trooped off to organise two coffees from a mobile counter that had 'Genuine Italian Coffee' emblazoned in large letters on a banner above it. As she queued, the prospect of her second conversation with Fiona Jones filled her thoughts. Sara blamed Drake's earlier impoliteness with Fiona on his irritation at being allocated a missing person inquiry. Reaching detective inspector inevitably meant a certain disdain for routine police work, and Sara resolved to take a greater part when they returned to break the bad news to Mrs Jones. Although Drake was her senior officer and vastly more experienced, Sara was convinced she could make a meaningful contribution and put Fiona Jones at ease.

Sara was becoming accustomed to Drake's idiosyncrasies. The occasional rudeness and intense silences had been difficult to fathom out and she had realised from the way he organised his desk how he obsessed about things.

She reached the counter and ordered a flat white and an Americano for Drake.

Returning to the car, she handed Drake his drink.

'Thanks.'

'Do we go and see Fiona Jones straightaway?'

Drake nodded but didn't say anything.

'Did you see all the antiques in her house? They must be worth a fortune.'

Drake eased off the top of his drink and gazed down at the surface. Sara immediately thought how fussy he could be about coffee. She had seen him leave dozens of half-filled mugs, sometimes even pushing them away in disgust.

'She reported him missing very quickly.' Drake used a tone that suggested he wasn't looking for a reply.

'What are you thinking, boss?' It struck her as normal that a loving wife would report her husband missing even after such a short period. But they were paid to be suspicious.

'We need to find out everything about Harry Jones. And about his wife too.'

Sara sat finishing her coffee as Drake made various telephone calls. He used formal, clipped terms as he spoke to his superior officer, Superintendent Price. Drake was more informal with operational support when requesting a mobile incident room and additional officers to be made available. Finally, he organised a family liaison officer for Fiona Jones.

'Do we wait for the pathologist to arrive?' Sara said.

Drake paused. 'Not this time, let's go and speak to Fiona again.'

Once Sara was back in the car after disposing of the plastic coffee mugs in a nearby bin they retraced their short journey to Fiona's home. Sara worried if she would ever get used to breaking bad news, whether it ever got any easier.

Before he tapped on the door Drake hesitated for a moment, composing himself. The door opened abruptly and Fiona Jones stared at them, wide-eyed.

'What is it? Have you found him? You've only just left.'

'May we come in?' Drake said.

Fiona stood in the doorway, her gaze darting from

Drake to Sara frantically trying to read their faces. 'Tell me, tell me now.'

Drake lowered his voice. 'We need to speak to you inside.'

He stepped over the threshold, forcing Fiona into the house. Sara followed him into the same room they had occupied earlier. A painting on the wall caught her attention – she saw the familiar signature of the late Sir Kyffin Williams, a well-known Welsh artist, guaranteed to be worth tens of thousands of pounds.

Once they were sitting down Drake cleared his throat. 'I'm afraid we have some bad news. We found a body this morning near the Quarryman's Hospital. The identification from a driving licence confirms it's your husband.'

Fiona blinked furiously, her eyes watering.

'There must be some mistake.'

Sara read the despair on the woman's face; it wasn't the look of a murderer. It was incredulity and a vain hope this was all a bad dream.

'I am most terribly sorry,' Sara said, moving towards Fiona along the sofa they shared. 'Is there someone we can call to be with you? A family member, perhaps. We've already arranged for a specially trained family liaison officer to be with you later.'

Now the tears and sobbing began as the terrible realisation struck home.

'My sister,' Fiona croaked. 'Please call her. My mobile is in the kitchen.'

Sara found it easily enough on the shelves of an old Welsh dresser. Finding a glass, she filled it with water before returning to Fiona who gratefully drank half before fumbling with the mobile and scrolling to her sister's number. Eventually, Sara spoke to her, telling her she was needed urgently.

'Mrs Jones, we do need to ask you some questions about your husband,' Drake said.

Fiona nodded.

'Do you know of anyone who might want to kill him?'

She doubled up in anguish as though someone had kicked her hard in the midriff. The word *kill* upset her. Sara wanted to shake Drake. At least he could have been a little bit more sensitive.

'Did he have any enemies?' Sara added.

'He ran a shop, and he was involved in all sorts of things, and he was on the parish council. I hardly ever saw him.'

Drake continued. 'Where was his shop?'

'In the village. Michael works for him.'

'We'll need the address. And when we spoke earlier you mentioned a council meeting. Do you know the name of the secretary?'

Fiona looked up and gave Drake a blank look. Sara sympathised with Fiona's anguish so she decided to seize the initiative before Drake asked a tactless question about Fiona's whereabouts the evening before.

'Mrs Jones.' Fiona moved her gaze to Sara. 'We have to establish your husband's movements last night so that we can get a clear picture of where he had been and who he was with. As part of that process we need to know where you were last night. It's just the routine inquiries we have to make.' Sara tilted her head and smiled at Fiona.

It had the desired effect.

Fiona maintained her eye contact with Sara. 'I

visited my mother; she lives near Bangor. I left here about five o'clock and called into the supermarket on the way to buy a lasagne ready meal she likes. I probably arrived a little after six.' Fiona ran out of energy as though the momentum of recalling her movements drained her.

Sara finished jotting notes, and cast Drake a quick glance; he nodded his encouragement for her to continue. 'What time did you leave your mum's?'

'I don't know exactly,' she stammered. 'But I was back home by about ten.'

Sara smiled again. 'Thank you, Mrs Jones. You've been very helpful.'

The sound of the doorbell took Fiona's attention. 'That'll be Ceri.'

Drake was the first to his feet. 'I'll answer that.'

Sara heard the brief exchange between Drake and Fiona's sister. Ceri entered the room moments later, ashen-faced, and hugged her sister tightly as both women wept. Drake motioned to Sara that they should leave. Neither Fiona nor Ceri paid them any attention.

Outside Drake called operational support, instructing them to find him the name and contact details for the local parish council. He turned to Sara. 'Let's call at his shop.'

Padarn Antiques occupied an old building on three storeys and as they walked down the side street Drake caught sight of the lake that gave the business its name. He hoped the crime scene investigators were making progress; he dipped a hand into his jacket pocket and found his mobile.

Foulds answered after a couple of rings. 'Anything to report?' Drake said.

'Still too early, Ian. But it looks as though he was shot – one bullet.'

'Close range?'

'I think so, but the post-mortem will tell you definitively.'

'Has the pathologist been?'

'He should be here any minute.'

Drake finished the call, wondering if Harry Jones's killer had got lucky with a single shot or whether it was a professional kill. He looked up at the building in front of him. The wooden windows had recently been painted, the external rendering a rich but neutral cream colour. The sign above the entrance door and shop window advertising *Padarn Antiques* in simple gold letters gave it a prosperous appearance.

He pushed open the door and Sara followed him inside.

The sound of a radio drifted from the rear and Drake followed a narrow path between the chests of drawers, grandfather clocks, shelving units and cupboards stacked with blue-and-white striped crockery. Delicate labels were attached with red ribbon to each but Drake didn't bother checking the prices.

In a makeshift office space butted to the rear, a man in his thirties, ponytail and trainee beard, was playing patience on a computer as the radio blasted out a Walter Trout song.

'Are you Michael?' Drake said.

'How can I help?' He gave his best customer-friendly smile and reached over to silence the radio.

Drake produced his warrant card. 'I'm Detective

Inspector Drake. This is Detective Sergeant Morgan. Your boss Harry Jones was killed this morning.'

The smile disappeared instantly. Michael frowned, his mouth fell open. 'I ... can't believe it.'

'Does Harry have an office here?'

Michael nodded as he scrambled to his feet. Drake continued. 'Please lock the premises before you show us his office.' Michael fumbled to find a set of keys from a drawer in the desk. He scampered off and Drake heard him struggling with the key; he scrutinised Michael's workspace – calendar, hole puncher, stapler and card machine, probably the most important part. Michael returned and gestured to the rear. 'It's this way.'

He led them through a stockroom piled to the ceiling with boxes and books and wooden crates.

'All this stuff needs to be sorted out,' Michael said.

He unlocked the room at the end. It smelled musty as though fresh air hadn't circulated for days. A lamp with a moss-green shade sat on a pedestal desk pushed into one corner.

'This desk was his pride and joy. HP said it was worth a mint.'

Drake surveyed the room – two filing cabinets, a small table with a kettle, various mugs, a jar of instant coffee and a packet of sugar. Despite the antique desk and lamp there were no domestic refinements for Harry Jones.

'Why did you call him HP?'

'It's his initials, Harry Paul.' Michael snorted. 'His nickname was 'hotpoint', after his initials.' Michael glanced at Sara and back to Drake. 'He liked the ladies: that's why everyone calls him 'hotpoint'.'

'But he's married.' Drake knew as soon as he made the remark that it sounded lame.

'It didn't stop hotpoint.'

Sara made her first contribution. 'We'll need your contact details.'

'Yeah, sure.'

'Do you know anyone with a grudge against Harry Jones?' Drake noticed that Sara emphasised his surname.

Michael shook his head. A message reached Drake's mobile and he read the name and number for the secretary of the parish council as Sara continued.

'What was he like to work with?'

'He was all right, I suppose. But I never knew what he was doing. He kept all these filing cabinets locked. He could disappear during the day. I didn't know where he went and some days he'd stay here until late. I've seen people call here late at night. And you should check out the lock-up he's got. He tried to keep it secret; he thought nobody knew about it. Everybody knows everybody else's business around here. Especially when hotpoint is up to his old tricks.'

'I'd like to know exactly where this lock-up is,' Drake said.

Chapter 5

Drake peered out of the windscreen of his Mondeo after he and Sara had locked the premises. Michael scurried away down the street. Drake presumed he'd go straight to his local pub ready to share the news with his friends. Llanberis was a tight-knit community, like many rural villages and towns in North Wales, so Harry's death would be the topic of every conversation. The hours were slipping by after the discovery of the body. Searching Harry's lock-up and discovering whether he was as much of a philanderer as Michael made out could wait. Establishing Harry's movements before he was killed was the priority.

Drake called the contact name on his mobile and spoke to a man with an elderly voice who sounded shocked. Eventually he agreed to call the other councillors and arrange for them to meet Drake later that afternoon at the community centre in the village.

He turned to Sara. 'We're seeing the councillors who were at the meeting last night.'

Sara nodded.

'Before that let's visit Fiona again.'

For the third time that day Drake stood outside Fiona Jones' front door; the sound of movement seeped through it. Footsteps on the tiled hallway, muted voices. The business of grieving and extending condolences was well underway. Drake recalled the activity at his parents' home when his father had died. It had exhausted his mother. Small communities had a habit of wrapping themselves around people's grief, well-meaning but tiring nevertheless.

He glanced over at Sara standing by his side,

pleased that her contribution to the second interview with Fiona Jones had helped. His initial irritation at being allocated the missing person inquiry had been ill judged.

Alison Faulkner, a family liaison officer Drake recognised, opened the door.

'Good morning, sir.'

Drake and Sara entered. 'How's Mrs Jones been?' Drake said.

Faulkner gave a world-weary shrug. 'As you'd expect.'

'Where is she?'

'She's in the kitchen.' Faulkner tipped her head towards a door at the end of the hallway.

Fiona sat at a table staring blankly at a piece of toast on a plate in front of her. Her sister was busying herself, finding things to do, stacking mugs into cupboards, clearing the draining board.

'We need to speak to Fiona again,' Drake announced. Ceri nodded and left the room, as Drake and Sara sat down opposite Fiona Jones. Drake took a moment to gather his thoughts.

'We've been to the shop and spoken with Michael. There are several locked filing cabinets. Do you know where the keys are kept?'

Fiona raised her gaze to Drake and gave him a puzzled frown.

'And he mentioned Harry owned a lock-up. We need to establish everything about your husband's background. Do you know where we can find keys to the lock-up?'

'Upstairs,' Fiona croaked. 'He's got an office in one of the bedrooms.'

Did she know anything about her husband's affairs, or his 'hotpoint' nickname? Until Drake had concrete evidence and not idle gossip, questioning Fiona about Harry's alleged infidelities could wait. Someone must have shared with her the details about her husband even if Fiona hadn't been able to sense it herself.

'He's got lots of keys in the drawers of his desk.'

Fiona wrapped her fingers around the half-empty mug of tea. Her gaze drifted back to the uneaten toast and then out through the window of the kitchen and into the far distance.

It occurred to Drake he needed more background information about her marriage, the antiques business and their life together. Somewhere they would find someone with a motive for his murder. He stared over at Fiona, wondering if she might be that person. After all, people known to the victim commit most murders and the level of domestic violence was shocking. Fiona's visit to her mother's home was hardly an alibi. It only explained the early part of the evening until she returned home.

The sound of the doorbell rang through the ground floor.

Fiona continued to stare into a space only she could see. Drake heard the exchange of conversation between Ceri and at least two other people. The intensity of the voices changed; Drake guessed Faulkner had ushered them into the sitting room. The family liaison officer would know not to interrupt him. But he was finished with Fiona for now and he nodded at Sara and they left.

'We'll be upstairs in Harry's office,' Drake said to Faulkner, who was waiting for him in the hallway.

'There are two neighbours come to pay their

condolences,' Faulkner said.

'I'll need a list of everybody who calls.'

Faulkner began. 'I don't—'

Drake gave her a sharp look and she said no more. He was paid to be suspicious, about everyone.

The balustrades and handrail of the imposing staircase were a deep mahogany and at the top a burgundy carpet covered the landing. Drake tried the first door, which opened into a bedroom with a double bed and heavy furniture. He turned on his heels and noticed Sara examining intently one of the paintings hanging on the wall.

'I'm sure this is a Donald McIntyre,' Sara said. 'My grandmother collected him.'

'I suppose it's to be expected from an antiques dealer.'

'And there was a Kyffin Williams downstairs.'

Drake stood and gazed at the oil painting. It was of an old farm in dark greens and blues and browns.

'Harry must have been loaded,' Sara said.

The second room was a bathroom, so Drake closed the door and turned his attention to the next two rooms. One was the master bedroom with the lived-in feel he'd expected. An electronic e-reader was charging on one bedside table, which Drake assumed belonged to Fiona, and on the other lay a hardback copy of the latest Ian Rankin novel sat alongside a cordless telephone.

The final room was large enough to be a double bedroom.

'I wonder if they have any family,' Sara said.

'The place doesn't have the feel of young children.'

'They might have already left home by now.'

Harry had a fondness for knee-hole desks and the second Drake had seen that morning was a more substantial version of the one in *Padarn Antiques*. It had fewer scratches, the brass handles glistened, and a pot of pencils and a stack of Post It notes were arranged neatly in one corner near a telephone. A faint smell of furniture polish hung in the air and Drake's immediate reaction was to approve of the order in the room.

Drake got to work on the drawers while Sara rummaged through the filing cabinets.

Various boxes storing paper clips, elastic bands of varying sizes and bits of stationery segmented each drawer. Drake's priority was to find a set of keys but before he started, he called Mike Foulds.

'What's the latest, Mike?'

'Give me a minute, Ian.' Foulds fumbled with the mobile as he shouted at somebody. 'Sorry, about that. We've had lots of rubberneckers, walking up into the woods taking photographs.'

'Have you found any keys with the body?'

'Nothing as yet.'

'Has the pathologist been?'

'He was complaining like mad because he's going on holiday tomorrow. And he's whingeing about hospital cutbacks making his life a misery. He's going to do the PM tonight.'

'What!' Drake could ill afford the time to be present at the post-mortem. They needed an exact timeline for Harry's movements for the night before, to build some sort of picture of his life, coordinate the local enquiries and hope they wouldn't miss anything in the vital first few hours. Now he faced spending two hours at the mortuary. The pathologist would have to wait until Drake was available later that evening. He tapped a message telling the pathologist to expect him by nine p.m.

'Anything wrong, boss?' Sara said.

'The pathologist wants to do the post-mortem tonight.'

'Do you need me there?'

Drake shook his head, much to Sara's relief. Drake returned to the drawers in the desk and after examining each one turned to Sara. 'Any keys for a filing cabinet?' She shook her head.

Drake turned his attention to a cupboard in one corner. Inside were various lever-arch files with neatly printed labels identifying the contents to be bank statements, letters from insurance companies and other investments. On the bottom shelf was a small safe, securely locked. It seemed unlikely Fiona knew the combination from her reaction to his previous questions.

He sat back in the upholstered leather chair. 'We haven't got time for this,' Drake said.

Forensics could break it open in due course. They retraced their steps back downstairs as the family liaison officer was seeing an elderly couple to the door.

Fiona perched on the edge of a sofa in the sitting room, having visibly aged since first thing that morning. The white wisps of hair were more pronounced and her cheeks looked more sunken. It wasn't easily faked, Drake thought.

'We found a safe in his office. Do you know the combination?'

Slowly Fiona shook her head.

Drake and Sara reached the mobile incident room installed at the far end of the car park near the entrance to the slate museum after a long session interviewing all the councillors gathered in the community centre. Drake had insisted on seeing them all in turn so that Sara could record an individual version of the events of the night before. He needn't have bothered; every version was similar.

A presentation by a company developing the site of an old quarry used as a bomb storage facility during the Second World War had started promptly. All the councillors were supporting the venture. It would develop a badly neglected area and create a handful of jobs. A councillor in his seventies with silvery hair was the only one who could confirm that the meeting had broken up by eight p.m. as he had wanted to return home to watch a gardening programme on television.

Mike Foulds stood with Drake and Sara in the mobile incident room. He gave them a detailed analysis of the immediate crime scene as the investigators in his team packed away their equipment and cameras.

'Do you want a full search completed of the area?'

Drake looked over Foulds' shoulder. The wooded escarpment behind the track leading up to the Quarryman's Hospital would be thick with vegetation, shrubbery and trees. Casually discarding the weapon used to kill Jones so close to the crime scene would be improbable. But there might be some other fragment of evidence, a piece of clothing snagged on a gorse bush or a shard of litter accidentally dropped.

Foulds would know the answer to his question. He was looking for confirmation from Drake.

Drake nodded. 'I'll make certain you get all the resources you need. Do a full sweep of the slate museum and as far as practical through the woods.'

Foulds stood and listened as Drake called operational support. He made clear he required every available officer to assist with the forensic search of the area. Drake looked at Foulds and noted the matter-of-fact determination on his face masked by the reality that finding valuable evidence was remote.

Drake finished the call and said to Foulds. 'Keep me up to date.'

Drake parked outside the mortuary a little before eight-thirty p.m. and sat in the car listening to his stomach growling. He picked up a message from Sian, his soon-to-be ex-wife, telling him she wanted to speak to him urgently, warning she would call first thing in the morning. Since their separation the routine of speaking to her on the telephone and collecting his daughters at prearranged times had developed too easily. His hope for reconciliation was proving more and more unlikely. He contemplated calling her but the prospect of a frosty conversation at the end of a tiring day filled him with dread.

Instead he walked briskly over the empty car park towards the mortuary. The usual insolent assistant had left for the evening and Drake made his way into the main corridor following the sound of classical music.

He pushed open the door. Dr Lee Kings waved his hands in the air, pretending to conduct an orchestra. As soon as he registered Drake the pathologist changed his smooth circular movements to a gesture of welcome.

'Good, you're punctual. I'm going on holiday tomorrow and can't bloody wait to get out of this place.'

Drake hadn't heard Lee Kings complain before. The pathologist struck him as a man dedicated to his work, passionate about dissecting dead people. Within a couple of hours Kings' work would be finished whereas Drake's was only beginning.

With a flourish Kings removed the white sheet covering Harry Jones.

'What were your first impressions when you saw the body?' Drake asked, stifling a yawn.

'That he was dead of course.'

Drake realised his lame question deserved an equally lame response.

The blood around the wound Drake had seen earlier had coagulated into sticky lumps. Kings started cleaning it, taking care to remove any possible fragments of hair and fibre – anything that could offer incriminating evidence. Gunshot wounds could always share with the investigating team details of the calibre of the gun used, its age, the manufacturer. The way in which the wound was formed could tell them how near the killer had been to his victim.

Thankfully, the use of firearms in Wales was uncommon, as it was in most parts of the United Kingdom. Acquiring a firearms certificate wasn't an easy task. Accessing the list of everybody authorised to own a firearm or shotgun in North Wales would be a priority the following morning.

Kings returned to the work in hand, moving quickly to dissect Harry's chest with a dramatic Y cut before attacking his sternum with a reciprocating saw, prising his rib cage apart to reveal his heart and lungs.

Once he finished cleaning the wound, Kings peered down into it. With a pair of tweezers he gently extracted the bullet and dropped it into a stainless steel bowl on a tray. It made a loud tinkling sound. It looked so small sitting in the tray, streaked with shards of bloody flesh.

'That's interesting,' Kings said, his earlier haste to finish the task in hand dissipated. 'I've never seen a bullet quite like that.'

'What do you mean?'

'I'm not an expert. But most of the gunshot wounds I have seen or read about don't have bullets that look like a museum piece.'

Kings pushed the small metal fragment around the tray.

'Once I've finished I'll get the bullet cleaned and sent for full ballistic examination. They should be able to tell you some more about the gun.'

Drake asked. 'How near was he to the victim?'

'There's no evidence of gunshot residue on the surrounding skin.' Kings tilted his head, contemplated his reply. 'I would say he was within a few feet of the victim when he pulled the trigger. Death was from a pericardial tamponade. The bullet lodged in his pericardium, and a small hole in his right ventricle allowed bleeding into the sack around the heart which fills with blood and strangles the heart, eventually stopping it from beating.'

'Did he die instantaneously?'

Kings pursed his lips. 'I can't be certain. Probably not, but he didn't live long – a few minutes. Do you have any suspects?'

Drake shook his head. 'Harry went to the Quarryman's Hospital to meet somebody. And that somebody produced a gun and killed him.' Drake continued to think aloud. 'So that suggests Harry Jones knew his killer.'

'I cannot comment on that.'

Drake nodded.

Kings peeled back the skin over Harry's head, clicking on the saw that enabled him to remove his brain, which he weighed and then carefully placed into another tray. It pleased Drake he hadn't eaten for most of the day. The post-mortem reached the stage where the body was treated as a collection of medical exhibits. Drake should have been accustomed to the mechanical nature of the exercise but it was something he found difficult to stomach.

After an hour a familiar, contented look came over the pathologist's face, a look that Drake had seen many times before. Drake left him and returned to his car. A fox scratched the undergrowth at the far end of the now empty car park before it saw him and scampered away.

Drake started the Mondeo, regretting he hadn't actually purchased an Alfa 159 he'd spotted in a local garage but it had streaks of rust around the wheel arch and one of the electric windows wasn't working. Even so, the Mondeo was a boring car to drive. He pointed the car towards the direction of the A55 and soon enough found himself parking outside his flat. Inside he cracked open a bottle of Peroni and sat at the kitchen table as he listened to the message from his sister telling him she was planning to stay for a weekend with their mother, although annoyingly she didn't say when it was going to be. He'd call her in the morning, although his mother would probably know the full details already. He had tried to rationalise with Susan, getting her to accept that with their father dead they had to build bridges with their recently discovered half-brother Huw Jackson, even get to know him. Persuading her that their father would have wanted them to have a relationship with Huw had proved difficult and it had been challenging to get his sister to speak to their mother about it.

Finding a loaf and block of cheddar in the fridge, he settled down to eat something. He could have a square meal tomorrow, maybe. In the morning, he'd be back in headquarters. It would be another twelve-hour day. It was the sort of routine that had ruined his marriage, resulted in him living in a flat in Colwyn Bay, eating toast and cheese before going to bed.

Chapter 6

Drake's mobile rang at 7.45 the following morning. He had already showered, chosen a sombre grey suit, a shirt with Bengal stripes matched with a navy tie. The brogues were his second-best pair, the shoes he had worn yesterday packed carefully in a box in the wardrobe ready to be cleaned. Drake thrived on order and routine, although it had been his obsessions and rituals in the past that so infuriated Sian. Counselling ordered by the Wales Police Service after a difficult case involving the murder of two colleagues had helped, but Drake had found himself recently ruminating more often than was healthy.

'Good morning.' Drake recognised Sian's number and tried to sound cheerful.

'I left you two messages yesterday.'

The implication that he had to be available to take her calls riled him. He offered his stock explanation. 'I was busy.'

'All day?'

He heard the impatience in the two words she stabbed out and decided against offering an explanation. His hunger that morning hadn't been satisfied by the bowl of muesli and an Americano, and a lingering headache reminded him it had been late when he'd returned to his flat.

'I'm going away for the weekend, and the girls are staying with Mum. But she forgot that on Sunday afternoon she and Dad are committed to some charity auction. I was hoping …'

It was a racing certainty he would be working this Saturday and Sunday. Unlike Sian he didn't have the luxury of being a GP with regular hours and weekends off. But he didn't want his daughters, Helen and Megan, shunted around while Sian was away. He could take them to see his mother.

'Of course. I'll make arrangements to collect them from your mother's place.'

'Don't forget, Ian.'

'Are you going anywhere nice?'

Drake thought it a reasonable enough request and he knew she had spent weekends away with some of her friends and with her parents in Berlin a few months earlier.

'It's a last-minute thing. Are you involved in that case in Llanberis?' Sian's clumsy attempt to distract him made him suspicious. Who was she going with? And was it any of his business?

Sian continued. 'My lawyers tell me you still haven't completed the forms they've sent you.'

Now Drake was certain she was being secretive.

'I'll deal with them over the weekend.' Drake had said this a dozen times before.

After finishing the call and clearing away the breakfast dishes, he checked that the kitchen was neat and tidy – he adjusted the dishcloths draped over the handle of the oven so that both hung down the same distance. Sian's habit of leaving them disorganised and untidy had always irked him.

In the hallway, he dragged on a light overcoat and glanced at the mirror before straightening his tie. He closed the door of the flat behind him and made his way down to his car.

Five minutes later he parked at the far end of the car park at headquarters in a slot certain to minimise the risk of scratches or accidental bumps to his Mondeo.

On the second floor, he pushed open the door of the Incident Room. He spotted that the image of Harry Jones pinned to the board was slightly off centre – he would have to move it, as otherwise it would play on his mind.

Gareth Winder stopped regaling Luned Thomas mid-sentence when he saw Drake. Luned's tightly wound arms and creased forehead suggested she wasn't enjoying the discourse from Winder. Drake had seen the tension between the detective constables previously. Winder was her senior by several years but no match for her sharp mind. Winder's chin under his round, flabby face seemed to have sagged and Drake thought he'd put on weight recently.

'Morning boss,' Winder said.

Drake nodded an acknowledgement. Luned uncrossed her arms. 'Sir.'

Drake walked over to the board and adjusted Harry Jones' photograph. As he finished, the door squeaked open, and he turned to see Sara shrugging off a red parka.

'The body of Harry Jones was found yesterday morning.' Drake gestured over his shoulder. 'A member of staff at the old Quarryman's Hospital in Llanberis discovered the body in their bin enclosure.'

'Any forensics, sir?' Luned said.

'Nothing so far. Definitely no murder weapon. There's a full CSI team at the scene today. They're going to search the surrounding woodland. The nearby slate museum is closed but there's a mobile incident room set up.'

'What did he do for a living?' Winder said.

'He was an antiques dealer in Llanberis. We need to build a complete picture of his life. We know he was married and that his wife Fiona was visiting her mother the night he was killed.'

'Is she a person of interest?' Luned said.

'I don't think so, but we keep an open mind. We'll need searches of the telephone records of both Harry and Fiona Jones. Somebody must have made contact with him to arrange to see him at the Quarryman's Hospital. And financial and banking details for Jones and do the Land Registry as well. And organise house-to-house at Llanberis.'

'All of the houses?' Winder said.

'Yes, Gareth. Llanberis isn't Manhattan. It's a small village.' Drake continued. 'A single bullet to the chest killed Jones. The pathologist thought the gun used might be quite old.'

Sara piped up. 'He certainly led a double life – the man who helped in his shop referred to him by his nickname *hotpoint* – apparently it refers to his initials HP but also to his reputation.'

Winder smirked. 'So, he was a player.'

'Typical chauvinist comment.' Luned sounded peeved.

Drake ignored her. 'I've organised for a forensic team to open a safe in his house this morning and they'll be removing various filing cabinets from his shop too. Sara and I will be visiting a lock-up Jones owned so when we're back I need progress reports.'

Drake drove into a large gravelled section of a small industrial estate that appeared deserted. As he slowed the car, Sara leaned forward and they craned to spot the search team near Harry Jones' lock-up. Behind him the towering presence of an articulated lorry flashed its lights, encouraging him to move out of its way. In a cloud of dust it drove past Drake and on towards a yard where Drake could see bags of builders' merchants' materials all neatly arranged in rows. A little way ahead of Drake's Mondeo were half a dozen wooden sheds and a sign advertising a company selling them. Alongside was a corrugated iron structure like an upturned boat, a single door in its gable. Only weeds thrived among the old pallets and coils of fencing material littered around the place.

In the distance he spotted an officer walking into view, peering over at them. Drake crunched the car into first gear and drove over the potholed surface. The man disappeared from view and it surprised Drake that the industrial estate stretched further than he imagined. They passed a dilapidated building that resembled an old railway station and Drake guessed the area must have been an old goods yard.

Two police vehicles were stationary in front of three corrugated iron structures, smaller but similar to the one at the beginning of the estate. Drake counted four officers and the uniformed sergeant who would be in charge of the search. Drake parked alongside one of the other vehicles and he and Sara left his Mondeo to join them. Three crowbars, two sets of enormous industrial pinchers and boxes of tools lay on the dusty ground nearby.

'Good morning, sir. Jack Evans,' the sergeant said. 'Any idea what's inside?'

'None.'

'It's just that a couple of the lads are on rest days today, which means a lot of overtime.'

It meant the bean counters at the finance department complaining about Drake's budget. Accountants would be the death of modern policing, Drake thought. The last thing he wanted to worry about was his budget or keeping the books balanced.

'I've got no idea how long this will take. Harry Jones kept it as a lock-up so whatever is inside must be valuable,' Drake said.

Evans nodded at one of the officers who came forward and snapped open the chain hanging over the door. Next, another officer worked on the lock. He reached for a cordless drill and a loud grinding sound filled the air. Eventually the door swung open.

Drake and Sara peered in, staring at furniture stacked floor to ceiling.

'Let's have a look,' Drake said.

Over to his left Drake saw a length of plywood screwed to an upright piece of timber with two old black switches. Fluorescent tubes high above them simmered into life once he switched them on.

'It looks like Harry Jones owned a lot of stock,' Sara said.

'How much stock does an antiques dealer in Llanberis need?' Drake said.

He walked down the aisle through the middle of the building, Sara following behind. There were chest of drawers, bookcases, wardrobes and shelving units full of boxes. Everything had been organised in neat rows allowing access to move any item easily.

Halfway down the row Sara detoured into an area with several metal filing cabinets. She opened the nearest and flicked through the contents of a drawer. She glanced over at Drake. 'There are some old books.'

'They must be valuable if he kept them under lock and key.'

Behind him, Drake could hear Evans dictating instructions for uniformed officers to start their work. He wasn't wasting any time, Drake thought. But he wondered if he was.

Sara had turned her attention to a metal storage cupboard. She eased open the unlocked door.

'This is like an Aladdin's cave,' she said. 'You should take a look at this, boss.'

By the time Drake joined her she held in her hand a picture frame with blurry images of two figures standing near a washing line, its contents being blown in the wind. Sara stared down at the painting. 'I'm sure this is by Kevin Sinnott.'

'Is it valuable?'

Sara nodded. 'He's an artist from South Wales – very collectable. This is probably worth thousands.'

She replaced the frame gently before examining others from inside.

'I don't recognise any of these. But we should get them all checked out in due course.'

'I agree,' Drake said.

Drake moved past her and further into the building. He spotted two polished dining tables and matching chairs. Alongside them were two desks with bowed legs and intricately inlaid surfaces. Drake imagined them having pride of place in some grand house in the English countryside. Behind him, Sara whistled under her breath and he heard her mention the name of another artist he hadn't heard of.

He opened the drawer of one of the desks, but it was empty. The second had scraps of newspapers from 1992 inside. Despite the autumn temperatures, the lock-up felt warm, and when Drake reached the end of the aisle he spotted a large space heater that Harry Jones must have used during colder weather.

Several antique chests were stored on a specially constructed vertical plinth screwed to the wall. It pointed to a professional operation. Drake wondered where Harry Jones had sourced all these items.

He turned his attention to an ornate cupboard with small delicate legs and colourful inlay in extravagant swirls across the drawer fronts. Sara joined him as he ran a hand along the surface.

'It looks French,' Sara said.

'How much is it worth do you think?'

'They look expensive. Do you think all this stuff belongs to Harry Jones?'

Drake shrugged. He had his doubts but without evidence they couldn't prove anything. He pulled out the top drawer and let his mouth fall open.

Sara peered in. 'Jesus Christ.'

The collection of hand guns inside looked like museum pieces.

Drake bellowed. 'Jack, get over here.'

Moments later the sergeant appeared at his side.

'Bloody hell. One of these could be your murder weapon.'

'Are any of your search team authorised firearms officers?'

Evans shook his head.

'Then call firearms and get an officer here who is. And nobody touches these until you're satisfied they are safe.'

A shout from an officer near the entrance took Drake's attention. 'Inspector, get over here.'

Evans and Sara followed Drake as he negotiated his way back towards the daylight. One of the search team stood looking at a table with two clocks standing on it.

'What's the problem?' Drake said.

'Paul Hughes, sir. I recognise these clocks. There was a break-in at my grandparents' home a couple of months ago. Both clocks are family heirlooms.'

'Can you be certain?' Drake said.

'I grew up seeing these clocks whenever I went to my grandparents' farmhouse. Taid used to show me how to wind them. Mam will be over the moon; she was really upset after the break-in.'

It was difficult to imagine Harry Jones as a burglar but handling stolen goods now looked very likely. Drake paused. It meant hours of work; every item would have to be photographed and fingerprinted, and the premises made completely secure until operational support could remove everything to a safe location.

'I want all these items seized then forensically examined.'

'That's going to mean a big commitment of resources.' Evans managed a mildly defiant tone.

Drake gave him a sharp look: budgets and protocols could go to hell. The killer might have handled any one of the items in the building, even a partial fingerprint might point them to a suspect.

Drake's mobile rang and he stepped into the sunshine to answer the call.

'Inspector Drake.'

'Alison Faulkner, sir.' It took a moment for Drake to recognise the name of the family liaison officer allocated to Fiona Jones. 'I think you should come to Llanberis. Fiona has run amok.'

Chapter 7

Drake jogged over to his car after jerking his head at Sara, indicating for her to follow him. 'Fiona left the house an hour ago and got into a scrap with a woman at the local supermarket.'

Sara clipped her seatbelt into place as Drake started the engine and sped off. 'Do we know who the other person is?'

Drake shook his head.

After each meeting with Fiona Jones Sara had become more uncomfortable about the grieving widow, but was her reaction tempered by what they had learned about Harry Jones? How much did Fiona Jones really know about her late husband?

The tyres of Drake's Mondeo kicked up a cloud of grit as he sped away for Llanberis.

Drake struck a disdainful tone. 'Apparently she told the family liaison officer she was going out for a walk. But she visited the local supermarket and got into an altercation with another woman and damaged her car.'

Near the imposing walls of the Vaynol estate that hugged the bank of the Menai Strait he indicated right and motored up the hill for Pentir, pressing on towards Llanberis.

A light shower of rain drenched the car and the wiper blades swished back and forth.

Sara continued. 'There is something a bit odd about Fiona Jones.'

Drake glanced over at her. 'Woman's intuition?'

Sara shrugged. 'How much did she *really* know about her husband?'

'A lot more than she told us at the start.'

A few minutes later Drake indicated right into the town and found the supermarket easily enough. It had a small car park – enough for a dozen or so cars. A marked police car had pulled up onto the pavement outside. A traffic cop stood by a Ford Fiesta, its windscreen smashed, the driver's side wing mirror hanging off limply.

There was no sign of Fiona Jones.

Drake double-parked and they joined the uniformed officer.

Introductions completed, the officer gave them a summary. 'Fiona Jones arrived to do some shopping. There was a confrontation between her and another customer. There was some shouting, pushing and shoving and things got a bit heated. From the eyewitnesses I've spoken to, Fiona Jones called her a slut and a tart – all the usual insults before rushing out and smashing the windscreen.'

'Have you notified forensics?' Drake said.

'They should be here any minute.'

'Is this other woman here?'

The officer dipped his head towards the shop building. 'She's with the manager.'

Sara followed Drake over to the automatic electric doors that pulsed open as they approached. In front of them was an aisle of refrigerated counters and a group of elderly women whose conversation abruptly ended as they noticed them. Sara looked to her left and spotted the checkout and the faces of two worried-looking teenagers wearing polo shirts advertising the supermarket brand.

Drake was ahead of her as he reached the

assistants. 'I need to speak to the manager.'

One of them buzzed an intercom. 'Can you come to the tills, Mr Patel?'

Seconds later a short man with heavy spectacles appeared from a doorway at the rear of the shop. He took a few steps towards Drake and Sara but when he realised who they were he waved them over. Patel led them into his office where a woman sat on a visitor chair.

'This is a Penny Muller,' Patel said.

Drake produced his warrant card. 'Detective Inspector Drake and this is Detective Sergeant Sara Morgan. Can you tell me what happened?'

Penny lifted her head and looked at Drake and then at Sara. Her eyes were smaller than Sara expected from her broad face and wide unsmiling mouth. The shoulder-length dirty blonde hair was curled into wisps, brushing the shoulders of her cream top with its scalloped neckline that showed a little too much tanned cleavage.

'I'd just finished some shopping.' The accent sounded educated; it wasn't local but neither was it Scouse, from the Liverpool area, which was prevalent in North Wales. 'I was taking my bags to the car when Fiona approached me.'

'Do you know her?' Drake said.

'Yes, of course.' Penny pulled the locks of hair that curtained the right side of her face behind her ear. There was a lot more to that reply, Sara thought.

'Is she a friend of yours?' Drake said.

Derision swept over Penny's face and Sara anticipated Drake had seen it too.

'I would hardly call her that.'

'Tell us what happened.' Drake folded his arms.

'She attacked me, Inspector. She started thumping me. My shopping fell to the floor. I don't know what possessed her. I dashed back inside the shop.'

Patel butted in, although Drake glowered at him. 'One of the staff called me and by the time I reached the tills Fiona was smashing the car windscreen and the wing mirrors.'

'How was she doing that?'

'She was using a hammer.'

'A hammer?' Drake exchanged a glance with Sara. It suggested premeditation; Fiona had left the house clearly intent on causing harm to something or someone. Sara frowned.

'Do you know where she's gone?' Sara said.

Penny shrugged; Patel did likewise. 'I told all my staff to stay inside. She left soon afterwards – jumped in her car and drove away.'

Sara looked at Penny, still troubled about her replies that suggested a lot more to her relationship with Fiona Jones. Sara adopted a soft tone. 'And why do you think she attacked you, Penny?'

'You'll have to ask her.'

Evasion was always a clear indication more digging needed to be done, Sara thought. Now she used a harder tone. 'Mrs Muller, I find that hard to believe. Mrs Jones has just lost her husband, surely you're aware of that? And yet she attacks you in broad daylight – why would she do that? Where do you live?'

Penny sighed impatiently. 'We live outside Llanberis. My husband and I run an alternative therapy centre.' Her tone irritated Sara, who turned to Patel.

'We'd like to speak to Mrs Muller in private.'

Patel glanced at Drake and then at Penny before leaving his office.

'What's the real nature of your relationship with Fiona Jones?' Sara said.

Penny cleared her throat. 'Is it any of your business? And in any event I didn't have a relationship with her. She's quite mad.'

'We'll be the judge of what is our business or not.' Drake raised his voice.

It didn't intimidate Penny, who sneered. For the first time Sara noticed her cold eyes and her distinctive jawline.

'Were you having an affair with Harry Jones?' Sara said.

For a brief moment, the veil of disdain and contempt that clouded Penny's eyes melted away into sadness. Sara waited for her to reply.

'It was a while ago.' She dipped her head and fidgeted with her fingers.

Sara wanted to interrogate her further, but Drake's mobile rang.

'Detective Inspector Drake.'

Sara watched him stiffen and he turned to Sara.

'We need to go.'

Drake sprinted to the car. 'Fiona's gone to the Mullers' place. And she's taken her hammer with her.' Drake reached his car first and jumped into the driver's seat before Sara could ask any questions.

Drake accelerated out of the car park. He tossed his mobile into Sara's lap as it bleeped. 'The message should have the postcode.'

Sara tapped the details into the satnav and waited for the directions to show up on the screen. Drake had already left Llanberis, heading west towards the coast. 'She drove to the Muller's property straight after the supermarket. All I've been told is that she was overcome by a couple of the employees.'

'What has she done?'

'She's smashed windows and various cars.'

'What did you make of Mrs Muller, boss?'

'You certainly gave her a hard time.'

'I hate it when people lie to us, when people go out of their way to be awkward.'

Drake nodded. 'It looks as though she was having an affair with Harry Jones.'

Sara nodded back vigorously. 'It doesn't give Fiona Jones any reason to smash up her car.'

'She's just lost her husband. People do odd things when they're under great stress. They never think straight.'

'Even so, boss …'

Drake took the junction towards Brynrefail before making another right turn for Deiniolen. The satnav took them to the outskirts of the small village and along a circuitous route Drake guessed would take them to the adjacent valley. A large enclosure of conifers came into view on his right-hand side. It was unusual for trees to survive on this wind-scarred landscape. The satnav bleeped that they had reached their destination and Drake indicated right into a rough drive. At the end they pulled up outside a Gothic-styled property of grey stone, enormous lintels covering wide doors and ageing wooden casement windows.

Drake left the car and nodded for Sara to follow

him round towards the rear. In a carport a burnt-orange Range Rover Evoque with a black top was parked next to a red Mercedes. A hammer had left clear indentations in the panels of both cars and the windscreens were smashed. The rear-view mirrors dangled against the paintwork of each. The cost of repair for vehicles like this would be astronomic, Drake thought. And each was a crime scene. The CSI at the supermarket in Llanberis could deal with them after he'd finished.

Over to his left Drake saw an open door.

'Let's go and see inside.'

The hallway felt colder than the season suggested. Red quarry tiles covered the floor and ran through into the main part of the building. A heavy Welsh dresser had pride of place against one wall. At the end of the hallway he could make out the bottom risers of a staircase. The sound of conversation emerged from the kitchen ahead of them and when they entered a tall slim man gazed over at Drake. He was fifty, give or take, with a head full of hair pulled back in thick waves. Its coiffured appearance reminded Drake of his mother returning from the hairdresser smelling of hairspray.

'Thank God. Are you the police?'

'Detective Inspector Drake and Detective Sergeant Morgan.' Drake didn't bother with his warrant card.

'Wolfgang Muller.' Wolfgang stretched out a hand, giving Drake and Sara a vigorous handshake. 'I'm so very pleased you got here so quickly.'

Drake gave Wolfgang a long stare. 'Can you tell me what happened?'

'Fiona Jones arrived a few minutes ago. She started smashing our cars, screaming like a banshee. I have never seen anything like it.'

'What was she saying? Any idea why she would do it?'

Drake hoped that Wolfgang would be a little more cooperative than his wife.

Wolfgang paused as he gathered his thoughts, composing his reply carefully. He straightened, as though standing to attention. 'She wants to blame my wife and myself for her husband's death.'

'Why would that be the case?' Drake said.

'It is no secret, Inspector Drake, that my wife had a relationship with Harry Jones. There was some unpleasantness between Harry and myself.'

'Unpleasantness?' Drake said. It was an oddly English word for someone with such a strong German accent.

'We argued. I told him never to come near her or myself ever again.'

'And did he?'

'On occasion I believe he did.'

'How did that make you feel?'

Wolfgang peered down at Drake, his eyes hardening. 'I wasn't pleased.'

'We found Harry Jones' body yesterday morning. Where were you the night before last?'

'I was here of course: all night, we had a house full of guests.'

'What exactly do you do here?' Drake glanced around the kitchen. It had an old range, at least a dozen pots hanging from butchers' hooks and cupboards with glass-fronted doors, its shelves filled with jars and dry goods.

'We run a centre offering yoga courses, alternative therapies and wellness clinics.'

'I see,' Drake said.

Sara made her first contribution. 'Where is Fiona now?'

'Follow me.'

At the far end of the room was a door that led into another corridor, equally cold, equally barren and inhospitable. Drake imagined some nonconformist industrialist from Lancashire in the Victorian era building the house as a holiday home that he used for a fortnight each summer, its hallways and landings occupied by surly servants complaining their master was too mean to keep the place warm.

Wolfgang led them past two rooms Drake thought had been part of the servants' quarters. At the end of the narrow corridor two men, both in their early twenties, stood sentry-like near a wooden door.

'You're not keeping her under lock and key, I hope,' Drake said.

Wolfgang shook his head. 'Of course not. We restrained her from causing any more criminal damage. We got her into the house and, well, as you can see, she started crying.'

Inside Fiona Jones was nursing a mug although she had long since finished its contents.

She saw Drake and Sara but her eyes didn't register recognition immediately. Then she frowned. 'I suppose you've come to arrest me.'

Chapter 8

Drake sat in the room of an off-duty sergeant at the police station in an anonymous industrial estate in Caernarfon. Unease filled his mind as he thought about the hours he was wasting on investigating criminal damage to three cars and an assault.

As a precaution Drake insisted Wolfgang Muller travel with Sara to the area custody suite in a marked police car. As she was doing that Gareth Winder and Luned Thomas were interviewing each of the guests at Bryn Hyfryd, the wellness centre Fiona Jones had vandalised. There was every chance Wolfgang was a real suspect and his reference to 'unpleasantness' between himself and Harry Jones made Drake suspicious.

Drake left the insipid-looking coffee Sara had brought from the canteen.

'Harry Jones had a colourful lifestyle.' Sara sipped on her tea – a strong brown colour.

'That's putting it mildly.'

'I wonder who else has fallen victim to his charms?'

'I want a full background search done on Wolfgang Muller and his wife in due course.'

Drake read the time on his watch. An hour had elapsed since his call requesting Fiona's lawyer to attend. They couldn't interview Fiona, sitting patiently in a cell in the custody suite, without him. Drake didn't expect her to be difficult. Six eyewitnesses confirmed exactly what had happened. In addition, the CCTV footage from the shop made the evidence against her overwhelming.

Deciding that he had to make progress, he called Paula Wendall, one of the local intelligence officers he knew. They were civilians, which meant a disregard for rank and hierarchy.

'Morning, Ian,' Paula Wendall said. 'I hear you're investigating the Llanberis murder.'

'Harry Jones,' Drake said. 'He was an antiques dealer. Have you got any intelligence to link him to known burglars?'

'I don't think so, but I'll check.'

'We also discovered several old pistols in a lock-up where he stored furniture. They looked like something from a Second World War film.'

'We don't get anybody using firearms around here, you know that. It sounds unusual; you're probably looking for a theft from a collector in one of the big cities. You might try John Edwards, the historian at the army museum in Caernarfon Castle.'

'Thanks.'

Drake finished his call as Sara's mobile rang, and he listened to her brief one-sided conversation.

She finished the call. 'The lawyer has arrived.'

Upton was an unusual name in North Wales and Dafydd was the son of the lawyer who finalised the probate papers for Drake's father's estate. He was a timid man in his early thirties, entirely unsuited to criminal work. It would only be a matter of time before he decided a career dealing with dead people was far more lucrative than spending hours in an airless claustrophobic interview room.

Once Drake got the formalities out of the way, he glanced at Fiona Jones. She looked pale sitting next to Dafydd Upton, her skin blotchy, her eyes bloodshot, as though she hadn't eaten for days. She held the plastic beaker full of water with both hands.

'Do you realise why you're here, Fiona?'

Fiona nodded.

'You were arrested earlier today on suspicion of criminal damage to vehicles belonging to Penny Muller and her husband Wolfgang Muller.'

'Yes, I know. I hate her so much. She wasn't like the others. She had control over him. He couldn't let her go.'

Drake paused; it was unusual for an interview to go so well at the beginning. Fiona admitted her involvement immediately. Neither he nor Sara needed to play the good cop/bad cop routine.

'Why did you take a hammer with you this morning when you left the house?'

'What do you mean?' Fiona looked over at him, puzzled. 'I went out for a drive; I needed to clear my head. Harry left some tools in the car. I saw her … I saw her arriving at the supermarket. My mind blanked out; all I could think of was Harry and her. And I've seen her with that husband of hers in the supermarket looking down their noses at me.'

'Where were you when you saw her?'

'I was just driving past.'

'Did you turn around?'

'I couldn't help myself.'

'Do you admit that you smashed the windscreen and dented the panels of her car?'

Fiona nodded.

'You'll need to say something for the recording.'

'Yes, I smashed her car.' Fiona used a tone that suggested she didn't quite believe it herself.

'I'm sure you agree, Inspector, that these are extenuating circumstances.' Dafydd Upton made his first contribution, which wasn't really helpful or constructive. He should have known such a comment was for the magistrates' court and not for the police interview.

By the end, Fiona Jones had made a full confession, making it one of the easiest interviews Drake had ever completed. He found himself feeling oddly sympathetic towards her. She knew her husband to be a serial philanderer, but his relationships had never been as intense as the one with Penny Muller. Somehow for Fiona it had been different and self-destructive. Before completing the interview, Drake asked one further question.

'Do you think Penny or Wolfgang Muller was responsible for killing Harry?'

'They were ruining our lives.' It didn't answer the question.

'Do you think Wolfgang Muller killed Harry? To stop him from having a relationship with his wife?'

Fiona gave Drake another of her confused, damaged expressions that he couldn't read. Had the thought not occurred to her?

The custody sergeant accepted Drake's recommendation that he release Fiona Jones on bail. Drake had no doubts the Crown Prosecution Service would press charges for criminal damage. In due course Dafydd Upton would get a chance to impress the magistrates with his plea in mitigation – maybe even get a mention in the local press.

'You're going to interview Wolfgang whatever-his-name-is?' The sergeant asked.

'I need to talk to my team first,' Drake said, heading out of the custody suite.

Winder was finishing a stale-looking Danish pastry when Drake arrived in the canteen. Luned was talking with Sara, empty mugs on the table in front of them.

Drake detoured to the counter for a bottle of water and returned to join the rest of his team. Winder dabbed a tissue to his mouth, a contented, fat-induced look on his face.

'So what did the guests at Bryn Hyfryd have to say?' Drake said.

Winder was the first to reply. 'There were a dozen guests – all a bit weird.'

'New-age people, sir.' Luned clarified.

Winder ignored her and carried on. 'They were all hippies. A yoga session run by Penny Muller finished about ten o'clock on the night Harry Jones was killed. A couple of them remembered Wolfgang being there. Some of them stayed around for chamomile tea – they made a point of telling us that.'

'Nothing wrong with herbal tea,' Sara said.

Luned nodded. 'I quite like the raspberry one myself.'

Winder grimaced, floundering as to how to react. 'Most of them were in bed by midnight and none of them recalled seeing Wolfgang afterwards. They were all staying there for a "wellness week", enjoying walking in the country, alternative pursuits and getting in touch with their inner selves.'

'So he could have left in the middle of the night. We'll need to establish if there are any traffic or CCTV cameras nearby.'

'Come off it, boss,' Winder said. 'It's like the wild

west up there. There are lots of these hippy communes in the mountains. Nobody knows what they get up to. And I wouldn't trust any of the witnesses to be reliable. Wolfgang could have slipped out any time.'

A search of the database of traffic cameras would give Drake the answer quickly enough. The Range Rover Evoque would have been too recognisable; Wolfgang might have used another car, a motorbike or a bicycle even. Drake made a mental note to get the route calculated. They needed an approximate time of death from the pathologist before they focused on Wolfgang Muller as a possible suspect.

Drake and Sara returned to the office they had used earlier. Wolfgang Muller was twiddling his thumbs in one of the conference rooms while communicating his impatience several times through the civilians working at the main reception.

Drake read Penny Muller's statement. It covered the basic facts and agreed with the sequence of events he had heard from Fiona Jones. Drake could have delegated the task of recording Wolfgang's statement to Winder and Luned. But his connection to Harry Jones made this different.

'We haven't got any evidence to suggest Wolfgang Muller is a suspect in the murder of Harry Jones,' Sara announced.

'I'm sure he'll want to make a formal complaint about the damage to his property,' Drake added.

Sara raised a carefully manicured eyebrow.

'And we can have a discussion with him about his relationship with Harry Jones at the same time.'

'It sounds like a fishing expedition,' Sara said.

Sara's comment signalled her growing confidence.

After several years of working with Caren Waits, it had taken time for Drake to become accustomed to Sara Morgan. There was a harder edge to her than Caren, not always as resourceful but tough nevertheless.

'We can't keep him waiting any longer.' Drake stood up, gathered his papers together, and nodded to Sara before leaving.

Wolfgang Muller was standing by a window when Drake and Sara entered. A china mug sat on a table, a distinct improvement from the plastic containers used in the custody suite. He frowned at Drake.

'Why the hell am I being kept waiting?'

'I am most terribly sorry,' Drake gave Wolfgang his best smile, waving a hand to the chairs around the table. 'I'm sure you can appreciate that investigations like this can take time. You know how it is these days. We have to handle things sensitively and be conscious of Fiona's role as the widow of the victim in a brutal murder.' Drake even surprised himself with his gushing obsequiousness, but it did the trick – Wolfgang's body language and challenging attitude dissolved into a matter-of-fact, cooperative expression.

'Is it going to take long?'

'Not at all. We want to formally record your complaint. It's all a matter of procedures, getting the protocols right. I'm sure you understand.' Drake rolled his eyes and gave him a man-of-the-world shrug.

Wolfgang read the time on his watch lazily.

'What time did Fiona arrive at Bryn Hyfryd?' Drake opened with a simple, softening-up question.

'I'm sorry, Inspector. I don't remember.'

'It must have been quite a shock when she smashed up your cars?'

'I told the guests to stay indoors. She was quite clearly deranged.'

'How long did her vandalism spree last?'

'A few minutes I guess.'

'It must have been very upsetting for you?'

'Yes, of course. But I was more concerned for the guests and their safety.'

Drake sat back in his chair for a moment. 'So why did you think Fiona decided to smash your cars?' Drake kept his eye contact firmly on Wolfgang's face, searching for any tell-tale signs, an indication of what was going through his mind.

'Obviously the loss of her husband is having a profound effect on her mental stability.'

Drake reached for a ballpoint on top of his papers and turned it through his fingers. 'Mental instability … and what do you think might have caused that?'

'I take it you are alluding to the fact that Penny had a brief …' Wolfgang fluttered his left hand in the air. '… affair with Harry Jones.'

'And what did you think of that?' Drake tried to make the question sound conversational.

'Penny and I agreed years ago not to make conscious moral demands on each other. In that way we can each fulfil each other's potential without being hidebound to the other. Loyalty and love mean so much more than simple fidelity.'

Drake spent time teasing out of Wolfgang as much information as he could about what he knew of his wife's relationship with Harry Jones. Occasionally Drake paused, retreated and regrouped until he could focus his questions on getting a clear picture of what Wolfgang really felt. By the end Drake wasn't certain he had achieved anything other than to listen to an explanation of a convoluted relationship that made no sense.

'We'll need full details in due course of the repair cost to your vehicles,' Drake said.

'I'll organise it in the next few days.'

Drake stood up and reached out a hand. 'Thank you, Mr Muller.'

Drake and Sara watched as Wolfgang left the police station. It had been a tortuous turn of events that day. The wife of a murder victim had been arrested for criminal damage. Her interview had taken place before Drake had completed taking statements from one of the complainants – Wolfgang Muller. Not that it made any difference; Fiona had made a full confession – enough for any CPS lawyer to decide that she be charged.

'What did you make of that boss?' Sara said.

'I think Gareth was right – we don't know what these people get up to. I want the mobile telephones of Wolfgang Muller and Fiona Jones triangulated for the day Harry died.'

Sara nodded. 'Conscious moral demands, it's like something those celebs said a few years ago when they split up – "conscious uncoupling".'

'It was Gwyneth Paltrow and Chris Martin from Coldplay.'

Drake disliked Coldplay: their music always struck him as so melancholic.

Drake and Sara said little on their journey back to headquarters. He pulled into the car park and once Sara had left he drove home. In the kitchen, he noticed the bleeping of the landline base, showing him there was a message. He listened to his mother telling him that Sian had contacted her about the weekend, and it piqued him that she had called his mother. Sian's plans must have been important enough to justify calling her. And that annoyed him. It made him speculate what she was doing, who she was seeing and where she was going.

He could always call Sian on the pretext of speaking to his daughters; ask some innocuous-sounding questions about her weekend. But it had been a long day and sitting by the kitchen table he finished a ready meal, and then polished off a bottle of German lager. Flopping into a chair in the lounge he flicked through the channels on his television before watching the news. He woke a couple of hours later to a documentary about the likelihood of a volcanic eruption around Naples. He switched the programme off and went to bed.

Chapter 9

The following morning Drake arrived at headquarters early. He took the stairs to the second floor two at a time to the empty Incident Room and his office. After draping the jacket of his suit over a wooden hanger on the coat stand he settled down at his desk. The columns of colour-coordinated Post It notes were shorter than usual but by the end of the day they would have lengthened as Drake got to grips with the investigation.

The rest of his desk was neat and tidy. He reached over and moved the photograph of Helen and Megan a few millimetres. Before switching on his computer, he pulled a duster from a drawer and cleaned the keyboard. Removing the dust gathered between each key and along the top rim above the F command keys before he could start work had become a recent habit he found comforting. Once satisfied it was clean he booted up his computer and waited for the monitor to flicker into life.

He deleted various emails from his inbox – but he lingered on the request from Superintendent Price for a meeting later that day. It would be his first opportunity to bring his superior officer up to date. He could imagine Price's reaction to Harry Jones' reputation. It would be a mixture of disgust tinged with an edge of jealousy.

The noise from bodies congregating in the Incident Room broke his concentration and he left his office and joined Winder and Luned as Sara entered and greeted everyone.

'Good morning,' Drake said to his team nearing the board.

'Any luck with Wolfgang Muller?' Winder said.

'We interviewed him yesterday as a witness. He admitted his wife had a relationship with Harry Jones and implied he was relaxed about it. He called it an absence of conscious moral judgements.'

Winder guffawed. 'You mean he was happy knowing that another man was shagging his wife?'

Sara made her first contribution. 'That seems to be the case.'

'I told you they were all hippies and dead weird.'

'We make Wolfgang Muller a person of interest in our inquiry. For most people family infidelity would be a perfect motive. So, I want to know a lot more about him. Dig into his past, establish full background details. And find a photograph for the board.'

Sara again. 'And the same for Penny Muller?'

'Yes, we treat everything she and Wolfgang told us with suspicion.'

Drake looked over at Winder. 'Were you able to check Fiona's alibi?'

'I spoke with her mother who confirmed the details Fiona gave you, boss.'

'One of you will need to take a formal statement from her in due course.'

Winder continued. 'It still means she could have killed Harry Jones when she got back.'

Drake thought the same. Fiona lived close enough to the crime scene for her to have lured her husband to the Quarryman's Hospital after arriving back from her mother's home. And a cuckolded spouse has the clearest motive in the world. It was a case where they had more than one.

Winder piped up. 'Perhaps Fiona simply got tired of his philandering. She snaps and kills him.'

'It's a bit too premeditated for that,' Drake turned to the image of Fiona on the board. 'We need to find out if Harry Jones made a will.'

'Is Fiona going to be charged with criminal damage, sir?' Luned said.

'She was bailed last night. We'll send the file to the Crown Prosecution Service; one of their lawyers can make the final decision.'

'And it would have been easy for Fiona to find a gun,' Sara said. 'She probably knew about Harry's collection'

Gun crime was practically non-existent in North Wales and when it did occur it made the headlines. The sort of coverage Drake had seen on the television where the reporters had interviewed the terrified residents of Llanberis – older citizens cowering behind their front doors, young mothers drawing children into a protective embrace.

Drake continued. 'He probably brought one home to show her.' Drake looked over at his team. 'We treat Fiona as a person of interest, too.'

Drake spent the next ten minutes allocating tasks. Winder was to coordinate the house-to-house enquiries. There would be dozens of statements from well-intentioned members of the public. The investigation might depend on some snippet of information from a jogger or a dog walker or secret lovers in or around the slate museum and the Quarryman's Hospital. Winder's shoulders sagged as he jotted down notes.

Luned was tasked with establishing the finances of Harry and Fiona Jones. Debt and the financial pressures it created were an obvious motive and Drake didn't want to dismiss the possibility that Fiona Jones killed

Harry without a complete investigation.

'One of the local shopkeepers rang yesterday boss,' Luned said. 'He saw Harry Jones leaving his shop at about 6.20 p.m. and he said he was heading to a council meeting.'

Winder moved his head to get Drake's attention. 'We had the preliminary financial reports on Harry Jones in too. He used his card in a supermarket on the day he was killed. I called them and apparently he bought flowers and wine.'

'And the time?'

'2.30 p.m.'

'Talk to the assistant on the till. You might get more details. And find out if he was with anyone.'

Back in his office Drake reached into a desk drawer and pulled out a pad before moving the Post It notes carefully to one side. He started by drawing two columns and scribbling 'time' on the top of the first and 'details' on the second. Then he read the details of the statement from the eyewitness who had seen Harry Jones leaving his shop.

Once complete, he rechecked the details and read them again.

Time	Details
12.30	HJ seen in shop by FJ and Michael
2.30	Supermarket – buying flowers and wine
5.00	Back in shop for closing – spoken to by Michael
6.20	Seen leaving shop by local shopkeeper.
8.00	Council meeting concludes

The absence of any details for the morning didn't trouble Drake. They had to establish where Harry Jones had been and, more importantly, who he had been with for two and half hours that afternoon.

There were flowers and wine involved so Drake guessed it meant a tryst. Drake sat back in his chair. Should he make a public appeal for witnesses to come forward with details of Harry's whereabouts that day?

He was still contemplating the answer when the telephone rang. He recognised the voice of Mike Foulds.

'I've been looking at those guns you recovered from that storage locker. They all look to be the genuine article. I was expecting them to be replicas or at least disabled. But they all could fire live ammunition.'

'Why would he keep those sorts of firearms?' Drake said.

'I'm going to send the bullet to a specialist forensic analyst I met at a course last year. He specialises in firearms and has a particular interest in World War II memorabilia.'

Drake imagined Fiona Jones finding the old revolver in the house; it gave her the ideal opportunity to kill Harry Jones.

'Yes, of course. Whatever you think best.'

He ended the call and his mind turned to the historian at the army museum he'd been referred to yesterday. He found the contact details and dialled the number.

'I'm Detective Inspector Ian Drake of the Wales Police Service. I need to speak to Mr Edwards on a police matter.

'I think I've got a number somewhere.' The receptionist dictated the details Drake scribbled down on his notepad.

After four rings, the call was answered but in the background Drake could hear voices and bleeping that sounded like a supermarket checkout.

'My name is Detective Inspector Ian Drake. I understand you have an interest in World War Two history. I hope you might be able to help us with identifying some firearms we've recovered as part of an investigation. I need you to examine some images.'

'I don't work at the museum every day. But I could see you tomorrow afternoon.'

He was already committed to babysitting his daughters tomorrow, but if he collected the girls in the morning he could take them to his mother's home for lunch and then travel into Caernarfon and meet Edwards.

'Will two p.m. be convenient?'

Drake rang off once Edwards confirmed the appointment.

Calling his mother to finalise the arrangements was straightforward. She sounded delighted at having them all for lunch. She dictated a possible menu and he salivated at the prospect of a decent meal. Reaching Sian proved more difficult. He left several messages for her that morning hoping she might return his call between appointments in her surgery. She eventually rang him back at lunchtime.

'I want to pick the girls up earlier than planned tomorrow,' Drake said.

'Why is that?'

'I'm taking them to my mother's for lunch.'

'I see.'

'When are you leaving for your weekend?'

Sian hesitated. 'We ... I'm leaving tonight.'

'Are you going far?'

'Look, Ian, this isn't a good time. The waiting room is full of urgent appointments.'

'Make sure you tell your mother to expect me early.'

'Yes, of course.'

Drake finished the call and slumped back in his chair. A mass of confused emotions trickled through his mind. He dismissed the notion he was jealous she might be going away with somebody for the weekend. After all, they had been separated for, how long? It annoyed him that he still expected Sian to share with him her family plans. The divorce had gone through, all that remained was to sort out the financial paperwork. Any prospect of reconciliation was a distant memory.

The demands of his working life had often meant that he worked long hours, arrived home late and left early. And talking about murder inquiries or difficult rape cases wasn't exactly the subject of household small talk. Glancing over at the photograph of his daughters on the desk made him realise how much he missed them: seeing them first thing in the morning, dropping them at school, sitting with them at mealtimes. The possibility Sian might have a relationship with someone else hadn't been something he had contemplated with any certainty. Now it appeared a more realistic prospect.

And his mother had made a comment recently that he shouldn't plan to live the rest of his life alone. It had even occurred to him to try one of the Internet dating sites that advertised regularly on the television. One of his colleagues was having a New Year's Eve marriage in a resort in the West Indies to a woman he'd met that way and Drake idly wondered what his daughters might say if he started dating someone.

Drake spent the next hour working his way through the list of individuals in North Wales who had licences for firearms, shotguns and revolvers. There were over a thousand, so he decided to narrow the search to those with addresses in Gwynedd, the county where Harry Jones lived, and the island of Anglesey. There were half a dozen gun clubs in the North West area of North Wales and Drake jotted down the names and telephone numbers for the secretary of each, knowing they'd have to contact them in turn. Someone would know of an individual with an interest in vintage revolvers.

He could sense the dull buzz of activity from the Incident Room beyond his door and hoped that the others on his team were making progress.

Sara appeared on the threshold.

'Would you like a coffee?'

Before answering Drake read the time on his watch and realised his meeting with Superintendent Price was imminent.

'No, thanks. I've got a meeting with the super.'

He got up and took his jacket off the stand, shrugging it over his shoulders.

It was a short walk through the corridors of headquarters to the senior management suite. Wyndham Price exchanged a joke with his secretary as Drake entered.

'Good to see you, Ian – go in.' Price nodded at the

door into his office.

Pride of place on the conference table was a glass vase with a bouquet of freshly cut roses still wrapped in its supermarket cellophane.

'It's a present for my wife; it's our wedding anniversary – thirty years.' Price made the final two words sound like a prison sentence. At least he managed to buy flowers, Drake thought, chastising himself about the frequency with which he had ever bought flowers for Sian.

Price sat down and dragged his chair nearer his desk. Apart from the piles of different coloured folders sitting discreetly on one corner, it was remarkably clutter free.

'Did you read the statement the public relations department issued yesterday?'

Drake nodded. It had been among emails he had read earlier. It contained the usual anodyne noncommittal language.

'Let's hope it helps.'

'Does it ever?'

Drake spent his allotted time explaining to his superior officer exactly how he intended to progress the investigation. Price nodded, agreed and made the occasional suggestion.

'Are you going to be organising a press conference?' Drake said.

A press conference was unavoidable, and the public relations department frequently suggested one be arranged although Drake never believed they achieved a great deal. After his initial nerves as a young officer Drake found engaging with the television reporters uncomplicated and, being bilingual, he was a regular with the Welsh language news broadcasts.

'Not at the moment. What concerns me is the use of a firearm. The press is making that into a big story. Have you made any progress with identifying the weapon involved?'

'We should have more positive identification by the beginning of the week.'

'Let's hope we can manage the press interest in the meantime.'

Drake stood up to leave; he cast an eye at the flowers.

'Are you going somewhere special to celebrate?'

Price smiled, and named an expensive restaurant that had recently won its first Michelin star. 'Keep me posted with developments.'

Drake drifted back to the Incident Room, regretting that his evening would be spent in front of his computer.

Chapter 10

When Drake arrived at the Incident Room the following morning the officers in his team were chatting amiably. A country and western singer would have been proud of the plaid shirt Winder wore that Saturday morning. Luned looked as formal as she did on a normal day. Sara had tied her hair in a severe knot behind her head.

Winder munched on a pastry and Drake guessed that the bag on the desk from a local bakery had more Danish and Chelsea buns to keep the young constable on a sugar high all morning. They exchanged the usual pleasantries, and Drake ignored a vague sense of guilt that he wouldn't be present all day, but at least his meeting with the historian that afternoon meant he was doing something constructive.

Standing by the board he examined the various photographs pinned to it. It was a motley selection of persons of interest. One of the team had pinned an Ordnance Survey map of Llanberis and the surrounding valley to the board. Although it was only a few miles from where he'd lived as a child it amazed Drake he hadn't heard about the bomb storage facility, even though it had been abandoned before he was born. The rural communities of North Wales could be self-contained, insular, isolated. The recent disclosures in his own family about his father's conflict with his parents had reinforced for Drake that his was a society that valued its secrets, frowned upon openness. Tom Drake had become a father as a young man but Drake learned nothing of his stepbrother until quite recently. It had been a shock, a secret that had rocked the family. His sister had still not come to terms with it.

Drake thought about Harry Jones' relationship with Penny Muller as he looked at Fiona's face. What did Fiona really think? People must have known, surely, Drake thought. At the heart of the secretive, quiet community was a festering hypocrisy. What else did they have to learn about Harry Jones?

Sitting at his desk he turned to the urgent column of Post It notes. The sound of clicking mice and paper being moved drifted into his room through the open door. He cast a glance at Fiona's image on the board in the distance and then at her name scribbled on a red Post It note. If she had murdered her husband, then her attempt at an alibi was ineffective – she could easily have killed him after returning from seeing her mother. The incident with Penny Muller pointed the finger of suspicion at Wolfgang Muller, but was it pre-planned and orchestrated to divert their attention from Fiona?

Drake turned his attention to Harry Jones' bank accounts. The antiques dealer had several – each with various names: business, property income, tax reserve, one marked *personal* and one jointly with his wife. A debit card on his personal account had been used for the purchase of flowers and wine on the afternoon before he was killed. Drake focused his attention on that account and jotted down the dates of other purchases in the same supermarket. Harry Jones wasn't buying flowers for his wife, Drake guessed, but who was the other person and why hadn't she come forward?

Soon a pattern emerged of weekly payments for sums approximately the same as the amount Harry Jones had spent on the day he died. Occasionally, more frequent. Drake made a mental note that he would have to ask Fiona if she was the recipient of Harry's generosity, but he doubted it. Trawling through someone's bank account was a small part of the investigation, a small cog in a larger wheel. Analysing all of Harry's bank statements would have to wait. As he read the time, knowing he had to collect his daughters imminently, he heard Sara's voice.

'Something you should see, sir.'

Drake left his office for her desk.

'The night Harry was killed he had typed out a message on his mobile – *Where are you?*'

'Who was the recipient?'

'The message was never sent.'

'So it could be anyone.'

Sara continued. 'And I've been trawling through the numbers in Harry Jones' mobile.'

Drake squinted down at her, expecting an important revelation from the tone of her voice.

'There are dozens of calls to a Richard Perdue.'

'And who is Richard Perdue?'

'I checked through the police national computer. He's got a number of convictions for handling stolen property and, more importantly, several acquittals for similar offences. There are references to intelligence reports from three other forces.'

Exchanging information with other police forces was crucial, but a reference to other forces suggested Richard Perdue was a person of significant interest.

Sara continued. 'I've still got at least three dozen other names to check out.'

Every contact on Harry Jones' mobile would need to be identified, followed up and spoken to.

Before leaving, Drake listened to updates from Luned and Winder and then scooped up his jacket and left the Incident Room, knowing his team had hours of work ahead of them.

When Drake arrived to collect Helen and Megan he made small talk with his mother-in-law although he didn't detect any warmth – not that he was offering any himself. He had never found it easy to get on with Sian's mother. Drake had harboured a suspicion she somehow thought Sian might have done better for herself, chosen a husband more wisely, as though she were assessing a thoroughbred racehorse. Sian's father was a lot easier, more easy-going, less judgemental.

It surprised Drake when she thanked him for taking the girls so she could attend the charity auction that afternoon. It also narked him that she thought it appropriate to thank him for taking his own daughters. Perhaps his lifestyle as a detective had come to this – making himself available for his children was an unusual occurrence.

He was later than he had hoped so a brief conversation with his mother on his mobile warned her they might be late. He drove down to the A55 and then westward through the tunnel under the Conwy estuary and then on towards the tunnels through the mountains. The traffic was light, and Drake tried small talk.

'Did you do anything interesting last night?'

'Nothing.' Helen said, uncommonly taciturn.

'We watched television. And we had pizza and Coke.' Megan piped up.

Both girls sat in the back returning their attention to the electronic gadgets on their laps.

'Has Mam called you?'

They shook their heads but said nothing. Drake had expected a little bit more information, but cursed himself for stooping so low to think he could interrogate them about Sian's mystery weekend.

After taking the junction for Caernarfon he skirted around the town, catching a glimpse of the castle's imposing turrets. He travelled the narrow country lanes to his mother's smallholding as he had done hundreds of times before. After a few minutes he reached the track that led down to the property. In the distance, storm-filled clouds gathered over Caernarfon Bay.

His mother was waiting for them on the threshold when he parked the car on the gravelled area near the back door.

'How are you, Ian?' She gave him a brief hug. She gave her granddaughters a more enthusiastic version.

The girls disappeared into the house.

'You look tired,' Mair Drake said before continuing in the same motherly vein. 'You're wearing your best suit.'

Drake wasn't going to embark on an explanation of the pecking order of the suits in his wardrobe. 'I told you I've arranged to see someone in the army museum this afternoon.'

Mair Drake rolled her eyes in feigned ignorance. 'Let's have lunch before you go.'

A warm, rich smell filled the kitchen. It reminded him how hungry he felt – grazing during the day was another unwelcome symptom of his busy schedule. The smell took him back to his childhood, of substantial roast dinners, serving plates piled with steaming potatoes and fresh vegetables.

'I've made beef stew.'

She told him about one of her neighbours who was waiting for an operation, and as Drake listened he realised how easy it was to relax in the house he once called home. Sitting around the table with his daughters was a simple family activity he missed. Although he hadn't valued it enough in the past.

By the end Helen and Megan had eaten far too much. The portions of fruit crumble and custard went unfinished on their plates. Drake helped his mother clear the dishes and her kitchen was returned to its usual neat and tidy order.

'Did I tell you about Susan?' Mair cast a worried glance at Drake. 'She's going to visit the weekend after next.' Apprehension was engraved into every word. 'I want her to meet Huw.'

Now there was a certainty and determination in her voice.

'You will be able to come, won't you?'

Drake smiled confirmation, hoping the demands of the inquiry would mean he could attend this family event where his half-brother would be present. He glanced at his watch and realised he was late.

'I need to leave. I won't be long,' he said, finding his jacket and reaching for the car keys.

It was a short drive down into Caernarfon where he parked on the quayside below the huge imposing walls of the mediaeval castle built by Edward I to subdue the querulous Welsh population. He strolled up to the main square, casting a brief glance at the platform upon which a historian had recorded that Edward introduced his firstborn son to the people of the town as the Prince of Wales.

At the entrance of the castle he paid the fee and

made his way inside. The scale and ambition of the building always made Drake pause. Tall polygonal towers loomed over the internal grassed area. It must have been an imposing, intimidating sight for the native Welsh population, Drake thought.

He followed the signs for the museum into one of the towers. Eventually he found a wooden door that filled a substantial stone arch. 'Staff Only' was printed on a thin metal sign screwed to the middle. A stainless steel ring hung to one side, the only clue as to how to open it. Inside, the warmth contrasted with the chill autumn air. The room was larger than Drake expected, and to his right a door led off up three shallow steps.

A man sat by a desk poring over books and journals. At the far end boxes were piled on top of a cupboard. Alongside it were stacks of plastic chairs. The collection of small tables and various filing cabinets completed the picture of an office-cum-junk room.

'John Edwards?' Drake said.

The man turned and looked over at Drake. He had a kindly warm face. He gave Drake a weak smile.

'Inspector Drake?' He stood up and reached out a hand. 'John Edwards, good afternoon.'

'Thank you for seeing me.' Drake dragged over a chair.

'How can I help?'

Drake sat down and dropped a folder onto the table.

'I'm conducting a murder investigation and we've discovered various old firearms in a lock-up storage unit that the victim owned.'

'I presume you're talking about Harry Jones, from

Llanberis?'

Drake nodded and rummaged in the folder for the photographs. Each gun had been photographed from every conceivable angle. Looking down the barrel, from the bottom of the handgrip, and from an elevated position.

'I've got photographs here and I was hoping that you might be able to identify these individual firearms.'

Drake handed a set of half a dozen images of the first revolver to Edwards who flicked through them slowly. He jotted something on a notepad on the desk. Drake passed him the rest of the photographs and for a few minutes Edwards said nothing, contemplated and made more notes.

The door behind them creaked open and a man entered carrying a tray with two steaming mugs.

'This is Glyn Talbot,' Edwards said. 'We meet on a Saturday to prepare articles for *Papur Padarn*.'

Drake recognised the name of the local 'papur bro' – Welsh language community newspaper.

Talbot wore a crumpled, dishevelled suit and an off-white shirt thin with age. The clothes matched the chubby-cheeked appearance. Talbot peered at Drake through half-rimmed spectacles.

'Inspector Drake.' Talbot offered a hand. He couldn't pronounce his 'r's correctly.

'Glyn, Inspector Drake wants help in identifying these pistols.' He pointed to the images on the table.

Talbot leaned over and gave them a half-hearted glance. 'They all look very old to me. I don't know anything about guns.'

Edwards nodded. 'They are all vintage revolvers from the period of the Second World War. The first one is a Walther P38 – commonly used by the German army before and during the Second World War and the second is a Mauser Hsc – it was in common use in the German army and navy as well as civilian use. The third is a Smith & Wesson that was manufactured in massive numbers by the United States.'

'Do you know of any collectors of these sorts of pistols?'

'Nobody locally. Have they been disarmed?'

'I'm waiting for the results of a full forensic examination.'

'There is a black market in these guns. Collectors who are prepared to take the risk. Normally the pistols would be rendered harmless by removing the firing pin. But certain people collect them despite it being illegal to do so.'

Richard Perdue might tick that box, Drake thought.

'I don't think I can add anything further,' Edwards said.

'Could there be any connection to the old bomb storage facility in Llanberis? Were any hand guns ever stored there?'

Talbot replied first. 'None and the place was left as a mausoleum.'

'If you're interested in Llanberis I can introduce you to Annie, who's researching the history of the village,' Edwards added.

Drake glanced at his watch, thinking that he didn't have the time to spend talking to a dry academic.

'Follow me.' Edwards stood up.

Drake gathered up his papers and joined Edwards, who strolled through into an adjacent room with long tables and glass-fronted cabinets filled with books.

A woman sitting at the far end turned and glanced over at Drake and Edwards.

'Annie, this is Detective Inspector Drake.' Edwards turned to Drake. 'Annie specialises in the history of the slate mining areas of North Wales.'

Annie stood up and reached out a hand. She gave him a perfect smile that lit up her broad, perfectly proportioned face and sculpted her cheeks into warm pockets. Dark auburn hair curtained her face. She dragged a lock of hair over her right ear. There was an intensity and warmth in her brown eyes that he hadn't seen in a woman's face since, well, he couldn't remember.

Introductions completed, Talbot made excuses and left, although Drake had paid him little further attention. From the curl of her mouth Drake realised he must have been gawping. She was the same height as Sian; why did he always compare women to her? And she had the same slim build. Perhaps that was why she was so attractive.

Drake found a chair and sat down.

'You're investigating the murder in Llanberis?'

Drake detected the sharp edge of a Cardiff accent as well as the rounded soft vowels of rural West Wales.

'Harry Jones.' Drake focused on making sensible contributions to their conversation. 'Glyn Talbot says you're an expert on the history of Llanberis.'

Annie smiled again. Drake smiled back, an instinctive reaction to the warmth of her face.

'I'm finishing a paper about the history of the labour conflicts in the various quarries in the Llanberis and Bethesda area and how they impacted on the communities.'

'Harry Jones' family was quite well-to-do at one time. I can certainly send you some details about them.'

It occurred to Drake to suggest that he collect them, but it would probably make him sound like a smitten teenager.

'Yes, of course.'

'Llanberis and the surrounding area is fascinating. There is so much history.'

Drake nodded, and listened as Annie told him about the development of the town from the Victorian era when the railway to the top of Snowdon was built and how the Dinorwig quarry produced vast amounts of slate.

Drake ignored the time, deciding he had a renewed interest in local history.

Chapter 11

Drake sat in his Mondeo staring at the Sudoku puzzle, realising that for a Monday morning he should have been more relaxed. Returning Helen and Megan to their grandmother's home on Saturday evening, it had occurred to him to suggest that they stay with him for the rest of the weekend. But he could imagine the cool reception such an idea would have encountered. Arrangements had been made, plans by Sian's mother forged in steel and, having taken the coward's way out, he regretted his decision that morning.

He discarded the newspaper on the passenger seat after managing a couple of squares and drove off to headquarters. Hopefully, he could find time during the day to finish off the puzzle – it was a moderate one after all. He reversed the Mondeo into a space at the end of the car park – the extra walking involved to reach the entrance might discourage others from parking too near his car. So far this approach had paid off; the bodywork was scratch free. He took the stairs to an empty Incident Room.

At the board Drake moved Harry's photograph, making it more prominent, right at the centre. He hated it when things appeared lopsided.

He had lost count of the times he had checked Annie's telephone number on his mobile since meeting her. Doubting himself that there were eleven numbers, he recounted them each time. He should have had the courage yesterday to call her – speak to her in person. That morning he looked at her number again and read the message he had tapped in at breakfast.

Would you like to meet for dinner Wednesday?

He had used the words *love to see you* but decided against it. And should he add an *x* at the end? Again, he decided against it. But did his message sound too cold? He added his name and pressed send. He sat back, wondering how he might feel if she didn't reply or simply said no thanks.

He didn't have time to answer himself as Mike Foulds appeared on the threshold of his office.

'I've been called to a burglary this morning in Wrexham so I thought I'd tell you in person that you need to check out the CCTV footage we found on the computer in Harry Jones' property.'

'CCTV?' Drake's interest was piqued.

'He had a small camera screwed to the storage cupboards on the back wall of his office. There are hours of coverage from the last few weeks. After three months the recordings are erased.'

'Is there anything of significance on them?'

'Come off it Ian. We haven't got time to go through CCTV recordings. You're the detective; that's your job.'

Drake followed Foulds into the Incident Room, almost colliding with Sara who entered at the same time. Foulds muttered an apology and Drake heard his muffled greetings to Winder and Luned, who soon traipsed in. Winder shrugged off his overcoat while Luned and Sara dumped their bags on their desks.

'The CSIs have discovered some CCTV recordings from Harry Jones' office,' Drake announced as three faces looked up at him trying to focus their attention. Drake could see Winder struggling to get his mind into gear. Drake read the time and glanced at Sara. 'We've got a couple of hours before our appointment in

Llanberis.' Sara nodded her recollection of their meeting that morning with the parish council chairman. Drake continued as he made for his room. 'In the meantime, we'll divide the coverage between us.'

He turned his attention to the emails in his inbox and quickly downloaded the attachment from Foulds. The digital recording had been stored in date order so Drake took a moment to decide how the coverage would be shared between the team before he called for Sara, Gareth and Luned to join him. They stood in the doorway listening to his instructions before they returned to their desks.

Finding the right speed at which to view the CCTV footage involved trial and error, and Drake didn't want to spend hours watching an empty office. It took him a while to find the correct setting and only when he saw Harry Jones or Michael the shop assistant did he play the recording in real time.

Following a murder victim going about his normal day-to-day business had an eerie quality. Drake rechecked the chronology for Harry Jones on the day he died. Sure enough, Harry appeared in the footage a little before 5 p.m. that fateful day. Michael came into the shot and spent a few moments, presumably discussing the day's takings; their body language suggested nothing controversial but without audio Drake had only half the picture. Harry Jones' departure matched up with the eyewitness evidence that recounted a meeting outside the shop at 6.20. It struck Drake he had started back to front for that day so he rewound the tape to 9 a.m. Harry turned up promptly at nine and began his office routine. He took telephone calls, swung his feet up onto the desk, made a coffee, left the room occasionally, presumably to talk to Michael because his absence wasn't lengthy. Mid-morning when the post arrived he used an antique letter opener, discarding the envelopes into a nearby bin while sorting the various contents into racks and the drawers of his filing cabinets. It appeared to Drake to be the dull routine of the small-businessman even though he knew Harry Jones was far from a model citizen. He hurried the tape on, but his attention was sharpened when he saw someone appear; he checked the time – 11.34. Drake paused the coverage and gazed at the screen. Two men and he couldn't instantly make out their faces. He knew he had seen one of them before – then he recognised the tired, old-fashioned looking clothes that belonged to Glyn Talbot, who he'd met at the army museum on Saturday.

He scrolled back until just before Talbot appeared.

He pressed play again. Harry Jones stood up. Making out the exact look on his face was difficult but Drake could tell that Harry was uncomfortable. He moved away from his desk and retreated from Talbot, who was a good two inches taller than Harry Jones and a bigger build. Drake jotted down the time when Glyn Talbot and Harry Jones started talking and when they finished – three minutes, twelve seconds. Drake froze the recording again: Talbot had made no reference to knowing Harry on Saturday. It was out of context, of course; he had been there to speak to Edwards but a grain of misgiving sowed itself in his mind.

A shout from Gareth Winder interrupted Drake's thinking. 'Something you should see, boss.'

Drake gave the static image of Talbot and Harry Jones another pensive glance as he left his desk. Sara and Luned had already joined a grinning Winder. Drake stood alongside both women as Winder clicked on his mouse. Staring at the screen for most of the morning made it easy for Drake to recognise the inside of Harry Jones' office.

'This was mid-week – three weeks before he was killed,' Winder said.

Drake glanced at the clock on the bottom of the monitor – 15.30.

A woman entered the room. It was difficult to make out her age – but she looked at least twenty years Harry's junior. She was slim, but making out her height was awkward. Harry pulled her close, drawing a hand up her right leg, hoisting her skirt to her waist, she offered no resistance and folded her hand across his face drawing him towards her lips.

'That's disgusting,' Luned said. 'He's old enough to be her father.'

Drake sensed Sara fidgeting in embarrassment as Harry propped the girl onto the table, forcing her legs apart before reaching for his belt buckle. Something interrupted Harry and the nameless girl, something Drake and his team could only guess at – noise, a shout, a knock on the door. She got off the table, straightened her clothes, Harry jerked towards the camera and the young woman hurried to the corner of the room.

'She's going into the cupboard.' Drake raised his voice to underline the incredulity.

Harry straightened the papers on his desk, and glanced at the cupboard. He stepped towards it and they could clearly make out that he dipped his head, obviously saying something to the girl secreted inside. Whatever was happening, she wasn't going to be included.

Harry left his office but seconds later he reappeared, losing his balance as though he had been pushed back into the room. He was followed by the outstretched arm of another man, clean-shaven, hair carefully trimmed to his skull, and wearing an expensive-looking leather jacket. He seemed mid-forties; thick lips gave his face a distinctive appearance. Although he wasn't much taller than Harry Jones, he started prodding a finger into Harry's chest.

The grainy coverage made it difficult to read the body language carefully, but from Harry's hand gestures and open mannerisms he was trying to win this man's confidence. Did Harry owe him money? Drake wondered. The man stood, wide-legged, glaring at Harry, obviously dictating a demand or at the very least instructions.

They stood in silence watching the final stages of the stand-off between Harry Jones and the mystery man. Eventually he left, and Harry hurried over to the cupboard. The girl emerged, seemingly unharmed; after a brief exchange, presumably for Harry to reassure her that he was unscathed, they continued where they had left off minutes earlier.

'I've seen enough,' Drake said.

Winder froze the screen, the girl's legs already intertwined around Harry's waist.

'Print off the image of the mystery man and the girl.' Drake nodded to Sara. 'Let's ask Michael – maybe he can tell us who these people are.'

Michael stood outside Padarn Antiques dragging on a

limp cigarette, a can of Irn-Bru perched on the windowsill behind him. Sara wondered who was now in charge of the business – had Fiona been along to check everything was running properly? When she and Drake got out of the vehicle Michael noticed their presence and quickly straightened, casting a guilty glance around the other shops in the vicinity.

Michael looked at them both impassively as they reached the front door of the shop.

The intimidating edge to Drake's voice had no effect on the young man. 'We need to speak to you.' He took a final drag of the cigarette, threw it onto the floor and ground it with the heel of his right shoe. Giving the can of Irn-Bru a hopeful sort of shake persuaded him it was worthwhile taking the dregs back inside. He led Drake and Sara to the small room he occupied.

Sara hadn't expected that anything would have changed.

Even the computer had a game of solitaire in suspended animation.

'Are you looking for a new job?' Drake said.

Michael gave him a half-hearted shrug. 'Mrs Jones says I can stay on until she decides what to do with the business.'

Michael perched on the desk; Drake squeezed himself inside the room while Sara stood on the threshold.

'Did you know Harry Jones had a CCTV camera in his office?' Drake motioned towards the rear of the building.

Michael's mouth fell open, the surprise genuine enough.

Sara continued. 'He was recording everything that

went on. He kept the coverage on his computer.'

'That's dead fucking weird. He could spy on anyone in his office? What about in here?' Michael jerked his head backwards, gazing around the space.

Drake now. 'Did you always see everyone who went into his office?'

'Yeah, I suppose.'

'What's that supposed to mean?'

'Dunno. Sometimes I heard him talking to people who came in through the back door. Then he'd lock the door into the shop. That was HP – thinking he could keep everything dead secret.'

'We've got some photographs. And we want your help.'

'I'm not going to grass anybody up.'

'Why? Do you think Harry Jones was into something illegal?'

'You're putting words into my mouth.'

'If you know something about Harry Jones' activities you'd better tell us now.' Drake stood up; it meant he was almost standing over Michael.

'I don't want to get involved.'

Sara opened the file she had carried from the car. 'We need to know if you recognise any of the individuals we have seen on the CCTV coverage.'

Michael didn't move. He darted a glance between Drake and Sara. Then she held out the first image.

'Have these men been to see Harry Jones regularly?'

'The tall one's Glyn Talbot. Yeah, I've seen him here a couple of times. He's another strange one. I've never seen the other one. He looks like a perv though.'

'Talbot called to see Harry at about half past eleven

on the morning he died. Do you know what they talked about?'

Michael shook his head vigorously. 'How would I know? He must have come in through the side entrance. And anyway I don't think I was here then. I didn't start early that day. I wasn't feeling well.' Sara recalled he appeared well enough the following morning, the morning they discovered the body at the Quarryman's Hospital. Probably a hangover, she guessed.

Drake motioned for her to move onto the next image.

Michael stared at the photograph of the man who had roughed up Harry Jones, interrupting his activity with the young girl. 'I don't want to get involved.'

'Do you recognise this man?'

'Like I said, it's nothing to do with me.'

'You worked for Harry Jones. That means you are involved.'

Sara folded her arms and glared at Michael, reinforcing Drake's message that he had to cooperate.

'He's called Richard Perdue.'

Sara stiffened, noticing Drake's brief frown as he recognised the name.

Sara tried a soft tone. 'What can you tell us about Richard Perdue?'

Michael shifted uncomfortably in his chair, darting glances at the immobile computer game on the monitor. His voice shook when he eventually replied.

'I don't want anything to do with him. He's a bad piece of shit. I don't know why HP got involved with him.'

'How often did he visit HP?'

Michael cleared his throat noisily. 'I didn't keep

count. But I've seen him here a couple of times late into the night when I was leaving the pub. The nights when HP was working late.'

'Did you ever see him threaten Harry Jones?'

'Like I said, leave me out of it. Seriously. I don't want anything to do with him.'

'Do you know where he lives?'

Michael shook his head.

When Drake glanced at Sara she made it clear that he should move on and dug into the file for the final photograph.

Both officers stared at Michael as he gazed, open-eyed, at the image of Harry and the young girl.

'The dirty fucking bastard.'

'Do you think he was telling the truth, boss?'

Drake and Sara sat in the car overlooking Llyn Padarn. Over the surface of the lake Drake could see the roof and chimney stacks of the old Quarryman's Hospital. He drank some of his Americano from a plastic beaker, the sort that made coffee tasteless.

Drake regretted his decision not to sit down in a proper café, but they needed to get on and speak to Glyn Talbot that afternoon.

'If he's lying then we can find out easily enough. We'll get the photograph circulated to some of the local uniformed lads – I'm guessing somebody will know who she is.' He stared at the mug as though sheer willpower would make the coffee improve. 'This coffee is awful.' He got out, paced over to a black bin filled to overflowing, and tipped the contents inside. Back in the car he switched on the engine. 'Let's go and see if

Michael was right about Glyn Talbot.'

High above the valley Drake threaded his way through a patchwork of detached properties, the occasional terrace and plots of derelict land. He parked outside a terrace of small stone houses with substantial slate roofs that couldn't hide the fact they needed a lot of care and attention. Paint flaked from windows; Drake spotted a loose gutter and downpipes ready to topple over onto an unsuspecting pedestrian.

Glyn Talbot opened the door after a delay that merited Drake and Sara exchanging a worried frown. He gazed at both of them impassively. He had the same old shirt that Drake had seen him wear in the museum but this time it was underneath a stained navy sweater.

'Detective Inspector Drake. We met on Saturday in the museum.'

Talbot didn't respond.

'I'd like to ask you some questions about Harry Jones. May we come in?'

Talbot hesitated.

'It really won't take more than a couple of minutes.'

'I was …'

Drake gave his voice a serious tone. 'This is an ongoing murder investigation. I'm sure you understand we have a lot of work to do.'

'Of course.' Talbot relented, easing open the door.

Immediately in front of them was a staircase and to the left the door into a downstairs reception room. The pungent smell of mothballs and ancient furniture tickled Drake's nostrils. A single bar of a double electric heater took the edge off an otherwise cold and unwelcoming room. A cabinet against one wall housed a collection of what looked like old-fashioned clocks and electrical equipment.

Drake sank further than he expected into the old sofa while Talbot sat on an upright Parker Knoll chair, its arms thin with age.

'How well did you know Harry Jones?'

'How well can one know anybody?' Even Talbot's accent sounded forced as though he had to be persuaded to elongate his vowels.

'So, what was your relationship with Harry Jones?' Drake was ready with a sharp reply had Talbot repeated the same response. 'What did you talk about when you visited him on the morning of his death?'

Talbot nodded serenely as though he were a pontiff accepting the supplication of a novice.

'He was the most vocal councillor in support of the development at the old Glyn Rhonwy quarry. I was hoping I could persuade him to change his mind.'

'Did you argue?'

'Of course not. It was a simple discussion. It's no secret, Inspector, that I have written articles critical of the proposed new leisure facility. There's a group of us who want to safeguard the rich heritage of our area and culture and language. There are many leisure facilities in North Wales – we don't need another one.'

'Who else is in this group?'

Talbot rattled off various names.

'I was with Tom Pritchard on the day Harry died. I'm sure he'll confirm the nature of our conversation.'

'I'll need to contact him.'

Talbot left them for the kitchen that was through the door at the end of the room. Sara and Drake took in the room. A necessary trait for any police officer. The walls needed painting – the paper peeled in one corner and the Artexed ceiling made the place feel oppressive.

Talbot returned and handed Drake a yellow Post It with a name and telephone number written on it.

'Thank you.' Drake struggled out of his chair and stood up. 'What do you do for a living, Mr Talbot?'

For a moment Talbot looked nonplussed. 'I'm retired.' He gave Drake another version of his Dickensian face, and Drake and Sara called it a day and left.

Once the door closed behind them they made for the car.

'That was a bit like stepping back in time, boss.'

'I can still smell those mothballs.' Drake shuddered.

He stretched out for the car door when a message reached his mobile.

Sorry, just seen your message. In meeting all day. Dinner Wednesday would be lovely. Axx

He smiled.

Chapter 12

When Drake arrived at headquarters the following morning, Sara had been busy at work for several hours judging by the mountains of files on her desk. She looked up at him as he checked his watch.

'Couldn't sleep?' Drake said.

Sara stretched her back, folding her arms behind her head.

'I wanted to get started on the paperwork operational support recovered from Harry's office.'

Drake nodded. 'There has to be something that links Harry Jones to Richard Perdue.'

The door of the Incident Room squeaked open and Winder and Luned breezed in, nodding greetings as they joined Drake and Sara.

'How did you get on yesterday, boss?' Winder said.

'Harry's assistant, Michael, couldn't identify the girl.'

Winder replied. 'Seems unlikely.'

'He confirmed the other man who interrupted Harry Jones and tried to rough him up was Richard Perdue.'

'He was the man Harry telephoned,' Winder added.

'So we need information on Perdue.'

Winder nodded as Drake continued. 'We spoke to Glyn Talbot about his visit to Harry Jones,' Drake said. 'They were trying to persuade him to change his mind and object to the plans for the old bomb storage facility.'

'I thought that proposal was supported by the local community?' Winder said.

'Talbot and a couple of his pals are dead against it.'
Drake nodded at Winder. 'I'll email you the contact
name for the other man with Talbot. Give him a ring
and check out the details.'

'Do we think either man was involved?' Luned
added.

'Neither of them have a motive as far as I can tell.
And have you both finished going through the CCTV
coverage?'

Winder and Luned managed to exchange a brief,
guilty glance.

'There could be somebody else of interest on that
tape.' Drake reprimanded. 'Yes, boss,' the detective
constables said in unison.

Drake spent a few moments scanning the various
emails in his inbox once he was sitting by his desk. He
ignored an invitation to a presentation about the latest
developments in pursuing cyber criminals. A brace of
circulars from his union would be checked later.
Usually they were complaints about additional
workloads and objections to changes in working
practices, and after giving them proper attention he
deleted most of them.

Sara had questioned the honesty of Michael after
their conversation yesterday and a quick search of the
police national computer told Drake he had no previous
convictions. He emailed the intelligence officers
responsible for the area that covered Llanberis asking
for any background about Michael and sending them
the image of the girl they had to identify.

Drake outlined on a legal pad the unanswered
questions from yesterday. Writing 'motive' under
Fiona's name focused his mind on the fact she had

tolerated Harry's infidelities for years, decades even. So why would she have murdered him now? Did she just snap? Had things come to a point where she could take no more? She would not be the first wife to have decided that enough was enough.

His preparation was interrupted by a call from one of the women on the front desk. 'A man called Councillor Evans wants to speak to you. He says it's urgent.'

She didn't wait for a reply and connected Drake. 'It's Councillor Evans. I'm the chairman of the Llanberis parish council. We met briefly when you interviewed the councillors on the afternoon you discovered Harry Jones' body.'

'How can I help?' Drake couldn't recall Evans as all the councillors appeared much the same – mid-seventies, paunches and double chins.

'I have left a message with the mobile incident room in Llanberis for you to contact me.'

Typical politician, Drake thought, getting his justification in first.

'On the night he was killed there was a council meeting where there was a presentation by the company planning the redevelopment of the bomb storage facility.'

'I do remember that. All of your colleagues recalled the meeting breaking up at about eight p.m.'

'Yes, of course; that's right. I wanted to tell you what happened. I'm surprised nobody has contacted me already.'

'Perhaps you could give me the details.'

'There's going to be a multi-million-pound investment to redevelop the bomb storage facility and quarry. There's going to be a visitor centre, a café and interactive suite that can be used for schoolchildren to learn about the industrial past of Llanberis. It's going to give a derelict site a new lease of life and make a positive contribution to reinvigorating an area spoiled by years of exploitation.'

More politician speak.

Evans paused for breath. 'Harry Jones was one of the most vocal and vociferous supporters of the proposal. He's appeared on television extolling the virtues of how the redevelopment will transform Llanberis.'

'I'm not certain how this is relevant to my murder enquiry.' Drake wanted to be as polite as possible but he was already planning how to bring the conversation to an end.

'I haven't finished yet. Harry's one-man campaign to have the place redeveloped made him enemies.'

Evans let the last statement hang in the silence. Drake heard his breathing.

'There were three protesters in the meeting the night Harry was killed and things got a bit heated. There was a lot of shouting. All of it directed at Harry because he'd been saying how important the development was going to be and how crucial it was for the future of the village. Some of the protesters hurled abuse at him. It all got very nasty.'

'Why didn't you tell me about this before?' Drake clenched his teeth.

'I reported it to the mobile incident room. I was expecting *someone* to contact me.'

Mentally Drake counted to five hoping to contain his annoyance with Councillor Evans. 'We'll need the names of the objectors.'

There was a rustle of papers as Evans dictated the information and Drake jotted down the details.

After returning home the previous evening Sara managed a five-kilometre run. It had helped her unwind and after finishing some cooling-down exercises she had showered, eaten a healthy meal of chicken and pasta and slept soundly, waking a little before six feeling refreshed.

An empty Incident Room meant she could get some work done without the distractions of Gareth Winder's fidgeting. She had hoped her irritation with the way he worked might have abated. But even after a few months he still got under her skin. She scolded herself that she didn't have the luxury of being able to choose work colleagues and recently she had resolved that as Winder was an experienced detective constable she had to tolerate him. Luned was different: a little stuffy perhaps but dedicated and intelligent.

Boxes of files transported from Harry Jones' office to headquarters sat in the storeroom having been archived and indexed by one of the civilians in operational support. She took the first box to her desk and reached down for the typed list. She read the details – sales reports, stock lists, rent receipts and auction particulars.

She was halfway through the various files when Drake entered, obviously surprised to see her in so early. Soon afterwards, Gareth Winder and Luned Thomas arrived, and she exchanged the usual morning pleasantries, making certain she appeared polite and professional. Drake telling Winder and Luned to finish checking the CCTV coverage had the desired effect of focusing Winder's attention. He settled down and all she could hear was the clicking from his mouse and the occasional pause for him to scribble on his notepad.

The files were the product of an organised and tidy mind. Sara read a list of items in the shop, and details of all card payments through his business and invoices from auctions where Harry purchased stock. She couldn't see any record of the items in the lock-up.

The second box that Sara looked in contained the financial documents Padarn Antiques needed. Bank statements printed from the Internet, draft accounts from a firm of chartered accountants, tax returns and circulars from the bank. It made her own banking arrangements seem pretty simple – one current account and a savings account into which she promised herself to pay money regularly but never actioned.

Tens of thousands of pounds sloshed around Harry's bank accounts. Fiona Jones wouldn't have any difficulty maintaining her lifestyle. Which begged the question whether Fiona was a realistic suspect?

When the name Wolfgang Muller appeared three times on the list in the third box Sara was checking, she was able to completely ignore the mid-morning coffee activity in the Incident Room. She reached down and pulled out the three files.

The first file contained letters from a firm of lawyers to Harry Jones. Wolfgang Muller had started a complex civil case against Harry Jones hoping to recover money invested in a company Harry had recommended. Sara turned her attention to the second file with the court documents. She focused her mind on trying to understand the basic allegation despite the obtuse language. Quickly she jotted notes hoping that she had understood the basis of the claim. Flicking through to the final documentation she read that Muller's claim had been dismissed and that he had been ordered to pay costs. Money was involved, a liability created – which made it the most obvious motive in the world. Drake had to be informed so she picked up the legal pad, pushed her chair backwards and at the threshold of his office rapped her knuckles on the door; he waved her in.

'I've been working through some of Harry Jones' papers. Wolfgang Muller was suing him over money he had invested. Apparently, the investment went sour and the company went bust. In the end Muller's claim was dismissed. It left him with a big bill.'

Drake whistled under his breath. 'Money makes one hell of motive.'

'Perhaps we can ask Fiona Jones for some of the details.'

Drake nodded slowly.

Alison Faulkner plonked the cafetière and a set of Lavazza cups and saucers in the middle of the pine table. Drake looked over at Fiona Jones. She looked tired, the bags under her eyes more prominent now.

'We have some more questions we think you might be able to help us with.'

Fiona plunged the cafetière and poured three cups. Drake pulled one towards him and fingered the rim of the cup hoping the coffee matched the logo on the surface. Fiona took a sip from her cup and glanced over at Drake, but he couldn't read her eyes.

'We were hoping you could fill in some gaps in our chronology for the afternoon Harry was killed.'

Fiona replaced her cup on the saucer and ran a carefully manicured finger along the handle.

'I've told you everything I can remember.' The replies sounded staged somehow, carefully rehearsed even. It made Drake think that she was hiding something and that if she wasn't more forthcoming she'd be at the top of the list of persons of interest alongside Wolfgang Muller and Richard Perdue.

'We've found papers relating to a dispute with Wolfgang Muller,' Drake said. 'Tell us what you know about it.'

Fiona glanced away and sighed as though replying was beneath her.

'That bitch Heulwen acted for Muller. He thought Harry defrauded him by dishonestly persuading him to invest in some company that went bust.'

'Why didn't you mention this before?'

Fiona shrugged.

Sara now. 'Who is Heulwen?'

'She's a lawyer who did the legal work for Muller. She should have known better.'

From the depths of his memory, Drake recalled meeting a Heulwen, who was also a parish councillor, on the afternoon Harry's body was found. 'Is she on the parish council?'

Fiona nodded.

Drake glanced at Sara before asking his next question. He wanted to see how Fiona would react. 'Were you aware that your husband had a CCTV system in his office?'

She blinked, too vigorously. He had his answer without Fiona saying anything.

'I'm sure there was a good reason for it.'

'Did your husband ever mention meetings with a man called Richard Perdue?'

'He had lots of business associates.'

'Is that how you classify his relationship to Perdue?'

Fiona shrugged.

'What sort of associate was he?'

Drake sensed that Fiona knew she had trapped herself.

'They did business occasionally. I know that Harry mentioned him.'

'Did Harry ever complain about him?'

Fiona frowned.

'There's an incident three weeks before he was killed where Richard Perdue appears to threaten your husband. Do you know what it could be about?'

Fiona shook her head. Drake paused, unnerved by her indifference. Was it behaviour she expected from Richard Perdue?

'You don't seem surprised. Have you met Richard Perdue?'

Another shake of the head. 'I think Harry was afraid of him. I don't think he wanted to do business with him any longer.'

'We need to know what sort of business he was doing.' Drake lowered his voice. 'It really is important, Fiona.'

'I don't know. I wish I could tell you. But it's not going to bring Harry back, is it?'

Drake drank more of his coffee after nodding to

Sara for her to continue. Hopefully she'd have more luck asking Fiona about the mystery woman recorded on the CCTV from Harry's office.

'I want to ask you about this person.' Sara pushed a static image over the table.

'Who is it?'

'We were hoping you could tell us. This is a printout from the CCTV coverage.'

Fiona inspected the photograph. She made a good job of hiding any recognition, Drake concluded. He didn't notice any flicker of acknowledgement in her eyes.

'Were you aware your husband was having a relationship with this woman?'

Again, Fiona's eyes didn't flicker; her face didn't respond. Drake glanced over at Sara; her puckered brow told Drake she shared his frustration.

'He …'

Drake wanted to butt in but decided against it when Sara moved her empty coffee cup to one side and lowered her voice. 'It must be difficult, Fiona, but it is important if you can share with us as much information as you can.'

'Harry was a good husband.'

Now Sara drew a long breath. 'On the afternoon that he died we understand he was in a local supermarket where he bought flowers and a bottle of wine. Do you know who that was for?'

'I don't think I can add anything else.' Fiona sat back, threaded the fingers of both hands together, and gazed at the floor.

Drake stood up. 'We may need to speak to you again, Mrs Jones.' He nodded at Sara, trying to hide his annoyance, and left the kitchen. On the driveway he stopped and turned to Sara.

'She's hiding something.'

'It could be she wants to blank out the truth about her husband.'

'Or else she killed him.'

Drake's mobile rang as he started the car and he fished it out of his jacket pocket.

'Drake.'

'Area control. You're needed at a possible crime scene. There are reports of shots being fired.'

Chapter 13

Drake didn't wait for the anonymous voice to give him instructions or tell him the postcode. He tossed the handset at Sara and slammed the car into first gear.

'There's been a report of gunfire at the bomb storage facility.'

'Christ, is anyone hurt or —?'

'I don't know. Armed officers are en route.'

Drake flashed his lights and sounded the horn at a car dawdling in front of him. He overtook and luckily the road was clear and he raced on.

The tyres screeched as he pulled into the junction for the bomb storage facility. He parked next to a marked police car. Two uniformed officers stood talking with a civilian.

The younger of the two looked relieved when he saw Drake walking up to them.

'This is Colin Paterson, sir.' The officer glanced at a forty-year-old, slim built, ashen-faced, wearing jeans and a fleece top under a red hiking jacket.

Paterson nodded at Drake.

'Has anybody been injured?' Drake said.

'No, sir,' the same officer replied.

Immediately Drake felt relieved. 'So, tell me what happened?'

'I was getting set up down there.' Paterson threw a glance over his shoulder. 'I'd been commissioned by this website to take photographs of abandoned and out-of-the-way places in Wales. Apparently, people like to explore them. Gives them a buzz, that sort of thing.

'It's a hell of a scramble to get down. I had my tripod and my camera and various lenses. I had taken a few images from the far end – the graffiti on the front of the buildings makes a great image. I decided to move over towards the entrance and that's when I heard someone moving. I could swear I heard breaking glass.

'I thought it was somebody poking around. There are photographs of the place all over Facebook. I even thought that another pair of hands might help with some special effects.'

Paterson paused for a moment, clearly shaken. 'Someone shouted at me. Telling me to get out.'

'Was it a man or woman?'

Paterson shrugged.

'Can you remember exactly what was said?'

'It was something like "leave me alone". At first I thought it was a bit of a joke.' Paterson stopped.

Drake heard a police siren in the distance and guessed the armed response vehicle was approaching. Drake turned back to Paterson who sipped from a bottle of water. 'What happened next?'

'I carried on. I took some photographs on the outside and walked over to the tunnel entrance. Then the voice shouted "fuck off out of here" and a second later there was a shot and a bullet flew past my head. I was petrified. So I picked up my rucksack and ran. I scratched my hands scrambling out of the place.' He held out bloodied and bruised hands.

'How many shots did you hear?'

'I can't be certain. Two, maybe.'

Paterson took another mouthful of water. 'What's going to happen to my kit? My camera is worth three grand.'

Paterson's equipment would stay exactly where it was, at least for the next few hours. The siren grew louder now and moments later a Series 5 BMW swept into the car park throwing up a cloud of dust as it braked. Two officers emerged; each nodded at Drake and Sara. It took them seconds to get their semi-automatic carbines readied before they joined Drake.

Once the armed response unit declared the place safe Drake scrambled down the rocks and gravel followed by the CSI team that had arrived while the armed officers finished their search. His brogues could be scuffed or, worse, scratched and it would mean cleaning them carefully before he could wear them again, so he took his time finding careful footholds.

At the bottom, he dusted off his trousers vigorously. Trees clung to the side of the facility and weeds thrust their way through the concrete at his feet. Along one side was the remains of a narrow-gauge railway that headed off into the tunnels that led underground. At the far end arched concrete sections identified where the Royal Air Force had stored their ordnance during the Second World War. Street artists had been busy daubing the walls with words and letters in a dozen colours.

'Why would someone take a pot shot at a photographer?' Sara said. She had managed to negotiate the screed of loose gravel more successfully than Drake. Behind her the two crime scene investigators dumped their bags of equipment by their feet.

'No wonder he was terrified.' Drake surveyed the surroundings. 'It's pretty desolate around here.'

'Why would someone try and frighten him off?'

'We could easily be looking at an attempted

murder here.'

Sara nodded.

'Let's take a look around,' Drake said.

The Ministry of Defence must have simply dumped the waste rock they had just scrambled down in a vain hope it would keep out trespassers. Rocks and gravel hit the ground behind Drake as Colin Paterson was the last to join them. More colour had returned to his cheeks.

Drake imagined the place as a whirlwind of activity in the war with ordnance arriving for storage deep in the bowels of the mountain. Now it was forlorn, neglected, ignored by its owners for decades. As he neared the entrance he could see a tripod and camera equipment standing upright, presumably where Paterson had left them. A shoulder bag with a bottle of water pushed into a side compartment lay to one side.

Drake turned to Paterson. 'I need you to remember everything that happened here.'

Paterson gave a nervous twitch before turning his head and nodding to an area behind his equipment. 'I was over there when I started taking photographs.'

'Show me,' Drake said.

They followed Paterson and when he stopped they turned to look back in the direction of the tripod and over towards the entrance of the tunnels. 'I took quite a few low shots from here. This is where I first heard the sound of movement. I didn't pay it much attention at the start.'

Paterson moved a few steps and paused, looking around as though he was smelling the atmosphere. 'I took some images from here, I changed my lens, added some filters hoping I could get more character into the photographs.'

'Did you hear anything while you were standing here?'

Paterson frowned. 'No, it was quiet.'

Back at the camera and tripod, Paterson reached up a hand, but before he could touch the camera, Drake raised his voice. 'Don't touch anything.' Paterson looked over, shocked. Drake nodded at one of the investigators who dumped his bag by the tripod's legs before snapping on a pair of latex gloves and starting the process of dusting for fingerprints.

'Was it here that you heard the shouting?'

Paterson nodded. 'And the sound of breaking glass.'

'Where did the sound come from?'

Paterson didn't reply; he motioned with his head unconvincingly towards the entrance where the railway tracks disappeared underground.

'You stay here,' Drake said to Paterson. He nodded for the second crime scene investigator to follow him and Sara. They walked over and peered down into the tunnel. Drake took a few steps inside.

'What are we looking for, boss?' Sara said.

'There were two shots. So if he used a rifle there is a chance he didn't collect the empty shells.'

It was easy to imagine the place being an attraction for children, drunks or even someone sleeping rough, but Drake couldn't ignore the fact that Harry Jones's death had been linked to his support for the redevelopment plans for the site. Was the firearms incident today mere coincidence or did it hold more significance to Harry's murder?

'But Harry Jones was killed with a revolver.'

'I know, but …'

Drake and Sara made their way slowly down underground, kicking the occasional stone and plastic bottle to one side, and as the light faded, a murky gloom wrapped itself around them. Eventually they used their mobile telephones to illuminate the concrete at their feet.

'Do you think we should get a full search team?' Sara said.

Drake stopped, drawing himself straight from the artificial crouched position he'd adopted to scan the floor.

'Two shooting incidents in Llanberis within a week of each other is too much of a coincidence.' Drake held up his smartphone, illuminating the walls. He caught the faint whiff of charcoal. Local kids would probably use the place for an impromptu barbecue, Drake thought.

The crime scene investigator was already a few yards ahead of Drake and Sara when he stopped and knelt. He scrambled in his bag for a pair of latex gloves. 'There's some glass over here.'

Drake and Sara hurried over and saw the fragments of a bottle lying next to some shrivelled-up cardboard. But once they focused on the concrete at their feet, glass shards glistened in the dirt.

'We'll need a full search team.' Drake cast a glance further down into the darkness and then back over his shoulders. 'The shooter could still be here hiding in the bowels of this place. And we can't rule out a connection to Harry Jones's death. So, we treat this place like a crime scene.'

Retracing their steps Drake squinted against the sunshine as they emerged from the tunnel. The wall of screed and rock seemed the only way out so there was a chance he was right about the shooter. Finishing a call to operational support formally requesting a full forensic search team, he turned to the armed officers.

'I'll need you to stay. The shooter could be hiding somewhere inside.' He jerked his head at the tunnel entrance. Both firearms officers tightened their grip on their weapons and nodded.

Drake strode away, Sara and Paterson following behind him. He emerged at the top and repeated the dusting down of his trouser hem. Drake made his way back to his car. Little had gone according to plan that day. A firearm had been discharged and he needed to establish who had pulled the trigger. It meant Harry Jones's killer was too far ahead of them and that only hardened the tightness in Drake's chest, a sign of his inner frustration.

He started the engine and headed for the A55 and back to headquarters.

Sara draped her jacket over the back of her chair and slumped down, gratefully accepting Luned's offer to make coffee. Drake had gone straight into his room clutching his mobile phone in his hand. Something had amused him from the message he'd received as he had smiled broadly, ignoring Sara's presence.

Sara had stopped Winder mid-sentence when he enquired about the events earlier that afternoon – he'd have to be patient. Sara wasn't going to repeat herself for his sake. Luned returned with coffees and a plate of digestive biscuits. Quickly Sara demolished one before starting on a second. She paused and drank a mouthful of coffee. She was about to start an explanation when Drake emerged. He reached the board and faced the team.

'There was a shooting earlier today in the bomb storage facility.'

Winder and Luned nodded, both eager to hear what had happened.

'Anybody injured, sir?' Winder said.

'No, thankfully.'

'Is it linked to the Harry Jones case?' It had taken a while for Sara to become accustomed to Luned's accent. It reminded Sara of actors from S4C, the Welsh television channel, which she watched occasionally hoping to brush up on her Welsh language skills.

'I don't like the coincidence of two shootings in Llanberis in a matter of days of each other. It's not the Bronx, after all.'

It struck Sara that Drake's attempt at humour was unusual. She took another mouthful of coffee and waited for him to continue.

'There's a full search team there at the moment. We'll be treating it as an attempted murder. So, let's hope there'll be some forensics.' Drake glanced over at Winder. 'In the meantime, have you had any luck with chasing down more information on Perdue?'

'I've spoken to a couple of the intelligence lads.'

Sara guessed that meant a long lunch or at the very least several hours away from the Incident Room.

'He's featured a lot in a number of previous inquiries. There a spate of burglaries of large detached properties in isolated spots several years ago. He was implicated in handling some valuable pieces of furniture but nothing could be proved. Since his conviction he's been very careful.

'What I did learn, boss,' Winder continued, 'is that some of the items we recovered from the lock-up owned by Harry Jones were stolen from stately homes all over the Midlands and the West of England.'

'Really?'

'I've made contacts with the serious crime teams in three forces and they've promised to get back to me soon as possible.'

Drake cast a glance at the board behind him. 'So, it looks like Harry Jones was connected with some heavy players. How did he fall under our radar?'

Sara had finished her coffee, and the benefit of the hot drink and two digestives invigorated her.

'We need to look in more detail at the development of the bomb storage facility,' Drake said. 'Tomorrow we'll talk to the objectors at the meeting the night Harry Jones was killed and then to the Big Thrill Company who are behind the proposal.'

'Do you think there's a connection, boss?' Winder sounded puzzled.

'I don't like coincidences.'

Drake's comment didn't invite a response from any of them. For a few seconds he stood staring at the board before his mobile bleeped. Sara paid it more attention than she would have normally, and Drake hurried away, looking energised, pleased with himself.

She wasted no time in hanging around the Incident Room any longer than she had to. Several routine emails were deleted and invitations to various training courses earmarked for discussion with Drake once the inquiry was over. Most detectives wouldn't have bothered to accompany crime scene investigators in the bomb storage facility and it was typical of Drake to spend that extra time.

Sara followed Winder and Luned out of the building exchanging small talk as they walked over to their cars. Once home she went straight for the bedroom and changed into her running kit before doing some warm-up exercises on the patio outside while deciding on the length of her run. It always helped her clear her mind, unwind effectively and ensure she had a decent night's sleep.

Chapter 14

Harry Jones's death had shaken Luned Thomas. It was a little too close to home for her liking. Her mother had been born in Llanberis and she remembered visiting the village as a child. She had found it difficult to detach herself from the community and look at the events through the prism of her training as a police officer. In the days after the killing she had dwelled on the circumstances, waking at night, the investigation invading her thoughts. It hadn't helped that a few weeks earlier she had visited the Quarryman's Hospital with her nieces from Adelaide.

Being familiar with the location of a murder makes it more real, Luned thought. Her mother had called her the same evening as the news broke about Harry Jones, and Luned had wanted to sound cool and professional but her mother's rising anxiety had played on her mind.

Yesterday she had spent far too long tracking down the lawyers who had prepared Harry's will. At first, they had refused to speak to her. After telling an aggressive-sounding secretary that it really was important, she had to listen to a lecture from a pompous lawyer explaining that he would need Fiona's written instructions.

That morning she detoured via Llanberis on her way into work to get Fiona's signature, before visiting Fiona's mother to confirm all the details of the woman's alibi for the evening of Harry's murder.

She parked outside the home of Fiona Jones's mother, as a slim woman with steely-grey hair and pronounced wrinkles bustled out. She stopped when she saw Luned and glared at her for a moment.

'She's in a foul mood this morning.' And with that she hurried off to her car.

The rear door to the house was open and Luned called out, 'Mrs Williams, good morning.'

'Who is it?'

The face at the kitchen door had wrinkled leathery skin, thinning white hair and the hardened look of old age. Determined eyes gave Luned the once-over. They also gave her warrant card a piercing stare.

'Did you pass that useless carer? She's really thick. I suppose you've come to ask me about Harry?'

'Can I come in?' Luned said. 'I'm part of the team investigating the death of Harry Jones. It's routine. We need to build a complete picture.'

'I know exactly what you mean. I've seen enough of those cop shows on television. You probably think Fiona had something to do with it.'

The old woman nodded to the inside of the house and Luned followed her into a parlour. Ornaments and figurines cluttered every surface; jugs and glass vases lined the windowsill. The room was hot. The newspaper, folded open at a crossword, sat on a table beside an upright chair.

'Can you tell me what happened on the night Harry Jones was killed?'

'What has Fiona told you?'

'I'm sure you know, Mrs Williams, that I need to get your side of things.'

'Fiona didn't kill him. All she's interested in is the money.'

Luned told herself to be patient. 'When did you last see Harry Jones?'

The older woman recalled all the details of a

Sunday lunch at a local restaurant – even commenting about the expensive jewellery and watch Fiona wore.

'How did you get on with Harry Jones?'

'It wasn't for me to get on with him; Fiona had to live with him.'

Luned was about to ask another question but Mrs Williams continued. 'Harry always looked after Fiona. She never wanted for anything, but I knew what he was like. He thought nobody knew about his other women. They were slags, ready to sleep with him for money – that was all it was.'

'That must have had an effect on Fiona.'

Mrs Williams launched into a reply. 'My daughter is independent; she can look after herself. She got used to it, tolerated it.'

Luned doubted Fiona's behaviour towards Penny Muller could be described in such terms.

'How many children have you got, Mrs Williams?'

'Fiona and Ceri and … Jean. She …' Luned sensed the old woman's discomfort, and recalled a woman called Ceri being with Fiona on the day they discovered Harry. 'She killed herself.'

Mrs Williams faltered. Luned saw the anguish still fresh in the older woman's mind.

'She was never right … And being married to Glyn … it would test the patience of a saint.'

Luned made a mental note to find out more about Jean. 'How often does Fiona come to visit?' Only one more question before getting back to the night Harry Jones was murdered.

'She's a good daughter, and so is Ceri.'

'I understand that Fiona came to see you on the night Harry was killed.'

Fiona's mother gave Luned a detailed minute-by-minute chronology, which all sounded very plausible. Either she had been coached effectively by Fiona or the version of events were accurate. It tied in with the CCTV coverage recovered from the supermarket where Fiona had bought the ready meal earlier that evening.

The older woman confirmed Fiona Jones's initial story – it didn't mean Fiona hadn't killed her husband, of course, but it did make her less challengeable. Luned thanked Mrs Williams and made to leave. On a cupboard near the door were several photographs and Luned noticed the smiling faces of Fiona and what looked like a sister. A young boy stood to one side.

'That's Matthew, my grandson.' Mrs Williams sounded genuinely pleased. 'He's a good boy. He takes after his mother, Jean, and my side of the family.'

Luned assumed the last comments made clear two of her daughters had made unfortunate marriages. 'You've only one grandson?'

'Jean only had Matthew.' She reached over for a photograph of another family scene, parents and three daughters, and showed it to Luned. 'That's Ceri and her daughters. And Fiona, well – Harry must have been firing blanks.'

The woman's belief in her own family's invincibility surprised Luned.

Back at headquarters Luned faxed the authority to the lawyers and got down to chasing the Land Registry for details of property owned by Harry, building a complete picture of his finances. It surprised Luned that someone would keep so much money in a current account. When she saw the regular stream of income it was obvious that finances weren't a problem to Harry

Jones. Perhaps he was money laundering through his business? She made a mental note to raise it at the next team briefing.

Across the Incident Room she heard Winder on the telephone but tried to ignore his conversations. She was certain he asked for a detective inspector whose name was unfamiliar. There was a brief conversation between both men, so it must have been important because Winder's demeanour changed. He became business-like, using 'sir' more frequently than he would normally.

It was almost lunchtime when an email reached her inbox from the Land Registry. She gladly put to one side fathoming out all of Harry Jones's finances and began assembling a spreadsheet of the properties he owned. There were eleven and it amazed her that someone could acquire so many houses. They were all in Harry's name apart from the house where he lived with Fiona, vested in their joint names, and another property a few miles from Llanberis in joint names with a Nancy Brown. A search of the telephone directory drew a blank for a landline number for Brown.

Winder stood up and exhaled loudly. 'You won't believe all this crap about Richard Perdue. I'm waiting for a call back from a superintendent in a police force in the Midlands.'

Winder's telephone rang on his desk. He grabbed at the handset. 'Detective Sergeant Gareth Winder.' He even managed to sound more professional.

She half listened to Gareth Winder's growing excitement, his conversation littered with frequent 'yes, sir's, his voice a little more raised than normal. Winder was still on the telephone when an email from Harry's lawyers arrived and she opened the attachment. Harry Jones's will appeared. She read the contents – more legal jargon, so she hit print and behind her the printer purred into life.

Winder was on his feet when she returned clutching the will. He was staring intently at the monitor before squinting up at her. 'I need to contact the boss.'

Drake sat in a café nursing a coffee mug and worrying that the time he had spent with the individuals objecting to the development of the old bomb storage facility had been worthwhile. Talking to the first couple had been a surreal experience – the wife had insisted on speaking Welsh to him while the husband spoke only English, and Drake doubted from the blank expression on his face that he understood a single word his wife had said.

The second pair had launched into a bitter and twisted tirade against everybody they thought had done them a disservice over the years. It included various Members of Parliament and members of the Welsh Assembly as well as every county councillor. Drake promised to consider everything they had said, made excuses and left.

'That was a complete waste of bloody time,' Drake said. 'They all knew Harry Jones. They all thought he was a scheming, crooked politician – all the usual phrases came out – nose in the trough etc. …'

Sara dabbed her finger to the side of her mouth as she finished the last of a scone. She nodded. 'They were all a bit … odd.'

'Let's hope the Big Thrill Company is bit more

positive.'

After paying the bill, they left and returned to Drake's Mondeo. The satnav led them to offices in a nearby business park.

A youngster on reception showed them into a conference room and soon the managing director, Ralph Erdington, joined them. Judging by the deformed cauliflower ears that stuck out almost at right angles from his head, Erdington must have played rugby with considerable enthusiasm and without the safety of a cap. He had a loud, booming voice, a crushing handshake and a physique that suggested he kept himself reasonably fit.

Drake pulled in his stomach and regretted his lack of exercise. The Big Thrill Company shared an office with a firm that designed websites where the staff wore T-shirts and jeans with prominent tears. Very few of the men staring at their monitors, clicking intently on their mouses, had shaved that morning.

Erdington sat down opposite Drake, the large, heavy watch on his wrist making a dull thudding sound as it hit the table top. Drake gave it a quick glance; it looked like a Breitling – he felt like the poor relation with his Omega.

'What can I do to help?' Erdington's rich vowels suggested the West Country. Somerset, maybe Devon, Drake thought.

'We're investigating the death of Harry Jones.'

'It's terrible of course, but I'm not certain how I can help.'

'He was one of the councillors in the community hall last week when you made a presentation about the development of the old bomb storage facility. I understand there were some people present who voiced their objections.'

'Our proposal is supported by everybody. The local county council are all in favour, as are local businesses. We've been very careful to seek support from the extended community. The Welsh government are supportive too.'

'What about the objectors present at the meeting?' Sara said.

Erdington opened his hands before shrugging his shoulders and then gently shaking his head. 'They've made comments about the disruption to their businesses but they were completely misguided. One of them has a smallholding and they think it might disrupt their farming activities; another has a local shop and café they've built from a converted chapel. They complain about the possible loss of business but they fail to see that this proposal will bring in hundreds of new visitors.'

'Apparently, there has been some debate in one of the Welsh language newspapers about the damage further developments might make to the character of the area.' Drake said.

Erdington adopted an earnest tone. 'We've made a commitment to employ local people and to provide all our signage bilingually. No community can stand still, after all. It's better to have jobs than see youngsters move away.'

It was the same argument Drake had heard every politician in the area articulate over the years. As most of the young people had left the area already he often wondered how many of the jobs actually went to locals.

'Have you received any malicious communications

– someone wanting to stop the development?'

Erdington shook his head. 'I'm sorry I can't be of more help. Everything about this project is uncontroversial.'

'Have you heard about the shooting incident?'

Erdington frowned. 'What do you mean?'

'A photographer was in the facility yesterday when he was shot at.'

Erdington leaned forward in his chair. 'Was anyone injured?'

'No one thankfully, but we are treating it as a possible attempted murder. The place will be treated as a crime scene.'

'Once we've completed the land acquisition we'll take steps to make the place more secure.' Erdington read the time on his watch but let his eyes gaze a moment longer than he needed. 'Unless there's something else I can do.'

Drake and Sara got up and Erdington showed them back to reception. Before they left, he handed them each a copy of the company's glossy brochure with a business card tucked into the flap inside. 'Do pay the centre a visit once it's finished.'

Drake flipped open the cover and noticed the image of Erdington and the local council leader, his chain of office resplendent around his neck, shaking hands enthusiastically.

As they made their way back to the car Sara turned to Drake. 'Do you think there's a connection to the bomb storage facility?'

Drake had learned that Sara measured her comments carefully, making certain that nothing was taken out of context. The old RAF base might have been a dangerous place but perhaps his initial instinct that something connected the murder of Harry Jones to the history of the place and the new development was misguided.

'I don't think Erdington is involved. Their proposal wasn't creating any real bad feeling apart from those few objectors.' Drake knew he hadn't answered Sara's question. And he didn't get an opportunity to elaborate as his mobile rang. He recognised Gareth Winder's number.

'I've had the details about the burglaries from the English stately homes. You need to get back here, boss. A chief super from Birmingham wants to talk to you.'

Chapter 15

Back at headquarters Drake spent fifteen minutes listening to Gareth Winder sharing what he knew about Richard Perdue and his links to certain organised crime groups in the Midlands. He read the time and, not wanting to be late, interrupted Winder mid-sentence.

'We need to leave.' It took Drake and Sara a few minutes to reach the video conferencing suite where a civilian was busy setting up.

'It looks as though we'll need to talk to Richard Perdue in due course,' Sara said after making herself comfortable at the table.

Drake didn't respond. The civilian fiddled with the equipment, making some final adjustments.

Moments later Sara and Drake appeared on the screen. Using modern communication systems meant significant savings in time and money for officers travelling around the country and brought a smile to the faces of accountants.

'Let's see what this detective chief superintendent has to say.'

Eventually the civilian checked her watch. 'It's time, Inspector.'

Drake straightened his tie, cleared his throat and fidgeted with the notepad in front of him.

Moments later the screen flickered into life and Detective Chief Superintendent Mitchell Overend peered out over the conference table.

'Detective Inspector Drake.' Overend had a strong Birmingham accent. He had rimless glasses, carefully trimmed short back and sides and a sharp jaw. Despite his rank he was in full uniform.

'This is Detective Sergeant Sara Morgan, sir; she's working with me on the case.'

'You're the SIO?

'Yes, sir.'

'Your superior officer is …?'

'Superintendent Wyndham Price.'

Overend nodded, jotting something on a notepad.

'We have an interest in an organised crime group with links to one of your suspects.'

'Not exactly a suspect as yet, sir. Perdue is a person of interest at the moment. Harry Jones was killed last week and we recovered stolen goods from a lock-up he owned.'

'Perdue is a low-life. But he's connected to some serious players. That's why I want you to be very careful how you deal with him. He's used by an organised crime group to dispose of stolen antiques and works of art. There have been a number of burglaries and thefts in stately homes over the West Midlands in the last eighteen months. We're talking of millions of pounds, Inspector.'

'Do you have evidence to link Perdue to these crimes?'

'I've got a team working on pinpointing his movements in relation to the other key players that we believe were involved. I've got printouts ten feet thick of triangulation reports, and hours of CCTV coverage which we need to analyse.'

'We haven't got a clear motive yet, but we need to understand his links to Harry Jones. We'll be interviewing Richard Perdue in due course.'

Overend paused. He tugged at his nose with his thumb and forefinger. 'The men he's involved with are dangerous. They wouldn't hesitate in using firearms or extreme violence. For some reason they take an interest in fine art and fancy pieces of furniture. We're not talking IKEA here; it's chairs worth thousands of quid. And they all go to mansions in the USA or the far east.'

'I understand, sir.'

'Be careful, Inspector. Make sure your team know Perdue is connected to some very unpleasant people.'

'Can you send me details of the individuals?'

Overend frowned, obviously troubled by Drake's request. 'I'll send you a briefing memorandum. And you can expect a couple of officers from my team to examine all the items you've recovered. I need your forensic reports too. In the meantime, I'd like you to keep me posted with every development in relation to Richard Perdue.'

'I'm not—'

'It's an operational necessity. I'm insisting. I'll email Superintendent Price with my clear instructions later. But I expect your full cooperation.'

Drake opened his mouth to reassure the detective chief superintendent but the screen at the other end of the room went blank.

'That went well,' Drake said.

Sara blew out a mouthful of air. 'Can he insist on be kept informed about our investigation?'

Overend was right – too many investigations in the past had been hindered by lack of cooperation between various police forces. Even so, it meant someone else looking over his shoulder.

Drake returned to the Incident Room, aware of the tension in his mind between his role as the senior investigating officer and the need to recognise the operational imperatives of a senior officer from another police force.

He pushed open the door and Sara followed him inside. Winder and Luned were making thinly disguised attempts to concentrate on the tasks in hand but both looked up immediately.

'How did you get on, boss?' Winder said.

Drake reached the board and tapped a forefinger on Perdue's image. 'Richard Perdue has some nasty friends in the West Midlands. We need to take it carefully. It looks as though the furniture we found in the lock-up owned by Harry Jones was stolen from various stately homes.'

'When do we interview Perdue, sir?' Luned said.

Drake was still staring at the image on the board. Ordinarily he would have responded by grabbing his car keys and driving straight to Perdue's house to interrogate him but Overend's words of caution rang in his ears.

'The DCS from Birmingham is sending me a briefing memorandum. Once we get that we'll pay Mr Perdue a visit.'

Winder piped up. 'I've had confirmation that the supermarket assistant where Harry bought the wine and flowers is working today. I was going to interview her later.'

Drake nodded, his mind still thinking about Richard Perdue.

Luned looked up. 'And Harry Jones has a lot of cash going through his business. He was making regular deposits into the bank. Perhaps he was laundering money.'

'We'll need more details. Talk to one of the lads in

economic crime – maybe they can assist.'

'A copy of Harry Jones's will arrived, sir,' Luned added. 'And I've put together a spreadsheet of the properties he owned.'

'Anything of interest?'

'One is owned jointly with a woman called Nancy Brown.'

Drake focused his attention on Luned. It was another new name associated with Harry Jones. 'Do we know anything about her?'

'Nothing. And I haven't been able to find a telephone number for her.'

'Where is the property?'

'It's in a village outside Bangor.'

Drake glanced at his watch. It made sense to see Nancy Brown, unravel another loose end in the life of Harry Jones.

'Give me the address and I'll go and see her.'

Sara stood up and reached for her jacket, but Drake held his hand up.

'You stay here for the rest of the afternoon. I've got a commitment later in Bangor so it suits me to go over there.' He glanced over at Winder. 'And email me the supermarket details – I'll call there too.'

Drake ignored Sara's disappointment and went over to his office. He left headquarters after emailing an updated progress report to Superintendent Price.

Thick grey clouds covered the sky as Drake drove over to Nancy Brown's home, but it was dry and the traffic was light. Despite the weather he smiled to himself. He felt like a teenager on a first date, but he was in his mid-forties, divorced with two daughters, harbouring piles of letters from lawyers about the financial arrangements – and it was the first time in twenty years he had a date. He worried what she might think of him, what she thought of police officers. Anxiety took over as he brooded over the possibility that his texts had been taken out of context. Surely he'd made it clear he wanted to see Annie Jenkins again not simply to learn about the history of the North Wales slate quarrying industry.

Imagining what Helen and Megan might say filled him with conflicting emotions. Was it apprehension? Or fear at what they might say and how they might react. A doubt crept into his mind that he was doing the right thing. A grudging acceptance replaced it, though; he now had to move on with his life, even if the tone of the lawyer's letters made him feel guilty. Sian's secrecy about her plans for the previous weekend forced him to realise she was making her own way in life, forging new friendships. Even so, he still fretted about who she was with.

Drake struggled to find the address where Nancy Brown lived. The postcode appeared to be inaccurate as it led him off down a narrow country lane. A tractor followed him towards a farmyard where Drake planned to turn round but when the tractor stopped and the driver got out and trudged off into a field Drake despaired – he would be late. He jumped out and ran off into the field, shouting after the driver but to no avail. The man vaulted over the gate into another field and Drake broke into sweat as he hurried.

Eventually he caught up with the man near an old barn.

'Who are you?'

Drake's breathing was laboured. 'You've blocked

me in.'

'What do you mean?'

'The tractor.' Now he produced his warrant card. 'Just move the bloody thing.'

Back in his car Drake switched off the satnav and threw it into the backseat. He was hot and sticky and hoped that he could calm down before seeing Annie. First, he had to speak to Nancy Brown.

Retracing his steps back to the main road he asked a man walking his dog for directions, who pointed to a house that Drake had passed once already – no number or name – and Drake cursed silently. He parked nearby and walked over. A silver Vauxhall Astra stood in the drive – six years old, alloys, recently cleaned judging from the absence of dirt around the wheel arches.

Drake didn't have long to wait after he'd pressed the doorbell.

'Nancy Brown?'

'Yes.' The woman gave Drake a puzzled frown. She inspected his warrant card carefully before he replaced it in his jacket pocket. He could see the realisation in her eyes about the purpose of his visit.

'May I come in?'

Nancy led him into a comfortable sitting room at the front of the house. The furniture looked modern. Nancy sat down and waved towards a sofa. Her chestnut hair fell loosely over her shoulders and Drake guessed that she was in her early fifties, although her sagging jaw line, vertical lines over her upper lip and the heavy crow's feet suggested age had been unkind to her.

'I'm investigating the murder of Harry Jones.'

Nancy blinked rapidly. Drake stared over more

keenly now. She looked grey, a sad gloomy grey, the sort of grey a death in the family causes.

'Can you tell me the nature of your relationship with Harry?'

'I was his common-law wife.'

Drake hadn't heard this description for several years. It was meaningless, of course, having no legal effect, but obviously it gave Nancy a false sense of respectability, Drake thought. She might well have used *partner* or *girlfriend* or maybe even *mistress*. What would Fiona think about Nancy's revelation? She'd probably stonewall them if they asked her.

'So, tell me about your relationship with Harry Jones?' Drake struck an emollient inquisitive tone.

'We lived together.'

Ordinarily he would have challenged such a bald statement, knowing that Fiona Jones had a respectable life as Harry's lawful wife in a substantial home in Llanberis with antiques and valuable paintings on the wall. Nancy Brown was another part of Harry Jones's life they needed to understand.

Nancy found a handkerchief from her bag and blew her nose noisily.

'I can't believe he's gone.' Nancy gazed down at her lap. 'How did he … I mean, did he suffer?'

'There are some things I can't discuss with you. Could you tell me a little more about your relationship with Harry? I need to establish everything I can about his background. And I'm sure you can help.' Drake smiled.

Nancy squinted over at him. 'He bought me this house. He would come and … visit me.'

For a moment Drake regretted Sara wasn't with

him. He could only imagine her reaction to Nancy Brown. Would it be incredulity or disgust?

'What do you do for a living?' Drake said.

Nancy's mouth fell open and she looked over at Drake astonished. 'I … Harry, … would look after me. I mean he paid for everything.'

Drake paused, before deciding that 'kept woman' would be a better description for this middle-aged lady.

'How long have you been in a relationship with Harry Jones?'

She changed her position on the chair, clearing her throat at the same time, giving her the chance to compose herself.

'It will be fifteen years next month.'

'Fifteen years,' Drake said, unable to hide the amazement in his voice.

Nancy pouted. 'We loved each other.'

Drake continued. 'When did you see him last?'

Nancy gathered her thoughts together. 'It was a couple of days before he was killed.'

Drake stared over at her. 'Where were you on the night Harry was murdered?'

Nancy didn't look up but fixed her gaze at a spot on the carpet at the far end of the room. 'I was here all night, watching television.'

Suspicion invaded Drake's mind. Everything about her domestic arrangements was odd but was it enough to justify his suspicions? He glanced at his watch; the tractor fiasco meant he had little time to spare and he didn't want to be late meeting Annie.

'Did you know anything about his business?'

Nancy shook her head.

'Did he ever discuss his family? His wife?'

'I never wanted anything different.'

'We'll need to take a detailed statement from you in due course.'

Nancy nodded. 'What's happening? I mean, have you found who killed him? I don't know what's going to happen next.'

Drake threaded the fingers of both his hands together. There was something rather sad about Nancy Brown and the whole set-up with Harry Jones. But was there more to this woman? Harry was her only source of income so why would she kill him? Suspecting her made no sense. But Drake was paid to be suspicious. 'I suggest you get some legal advice.'

Nancy Brown choked back the tears.

Drake got to his feet. 'Thank you for your time. I'll get one of my officers to come and take a statement from you.'

Outside Drake sat in his car digesting what he had learned, thinking how much more they had to discover about the mysterious Harry Jones.

Chapter 16

Drake arrived early at the restaurant. He parked and sat in the car for a few moments looking out over the Menai Strait. A yacht, sails furled, was taking advantage of the north-bound current. A young couple in their twenties, in skinny jeans and colourful tops, sauntered past hand-in-hand exchanging a new-lovers smile. He reached for his mobile telephone and found the messages he'd sent Annie. He could still remember the warmth of her smile, the way her eyes lit up. The first message suggested they might meet for dinner. He had even added he was keen to learn more about the history of slate mining in North Wales. It made him cringe. Texting had a certain anonymity that didn't replace the intimacy of a nervous telephone call or a face-to-face request for a date. When he read the second and third messages again he smothered the urge to drive off, to send her another message that he had been called away.

It was too late to change his mind.

He was old enough to deal with the embarrassment.

Glancing in the rear-view mirror he decided to discard his tie, too formal-police-officer mode. Nobody wears ties any more in restaurants, Drake reassured himself. Wanting to make certain he arrived before Annie, he left the car and made his way to the entrance.

A girl with an enormous pair of spectacles checked his name off a list. When Drake explained that Annie had yet to arrive she asked him to wait by the bar. He sat on a wooden stool and surveyed the tables. Scanning the few other diners, Drake realised that even tie-less he was overdressed. He ordered a beer, scrutinising the menu without paying it much attention.

What was the protocol for the greeting? Should he take the initiative and kiss her on the cheek? Or was that too forward? And at the end of the evening? Another thing that troubled him was whether it should be a kiss on both cheeks. Brits only did one, Drake concluded, although his sister had adopted the continental habit of kissing on both.

He would have to tell her about Helen and Megan, of course. Did he tell her about his marriage or Sian? He hoped he could find a way without blurting it out. Halfway through a glass of beer he realised he was drinking too quickly. Nerves had torn to shreds the small talk he had been rehearsing for the past few hours. A barman looked over at him clearly hopeful of another sale, but he ignored him.

Drake scrambled to his feet as he saw Annie walking towards him.

She beamed; he smiled back.

The sleeveless red dress fitted flawlessly; a discreet bangle hung from a chain around her neck. Drake could only guess at the time Annie had taken with her make-up because she looked sensational. Drake found himself staring at her. She spared him the trouble of deciding on the right protocol by placing a hand on his right arm and giving his left cheek a glancing kiss.

Annie pulled herself onto the stool next to Drake and crossed her legs, displaying a perfectly proportioned amount of well-toned thigh.

'Have you been waiting long?'

'No, I haven't been here long. Just enough for a mouthful of beer.' Drake reached for his glass, hoping he didn't sound too nervous.

A waiter came over to tell them their table was ready, and Annie followed him towards a table in the window looking out over the Strait. Drake noticed the modest heels that accentuated her legs. They exchanged small talk as they read the menus, exchanging comments about the selection of starters, remarks about the various main courses.

'Have you been here before?' Annie said.

Drake seized the opportunity. 'About a year ago. I brought my daughters here with my mum.'

A sense of achievement came to his mind. He had told her early about Helen and Megan. Now he'd have to deal with her questions.

'How old are your daughters?'

'Helen is ten and Megan is eight. I've been separated some time.'

'It must be lovely having children.'

'Do you have any family?'

'No. I've been too busy with my career I suppose.'

A waiter appearing at their table brought the conversation to a natural close.

Drake settled on the liver pâté – one of his favourites – while Annie chose an assorted seafood starter. Gradually his tension relaxed as small talk came easily enough. She smiled broadly, laughed at his occasional lame jokes and he realised she was treating it as a proper date. Her move to Bangor was recent. A professor at the history department had died earlier in the year, which meant a reorganisation that allowed them to advertise for a new lecturer. Her interest in the slate mining communities of North Wales made the role a perfect choice.

'I wanted a change from Swansea University,'

Annie said, running a granary roll around the edge of her plate.

'Have you worked at Bangor before?'

Annie shook her head. 'After graduating from Oxford I returned to Wales and I did a PhD in Cardiff.'

Drake couldn't remember meeting a doctor of history before.

'What did you study at university?'

It pleased Drake that she automatically assumed he had studied before joining the police force – although not all senior officers were graduates.

'I read international politics at Aberystwyth.'

Annie did a double-take. 'Really? That's a very well-thought-of department.'

He could see her mind thinking, why join the police force?

A waiter returned to their table to clear away the empty starter plates and she leaned forward.

'Did you always want to be a police officer?'

Drake couldn't recall when he last discussed with anyone his educational achievements or his decision to join the Wales Police Service. It felt refreshing, as though he was rebooting his own personality, adding to it, making himself more relevant. He enjoyed it.

'Are there a lot of police officers in your family?' Annie continued.

'My parents ran a smallholding near Caernarfon, although my father is dead.'

'I'm sorry, he must have been quite young.'

Drake reached out to move his knife a few millimetres.

'He died of cancer. It was all a shock and very sudden. After leaving university I wasn't certain what to do. Some of my friends went to work in public relations or for various political parties. I suppose I wanted to make a difference, I know it's a cliché, but I wanted to help catch the bad guys.'

A waiter returned with steaks and bowls of salad and French fries.

Drake and Annie took a brief hiatus from gathering information about each other, at least for a couple of mouthfuls.

'My grandfather ran a farm in Carmarthenshire,' Annie said.

She shared with Drake details about her family in an unhurried, unforced way and Drake relaxed, enjoying listening to her. Her father worked as a civil servant with the Welsh government and he was retiring in three years. Annie rolled her eyes when she added that having her father at home would drive her mother mad.

Drake polished off his steak, regretting how quickly the evening was passing.

He finished a second glass of beer while Annie drank a glass of Merlot. The waiter cleared the dishes and then returned with the dessert menu. Drake shooed him away, telling him to return in a few minutes.

'Do you enjoy being a policeman?'

It wasn't a question Drake had asked himself for years.

'I enjoy the challenges. I don't enjoy all the paperwork and form-filling and politics that goes with the job.'

It struck him that so much of what he did was routine.

'It must be terribly exciting when you get a murder

case. Have you found out who killed Harry Jones?'

An innocent enough question: his mother would often ask them.

'We are pursuing our usual lines of inquiry.'

Annie giggled, covering her mouth with a hand. 'You sound like someone from one of those television crime dramas.'

Drake blushed and stammered a reply. 'I'm sorry … you trot out the same replies.'

Annie excused him with a tut-tut. 'I understand.'

'So, tell me why Llanberis is so interesting for historians.'

Annie's face lit up. 'The slate mining industry had a massive impact on the history of North Wales. At one point the Dinorwig quarry employed thousands of men. There are some lovely walks around the inclines and the tracks where the men worked.'

'I went up there years ago as a boy.'

Annie gazed over at him open-eyed. 'You must go again. I'll organise to take you one weekend.' She smiled at him. 'I can show you the Anglesey barracks where men stayed during the week.'

'I'd love to.'

'It's amazing,' Annie continued. 'To think there is a huge hydroelectric scheme in the middle of the mountain. And they were thinking of establishing a second one in the old Glyn Rhonwy quarry before the plans for that adventure playground.'

'There was an incident in the old bomb storage facility earlier this week.' Drake knew the press had reported the shooting so he wasn't sharing a confidence. 'Someone fired off a few rounds.'

'I heard about it on the radio.'

Drake sensed she wanted to ask him if they knew who was responsible but she kept quiet.

'We're not certain if it is related to the death of Harry Jones but it's certainly an odd coincidence.'

The waiter returned and gave Drake an impatient look when he realised they still hadn't decided. He stood and waited. Drake shared a self-conscious glance with Annie before they gave him their orders and the waiter scuttled away.

They resumed without any hesitation, Drake finding the whole experience of spending time with Annie a joy. She turned the conversation to visiting Snowdon, telling him she had walked the Llanberis Path and that she hoped to do the other paths soon.

'I haven't been to the top of Snowdon since my father died. My grandfather's favourite route was always the Snowdon Ranger path.'

'You will have to show me that one day.' She tapped two fingers on the back of his left hand resting on the table. Even that fleeting touch made his skin tingle and he wondered if she was teasing him or starting a joint to-do list. Before he responded the waiter arrived with panna cotta.

Drake ordered coffees, instinctively hoping to delay the end of the evening.

They filled in the various gaps in each other's knowledge of their respective families. He'd mentioned little of the relationship he had with Susan, his sister in Cardiff, and decided that Huw Jackson, his recently discovered half-brother, would be a topic for another date. Once they finished Drake insisted on paying and realised he was fretting again about the end-of-the-evening, shall-I-see-you-again protocol.

They made their way out towards the entrance.

Annie shrugged on her coat, glancing over at Drake. He smiled back. Protocols could go and hang themselves. He was going to take the initiative and kiss this woman before she left.

'I've had a lovely evening,' Drake said.

He leaned down and kissed her on the lips and she kissed him back, really kissed him back. It made his skin feel as though dozens of small needles were prickling him all at once. He pulled away, self-conscious about the other diners milling around, but no one paid them any attention. He could see the colour of her eyes and that wonderful smile again.

'Can I see you again sometime?'

Annie smiled. 'I'd like that.'

Chapter 17

Drake woke in a sweat. His pillow felt damp and he sensed his pulse beating wildly. Realisation that he had forgotten something struck him like a blow to the chest. He grabbed his smartphone from the cradle near his bed and fumbled to switch it on.

He scrolled to his emails and read the details of the shop assistant he should have interviewed yesterday. But he had clean forgotten in his enthusiasm to see Annie.

Why the hell hadn't he rung to cancel or postpone their dinner for an hour? The assistant could be an important eyewitness. She might have some crucial evidence that could crack the case wide open. He had only himself to blame and he tried not to think about the consequences.

He read the time – 6.45 a.m. – too early to call, so he cursed silently.

He flopped back onto the bed before fisting a hand and thumping the duvet. He should have known better.

After a shower and dressing, he drank water and made a coffee but he didn't feel hungry so he listened to the morning news.

At 7.25 he tried the supermarket. An answering machine told him they would open at 8.30. If the assistant was working, he would see her straight away.

He left the house feeling empty.

He had never let his personal life impede an investigation before. His stomach churned and by the time he reached headquarters he was thirsty again. He took a glass of water to his office and sat down. A little before eight o'clock he tried the number again – just in case.

The same message replayed over the telephone.

He tried to concentrate on work, but he kept checking his watch.

Finally, he got through to someone at the store, but his lips were dry and he sounded garbled asking for the manager.

'Peter Green. I'm the manager. How can I help?'

'I'm Detective Inspector Drake – I was due to interview Vera Alton, one of the assistants yesterday, but my meetings ran on. Is she in this morning?' Drake chided himself for the casual lie.

'Just a moment.'

Drake's pulse hammered in his neck.

'I'm sorry,' Green said eventually. 'She's not in until the night shift on Tuesday. Apparently she's gone on a hen do to Tenerife.'

'What?' Drake's insides quivered.

'A girl's weekend away – before a wedding. Like a stag do.'

'I know what a hen do is,' Drake snapped.

'Keep your shirt on – you asked.'

'When is she back?'

Once Green had confirmed she was away for a very long weekend Drake slammed down the telephone.

He turned back to work. Before Tuesday, he had to make progress.

He found the report from Detective Chief Superintendent Overend in his inbox. The clear, stark language made chilling reading. Richard Perdue was connected with some seriously unpleasant gangsters from Birmingham and Nottingham. One was suspected of being involved with drug importation involving millions of pounds of Class A drugs. The second gangster linked to Perdue had an unhealthy interest in trafficking young girls from Eastern Europe and a fascination with guns. Chillingly all the men were implicated in half a dozen unsolved murders. Drake focused on Perdue's connection to burglaries in various stately homes. Valuable furniture and chattels had been stolen, and despite every attempt to trace the items through 'the usual channels', which Drake took to mean intelligence sources, nothing had been recovered. Shipped out of the country to the mansions of Mafia bosses, Drake thought.

Overend speculated that various accommodating dealers throughout the UK had disposed of the rest. Harry Jones was simply a small cog in a large illegal wheel, Drake thought. He probably recycled the small items, making sure every item of stolen goods produced income.

When his team arrived Drake had decided that a meeting with Perdue was overdue. Winder was the first to appear in his doorway. 'Good morning, boss. How did you get on with the girl in the supermarket?'

Typical, Drake thought; it had to be Winder asking. He thought about making some comment that Winder hadn't shaved for three days but at least he was wearing a tie so on balance Drake decided against a pithy remark.

'My meeting ran late so I missed her.'

'Oh.'

'She's back on Tuesday. We'll see her then.'

Winder frowned, and Drake raised his voice. 'We'll need a full financial and background check on Nancy Brown. She was Harry Jones's mistress, although she called herself a common-law wife.' Drake dismissed Winder with a curt nod and called out over his shoulder. 'Sara, get in here now.'

Winder left, and Drake drew his chair nearer the desk. He waved for Sara to enter.

'We are overdue a discussion with Richard Perdue.'

'Yes, boss. Did the Midlands police have anything useful to tell us?'

Drake gave her an executive summary of the complex web of criminals linked to Perdue. Occasionally Sara nodded, tut-tutted or simply rolled her eyes.

'I understand now why that detective chief superintendent told us to be careful.'

Drake stood up. 'Let us go and see what Perdue has to say.'

A few minutes later they were walking out of headquarters and down to Drake's Mondeo. Inside it felt reassuringly antiseptic. He drove down to the A55 and indicated west.

'What could be Perdue's motive for killing Harry?' Sara said once they were clear of the final tunnel at Llanfairfechan.

The same thought had occurred to Drake. 'Perdue was connected with some people who don't need a motive for murder.' It sounded chilling. Reading the reports from Overend that morning had only highlighted to Drake there were some serious gangsters in the inner cities of England.

'Harry Jones got himself involved with some real villains. Maybe he thought he was too clever for them – tried to diddle them. They discovered he was on the take – I don't think they'd react too kindly to that.'

Sara nodded but said nothing. Drake couldn't quite make out if she thought his argument had little value.

Crossing over the Britannia Bridge and onto Anglesey, Drake cast a quick glance down towards Plas Newydd, the ancestral home of the Marquess of Anglesey with its lawns that reached down to the edge of the water. He took a left off the bridge and after half a mile indicated again to his left. The route took him past the entrance for Plas Newydd, and the satnav bleeped with instructions for him to turn right. He followed the road as it narrowed, leading to more bleeping from the satnav instructing him to take a left down a narrow country track, the grass that was growing in the middle brushing the underside of his car. At the end, the lane opened out into a gravelled area in front of an old farmhouse, recently refurbished by the clean render and glistening windowpanes.

A Porsche 4x4, two years old from the number plates, stood outside a double garage. Drake drew up alongside and he and Sara got out. The main door's black paint glistened and the locks looked expensive. Drake glanced upwards and noticed the CCTV camera screwed to a bracket high above them. What other security arrangements had Richard Perdue added to the property?

A man in his late forties with protruding eyes and thick lips opened the door and stared at Drake and Sara. His features were the sort that made it difficult to read his emotions, Drake thought, knowing he had to be careful. Perdue's carefully ironed shirt looked expensive and matched his designer jeans.

'Richard Perdue?'

'And who are you?'

Perdue gazed inquisitively at both warrant cards. He was either buying time or wanted to fix the details in his memory. 'What do you want?'

'We'd like to discuss your relationship with Harry Jones. May we come in?' Drake kept direct eye contact with Perdue but struggled to read any recognition or realisation of why he and Sara were there. Perdue hesitated. Was he going to try denying he knew Harry Jones? That would be foolish, really stupid, Drake thought.

'Of course, come in.'

Perdue led them into a room at the rear. The entire gable had been converted into a window with large panels. If Perdue ever sold the property the view over the countryside towards the mountains of Snowdonia would probably command a high asking price.

Perdue made no attempt at small talk, no offer of coffee or tea.

He sat down but didn't suggest that Drake and Sara did likewise. The eyes still bulged and his lips barely moved.

Sara examined every piece of furniture in the room; Drake had sensed her slow pace as they followed Perdue from the front door, allowing her to glance into the other downstairs rooms. Luckily the doors were open; clearly Perdue hadn't been expecting two officers from the Wales Police Service to arrive on his doorstep.

'Harry Jones was killed, shot, last week near the Quarryman's Hospital in Llanberis.'

Perdue barely blinked. 'It is very sad.'

Drake tried to read the emotion in the voice. It wasn't easy, neutral like an announcement at a railway station.

'How well did you know Harry Jones?'

Perdue blinked this time and his lips moved slightly but darkness lurked behind the eyes. 'I bought some pieces from him occasionally. He was a very well-established dealer.' The accent was undiluted cockney. Drake guessed it would only be a matter of time before there'd be some rhyming slang, intended to confuse but which he always found grating.

'How often did you make contact with him?'

'Not often – I can't remember when I last spoke to him.'

'What do you do for a living, Mr Perdue?'

'This and that, know what I mean?'

Drake didn't know what he meant but he wasn't going to be goaded.

'Perhaps you could explain.'

'Just a bit of trading, occasionally I make a profit, which pays for all of this.' Perdue raised a hand in the air like a member of the royal family. 'A mate of mine might ring me with an offer of a juicy deal. We buy and then sell at a profit. Easy peezy, jobs a good un.'

In five minutes flat Perdue was crawling under Drake's skin.

'Did Harry Jones ever offer you a "juicy deal"?'

'No, can't say that he did.'

'Did you ever offer him a "juicy deal"?'

Perdue shook his head.

'Did he owe you money?'

'Don't be silly.'

Drake squinted at Perdue, uncertain whether he was suggesting it was preposterous that anyone would owe him money such was the risk involved or whether the suggestion itself was preposterous.

'So, you have no recollection of when you met Harry Jones last?'

Perdue feigned seriousness, frowning. 'A few months ago, yeah, that's right, I bought a small clock from him. I love clocks, don't you? Do you want to see the receipt?'

'So, it wasn't in the last month?' Drake asked slowly giving Perdue enough time to hear and understand every word.

Perdue pretended to think. 'I'm not a man for diaries, Inspector.'

Hedging his bets, Drake thought. Perdue knew it wasn't an interview under caution. Sara scribbling in her police note book would be the only record of their conversation.

'From Harry Jones's mobile records we've been able to establish that he called you several times in the past few months, and a number of times in the past few weeks. What did you talk about?'

'Nah, there must be some mistake. You know how these mobiles can make these fake calls. What do you call them? Pocket calls or something – when you've got your mobile in your pocket and you accidentally press it.'

Drake took the call log out of the folder on his lap. 'All the calls seem to be of a reasonable duration. The last one was forty-five seconds, one before that ninety-three seconds and several before that of over a minute.'

Perdue averted his eye contact; the whites of his eyes shone. 'Technology.' He managed a jocular mood. 'What can I say?'

Drake kept his frown to himself. The more Perdue

was lying to him the more it was likely that he would be a formal suspect to be interviewed under caution at some point.

'Are you married, Mr Perdue?'

'Not for me, mate.' Perdue winked at Drake. 'Play the field, that's for me, mate. I don't like to be tied down to one person. I like to have a bit of a change.'

'Can you tell us where you were on the night Harry Jones was killed?' Drake dictated the date.

'Last Tuesday?'

More hesitation. 'I remember. I was here all night. I watched TV, had a couple of glasses of wine, went to bed early.'

Now Drake hesitated. 'So, there's nobody that'll confirm your movements?'

Perdue shrugged. 'On me lonesome, I'm afraid, Detective Inspector.'

'Do you know where the bomb storage facility is in Llanberis?'

Perdue looked puzzled. 'Never heard of it.'

Drake decided that for now he had had enough of Richard Perdue. 'Thank you for your time.' Drake stood up; Sara followed suit.

Perdue saw them to the front door. 'If you need to speak to me again, just call.' Perdue stretched out his thumb and little finger to mimic a telephone handset. He managed to mangle the word call into *cawl*.

Once they were inside Drake's car, Sara turned to him.

'I think he's lying through his teeth. Why didn't you show him the photograph?'

'I wanted to wait until we've seen all the footage. There may be more images of Mr Perdue.'

Sara nodded.

Drake started the engine. 'The next time we speak to him will be at area custody – once we've arrested him.'

They drove away leaving Perdue still standing on the threshold in front of the glistening black door.

Chapter 18

'I need a word.'

Drake waved Mike Foulds to a chair.

'This is the forensic report on the bullet that killed Harry Jones.' Foulds dropped a sheaf of papers on top of the morning's newspaper Drake had left on his desk. The Sudoku had proved particularly challenging and Drake had promised himself he'd tackle more of the puzzle later.

As he read the first page of the report, Drake recalled Foulds' belief that the bullet could have been fired from an antique pistol.

Foulds continued. 'The bullet came from a revolver that was around during the Second World War. And it's very likely the gun was of German origin. And none of the pistols we recovered fired the shot that killed Jones.'

'Thanks, Mike.'

Foulds left and even though it was too much to expect the murder weapon to have been stored back in the lock-up, Drake felt disappointed. Establishing who knew about the pistols was a priority. Perhaps Richard Perdue knew about them, was implicated somehow in the thefts of the handguns. And Harry might have shown them to his wife and even to his 'common law wife'; Drake couldn't dismiss either woman from the inquiry.

Drake turned his attention to Harry Jones's will.

The document was written in standard legal language. An accountant, Dan Caird, based in Llandudno, was the executor. The next two pages were taken up with a complex clause that Drake didn't follow. At the top of the next page was a substantial gift to the Harry Jones No. 1 Trust and directions that the money should be held in accordance with the existing trust document. Drake would need more information about the anonymous-sounding trust.

He decided to call the executor. A bored receptionist connected Drake.

'Mr Caird, I'm investigating the murder of Harry Jones.'

'It's terrible. Awful. But I don't know how I can help you, Inspector. I was Harry Jones's accountant. I liked him, although I didn't know him that well.'

Drake struggled at the start to understand Dan Caird's thick Scottish accent.

'But you must know a lot about his financial position as you were appointed his executor.'

'I'll do what I can to help.'

Caird was simply being cautious, Drake concluded. 'I'm trying to trace the details about a clause in his will. He left money to the Harry Jones No 1 Trust.'

'Yes, of course. I know all about that,' Caird said energetically. 'A financial adviser persuaded him a few years ago to put money into a trust fund in order to avoid tax. He sold a couple of properties and there was of lot of surplus cash Harry didn't need at the time.'

'How much was involved?'

'Over £200,000.'

'And who are the beneficiaries of this trust?'

'You'll have to talk to the financial adviser who set the whole thing up.'

'Do you have his contact details?'

'Yes, give me a minute.' Drake heard Caird breathing down the phone. He dictated the number.

Without pausing, Drake called the financial adviser. A smooth, confident recorded voice offered apologies that he couldn't take the call in person and urged a message be left. Drake duly obliged, asking Malcolm Walker to return his call.

Drake assumed the will used standard legalese but he wanted to be reassured, so he emailed one of the lawyers in the in-house legal department. After pressing the send button he sat back, and it struck Drake as odd that there was no provision in the will for Nancy Brown.

Drake parked it in his mind for now and read on. Financial legacies were the next item in the will. Harry left several gifts of £500 to various small charities in and around Llanberis. Drake calculated the total – £10,000.

In addition, Harry Jones had included a full page of gifts to individuals ranging from £50 to £500. Again Drake added the sums together – over £40,000. He paused: Harry had gifted a lot of money. How would Fiona Jones feel, Drake thought, when she'd learn about these legacies. Drake guessed Harry had more than enough money to ensure his widow could live comfortably.

The individual recipients meant little to Drake; he presumed Ceri Parkinson was Fiona's sister – and then her children Lowri, Anna and Gwenllian. Next were varying amounts to a Donna Jones, Jennifer Howard, Lily Rogers and Matthew Talbot. Harry even left a legacy of £1,000 to Michael, his shop assistant, and similar sums to his family doctor and dentist.

Drake sat back; Winder standing in his doorway interrupted his deliberation.

'I've been working on the CCTV coverage.' Reading the time, Drake realised he only had a few minutes before his meeting with Superintendent Price. Winder made the statement sound like an invitation so Drake followed him into the Incident Room.

'This needs to be quick,' Drake said.

Winder settled down in front of his computer.

'I've been back through all the coverage from Harry's CCTV camera. I've discovered he regularly saw Richard Perdue. At least twice a month and three months ago he saw him with another man.' Winder clicked the monitor into life and a grainy image filled the screen.

Drake's regret about the shop assistant, which had played on his mind, was now displaced by realising he had been right to hold back with Perdue.

'Good. Perdue lied to us and that puts him in the frame – get these images sent to Detective Chief Superintendent Overend. Let's hope he can identify this man.'

He got back to his office and finalised scribbling some notes before heading to the senior management suite. He detoured to the bathroom on the way. He took a moment to straighten his tie, wash his hands, and drag a comb through his hair.

Drake settled into a visitor chair in the superintendent's office and balanced his note pad on his knee. Price kept his eye contact direct as he listened intently to Drake. Occasionally the superintendent asked for clarification. Price could be hot tempered, intolerant, but when he made a decision he stuck to it and Drake always welcomed his support for his team.

'So, the persons of interest are Perdue and Muller,

whose motive is likely to be as a jealous husband and having been diddled by Harry over some investment. And we have Fiona Jones and his mistress Nancy Brown. I can see Fiona's motive – something happens in her mind, and suddenly she snaps and bang, Harry is no more.'

Drake nodded. 'Yes sir.'

'And have you anything on the shooting in the bomb storage place?'

'Nothing.'

'Is it connected to Harry's death?'

'It's impossible to tell. But two shootings in Llanberis within a few days of each other is a coincidence.'

Price continued. 'It strikes me Richard Perdue and his connections to the organised crime groups in the Midlands are your best bet.'

Drake couldn't help but notice that Price's complexion was a paler shade than usual. He knew the superintendent worked long hours and had little social life apart from the occasional trip to the golf club. Mrs Price appeared to be a remarkably dull woman with little small talk, who Drake recalled meeting at an event organised by Northern Division. She smiled occasionally, fiddled with her hair regularly, but was clearly ill at ease. What would Price do after he'd retired, Drake thought.

'Keep me posted,' Price said as he returned his attention to the piles of paperwork on his desk.

Drake wandered back through the corridors of headquarters. He was seeing Helen and Megan on Sunday. He would take them for lunch in a local pub that had a generous carvery. Then perhaps a walk along

Llandudno pier, an ice cream at the end. But there was Saturday night before that and, finding his mobile, he tapped a message to Annie. Would he sound desperate texting her to confirm their date for Saturday evening? He hit send as he approached the door to the Incident Room. Then he heard laughter and a baby cry.

He pushed open the door and smiled as he saw Caren Waits, his former detective sergeant, standing with Sara, Winder and Luned, her baby cradled in her arms. Caren looked well; her appearance was still dishevelled and her clothes a mass of different colours and textures, but motherhood clearly suited her. He gave her a quick peck on the cheek.

'This is Aled,' Caren said proudly. 'He's a month old.'

Sara reached over and ran a finger over Aled's cheek. He gurgled.

Luned and Winder managed a stream of small talk – babies always had the effect of being able to get everyone talking. It amazed Drake that Winder could seem so paternal. Caren doted on all the attention.

'I've got some news, boss,' Caren said. 'I passed the inspector's exams.'

A mix of emotions swirled around his mind, pleased for Caren – but disappointment too that she wouldn't be returning to his team. Although she would be on maternity leave for a few months, by then Northern Division would have found an opening for her at inspector rank.

'Congratulations, well done. I'm sure Alun and your family must be very pleased.'

Caren smiled. Now he realised how much he missed working with her. Perhaps he had been too reluctant to accept her idiosyncrasies – eating with her mouth full and her scruffy appearance, all of which could irritate him.

'Are you investigating the Llanberis murder?' Caren glanced over at the board.

'Harry Jones was shot with a revolver near the Quarryman's Hospital,' Winder said.

Drake butted in. 'Forensics think the bullet came from a Second World War German pistol.'

'It sounds interesting. Nothing ever happens in Llanberis.'

Drake made excuses and returned to his office. The forensic report delivered by Mike Foulds was still on his desk. He called Barnes again: still unavailable. Drake sat back in his chair, annoyed. The telephone rang; he hoped it was Walker returning his call. He was disappointed. He recognised the deadpan tone of area control.

'We have a report of a homicide. Can you take the details?'

Chapter 19

'Sara,' Drake bellowed, standing at the same time, his chair jerking away behind him. He reached for his jacket as Sara appeared in the doorway.

'Heulwen Beard has been killed.'

'Who?'

'She was one of the parish councillors we met in Llanberis – and she was the lawyer that worked for Muller when he sued Harry Jones.'

Sara joined Drake as he ran out of headquarters. His coat flapped by his side as he headed for his car.

'Where did she live?' Sara said.

Drake aimed his remote at the car; it bleeped open. He thrust a hand into a jacket pocket and tossed his mobile at Sara. 'The postcode should be on the last message from area control.'

Inside Sara fumbled with the satnav as Drake accelerated down to the A55. Traffic on the dual carriageway delayed his journey but once he was clear of the fifty miles per hour speed restriction he hammered the Mondeo towards the tunnel under the Conwy estuary.

'Find out what you can about the scene,' Drake said.

Sara started making telephone calls. Drake listened but his irritation grew at the one-sided conversation. Sara had the annoying habit of sounding too professional, too detached as she replied. The signal died as Drake drove through the mountain tunnels and Sara fell silent.

'So what are the details?' Drake said impatiently.

'Apparently someone calling at the house found

her badly beaten body.'

Once he negotiated the roundabout for Llanfairfechan Drake floored the accelerator and the car flashed past various vans, articulated lorries and the occasional caravan as he reached almost a hundred miles an hour. It was a journey he had done many times before. Thick clouds gathered, although the forecaster's promise of rain had materialised only in a brief shower earlier that morning. As they approached the junction for Caernarfon the sky cleared, and a weak sun broke through, but the clouds soon returned to obliterate the autumn sunshine.

Another left turn took him towards Llanberis via Pentir and the back roads. Apart from the postcode, there was a house name – Gwelfor. The satnav bleeped instructions for Drake to follow the signs for Deiniolen but he wasn't familiar with the route. After a few minutes he slowed and pulled the car into a space, allowing a minibus to pass the car. He gazed down into the valley. A sheet of sunshine drew itself across the opposite side. Drake peered up and saw the summit of Snowdon glistening, and towards the top of Pen y Pass rain dissected the slate-grey sky.

Most of the small stone houses that clung to the steep valley side had been built for workmen in the local quarries. At the time no one thought a wonderful view would command a premium but judging by the rooflights and the glazed extensions and expensive cars in discreet off-road parking spots, few locals could afford to buy houses here any longer.

Gwelfor was a more substantial property than its neighbours and stood a little further back from the main road. A drive led up in a sweeping arc to the side of the building. Drake parked next to a marked police vehicle. As they got out a uniformed officer appeared on the doorstep. Drake paused for a moment to look out over the valley. A covered veranda ran along the front elevation of Gwelfor and took in the entirety of the spectacular view.

Behind them, set back from the property, was another police car, and the crime scene support vehicle.

Drake briefly flashed his warrant card at the uniformed officer, barely giving the man an opportunity to check the details.

'She's in the study, sir.'

Drake and Sara followed the officer into the hallway. Judging by its dark colour the parquet flooring hadn't been polished or cleaned for years and loose sections shifted under Drake's shoes. The wooden panels adorning the walls were similarly aged. Sara paused briefly to inspect several watercolours of sweeping landscapes hanging from a picture rail. The house smelled heavy.

At the end of the hallway, Drake heard activity. The officer stood to one side and gestured inside, where Mike Foulds and an investigator were establishing the immediate perimeter of the crime scene.

On the floor in front of a carefully carved wooden mantelpiece was the body of Heulwen Beard.

She lay face down, one arm lying by her side while the other was draped across a brass companion set, its contents spread over the hearth surround. Her claret blouse under an old thick cardigan matched her pleated skirt and shoes straight from an *Agatha Christie* television drama.

Drake snapped on a pair of latex gloves, stepped

towards her, and knelt down.

Her head lay against a heavy, squat finial. A pool of blood gathered below it.

'It looks like she was struck with something heavy – probably the ceramic bust on the floor behind the desk.' Foulds said. 'And she fell, hitting her head on the surround. That's why there's no blood splattered all over the place.'

Drake gazed down at the lined face. He recalled the brief conversation he'd had with her only days previously and he was reminded of how much more professional she had seemed than the other councillors. He stood up and moved back.

'Have you been into any of the other rooms?' Drake said.

'Not in detail. Once we've finished this crime scene we'll work our way through the rest of the ground floor.'

Every killer leaves a trace and every murder has a motive, Drake reminded himself. The killer would have left something behind, a fragment, and they would have to find it …

Sara piped up. 'Has the pathologist been? We need a time of death.'

Foulds shrugged. 'He should be here any minute. But my guess is she was killed earlier today at some point.'

'Who found the body?'

'Some bloke who was calling to see her. He's quite cut up. He's with one of the uniformed lads.'

Drake and Sara left Foulds to his gruesome work. It would take hours and would probably mean working until late into the evening and then restarting in the morning. Retracing their steps to the front door, Drake joined the second uniformed officer in a room off the hallway; he was chaperoning a man huddled on an ancient sofa.

Drake recognised the frightened face of Glyn Talbot. His eyes darted around the room and he clasped a book and various sheets of paper in his hands. Drake sat down on a chair opposite Talbot, and Sara joined him. French windows led out onto the veranda. Velvet mocha curtains that draped either side matched the morose feeling about the house. It wasn't a place where a family or children had lived for a long time, Drake thought. If there were ghosts, they were all thoroughly miserable.

'I understand you found the body?'

Talbot looked up at him slowly, blinking rapidly. His voice was shriller than Drake recalled. 'I called to bring her this book and to show her my article.'

Talbot's movements were jerky as he raised a hand with the papers he clutched.

'Was she expecting you?'

'I spoke to her last night. I told her I would be calling. She is the editor of *Papur Padarn* – the papur bro,' Talbot continued. 'I've written this article about the history of one of the local chapels. I wanted to get her to read it so it could be included in the next edition. We're going to press in less than a week.'

'What time did you arrive?'

The sound of activity as more crime scene investigators arrived unnerved Talbot. 'I don't know, an hour ago, maybe longer. I can't be certain. I wasn't paying any attention to the time.'

'I'd like you to explain exactly what you found

when you arrived.' Drake managed to slow his voice. Talbot's evidence might be crucial.

'The door was ajar. I didn't think that was unusual. Nothing much happens around here and I know people leave their front doors open during the day. I've called to see her many times. She is the editor of the *Papur Padarn*. I write articles sometimes.'

'You've told me that already,' Drake said. 'I want to know what you saw.'

'I walked down from my place.' Talbot jerked his head, indicating northwards. He ran an erratic hand through his hair. 'I thought I would get some fresh air. It's not far.'

Drake sensed Sara staring at Talbot who was certainly making heavy weather of giving them a detailed explanation.

'Did you see anyone else when you were walking from your home?'

Talbot gave Drake a puzzled look.

'What do you mean, people walking, or cars? There are tourists around all the time. We get hikers going to the old quarry and visitors driving around. Is that what you mean?'

'Mr Talbot, did you pass anybody?'

Using a firm tone and a formal address did little to encourage Talbot. His gaze continued to dart around the room.

'I spotted a van from one of those outward bound walking centres.'

'Did you notice anybody you recognised?'

'No, I don't think so. What do you mean, somebody local?'

'Was there anybody leaving Mrs Beard's home?

'Nobody ... there was nobody here.'

'When you spoke to her last evening what did you talk about?'

'It was ordinary stuff about the *Papur Padarn*. She wanted to give up being the editor and there's nobody else, nobody who could do the job. I was going to persuade her to continue; she had to carry on.'

Talbot struck Drake as a sad, lonely character.

'We shall have to speak with you again.'

Now Talbot hesitated, widening his eyes. 'You know where I live.'

Drake got to his feet and Talbot left the room still clutching tightly a hardback book and sheets of paper. Drake and Sara followed him outside.

'He was quite shaken up,' Sara said.

'He comes across as a bit strange, eccentric.'

'Do you think he could be involved?'

Drake walked over to the rear and looked over a garden of neglected uneven terraces clinging to the hillside.

'Unless he has motive, I think we can rule him out.'

'He's too timid to be capable of murder.' Sara stood a couple of feet behind Drake. 'Do you think her death is connected to the murder of Harry Jones?'

'Everyone seems to be connected in Llanberis,' Drake replied without answering the question directly.

Drake wandered around the garden for a few minutes, casting the occasional glance towards the house, its sombre stone exterior hiding the high-tech activity inside. By the back door, he noticed a plastic bag, the sort that supermarkets were trying to phase out. It caught his attention and he turned to Sara.

'Something by the back door.'

By the rear door a flat piece of slate wedged the bag securely, suggesting its contents had value. Drake knelt down, reached for another pair of gloves from his pocket and removed the slate to one side before opening the bag. Inside, wrapped in another bag, were two fresh salmon.

Drake got to his feet and turned to Sara. 'There are two salmon here.'

Sara looked puzzled. 'What do you mean? Why would she leave them outside?'

'I don't think Heulwen Beard left them outside. Probably one of her neighbours. We'll get the house-to-house team to ask around.'

Drake read the time on his watch; they had hours of work ahead of them.

'Let's get started.'

Stephen Puleston

Chapter 20

Drake woke from a dreamless sleep. Then he remembered watching a documentary about mediaeval France the evening before that had a soporific effect.

A text message from Annie reached his mobile.

It told him how much she looked forward to seeing him that evening. A yearning blossomed as he thought about what she was doing that morning. Was she curled up in bed texting him? What was she wearing? For a moment he allowed his mind to wander, his emotions to develop, his desire to feel the warmth of a woman's body next to his once again. He cursed himself when he realised that keeping his date would be practically impossible.

He tapped out a reply to Annie but the words appeared unforgiving.

He would call her later. Speaking to her was so much better than an anonymous text. But he might forget, so he tapped out another message but deleted that too in a burst of annoyance. He glanced at his watch. Unless he left he was going to be late for the post-mortem so he fiddled with the phone, setting himself a reminder to contact her.

Three hours later Drake sat in his car outside the mortuary.

No matter how many post-mortems he attended there was a lingering smell that stuck to his clothes, invaded his nostrils. He supposed it was a mixture of decay and blood and the sterile conditions. It still amazed him that pathologists could develop a robust, detached attitude to their work. Most thrived with a saw or a drill in their hand.

The locum pathologist had a strong Irish accent and Drake struggled to understand him as he explained that the first blow to her head had knocked her unconscious. 'She has a large depressed skull fracture to her occiput, consistent with blunt force trauma, possibly being struck from behind with a heavy object. I've opened what's left of her skull for you, Ian.'

He had pointed at a mass of grey tissue and congealed blood. The back of the head looked like a broken eggshell.

'The blow caused catastrophic damage to her brain; this would have knocked her unconscious immediately and despatched her fairly swiftly after. She then struck the finial on her way down, causing this nasty gash to the side of her head, severing the temporal artery. This would have caused some impressive bleeding, accounting for the pool of blood at the scene. But it was the initial blow which killed her.'

The pathologist had studied the image of the bust found at the crime scene intently before confirming that he thought her injuries compatible with a blow from it.

It all suggested an angry assault from someone with a violent temper.

Someone like Fiona Jones, Drake concluded.

Drake glanced out of the windscreen and an ambulance sped towards the entrance of the accident and emergency department immediately followed by a police car, its lights flashing. He found his mobile and called Sara.

'Morning, boss,' Sara said. 'How did you get on with the post-mortem?'

'Severe blunt force trauma to the skull. She didn't stand a chance.'

'Confirms what we suspected.'

'The pathologist confirmed the bust at the scene was responsible for the injury.'

'She probably knew her attacker.'

Everything suggested that Heulwen had invited her assailant into the house. Somebody with a short fuse.

Drake watched as paramedics supervised by two uniformed officers pulled a patient from the ambulance and wheeled him inside. Another eventful morning for the medics. He rang off after arranging to meet Sara at the offices of Heulwen Beard.

The legal firm of Beard and Beard occupied an imposing building on a quiet street in Bangor. Drake hammered on the front door, but it remained firmly closed. Sara stood behind him peering up at the first floor. Seconds later the door creaked open and a woman with dank, lifeless hair and bags under her eyes appeared.

'Julie Hall?' Drake said, holding out his warrant card.

The woman nodded lifelessly. 'Detective Inspector Drake. We spoke briefly last night. I need to go through Heulwen Beard's paperwork.'

Hall's chin wobbled when Drake mentioned her late employer's name.

'May we come in?'

Hall opened the door and Drake and Sara followed her into the hallway that led into an equally depressing reception room.

Hall appeared lost; she stood staring at the desk where Drake presumed she worked. A monitor was propped up by old magazines, the computer out of sight. Behind her was a corkboard, a mass of printed sheets, including a schedule of postage costs and notices from local authorities. A threadbare mat sat in the middle of the floor. An ancient gas fire flickered silently as it warmed the room.

'We'll need to see Miss Beard's office,' Drake said.

Hall gave him a puzzled look. 'Of course. I'll show you.'

Beard's office was a mirror version of the study at her home. The walls hadn't seen a coat of paint for years. Pictures hung crookedly exposing the unfaded wallpaper behind them.

'Does Miss Beard have a diary?' Drake sat down on an old leather chair behind a desk strewn untidily with files and folders. He didn't know where to start – the whole place was disorganised and he couldn't imagine anyone working in the circumstances, let alone a lawyer who needed to be orderly.

Sara flicked through a shelving unit stacked with paperbacks and DVDs.

Drake continued. 'What sort of work did Miss Beard do?'

When Drake heard a sniffling sound, he raised his gaze and saw Hall dabbing a handkerchief to her eyes. 'It was mostly conveyancing or dealing with probate work or writing wills for people.'

Sara turned to Julie, dusting off her hands. 'Miss Beard worked for a Wolfgang Muller when he sued Harry Jones.'

Julie shook her head. 'I think she regretted ever agreeing to do that case.'

'We'll need the file.'

Julie scurried off and Drake sat at Heulwen's desk and pulled out a narrow drawer on the left-hand side with ballpoints and pencils scattered inside. Using an old ruler he prodded around among the stationery as Sara dragged open drawers from filing cabinets lined against one wall. 'These are all filed in alphabetical order.'

Drake reached the second drawer, full of old diaries.

The final drawer on the left-hand side of the desk had a pot of moisturiser and a box of tissues. He turned his attention to the drawers on the right-hand side.

'Anything of interest?' Drake said, working his way through some back issues of *Papur Padarn*. He recognised the articles written by Glyn Talbot and then Heulwen's name as the editor. When he visited his mother he'd occasionally scan the papur bro, which reported the local gossip; he recalled fondly how his grandparents would dote when his photograph from a school activity appeared in the paper.

Sara had stopped at the third drawer of the first cabinet. 'I don't think she stores any files. Some of these are years old. They all deal with people buying or selling property or making wills.'

Drake finished Heulwen's desk and debated whether it was worthwhile turning his attention to a glass-fronted cupboard lined with legal textbooks as Julie returned to the office carrying an armful of files. She dumped them on the desk.

'Here are the files you wanted.'

Drake opened the first, fingering the pile of paperwork. 'Do you know anything about this case?'

'Muller sued Harry Jones over some money they'd both invested. He thought Harry had defrauded him.'

'We'll need to take the papers with us.'

Hall shrugged.

'Do you know if she had any enemies or anyone that might have a motive to kill her?' Drake said.

Hall's chin and lips quivered in tandem. She gasped for breath. Getting useful information from the secretary was going to be difficult if she carried on with this melodramatic reaction.

'I don't know anyone who would want to kill her,' Julie sobbed.

Even the simple questions about how long she had been working for Heulwen Beard were met with obfuscation. He checked his watch, amazed at the time he had spent at the offices already. Judging by the grumbling sounds coming from his stomach it was nearly lunchtime. Drake lost his patience, and found himself raising his voice, sounding irritable even to himself. Eventually he coaxed out of Hall that she had worked for Beard and Beard for fifteen years. Hall admitted she liked Heulwen Beard's father much better than her.

Drake glanced over at Sara who was still working her way through the filing cabinets.

'Do you have a list of your clients?' Drake said.

'It's in a book in reception.'

'A book?'

'Miss Beard didn't trust computers.'

Drake heard Sara struggle with one of the drawers.

'I don't believe it.' Sara raised her voice, and turned to Drake. 'Boss, something you should see.'

By the time Drake reached Sara she had pulled out

a file onto the top of the drawer. Stencilled in clear letters was the name *Richard Perdue*.

Chapter 21

After texting Annie to apologise that he couldn't keep their date that evening Drake spent the first few hours of the afternoon reading the Muller papers. Sara had the Perdue file while the rest of the team were coordinating the immediate work needed following the discovery of Heulwen Beard's body.

Drake found a twenty-page document signed by Wolfgang Muller with a large scrawl that stretched over most of the final page. Legal jargon and complex phraseology made the court documents heavy going so reading Muller's statement was straightforward.

Harry Jones had persuaded Muller to invest £30,000 in a company that owned a high-tech piece of equipment used in the car industry to prevent thefts of vehicles. Muller alleged Harry Jones had personally guaranteed he wouldn't lose his money. When the business went bust all the investors lost out, including Muller and Jones. It wasn't clear from the paperwork how much Harry Jones had invested but if it was the same as Muller, Drake guessed Harry wouldn't be troubled by losing £30,000. From the tone of Muller's statement, he wanted his money back, really badly.

At the end of the afternoon Drake spent an hour with Philip Hughes, a lawyer from the legal department. Hughes complained like hell that Drake's insistence he attend at headquarters to read the papers ruined his participation in a golf tournament.

'This looks like the classic case of one person's word against another,' Hughes said. 'Muller betted the judge would believe him and not Harry Jones. There is nothing in writing. The claim relies on the judge deciding which of them is telling the truth.'

'So, Wolfgang Muller is left out of pocket to the sum of £30,000. And presumably he has a lot of costs to pay. It must have made him incandescent when his wife started an affair with Jones.'

Hughes was on his feet. 'Both those things together would give Wolfgang Muller a motive to kill Harry Jones.'

Before they could justify an interview with Wolfgang Muller the team would need to dig into the financial background of Mr and Mrs Muller.

Hughes turned to Drake by the doorway. 'Unless Wolfgang Muller was really pissed off with Beard for cocking up the case, you don't have a motive for him to be her killer.'

'There's nothing to suggest both deaths are linked at the moment.'

Hughes gave Drake a doubtful eye-roll.

Sara struggled to block out the activity in the Incident Room. Winder's voice grated as he spent all his time on the telephone or so it seemed. Even Luned's presence irritated Sara although she was guilty only of incessantly clicking on her mouse.

Sara removed the contents from one of Richard Perdue's files they had taken from Beard's office. She placed the various sections on the desk. There was a bundle of correspondence, some legal-looking documents and a sheaf of papers produced by one of the local councils.

Richard Perdue bought land speculatively with a view to gaining planning consent and then selling at a profit. But things hadn't gone according to plan. Objections were raised by the local authority about the density of the proposed development and the means of access to the main road, and they suggested his plans were generally out of character with the entire locality.

Scanning various experts' and architects' reports, Sara realised Perdue had invested a lot of time and money in the proposal. She counted over a dozen letters of objection, in Welsh, some stretching to two pages, so she read the translated versions. Nobody in the local community supported Perdue's plans.

After two hours Sara's concentration drifted so she organised coffee. Deciding Hall might know more of the background, she called the secretary.

'I wanted to ask you about Perdue's planning application.'

Hall sounded tentative. 'Miss Beard warned him not to buy the land on spec but he was determined to go ahead. She got involved because he thought a local professional might assist. Everybody else involved came from London.'

'And that didn't help?'

'It probably alienated a lot of the locals. It's what happened afterwards that caused the problem.'

'And what was that?'

'It's in the file. You can judge for yourself.'

Intrigued, Sara found the correspondence easily enough. She started with the record of the conversations between Beard and Perdue. After selling the land at a substantial loss to a farmer Perdue was out for blood once he discovered Harry Jones had submitted a planning application that included Perdue's land with adjacent land Harry owned.

Perdue wanted to sue the local authority, take out an injunction against Harry Jones doing anything further with the land, make a complaint to the local government ombudsman, find someone to blame. The tone of his correspondence and emails to Heulwen Beard had a nasty, aggressive streak. Sara rang Hall back.

'Perdue wasn't happy,' Sara said.

'Every time he came in here he got nastier. It upset Miss Beard; after all she had done for him in the past.'

'What happened to the land in the end?'

'When Richard Perdue found out that Harry Jones made a profit of almost a quarter of million pounds he came in here in an uncontrollable rage. He said he was going to expose everyone in the community and that we were all small-minded sheep-shaggers. I told Miss Beard to call the police.'

'Did she?'

'No.'

'Is there anything else?'

Hall paused. 'I didn't pay it much attention at the time, but I heard him shouting at Miss Beard during their last meeting. Telling her he was going to get people from London to sort everyone out.'

Sara recalled Perdue's face and chilled – was it more than an empty threat?

Drake stood by the Incident Room board suppressing a yawn. Three sets of tired eyes looked back at him. Empty mugs and plates littered the desk. They had a full day of work ahead of them tomorrow even though it was a Sunday.

The image of Heulwen Beard had been pinned to the board alongside Harry Jones. Underneath were photographs of Fiona Jones, Wolfgang Muller and Richard Perdue. Nancy Brown occupied a less prominent position.

'Harry Jones.' Drake turned to tap a ballpoint on the photograph before scanning the other faces. 'One of these people has a motive to want him dead. Wolfgang Muller hates him for sleeping with his wife and for defrauding him of £30,000.'

'Allegedly.' Winder pushed back in his chair.

'But it gives him a motive. And he finds out Harry Jones has been seeing his wife despite Muller warning him off and he snaps …'

Sara added. 'But does that give him a motive to kill Heulwen Beard? We don't have any evidence Muller has a temper. Although Fiona does.'

Drake nodded. 'Muller instructed Heulwen to sue Harry and he loses. He blames Heulwen for the case collapsing and landing him with a massive bill for costs. The red mist descends on him …' Drake clicked his middle finger and thumb together.

'We don't have any evidence Muller was near Beard's place,' Sara said.

Drake turned his back to the board. 'We need to triangulate his mobile telephone for the day to see if he was near Heulwen Beard's home.' Drake peered at Winder. 'Have you traced the minibus from the outward bound centre Talbot referred to?'

'Not yet, boss. I telephoned three and I've got at least another twelve to contact. And that's only the ones based in Snowdonia. If it travelled here from outside the area we might never identify it.'

Drake ignored the despondency in Winder's voice.

'And we need to know more about Glyn Talbot, who found the body.' A fragment of recollection reminded Drake he had overlooked something from the day before – he had read the name Talbot just before Foulds had interrupted him. 'Harry left a legacy to a Matthew Talbot. We need—'

'That must be his nephew,' Luned spluttered. Three pairs of eyes gazed over at her. Luned trawled her memory. 'When I spoke to Fiona's mother she said that her daughter Jean had been married to a Glyn but she never mentioned a surname and she implied he was difficult to live with. Jean committed suicide and when she was talking about it, it was the only time Fiona's mother showed any emotion. There was a photograph of her grandson Matthew on a cupboard.'

'Luned, check out the connection. Get some background on Glyn and Matthew Talbot. There wasn't any sign of anyone living with Glyn when we visited his house and, Gareth, you chase Harry's financial adviser for details of that trust he established.'

Drake turned back and stared at Richard Perdue. 'Perdue is dangerous. He has to be the main focus for us.' Drake paused. 'We need a full background on him.' He glanced at Luned who nodded back. 'And chase the Midlands police about the image of the man with him when they visited Harry Jones.'

He realised something was missing. Finding a scrap of paper in the nearest desk, he scribbled something on it and pinned it to the board.

It read 'unidentified girl'.

'And we need to find that girl from the CCTV coverage.'

Drake settled back at his desk and moved the columns of Post It notes to one corner. From a drawer he found several sheets of paper and started a mind map on one page. It always helped him. There was something therapeutic about the physical act of grasping a ballpoint pen and scribbling.

He wrote Harry Jones's name in the middle of the first sheet and added Fiona's in a bubble to the right, then Nancy Brown's underneath before filling an empty bubble with a question mark at the bottom. He paused for a moment, thinking about the unidentified woman recorded on the CCTV coverage from Harry's office. Turning to the report from the sergeant in charge of policing Llanberis, he reread the details. It sounded bland, disinterested – 'the usual channels have been explored', 'shopkeepers and local publicans and staff interviewed' as well as 'approaching known human intelligence sources'. The report had no details about how many officers had been deployed and a suspicion niggled its way into Drake's mind that his request for assistance had been given a low priority.

On the left-hand side, he wrote the names of Muller and Perdue and drew arrows from their names to Harry's.

A second sheet of paper was dedicated to Heulwen Beard. Bubbles on the right of that page had Muller and Perdue written inside them and on the left he jotted down Harry's name, underlining it three times. Recalling the chalky face of Glyn Talbot reminded him that murder in the close-knit community of Llanberis was like an unwelcome ghost disturbing quiet certainties. He pushed both sheets together and Muller and Perdue's names mirrored each other.

On the third sheet he wrote 'bomb storage facility'. Was the incident there earlier that week connected to the two deaths? He had nothing to suggest it was. But he hated coincidences and the possibility that a shooting and the incident in the bomb storage facility could be unrelated seemed unlikely. Turning to the monitor he accessed the CSI report. If they could establish who had discharged the firearm he could interview him or her and build a case for a charge of attempted murder. He read the conclusions of the report twice – no evidence of any firearm and nothing to identify the culprit. The CSIs had discovered broken bottles and empty cans of lager and cigarette butts and discarded chocolate wrappings. Superintendent Price had called off the search once it was clear that valuable resources could be wasted.

Nothing in the background checks into the photographer suggested anyone would want to kill him. The significance of the bomb storage incident would have to be parked for now. The Incident Room had emptied by the time he finished scanning the photographs from the site. The graffiti and weeds and dereliction only reaffirmed that despite being near the town of Llanberis, it had somehow been forgotten.

A silence crept into his office, taking him back to evenings when his rituals could keep him at headquarters too late. Often Sian telephoning and insisting he get home would be the only check on his obsessions. Now he didn't even have that, so he promised himself that once he'd checked the house-to-house reports he'd leave.

Officers had tramped around Llanberis, and the summaries produced suggested a community jolted by

Harry's death. Nothing of significance had been discovered and the preliminary reports of the house-to-house inquires around Heulwen Beard's property were much the same. One of the officers had noted that a neighbour was a fisherman, who suggested the salmon might have been poached.

Drake looked again at the results of the triangulation reports of Fiona Jones's and Wolfgang Muller's mobile telephone numbers on the day Harry was killed but he knew the science was inexact and that pinpointing a telephone, even if it was switched on, was like searching for a small needle in large haystack. He dragged from his mind that Harry had an unsent text stored as draft on his mobile when he was killed.

Drake found the details – 'where are you?'.

Finding Harry's murderer would be easy – all they had to do was fathom out who the intended recipient was.

But was that the same person who killed Heulwen Beard?

Chapter 22

Drake drove the short distance from his flat to the estate where he had lived for so many years and parked his car next to Sian's BMW. She gave him a courteous nod as she opened the door, and he followed her into the kitchen.

'I hope this isn't going to take long. I'm collecting the girls from a sleepover.'

It looked a typical Sunday morning; the remains of breakfast on the round pine table. Drake ignored her flouncy gesture of looking at her watch and sat down.

'Susan is coming to stay next weekend with Mam. She's bringing both boys with her. And my mother is planning a family party.'

'Does that include …?'

Drake hesitated. 'Mam has made a lot of effort to get Susan to agree to meet Huw.'

Sian flicked on the electric kettle on the worktop. 'Do you want coffee or something?' Drake sensed the sharpening edge in her voice.

'No, thanks. It would be the perfect opportunity for Helen and Megan to meet Huw. After all—'

'Don't give me that stuff about him being family.'

'But he is,' Drake replied firmly. 'And they know Susan and the two boys. And they haven't seen them for a long time. In fact, I can't remember when they last saw their cousins.'

Sian sighed, heaping instant coffee into a mug followed by hot water.

'It's just … I think it is too soon.'

'You're being overprotective.'

'Hardly. We don't know anything about this man.

He comes into your life, upsetting things, badgering your mother, who seems to be completely oblivious to the impact it might have on the family.'

'Helen and Megan have faced our problems. And dealt with it.'

Sian gave him a sharp look. She remained standing by the kitchen worktop, coffee mug in hand.

'This is different.'

'I don't agree,' Drake said. 'Helen and Megan will have to get used to changing circumstances. What if you started a relationship with somebody else?'

'I don't know what you mean,' Sian stiffened. Her discomfort reinforced Drake's suspicion there was someone new.

'Come on Sian, be sensible. We can't protect Helen and Megan indefinitely. They both realise that we've moved on.'

'I'm still not certain it's the right thing.'

Drake paused. 'Keeping the secret about Dad's relationship wasn't right. It's caused all this difficulty now and I don't want to hide it from the girls any longer.'

Sian sipped on her coffee. He knew he was winning the argument. Sometimes doing the right thing meant making difficult decisions.

The chair scraped on the tiled floor as he stood up.

'I'll let you know what the arrangements will be.'

Sian put her mug down. He could see the vulnerability in her face; her careful orderliness was being challenged. If Susan, his sister, could face meeting Huw then Helen and Megan would take it in their stride.

'Where is it going to be, this family party?'

'Probably at the farm.'

'I'm still not completely convinced.'

'This is my family, Sian. I want Helen and Megan to meet their uncle.'

Sian followed Drake into the hallway. He opened the front door and paused, looking back at Sian. 'It's time to move on Sian. I'll call you next week with the details.'

She gave a brief, puzzled frown and tilted her head. 'Are you wearing aftershave?'

His cheeks flushed and he mumbled a reply before walking over to his car, starting the engine and driving away, realising it really was his former home. He was moving on with his life, resolving to make things better, different. Facing the challenges after his father's death with confidence. Even if he was uncertain how things would turn out.

He glanced over at the board when he arrived at the Incident Room and spotted that the image of Harry Jones's mystery love interest had replaced his handwritten sheet. Before he settled down to work, his mobile rang. Huw's number appeared on the screen.

'Morning, Huw.'

'Ian. I wanted to talk to you about next weekend.'

'Mam's looking forward to it.' It wasn't strictly true as Drake was convinced she was apprehensive.

'She's asked me to bring Sioned and Wil but I'm not certain it's the right thing to do.'

It was more a matter of how Susan, his, *their*, sister might react.

'If Mam has invited them then I'm sure it will be

fine.'

Huw paused. 'Are you in charge of the murder investigations in Llanberis?'

'Yes.'

'Sioned is working in one of the hotels at the moment – she's taking a year out. Can you keep an eye out for her?'

It was a father's natural concern for his daughter and probably the real reason for Huw's call. He sensed Huw wanting reassurance that there was nothing to worry about. He would be the same if it were Helen or Megan.

'Of course. Where is she working?'

'The Fox and Hounds. She told me that the locals are pretty spooked. Everyone knew Harry Jones.'

An idea formed in Drake's mind. 'How long has she been working there?' The locals of the pub might have more luck than the local uniformed officers in identifying the mystery woman.

'A few months. She really enjoys it.'

Drake promised to contact his brother about the final arrangements for the following weekend and as he finished the call a message from Annie reached his mobile. *Really sorry. Can't make it tonight. I've got to go back to Cardiff. Back Tuesday – see you then xxx.*

He recalled his brief conversation with her the previous afternoon when he explained that he couldn't see her. The usual platitudes about 'something having come up' and that he was very sorry sounded hackneyed. The sort of phrases he had trotted out to Sian repeatedly during their marriage until they became meaningless. Was he being unrealistic to hope that things could be different with Annie? Now he wanted things to change.

He read the message again. He wondered why she had to go back to Cardiff. Had his feeble excuses for last night been enough for her to realise a relationship with a police officer wasn't for her. How could he reply? Maybe he should ring her and find out what was happening. But he'd sound pathetic. It was only their second date – even thinking that word –'date' – made him uncomfortable. He tapped out a reply: *Looking forward to seeing you xx*. Then he decided to add – *Safe Journey* and toyed with the idea of asking – *Everything ok?* Deciding it was none of his business, he deleted the question.

He pressed send and sank back in his chair.

Visiting The Fox and Hounds suddenly sounded more interesting than poring over his desk so he gathered up his car keys and left headquarters before the rest of his team arrived.

A call to the pub told Drake Sioned wasn't working until later that morning so he detoured around Deiniolen and drove towards Heulwen Beard's home. The lawyer had lived in this rural community all her life, as had her father before her.

He stopped briefly at a passing slot for cars and took in the view, realising why it enthralled city dwellers. Foulds and the CSIs were still working through Gwelfor when Drake arrived.

'Back again?' Foulds said.

'In the neighbourhood.' Drake tried some humour.

'Yeh, I bet.'

Drake stood in the hallway admiring the oak panels. He could imagine local joiners fashioning them with chisels and round wooden mallets. It had taken precision and care to finish the substantial staircase, balustrades and handrails. He reached the first floor. It must have been an empty, lonely existence for Heulwen Beard, living in such a place on her own.

A musty carpet covered the landing and stretched into the first bedroom, which had a mahogany suite, with an empty wardrobe, a double bed with an ancient eiderdown and a chest of drawers – also empty. Drake shivered; the place felt soulless. New owners would soon discard the furniture into a skip, throw away the carpet, replaster all the walls and paint everywhere a brilliant white.

A makeshift study occupied the smaller bedroom. He sat down in front of a desk with a curved rolltop. A small key protruded from a hole at the bottom. He opened it and pushed the rolltop into its cover.

A pile of recent editions of *Papur Padarn* were stuffed into one corner. Alongside them were printed sheets with double-spaced type covered with red scribbled editing comments. Clearly Heulwen Beard had preferred to edit the old-fashioned way. Drake speed-read an article by Glyn Talbot about the history of the bomb storage facility. And another about the local railway that skirted the lake. More highbrow stuff.

Drake worked his way through the various drawers. He paused to admire the craftsmanship that had gone into assembling the dovetail joints in the drawer. There were letters in scrawny handwriting, one of which was addressed to Mr Beard. In the final drawer he fingered the plastic exterior of several photograph albums.

His interest piqued, he lifted them onto the desk.

It was a bespoke album – the words 'Windermere

1980' etched in faded gold lettering. It was like stepping back in time in more ways than one. Nobody does photographs any longer; cameras replaced by smartphones. He sensed the albums hadn't been opened for years. Drake wondered what memories it rekindled for Heulwen Beard. He found out soon enough when he saw her face and that of Harry Jones as an unmistakable teenager peering at the camera.

All the images were of two young people clearly infatuated. And in the age before the selfie. Another holidaymaker must have taken the pictures of Heulwen Beard and Harry Jones holding hands, his arm threaded behind her back, pulling her close. Beard sat smiling on a steamer on Lake Windermere, eating a cream tea in a café, walking up one of the fells. It appeared blissfully innocent.

Drake worked his way through all of the photograph albums. There was a similar one for the Yorkshire Dales a year later. But when he tried to discover the albums for any subsequent year there was a gap – until he found an album, no expensive embossed name and year this time, simply a collection of photographs of Heulwen Beard and her father. The location looked vaguely continental. He noticed the occasional palm tree but he noticed a sign advertising Torquay.

At the bottom of the final drawer lay a carefully folded letter.

Drake opened and read with increasing astonishment a letter from an adoption agency – the language formal but polite. Did she want to have contact with her daughter? The girl had recently contacted them and wanted to meet her birth mother.

Immediately Drake thought about the images of Heulwen and Harry. Was he the father? Another secret the family didn't want to share? He found an envelope for the letter and stored it safely in a pocket.

In a cupboard behind him were more of Heulwen Beard's personal memorabilia. Photograph albums of her father and mother. Some old books wrapped in tissue paper. She had kept the record of her trips to Windermere and the Yorkshire Dales close. Immediately to hand, somewhere she could access them whenever she wanted. It must have been a reminder of something special and valuable, but also something she had lost.

Heulwen Beard's bedroom proved a disappointment after the small study. Dowdy old-fashioned clothes filled the wardrobe and a faint smell of mothballs tickled his nostrils. Back downstairs he made a cursory examination of the books in the main sitting room. Looking out from the French doors, he decided on a whim to walk out onto the veranda; he struggled with the lock, which eventually gave way.

After the musty atmosphere inside he welcomed the cool fresh air against his face. Harry Jones had worked all his life in Llanberis, the village Drake could see on the valley floor, and Heulwen Beard was a pillar of the local community – a respected lawyer from an old family.

Both were linked inextricably. Her daughter would have to be traced and identified.

A chill wind whipped up, sending swirling columns of mist high into the sky. Drake drew his jacket collar to his cheeks. Their only real suspect was a cockney with a reputation for dodgy business deals and gangster friends, but Drake couldn't ignore Wolfgang Muller and his grudge against Harry and a link to Beard. Drake gazed down and thought about Fiona in her comfortable detached property, consciously ignoring her husband's failings. Did she know about Harry and Heulwen? More importantly, did Richard Perdue?

As Drake looked over the valley it struck him that seeing Heulwen Beard and Harry Jones hand-in-hand as young lovers meant he might have to look for the culprit much nearer to home.

Chapter 23

Drake reached the car park of the Fox and Hounds and found a slot at the far end before leaving the car. A sign at the entrance advertised 'Sunday Carvery' and 'Live Music'. The smell of stale chip fat drifted through the air. Condensation covered a window and from the shadowy figures behind it Drake guessed it was the pub's kitchen.

Drake pushed open the outer door and after a narrow porch he reached the main pub area. Tables were being laid with menus and condiments. It had been a while since he had met Sioned but he soon recognised her as she sorted glasses behind the bar. She gave him a brief nod of acknowledgement – his message to the landlord for her to expect him had been relayed. She waved him towards a stool.

'The boss said you'd call,' Sioned said, joining Drake. 'We're going to start lunch soon. It can get really busy.'

'I'm in charge of the Harry Jones inquiry and I need help to find someone.'

'I can try. Everyone is talking about it and now with the second murder, it's terrible.' Sioned lowered her voice. 'Nobody likes Fiona Jones very much. I think she's a bit stuck-up.'

From an envelope Drake pulled out the photograph of the girl they had to trace.

'We need to find this girl.'

Sioned gazed at the figure. 'Lots of people come in here. She looks sort of familiar. She might have been here on a Thursday evening for the Pie and Pint Night. It's always rammed because it's so cheap.'

Sioned stared at the girl again and frowned.

'We could ask some of the other staff.'

Sioned jerked her head at Drake for him to follow her as she eased herself off the stool. 'They'll be having a sandwich before lunch service – you can ask them all.'

A group of four girls and a youth in his early twenties sat around a table eating a plate of sandwiches while intermittently dipping into a bowl full of crisps. Only one of the girls looked up at Drake while two of the others played on their mobiles.

'This is Detective Inspector Drake.' Sioned's announcement got their attention.

Chewing stopped and five pairs of eyes fixed on Drake.

'I'm investigating the murder of Harry Jones and we need to talk to this girl.'

The first girl gave the image a cursory glance. The second took more time but the third quickly passed it on until it reached the man at the end who dropped his mobile onto the table. He stared at it and then dipped his head, squinting his eyes.

'She's been in a couple of times.'

'Do you know her name?' Drake hoped he was hiding the urgency in his voice.

'Sorry. But you should talk to Emyr. He was with her.'

The man got back to texting. Now Drake raised his voice. 'This is a murder inquiry. Where can I find Emyr?'

The man sneered.

'What's your name? I need to know the name of anyone who obstructs a police inquiry.'

'All right. Fuck's sake. He lives down near the old mill.'

'I think you can come with me and give me directions.'

He squirmed in his chair. 'What and miss my shift?' He glanced over at the bar. 'I'll get the sack.'

Drake gave him a weak smile. 'Then I want an address and a number.'

The man snatched at the mobile and frantically scrolled until he found a number he dictated to Drake. He gave semi-garbled instructions for the property where Emyr lived. 'Can I go?'

'Off you go,' Drake said.

The girls exchanged amused glances as he scurried off.

Drake hurried out to his car, leaving Sioned frowning at the door of the pub. His annoyance turned to anger that the sergeant in charge of Llanberis and his officers hadn't been able to trace Emyr, and he composed the outline of an email complaining and demanding an explanation. He shot past a junction across from a dilapidated building and, remembering the instructions to turn right, he braked hard. The road took him down a narrow track that eventually widened by a bridge; a rusty telephone kiosk stood near an old property tucked onto the bank of a river.

He pulled the car into a weed-infested driveway. The main door was slightly ajar. He called out – no response. Drake thought about calling the mobile number he'd been given but when he heard music he shouted Emyr's name.

He pushed the door open and ventured inside.

Thick walls and small rooms with limited

headroom gave the place an oppressive feel. A parlour had two small windows opposite each other; a log burner filled the room with a dry, warm heat. By its side were piles of logs.

The sound of a television drifted in through the open door in the corner. Drake assumed Emyr was the man playing a videogame on an enormous screen hanging on the wall. He gave a start when he saw Drake and jumped to his feet.

'Who the fuck are you?'

Emyr peered at Drake's warrant card. He had small eyes and a blotched complexion.

'I'm investigating the murder of Harry Jones.'

'What about him?'

Emyr stood now, feet apart. Drake needed this man's cooperation and having him strutting like a prizefighter wasn't going to help. Drake sat down, resting an envelope on his knees. 'I believe you may be able to help.' Drake nodded at the chair Emyr had vacated. Emyr shrugged before sinking back into it, allowing his legs to splay like a man sitting on the toilet.

A softening-up question first: 'Did you know Harry Jones?'

'Yeh, sort of. Everyone knew HP. He gave me some jobs years back.'

Drake pulled out the photograph and handed it Emyr. 'Do you recognise this woman?'

'Might do. Is she in trouble? Fuck me – you don't think she killed HP do you?'

'You were seen with her in the Fox and Hounds.'

Emyr gazed at the photo. Drake leaned forward. 'I need a name, Emyr.'

'Where was this taken?'

'Who is she?'

'It's Carol.'

Progress. He needed an address or at least a contact number.

'Where can I find her? Do you have her mobile number?'

Emyr still stared at the girl. 'Was HP shagging her too?'

The youngster knew more about Carol than he was letting on, and Drake wondered how he might get him to cooperate.

'Is she your girlfriend?'

Emyr guffawed. 'She stood me up. We were supposed to meet up one night last week but she never showed up. Made me feel like a right fucking lemon.' Emyr continued. 'Harry couldn't keep his hands off anyone. If it had a pulse it was fair game. He was shagging that German bloke's bird wasn't he?'

Drake didn't stop Emyr, sensing more to come.

'That's why Fiona smashed her car up wasn't it?'

'So tell me what happened the night you were stood up by Carol.' Engaging Emyr might help him volunteer Carol's number.

'I saw Harry. Him and that German. He was shouting like someone demented.'

'When was this?'

'Last week.'

Drake leaned forward. It had already been almost two weeks since Harry had been killed so he needed an exact date. 'Can you be more precise about when?'

Emyr shrugged before a recollection triggered a response. 'I missed Man Utd's FA Cup fixture to see her. I got back here in time for the second half.'

Drake reached for his mobile and googled the Premiership side's fixtures.

He had to read the date twice before it sunk in. It was the evening that Harry Jones had been killed. He gazed over at Emyr. 'Are you sure?'

'Of course. I've been following Man Utd since I was a kid.'

Drake focused on what else Emyr had told him. He had to take this slowly, getting to the truth. 'What do you mean "that German"?'

'It was that fucking German. I saw him in the car park having a go at HP.'

'Wolfgang Muller?'

'Yes, he's a real shit-bag.' Emyr spat out the reply.

'Did you hear what they said?'

Emyr shook his head. 'They were too far away.'

'Describe what happened.'

'They were fucking arguing, like I said. Muller shoving him around.'

'Did you see Muller leaving?'

Now Emyr sounded confident. 'I left. I was getting nervous.'

'How well do you know Wolfgang Muller?'

He hesitated again, chewing his lower lip. 'He's a gangster, I hate him.'

Drake was intrigued. 'What has he ever done to you?'

'He beat me up last year. I haven't done anything to him, absolutely fuck all.'

'Then why did he assault you?'

'He broke Frank's arm. I heard the bloody crack. Just because Frank tried it on with his daughter. He found us one night drinking by the lake; that's when he assaulted Frank. He landed up in hospital, for fuck's sake.'

'Did you report this?'

'Did I fuck. Who would believe us?'

'What's your friend's name again?'

'Frank Smith.'

'I'll need a statement from you and your friend.' Drake reached for his mobile, ignoring the scornful look on Emyr's face.

Sara spent most of the morning tracking down the right contact at the Metropolitan Police who could access intelligence about Richard Perdue. Being passed from one person to another frustrated her and made her realise the challenge of working in an organisation as large as the police force that covered London.

The reports she had read, that Inspector Drake had circulated after his discussion with a senior officer from the Midlands police, emphasised the violent background of Richard Perdue's associates. Major organised crime wasn't a significant part of the work of Northern Division of the Wales Police Service and she liked it that way.

The first officer she spoke to soon had her checking back over her records. 'We'll need an address. We can't do anything without an address. Or at least a borough.'

His birth certificate recorded the event in the London Borough of Hackney, so she started with that address. A search of the electoral roll soon turned up the Perdue family. She followed the records until she produced a list of three addresses, and she called her contact again.

'Well, you've been busy.' Chris had a thick cockney accent. 'Let me see what I can do. I'll get back to you.'

His accent reminded Sara of the students from London studying with her at university. They all had an inflated opinion of their self-importance and spoke a couple of decibels too loud, as though Welsh people were hard of hearing and a little backward.

Sara sat back in her chair. There was progress, of sorts. Drake's cryptic message to her mobile earlier that morning about visiting Llanberis suggested he was preoccupied. Recently she had noticed the occasional flash of humour and a grin when he read text messages, all of which were out of character.

Winder was busy staring at some CCTV footage he had uncovered. Instead of his usual enormous mugs of tea or coffee he had been sipping constantly on a bottle of water and running his hands over his face and shaved head. Sara dismissed it as an affectation that helped him concentrate. But it kept him quiet and that suited her. He could be quite the most annoying man and it surprised her how his girlfriend found him attractive.

She didn't have to wait long until her inbox pinged into life with an email and several attachments. She read about the Perdue family having been a source of considerable interest to the serious crime divisions. Sara couldn't follow the differing titles of the various divisions but she guessed the Metropolitan Police was the subject of constant reorganisation.

The Perdue family was suspected of being involved in drug dealing and several robberies but from behind the facade of a respectable public house and six Chinese takeaways they frustrated every attempt to acquire the evidence to bring a case to court. An Inland Revenue inquiry into their businesses proved to be a dead end too.

A reference to their business interests in Southend-on-Sea caught her attention. A Google search told her the seaside town was a mecca for retirees and commuters alike. It had a famous pier and lots of amusement arcades. And businesses that thrived on cash – ideally suited for money-laundering.

It took another hour to track down the right contact at the police force covering Southend-on-Sea. She had to follow another protocol, this time for a Jamie who had a strong Geordie accent.

'I'll need a full name, date of birth and an address in our force area,' Jamie said.

Sara dictated the details.

'Give me a minute.' Sara became increasingly frustrated at chasing Richard Perdue around Southern England.

Sara heard the sound of breathing on the other end of the telephone and luckily he was as good as his word. 'You're in luck. I've got some details I can send you. And I know a DS who might help you.' Sara straightened in her chair, encouraged she could actually talk to a serving police officer about Richard Perdue. 'Hang on, I'll put you through.'

The line went dead for a moment, no sound. She didn't have to wait long. 'Detective Sergeant Clawton. I understand you've spoken with Jamie about the Perdue family.'

'He's a person of interest in a double murder

enquiry. I want to build some background.' Sara tried to sound professional, matter-of-fact.

'I'm retiring next month, and one of the biggest regrets of my career is that I was never able to prove anything against the Perdue family. They've had their noses in all sorts of shit. But they were clever enough or maybe lucky enough to keep themselves out of trouble.'

'Did you meet Richard Perdue?'

'Of course I did, man and boy. It certainly feels that way. I was a young constable when he and his family muscled their way into some of the businesses in Southend. Occasionally Richard Perdue would lose his temper and crack a few heads together. But there were never any complaints. Nobody would say a word against them. I reckon Perdue was some sort of psychopath or he's got some personality disorder. Once he gets a bee in his bonnet there's no stopping him. People left Southend because they were frightened of him, good people, people who lived here all their lives –and then they up sticks.'

Clawton was clearly venting his spleen. Sara glanced at the clock on her screen wondering how long she had been talking with him. He gave a heavy sigh down the telephone line. 'And another thing – Mr and Mrs Perdue senior died in very odd circumstances. We couldn't prove anything – the forensic analysis was inconclusive. And Richard Perdue had an alibi. But we reckoned he was behind their deaths. Our informants told us his parents had objected to the way he managed the business. There were blazing arguments. And that all stopped when they died.'

'Can you send me the details? It might be very significant,' Sara said.

'I have no doubt it is knowing Richard Perdue,' Clawton said. 'You should check out the *Southend-on-Sea Observer*. They ran a campaign to give the case lots of publicity. All helped by some discreet disclosures by the investigating team. We hoped that somebody might come forward but the thing was a complete waste of time. Richard Perdue moved away after a couple of years. Thank Christ for that.'

Drake ran over the car park taking the stairs to the Incident Room two at a time and pushed open the door, letting it bang against the wall. Three pairs of eyes followed him to the board.

'I've just spoken to someone who can identify the mystery woman from the CCTV.' Drake jerked a finger at the blurry image. 'Apparently her name is Carol and I have a mobile telephone number for her, but it keeps ringing out.'

'How did you trace her?' Sara said.

'It's a long story. But the person who identified her is also an eyewitness to seeing Wolfgang Muller and Harry Jones arguing on the night Harry was killed.'

Winder whistled under his breath.

Luned nodded sagely.

'And the same eyewitness has evidence of Wolfgang Muller's temper. Muller assaulted Emyr – the eyewitness – and a friend of his.'

'Why the hell hasn't he come forward already?' Sara sounded suspicious.

'Muller lied to us about when he last met Harry Jones and now we've got direct evidence he has a short fuse.'

The team waited for him to continue.

'Gareth and Luned – we need to talk to Carol. I want full triangulation reports on her mobile telephone. I want to know where it is, now, yesterday and who she's been calling. All the usual stuff. And one of you talk to Michael – I don't think he was telling us the truth about knowing Carol. What other progress have you made?'

Winder responded. 'Do you still want me to interview the financial adviser?'

Drake shook his head. 'We need to find Carol.'

Luned responded. 'I've been putting together some background about Glyn Talbot and the extended family of Harry Jones. I should have it finished tomorrow.'

'Good. Anything promising?'

'The families have been around a long time. My mother even knew Harry Jones faintly when she was younger. And she'd heard of the Talbot family. There was some gossip years ago about bad feeling between them. But there was a lot of feuding historically between some of the villages going back decades.' Luned sounded matter-of-fact.

A developing snicker crossed Winder's face, presumably about Luned's reference to her mother knowing Harry Jones, but good sense prevailed and he smothered it. A simple jerk of Drake's head told him an update was wanted.

'Nothing yet from the CCTV, boss. But there aren't many cameras in that area.'

'Yes, of course.' Drake sounded exasperated. 'So, concentrate on the cameras offering coverage of the routes into the Llanberis. We need to know how Muller got there.'

Sara again. 'Are we going to talk to Wolfgang Muller?'

Drake turned to face Muller's photograph. 'Dead right.'

Chapter 24

Drake arrived at headquarters before seven the following morning. He spotted Wyndham Price's glistening blue Jaguar; reaching superintendent rank required early mornings, late evenings and little social life. Perhaps he had reached that stage already, Drake thought. He didn't want to be the sort of grey bureaucrat Price had become. Not even a luxury car would be compensation for so little family life. He shook off his rumination, got out of his Mondeo and walked quickly up to the Incident Room.

Drake exchanged pleasantries with Sara and Luned. He smarted at the acrid taste of the instant coffee Winder produced. Pinned to the board was a plan showing Wolfgang Muller's home address with the various roads leading to it. Drake had finalised preparing for the arrest late the previous evening. Now he took a few moments to summarise everything again. 'Sara and I will take him to the custody centre in Caernarfon. We can hold him for twenty-four hours, which gives the search team time to execute the warrant.'

Drake cast his gaze at Winder and Luned before reminding them of their tasks that day. The arrest of a suspect was always a turning point in any case. It was the moment when things got serious. Everything changed after an arrest.

He nodded at Sara. 'Let's go.'

Drake detoured into the bathroom on the way to the car park and after washing his hands he stared at himself in the mirror. He adjusted his tie; his shirt looked a little tired but the navy suit, his second-best kept for interviews, had been recently cleaned. It was going to be a long day.

He joined Sara in reception and they walked out to his car.

They reached the tunnel under the Conwy estuary before Sara said anything. 'This is always the part I like best. It's when you realise how much power we've got.'

At six minutes past nine they indicated for the turning into the drive up to Muller's wellness centre. The gravel crunched under Drake's brogues as he left the car. The search team arrived soon afterwards. It was a crisp autumn morning. It hadn't rained for a couple of days. Sycamore seeds drifted against a length of box hedging.

Drake hammered on the door, Sara by his side.

He banged on the door again. Then he heard an exasperated shout. Muller appeared in the doorway looking first at Drake and then Sara.

'Wolfgang Muller, I'm arresting you on suspicion of murder.'

'You must be crazy, every one of you.'

'You don't have to say anything but anything you do say …'

Reciting the standard words of the official warning made Muller shut up.

Drake bundled Muller into the car and drove the short distance to the custody suite in Caernarfon.

It was late morning by the time they'd completed all the protocols and settled Muller into a cell. When it became clear the lawyer Wolfgang Muller requested wasn't available until early in the afternoon Drake took the opportunity to return to Muller's property. He gave the various guests a kindly, avuncular smile, reassuring them their visits would be uninterrupted. A tall, attractive woman from Brighton with an extremely plummy accent thought the events were 'awfully tiresome', explaining she had come for some 'good clean Welsh air'. Drake doubted she would mix easily with the two Geordie girls who had nose rings, studs in their upper and lower lips and an assortment of fastenings in both ears. An American couldn't get over the fact that Drake nor the other officers were armed.

Drake found the search team supervisor working his way through Muller's office.

'Any sign of a firearm?' Drake said.

'No, but there is a lot of memorabilia from the Second World War – knives, photographs, and an old uniform. What exactly do they do here?'

'They run courses for making people feel better about themselves.'

'Four pints of lager and a good curry does it for me.'

Drake spent an hour walking through the wellness centre. A guest explained about the pressures and stresses of life and finding their inner selves had been the whole purpose of their trip to North Wales. Cynically Drake couldn't help but think Muller sold modern-day snake oil and preyed on vulnerable people.

He returned to the custody suite with a boot full of military souvenirs ready to face Wolfgang Muller.

Formalities completed, Drake collected the tapes and headed for the interview room. It had uncomfortable plastic chairs, a battered table barely enough for his file of papers and a tape machine screwed to the wall. The air conditioning hummed in the background.

Wolfgang glared at Drake as they entered and sat down.

Drake turned to the lawyer sitting next to Muller. Pat Stokes was one of the regular criminal lawyers Drake came across frequently. She had disorganised blonde hair, broad cheeks and a pasty windswept complexion. 'Hello, Pat.'

'Inspector Drake,' she replied.

'You know Detective Sergeant Sara Morgan?'

Stokes twitched her lips at Sara.

Drake slotted the tapes into the machine and waited for a buzzing noise before turning to Muller. 'Do you know why you're here?'

Stokes interjected. 'You can dispense with the formalities at the start. We know exactly why we are here. You've arrested Wolfgang for murder.'

Stokes' early interruption put Drake on edge.

'How well do you know Harry Jones?'

Muller turned to Stokes who nodded briskly.

'He was a shopkeeper in Llanberis.'

The German accent made the word shopkeeper sound like an insult.

'Describe your relationship with him?'

'We did not have one.'

Drake glanced at Stokes. Her eyes weren't giving anything away.

They might be here all day if Muller was going to be monosyllabic in his replies.

'I understand you've lived at Bryn Hyfryd – your wellness centre – for fifteen years. Is that correct?'

'Yes.'

'And you must be familiar with Llanberis.'

It wasn't a question but Muller replied. 'Of course

I am.'

'Harry Jones ran an antiques shop in the village. And he was a parish councillor so he was well known in the area. And he owned several properties.'

Muller sat back, folding his arms in front of him, but said nothing.

'And it would be fair to describe Harry Jones as something of a ladies' man. He had lots of different relationships in the past and several recently. One of which was with your wife. How did that make you feel?'

'The answer is no.'

'No?'

'What you're really asking me is did I kill him because he had sex with my wife.'

Mentally Drake counted to ten. It was always the risk when interviewing intelligent people that they answered the next question.

Muller continued. 'I explained to you that my relationship with Penny is grounded in complete and mutual self-understanding; sexual fidelity as normal people would understand it has no meaning for us.'

'Does that mean you have sex with other women?'

'None of your business.'

'Most people, most ordinary people, most normal people would be appalled if their spouse had an open, talked-about, gossiped-about relationship with somebody else so publicly. And you expect me to believe it didn't upset you.'

'You can believe what you want.'

'I'm asking for your explanation, Mr Muller. I think knowing your wife was having such a brazen affair would be humiliating.'

'And your question?'

Drake paused, resisting the temptation to shout at this man. Instead, he narrowed his eyes, glaring over at him.

'Were you humiliated enough to kill Harry Jones?'

'It is beneath contempt to even reply.'

Drake nodded over at Sara who picked up the questioning.

'You're lying to us about your relationship with Harry Jones.'

Sara's statement caught Muller and Stokes off guard for a second. She sounded confident, definitive. Now she had to back it up.

'You initiated a complex court action against Harry Jones in relation to an investment in a technology company. In the court papers you allege you had several meetings with Harry Jones where you discussed your investment. I would say that that means you had a very close relationship with him.'

It always amazed Drake how suspects, even intelligent suspects, were surprised when the police did their job, finding evidence, building a case.

'That was different of course.'

'Perhaps you can explain how it was different.'

Drake heard the irritation in Sara's voice; he shot her a glance telling her to be patient.

'It just is, Sergeant,' Muller said. 'We had a few meetings about a possible investment. I would hardly say I *knew* Harry Jones. And really it was very far from that. I didn't know what he was like as otherwise I would never have made that investment.'

'Where did you meet?'

'I ...'

'Was it at his home?'

Drake saw Muller calculating whether to lie as his eyes darted round, his face twitched.

'Perhaps at your home?'

'I can't remember.'

Sara read her notes – she knew the details better than Muller who couldn't remember what he had said in his statement. Because it had all been a lie.

'Did you meet in some of the local hotels?'

'It's such a long time ago I can't possibly remember.'

'But you sued Harry Jones. It must be something uppermost in your mind. It was a complicated court action.'

'I lead a simple life, Sergeant.'

Now Sara glanced at Drake.

Describing himself as leading a simple life was one the biggest exaggerations Drake had heard for some time.

'I'd like you to try and remember – rack your brains. Where did you meet Harry Jones?'

'I'd need to check my records.'

Sara tried the same tack Drake had used earlier. 'I think most normal people would think that several meetings to discuss a business investment could be described as a relationship. And I think most people would remember where those meetings took place.'

Muller pouted.

Drake took over. 'The result of your court action against Harry Jones was abject failure. You lost tens of thousands of pounds. How did that make you feel?'

'How do you think?'

'Answer the questions, Mr Muller.'

'I had been swindled. Defrauded by that man. I was angry, I admit it. But money isn't everything, is it?'

'Before we discuss your financial position I need to cover some background.'

Muller fidgeted with the nails of his left hand.

'I understand you have an interest in military memorabilia.'

Muller continued his grooming.

'What's your connection to the military?'

Muller admired his hands.

'Did any of your family serve in the Second World War?'

Muller lifted his head and peered at Drake. A nerve had been struck. Drake continued. 'Do you have any pistols from that period – perhaps your father or a near relative was in the German armed forces. We shall be asking the German authorities for the records in due course.'

'You can go and rot in hell.'

Drake was unimpressed. 'The gun used to kill Harry Jones was a German make, common in the Second World War. So, I think you may well have such a weapon especially with your interest in relics from the war.'

'Do you have the murder weapon?' Stokes sounded irritable.

Drake moved on. 'This might be a good opportunity for us to discuss your financial position.' Drake saw the shutters come down in Muller's mind. The pretence at cooperation soon evaporated.

Muller avoided answering any questions about whether his wife was aware of his substantial debts. Every time Drake challenged him about his financial affairs, Muller had some clever explanation, throwing sand in Drake's face. And each time Drake brushed them away and refocused attention on exposing the thin veneer of reality Muller wanted to drape over himself.

After an hour, Stokes interrupted. 'Unless you have some direct evidence against my client you should release him immediately.'

Drake smiled at her – and then at Muller. 'I am also investigating the death of Heulwen Beard.'

'Surely you don't suspect my client to be involved?' Stokes managed to sound exasperated.

Drake ignored the lawyer, staring over at Muller. 'She didn't do a very good job did she? The court case was a disaster, you lost a lot of money and you blamed Heulwen Beard.'

'Don't be absurd. This is becoming a farce.'

'So, with Heulwen Beard out of the way you don't have to pay her costs. I think you went to see her, tried to get her to forget them altogether so you would be off the hook for her fees. But she refused – her papers make clear she warned you your case was hopeless.'

'No, she didn't.'

'Did you know Heulwen Beard and Harry Jones had been in a relationship years ago?' Drake struggled to read Muller's reaction. Drake kept his eye contact direct and realised his disclosure about Beard and Harry Jones didn't come as a surprise. But now there was panic on Muller's face. Muller feared the worst – he was losing control over the interview.

'You were furious with her. When she refused to forego the costs, you took a ceramic bust and killed her.'

'I've never been to Heulwen Beard's place.'

Stokes piped up. 'Have you got any evidence my client visited Mrs Beard's property?'

Drake ignored her and turned his attention to the folder in front of him.

'Where were you on the night Harry Jones was killed?'

'I've told you before.' Muller raised his voice. 'I was at the centre.'

'Did you leave at any time?'

'I was there all night. How many times do I have to tell you people the same thing.'

'We have an eyewitness confirming seeing you talking to Harry Jones in Llanberis on the evening he was killed.'

Muller tugged nervously at his right ear lobe. Then he scratched the skin of his neck.

'I ask you again, Mr Muller – were you in Llanberis on the evening Harry Jones was killed?'

Muller opened his eyes wide. There was panic behind them.

'There's no doubt about the eyewitness. You assaulted a friend of his, broke his arm.'

Muller blurted out. 'Frank Smith is lying. And he's a scumbag.'

Muller ran a hand over his lips, glanced at Drake and Sara, and then at Stokes.

An uncomfortable silence enveloped Muller and Stokes broken by a uniformed officer entering the interview room and gesturing that he needed to speak to Drake.

'I'm suspending the interview,' Drake said, leaving with Sara.

The custody sergeant stood by the counter, a heavy

damp patch discolouring each armpit. 'Mrs Muller and a lawyer from up the coast are here. Demanding to see you.'

Drake turned to Sara. 'Let's go and see what they want.'

Streaks across the laminate table surface suggested recent cleaning and as Drake sat down he ran a finger along the edge of the conference room table. Nicholas Frobisher had a severe cutaway collar to his brilliant white shirt and Drake reckoned a skilled tailor had made the suit that fitted his slim build perfectly.

'I understand you have Mr Wolfgang Muller in custody.' He had a cultured, rather deep voice that gave his words an incredulous edge.

'He is assisting with inquiries.' Drake folded his arms thinking he'd need a coffee before resuming with Muller.

Frobisher pushed a sheet of paper towards Drake. 'Mrs Muller has prepared this statement that I think you should read.'

Drake read the statement that confirmed in clear terms she and her husband had been at home throughout the day of Harry's death and that she knew all about her husband's failed investment. Drake reminded himself about Emyr's evidence; he might make an unreliable witness but once they had traced Frank Smith and taken a statement from him there'd be two witnesses to Muller's temper.

'Mrs Muller hopes that this unpleasantness ...'

Unpleasantness – that word again, Drake thought angrily.

'... can be put to one side and that Wolfgang can be released forthwith.'

Drake slid the statement over the desk at Sara and smiled insincerely at Frobisher, buying time for a reply while she read the details. Sara gave Drake a noncommittal serious nod.

Drake stood up. 'It's very kind of you to come in and bring us this statement.' He shared a disdainful glare between Frobisher and Penny Muller. 'I will consider it most carefully.'

Sara followed Drake to the door where he turned. 'I'm sure you can see yourselves out.'

In the canteen, Drake ordered a coffee, two scoops of instant, and sat down.

'What did you make of the lawyer, boss?'

'Fucking useless …'

'We'll have to release him.'

Drake winced as he sipped his drink. 'He can spend a night in the cells. See what his lawyer makes of that.'

Chapter 25

Luned parked in a layby after passing Nancy Brown's address.

Her decision to establish a pattern to Nancy Brown's movements had been made without consulting Drake or Sara and as she drove from headquarters her confidence that this was worthwhile had ebbed. Brown was part of Harry Jones's extended family after all, but his set-up with Brown felt wrong, Luned rationalised. It had bothered her that a search of Brown's financial record had turned up so little – only a single bank account, no loans or credit cards.

And she could double-check on Harry's movements too she reassured herself.

The bungalow was a discreet distance from the nearest property, enough Luned concluded to persuade Harry Jones he might be able to maintain a degree of privacy when he visited. She left the car and headed to the first of the adjacent homes.

The woman who opened the door in the first property had a large hearing aid in both ears. She invited Luned into the kitchen with a yell. After ten minutes Luned had managed to ask only one question – the woman's name – in a voice that increased until she feared the neighbours might hear her. Each reply had been convoluted so Luned made excuses and left.

An elderly couple lived in the second property. The husband introduced himself as Mr Watkins, his accent straight from one of the suburbs of Liverpool.

'How long have you lived here?' Luned said before venturing over the threshold.

'A couple of months. We love it. All this fresh air

and the great outdoors. We should have moved years
ago.'

Luned declined an offer of coffee. Mr Watkins
shook his head when she asked about Harry Jones and
looked puzzled when she mentioned Nancy Brown.
'Don't know who you mean, love.'

Luned smiled and thanked him before heading for
the next property.

Would it help to establish a pattern to Harry
Jones's visits to Nancy Brown? She rebuked her
cynicism: detective work was about building a picture,
gathering information, uncovering facts.

Luned called at two other properties and both of
the occupiers knew Nancy Brown. But only as some
sort of recluse who rarely went out and had
supermarket deliveries each week. It amazed Luned
how anyone could know so little about their neighbours
before deciding to try one final property.

She rang the doorbell and heard a shout from inside
and then footsteps. A woman with curlers in her air
who looked like an extra from a comedy drama stood
on the threshold. She seemed at least fifteen years
younger than the other homeowners Luned had
interviewed. The woman gave her warrant card a
cursory glance and waved her in.

'I'm part of the team investigating the death of
Harry Jones in Llanberis,' Luned said as she followed
the woman through the hallway.

'That was terrible.'

In the kitchen another woman stood next to a chair;
scissors, combs and brushes lay on a black cloth on the
nearby table.

'I'm having my hair done. Donna comes every

fortnight.'

Donna smiled.

'How long have you lived here?'

'Fifteen years although it seems like yesterday when I first moved in.'

'Do you know Nancy Brown?'

Mrs Harrison rolled her eyes. 'She's a strange one. Keeps herself to herself. You tell her, Donna.'

The hairdresser pitched in. 'I called to see her, thinking she might like to have a perm at home. I could always do with new customers. She couldn't even open the door properly – she peeked out. She was polite enough – told me she wasn't interested.'

Luned produced a photograph of Harry Jones. 'Did you ever see this man calling at the property?'

Harrison nodded. 'He used to park on the drive until he had the electric garage door installed.'

'What do you mean?'

'About a year ago they had one of those fancy electrical doors fitted to the garage. You know, it's all in sections, you press a button, and it opens automatically. He could drive straight in then. But tell her what you thought, Donna. Tell her you thought she had a new fancy man.'

Luned didn't have to trouble herself with coaxing a response from Donna.

Donna continued as though they were talking about a close friend. 'Well, I can remember it like it was yesterday. I was coming up towards her place when I saw the BMW and noticed a personalised plate. My John wants one with his initials on it. Something like JLD – John Lloyd Davis – but last time he checked they could be dead expensive – so he's saving at the moment. He says he can get me one for my Fiesta too.'

'Do you remember the number plate?' Luned said.

'The letters were K.E.V. That's my dad's name – Kevin, I mean. He's dead.'

Luned frowned. 'And do you remember the numbers?'

Donna chortled. 'No, don't be silly.'

'Have you seen the vehicle there again?'

Harrison pitched in. 'Nobody gets a chance. Because she has this electric door and the car goes straight inside the garage. Sometimes I try and look out but it's all too quick. And I don't want to be a busybody.'

'Of course not.' Luned hoped she didn't sound sarcastic.

'We want to know what she gets up to.' Donna sounded titillated. 'She must have this power over men if they can just turn up. We've often thought that she might be … Well, you know … on the game … getting them to pay.'

'This is a respectable neighbourhood; we haven't got any ladies of the night working here,' Mrs Harrison said.

Despite being entertained by Donna and Mrs Harrison, Luned wanted a description. 'Could you describe the man in the BMW?'

Donna paused, frowning. 'He looked middle-aged. And he wore sunglasses. And the car had tinted glass. My John goes on about having tinted glass in his next car all the time.'

'It'll make him look like a drug dealer,' Mrs Harrison said.

'Don't be stupid.' Donna sounded hurt.

Luned tried again. 'And how old was he? In his twenties?'

Donna shook her head.

'Was he in his thirties?'

Donna took a moment before replying. 'He was probably forties or fifties.'

'Would you be able to recognise him again?'

Luned's serious tone voice made both women stare at her. Donna blinked repeatedly. 'Suppose so.'

Luned drove back to headquarters pleased with her progress – a car registration number. By the following morning, the DVLA would confirm the identity of the owner. She stopped in a supermarket, bought a sandwich and a soft drink and arrived back to an empty Incident Room. She ate her lunch in a quiet Winder-free environment. If only every day in the Incident Room could be this hassle free, she thought.

She made her notes from that morning, diligently following all the correct protocols. Then she searched through the CCTV coverage from Harry's office, jotting down the date and time when Perdue had visited Harry Jones with his anonymous friend. It took her longer than she expected to trace the static image she needed. The memorandum from Detective Chief Superintendent Overend gave her the name of a detective constable, Jason Hardcastle, as their contact in the Midlands police. She dialled his number.

'Hardcastle.'

'My name's Detective Constable Thomas, Wales Police Service, Northern Division. I was given your name as the contact dealing with the Richard Perdue inquiry. Are you able to identify the man from the image we sent you?'

'What man?'

'We sent an email with an image of a man we need to trace.'

'Sorry, love. Don't know anything about it.'

Establishing when the original had been sent and where the blame lay for the delay could wait.

'I'll send you another.'

She double-checked the email address, finished the call and typed up a message she marked as urgent before attaching the image. She even called Hardcastle back to check her email had arrived. He promised to call her back as soon as he had any information. For the rest of the afternoon she intended to finish the background on Glyn Talbot that Drake wanted. She guessed Drake and Sara would be back by late in the day but it would be a racing certainty Winder would return before them, complaining about his workload.

She had achieved very little when the telephone rang.

'DC Thomas.'

The voice at the other end boomed in a distinct Birmingham accent. 'Detective Chief Superintendent Overend. Are you the officer that's been in touch with Hardcastle?'

Luned stood up, her chair rolling away behind her. 'Yes, sir.'

'You sent a photograph through to us.'

'That's correct, sir.'

'Where the bloody hell did you get this image?'

'We recovered CCTV coverage from the office of Harry Jones. Richard Perdue appears at least twice and on one occasion he was accompanied by this unidentified man.' Luned prayed her voice didn't sound too nervous. 'We were hoping you might be able to identify him.'

Overend guffawed. 'We can do more than that, Detective Constable. Is Inspector Drake available?'

'He's interviewing a person of interest.'

'So, he's making progress then?'

Luned wasn't certain whether he expected a detailed reply, so she decided on a noncommittal answer. 'Yes, sir.'

'I'll send you details about your unidentified man. His name is Patrick Lennon. You'll find his record of previous convictions interesting – top of the list is a decent stretch for armed robbery. Have Drake call me when he returns.' Luned continued to hold the handset of the telephone for a minute after Overend had finished the call. She couldn't remember ever speaking to a detective chief superintendent before. It took a couple of minutes for her pulse to return to normal.

Winder breezed in late afternoon, an enormous bottle of Diet Coke in hand, and fell into his chair, loosening his tie, and blew out a mouthful of air.

'You wouldn't believe the time I've wasted today.'

Sympathy was the last thing Luned would offer. She glanced at her monitor expecting an email from Hardcastle or Overend to appear. Winder continued.

'I've been trying to find Michael, who worked for Harry Jones.'

'Any success?'

'He wasn't at home, which is a crummy flat in one of those big houses converted into dingy bedsits. One of the other tenants gave me the run-around to a property in Caernarfon and then back to a place in the mountains.'

Luned half listened to Winder, concentrating mostly on glancing at the screen on her desk. She had already decided she wouldn't share any details about Patrick Lennon with Winder until Drake and Sara arrived back.

'It took me bloody ages to track down Michael's mother. And guess what – when I showed her the picture of Carol she told me that Carol had been Michael's girlfriend.'

Luned made a double-take. 'So, he knew who she was?'

Winder nodded.

'We need to find him.' Luned stared over at Winder.

'I spoke to a friend of his who hasn't seen him for a couple of days. They go to a pub quiz together once a week – but he hasn't heard from Michael. And apparently he can go hiking over the mountains – takes a tent with him and takes photographs.' Winder shivered at the thought.

He reached over for the soft drink and took a large mouthful before wiping the back of his hand over his mouth and then hauling his feet onto his desk. He didn't have a chance to get comfortable before the sound of Drake and Sara in conversation drifted in as they approached the Incident Room door.

Sara looked pasty, the sort of complexion that sitting for hours in an interview room can cause.

Drake went to stand by the board.

'We've just finished with Wolfgang Muller.'

Sara shrugged off her red parka and sat down by her desk next to Luned.

'Mrs Muller turned up with a fancy lawyer and

gave her husband an alibi for the afternoon and evening that Harry Jones was killed.'

'Does that mean he is in the clear, boss?' Luned said.

'We all know what alibis from spouses are like. We've got first-hand evidence from Emyr that Wolfgang Muller was in the village the night Harry Jones was murdered *and* that he has a hell of a temper. And we'll need to speak to Frank Smith in due course. Muller has got more than enough motive to kill Harry Jones and Heulwen Beard. But we'll hold Muller overnight and release him on bail in the morning. The search of his property might even turn up something.'

Winder was the first to contribute. 'I haven't been able to track down Michael, boss. But I did talk to his mother who confirmed that Carol was his girlfriend at one time.'

'So he lied to us. He knew her all along. We need to find him.'

'Yes, boss.'

'There's been another development, sir.' Luned struck a serious tone. 'Detective Chief Superintendent Overend wants you to call him urgently. He sent the details this afternoon of our unidentified man who accompanied Richard Perdue to see Harry Jones. He's called Patrick Lennon and he's got a string of convictions including one for armed robbery.'

'Jesus Christ, why the hell was Harry mixing with these people?'

'It makes it even more important to track down Carol,' Sara said. 'It looks like her evidence will be crucial.'

Chapter 26

Drake parked outside Malcolm Walker Associates, Harry Jones's financial adviser, early the following morning. The messages left on the answering service had so far been ignored and Drake was annoyed. After the interview yesterday, he still believed Muller and his wife were hiding something. Despite Muller being released on bail later, Drake still hoped that the ongoing search of his property would be fruitful.

Two men in smart dark suits and slicked-back hair entered the offices followed by a slim woman with high heels and a severe ponytail that swung assertively behind her head. Drake left the car.

Gold lettering stencilled on the window advertised 'wealth management' and 'financial planning' services. The pony-tailed woman looked younger and less smart now she was sitting behind the desk at reception, although her name badge – Angelique – suggested someone exotic.

'Good morning.' He held out his warrant card. 'I'm Detective Inspector Ian Drake and I want to speak to Malcolm Walker.'

'Do you have an appointment?' The coarse Scottish accent ruined the carefully constructed appearance and the immaculate make-up.

Drake gave the girl a hard look. 'I'm investigating a murder. I don't think I need an appointment.'

She blinked. 'Please take a seat.' She regained her composure and reached for the phone.

Drake sat in a faux leather chair with floppy arms and deep cushions. *Cheshire Life* and *Good Housekeeping* magazines were stacked carefully on the table next to him. He found their neat symmetry reassuring.

Drake hadn't been seated long when a door behind Angelique opened and a man, at least two stones overweight, wearing a navy pinstripe suit and matching waistcoat bustled over to Drake.

'Malcolm Walker.' He held out a hand. 'I'm sorry for not getting back to you. I have been so busy. Come through to my office. Coffee please, Ang,' Walker said without looking at the receptionist.

Walker's room overlooked the busy street where Drake had parked.

'Sit down.' Walker pointed to a chair.

'I've left several messages about Harry Jones,' Drake said.

'As I said, things have been frantic.'

Ang appeared with coffee on a tray with a milk jug and sugar.

'Nothing better than coming to work and having something gorgeous to look at.' Walker winked at Drake after she left.

Drake ignored him. 'How long were you Harry Jones's financial adviser?'

'A good few years. His death was tragic. Do you have a suspect?'

'We have numerous active lines of inquiry. Several years ago, you advised Harry to create a trust.'

Walker nodded. 'He wanted to protect his capital. Nobody wants to pay inheritance tax if they can avoid it.'

'Of course.'

Walker helped himself to a coffee; Drake did likewise. The cheap instant didn't go with the image

Walker was cultivating.

'Harry had sold a property and he didn't need the money so he salted it away in a trust we established. All above board and legal. Nothing dodgy, Inspector. It wasn't tax evasion in any way, shape or form.' Walker adopted a serious voice. 'I wouldn't get involved in anything illegal.'

'Of course not. Who are the beneficiaries of the trust?'

Walker opened a file on his desk.

'Apart from himself and Fiona he nominated a Matthew Talbot.'

'Did Harry explain why he wanted to nominate Matthew Talbot?'

'No, sorry. I never asked. Harry could be secretive sometimes. I didn't think anything of it. After all, I just give advice and act on my client's instructions.'

'What else can you tell me about his financial position?'

'He had been quite a successful businessman and we managed a substantial portfolio of different investments. We also organised all the insurance for him on his various properties. Most were let long term to reliable tenants. One of the houses was held jointly with a woman called Nancy Brown.'

Drake nodded. 'Do you know anything about her?'

'Not really ...' Walker paused to find the right words. 'I never knew the precise details of their relationship ... but I assumed she was ... how shall I put this ... a girlfriend? Mistress sounds such an old-fashioned sort of word.'

'Is that how Harry described her?'

'I don't think he did. I mention it because we wrote

a life policy in Harry's name where she is the sole beneficiary.'

Drake straightened in his chair. 'Why the hell didn't you tell us about this before?'

Walker looked flustered. 'I'm sorry ... I didn't think it was relevant.'

'How much was the policy worth?'

'From recollection, £300,000.'

'How much?' Drake couldn't hide his surprise. 'I'll need all the details about this policy emailed to my office immediately. Is that clear?' Drake stood up.

'One more thing, Inspector. Harry recently asked me about changing the trust. He wanted to add a beneficiary. I told him he'd have to start a new trust. I warned him there would be fees involved and it might be quite expensive but he didn't seem to mind.'

'Did he give you a name?'

Walker shook his head. 'Sorry.'

'Did you ever meet Fiona Jones?'

'I met her once when she attended a function with Harry we were sponsoring – you know, networking. It all helps our business.'

The beneficiary of Harry's generosity wouldn't have a motive but whoever lost out, and that included Fiona Jones, certainly would. 'Did you make any assumptions about the identity of the beneficiary from what Harry told you?'

Walker gave a light shrug.

'I'll need your file of papers.'

'I understand. I hope you catch the killer.' Walker stood up.

'If you think of anything else then contact me or one of my team. Don't assume that it could be irrelevant.'

Drake left and sat in his car letting his anger at Walker dissipate. He checked his watch again for the umpteenth time that morning. The shop assistant he had forgotten about in his haste for his first date with Annie was back that afternoon for her nightshift at the supermarket. He would interview her before his second date with Annie that evening. Beard's murder two days *after* the missed appointment had preyed on his mind. What if the woman had some crucial evidence that might have prevented Heulwen Beard's death? How would he live with himself?

He tapped out a message to Annie – *really looking forward to this evening. I might be a little late xxx.*

Before he drove away Drake solved two more squares of the Sudoku puzzle in the morning newspaper. It had the desired effect of making him feel more in charge, and when a message reached his mobile from Mike Foulds asking that he call at the CSI department he sent a reply telling the crime scene manager to expect him once he was back.

It was a short drive and Drake listened to a few tracks from *Dark Side of the Moon* before parking. The forensic lab was a hive of activity – a team of white-coated investigators ploughed their way through the evidence recovered from Muller's property. Drake hoped that Mike Foulds had made a breakthrough – something definitive to link Muller to Harry Jones's murder.

When Foulds saw Drake he waved him over.

'I wanted to tell you as soon as I'd heard. We got a fingerprints match from the furniture you discovered at Harry Jones's lock-up.'

Foulds patted a stool by his side. Drake made himself comfortable. 'Fingerprints?' Drake wanted confirmation he understood Foulds correctly.

Foulds sorted the paperwork in front of him as he spoke. 'We recovered over fifty sets of prints. It's taken us days of work. Most probably belong to the owners of the property. There were sets belonging to a couple of convicted drug users – mostly recreational stuff and several drink drivers. But it's the last two that I thought you might be interested in.'

Drake glanced at the clock on the wall hoping Foulds would get on with it. He hadn't got all day.

'There are fingerprints from Richard Perdue and a man called Patrick Lennon.'

Drake's mouth fell open. 'Are you certain?'

'I thought those names would interest you.'

'And you haven't got any evidence from yesterday's search of Muller's property?'

Foulds shook his head. He pushed over the detailed results. Drake touched his parted lips with the thumb and forefinger of one hand as he read the details, blanking out the noise and activity in the forensic lab. He slid off the stool once he'd finished, thanked Foulds and left.

Winder jumped to his feet when Drake arrived in the Incident Room. 'I've just taken a statement from Frank Smith, boss.'

Drake ignored him. From the desk nearest the board he found a sheet of paper and scribbled a name on it. He pinned the paper alongside the image of Richard Perdue before he turned to face the rest of the team. 'All in good time, Gareth. I've been to see Mike Foulds and they've had the results of the fingerprint examination of the furniture we discovered in Harry Jones's lock-up. And guess whose fingerprints are all over an antique table.' He tapped a ballpoint to Richard Perdue's face, and then on the name Patrick Lennon written in large letters.

'We'll need to speak to Richard Perdue again,' Sara said.

Drake checked his watch, conscious he had to give himself enough time to arrive at the supermarket on time. And conscious too that Detective Chief Superintendent Overend had warned him about the company Richard Perdue kept. 'And Patrick Lennon in due course. Get a copy of his picture onto the board.'

Luned got to her feet as though she were making a formal announcement. 'There's more, sir. When I spoke to Nancy Brown's neighbours yesterday, one of them remembers a car with the registration letters KEV calling at the property. The result of a search of the DVLA came back this morning and Richard Perdue owns a car registered with those letters.'

'Perdue knows Nancy Brown. What the bloody hell is going on?' Drake said.

Drake looked over at Luned. The detective constable had a natural authority. She sounded confident. It was the second big case since she had joined his team and now he felt she was slotting in, finding her feet.

'And I established that Harry Jones created a trust that benefits his nephew Matthew Talbot, so, Luned, email me any background you've got on him.'

Luned buried her head in a notepad, scribbling notes.

'And Nancy Brown is the beneficiary of a policy

worth £300,000 on Harry Jones's life.'

Winder whistled under his breath. 'If Nancy Brown and Perdue are an item then that gives them both a massive motive.'

Sara grabbed Drake's attention. 'I've been doing some digging around into Richard Perdue's background. I made contact with the Met and eventually I tracked down some of the family history to Southend-on-Sea.'

'Go on,' Drake said.

'The police in Southend have never been able to prosecute Perdue successfully. I spoke to one sergeant who sounded like he'd give his pension to have convicted Perdue.'

Drake noticed Winder's look of boyish anticipation. 'Gareth, tell us what Smith said.'

'He'll make a great witness.'

'Tell us what he *told* you.'

'Sorry, boss. Muller broke his arm when he assaulted him. Smith told me he was in one hell of a temper.'

It wasn't going to be enough to prevent Muller's release on bail. If the new leads pointing to Richard Perdue led nowhere then the Crown prosecution lawyers could decide about prosecuting Muller.

'Good work everyone.' Drake fastened his jacket. 'I'll inform the super and I'll call Overend about the fingerprints.'

Chapter 27

Wyndham Price nodded and grunted occasionally as Drake explained the basis of his decision that Perdue had to explain himself and that he had to do so under caution in the custody suite having been arrested on suspicion of murder.

'I hate these gangsters coming to North Wales thinking we've got straw between our ears.' Price hesitated. Drake could see him thinking around the problem. 'And have you spoken to DCS Overend?'

'Not yet.'

Price reached over for the telephone on his desk. He dialled a number. 'Andy, I've DI Drake with me.'

Drake recognised the Christian name of a senior Crown prosecutor.

'I need to organise a meeting tomorrow for an urgent serious case review.'

The superintendent used a fancy-looking fountain pen to jot the details on a yellow Post It note.

'You'd better call Overend before our meeting,' Price said, giving Drake a look that said he had finished.

'Yes, sir.' Drake got to his feet.

Threading his way back to the Incident Room he wasn't certain what Price thought. Would he support arresting Perdue? Or would he wait and see what Andy Thorsen might say? It made him uneasy. There was lot that Perdue had to explain. Drake sat at his desk, wondering if arresting Perdue was justified.

He shook off his doubts and called Overend.

'I anticipate arresting Richard Perdue on suspicion of murder,' Drake said, hoping he sounded confident.

Detective Chief Superintendent Overend, listening at the other end of the telephone line, didn't react immediately.

'Our forensics team have discovered fingerprints belonging to Perdue and Patrick Lennon on the furniture we recovered from Harry Jones's lock-up.'

'I see.'

'There's a clear picture emerging that Perdue met Harry Jones and lied about it. We believe Harry was involved with Perdue and Lennon.'

Drake sensed the exasperation from the other man down the telephone.

'And there's a lot of intelligence to suggest Perdue is more than capable of murder.'

'Southend.' Overend announced flatly.

Drake paused, his momentum broken. 'We shall need to interview Lennon in due course.'

'Has this been authorised by your super?'

'We've got a senior case review meeting with a Crown prosecutor tomorrow.'

Overend said nothing for a few seconds and Drake assumed that his reference to the lawyer gave him little room to criticise the approach. Price had been right, of course, even if he was covering his tracks.

'Keep me posted.' Overend finished the call abruptly.

Drake glanced at the time. He would have to leave soon to meet the shop assistant before seeing Annie later that evening. Guilt wriggled around in his mind again about the first meeting he had missed but he didn't have time for it to develop as Winder stood in his doorway.

'I've identified the minibus Talbot saw on the

afternoon Beard was killed. I'm going over there later.'

'Good.' Drake got to his feet and followed Winder out into the Incident Room.

'I'm going to see Vera Alton, the shop assistant,' Drake said.

'Do you need me to come too, sir?' Sara said.

'No, I've got a family commitment later.'

He noticed Sara share a glance with Winder that he couldn't immediately interpret. He didn't want to explain about Annie and he had hoped that 'family commitment' might imply he was seeing his mother. Now he wasn't so sure.

Drake arrived at the supermarket half an hour before Vera Alton's night shift started and waited in his car. Sitting watching young mothers struggling with their bags and screaming children made him think about Fiona Jones. It must have been galling for her to be subjected to the gossip from the local community about her husband's indiscretions. Did his money and wealth buy her peace of mind? Had she become bitter and twisted enough that her love for Harry had turned into hatred, intense enough to kill him.

Two emails arrived on his mobile. He opened the first from the adoption agency confirming Harry Jones as the father of Heulwen Beard's daughter. Was Fiona aware Harry and Heulwen Beard had been an item and that their child had been given up for adoption? Drake found his mind joining too many dots as he contemplated the possibility that the new beneficiary Harry was planning for his trust was actually Harry's child with Heulwen Beard. Perhaps the child had made contact with him, hoping to re-establish a relationship with her birth parents. Fiona must have found that galling too.

Drake turned his attention to the email from Luned with the report on Glyn Talbot's background and Harry Jones's extended family. Matthew, Glyn's son, lived in Bangor and worked in the property department of the university and Luned had discovered that father and son had little to do with each other, which didn't surprise Drake from what he knew of Glyn Talbot.

It intrigued him why Harry Jones would have created a trust fund for his nephew. Glyn Talbot had made no mention of his family connection to Harry Jones when he first met Drake in the army museum nor when they questioned him about his visits to Harry Jones on the morning Harry was killed. Talbot had recently been made redundant from the slate museum but not before complaints from staff members that he had acted aggressively towards them led to disciplinary proceedings.

Luned's summary confirmed Drake's impression that Talbot was an eccentric loner living in a small confined world of writing historical articles for a local paper that probably few people read. When Drake tried to read one of his articles he found the language obtuse and highbrow. Drake read on and noted the details about Jean Talbot's suicide and he realised Luned had used her initiative to dig further and deeper into the family background. Something must have troubled Jean deeply, Drake thought, as he imagined the impact on Matthew and Glyn Talbot. Father and son had lost a wife and mother; as he mulled over the details of the inquiry and everything he knew about Harry, a dark scenario developed in his mind. It answered the question as to why Matthew was the beneficiary of

Harry's generosity.

Matthew was Harry's son and the guilt had driven Jean to suicide. Did Fiona know? Only asking her would give them the answer.

He glanced at the clock on the dashboard and decided he couldn't be late so he made for the entrance of the supermarket. A tall man with glasses and close-cropped hair stood by customer services scanning the shoppers as Drake entered. He gave Drake an enquiring look, searching for recognition that turned to relief when Drake approached him.

'Detective Chief Inspector Drake? I'm Peter Green, the manager.'

'Inspector,' Drake replied. 'Is Vera Alton here?'

'She's in the staff room. Follow me.'

At the rear of the store a door by the pharmacy led to a staircase and then down a short corridor. Green pushed open a door into a large room dominated by a table and a dozen office chairs.

Vera Alton cradled a plastic cup of a hot liquid in one hand. She had jet-black hair, a puffy complexion and far too much make-up. She made to stand up; Drake fluttered a hand telling her to sit down. Green sat on a chair at the far end of the table.

'I'm investigating the death of Harry Jones. I understand that on the afternoon he was killed you served him.' Drake recited the date and time and pushed over the table an image of Harry Jones.

Alton stared at the photograph and then glanced up at Drake. 'I've seen him a few times. He's a regular.'

'On the day of his death he bought flowers and a bottle of wine.'

Alton nodded.

'Have you served him before?'

'Yes, I think so, quite often. In fact I don't remember him buying anything else – perhaps chocolate sometimes.'

'Was there anyone with him?'

She frowned, taking time to think.

'I don't think there was anyone else with him. But I can't be certain.'

Drake turned to the manager. 'Do you have CCTV?'

'Yes, but it's only of the entrance and the car park. We don't film every checkout.'

'I'll need to see it.'

'Well, it might take some time.'

'Now. I need to see it now.'

Green blinked nervously, fidgeted with his fingers. 'I'll see what I can do.'

Drake followed him back into the corridor and then passed other offices until he pushed open a door. Inside was a bank of monitors showing the live coverage from several cameras pointing at the main door near the till area.

Green sat down and pulled a chair nearer the desk. 'What were the details again?'

Drake dictated the date and time, becomingly increasingly irritated as Green fiddled with the controls, inputting the incorrect information. Drake repeated the right data in a loud voice that earned him a sharp look from Green.

Drake read the time again. If he was going to be delayed much longer he might be late for his date with Annie. So he would have to text again. No, call her this time; he'd love to hear her voice. Looking down at the screen Green swore under his breath and announced. 'I don't usually do this.'

Drake didn't reply; he kept staring at the monitor.

Eventually the correct date appeared in the top right-hand corner.

'It was afternoon,' Drake dictated the exact time. 'Go back half an hour before that.'

Green nodded.

'Is there some way to speed up the footage?' Drake said.

Green did as he was told and the images sped along like an old-fashioned movie.

Drake's adrenaline spiked when he saw Harry Jones walking into the store a few minutes before his purchase. But it was his companion that really caught Drake's attention. Penny Muller ambled in alongside him as though they were any ordinary couple going shopping one afternoon.

'Stop that.' Drake's shout unnerved Green who fumbled with the controls. 'I'll need a copy of this footage.'

Now Drake had concrete evidence that Penny Muller had lied to him about her whereabouts that afternoon. What else had she lied about? Perhaps she and Wolfgang had conspired to kill Harry Jones?

'Run the tape on in normal speed until they leave the store. And have you got any images from outside?'

Drake folded his arms, standing over Green as he scrolled through the various cameras until he could show Penny Muller and Harry Jones leaving together and heading for the car park. The footage switched to the cameras on the exterior of the building. Drake watched as Penny and Harry Jones laughed and joked.

'Stop, there.'

Where were these two going? Drake allowed his gaze to scan some of the other vehicles parked nearby. One in particular caught his attention. He leaned over Green. 'Do you see that Range Rover Evoque? Can you zoom in onto that vehicle?'

More fumbling with the controls ensued but Drake kept his irritation in check. The screen filled with an image of the car. It was grainy, but even so Drake recognised Wolfgang Muller.

Annie sat opposite Drake in a pub with a wood fire burning in an open hearth. There was an occasional hiss from a damp log. The place was busy, most of the tables occupied, a group of regular drinkers sitting on stools by the bar. Nobody paid them any attention. They looked like any other early middle-aged couple enjoying an evening out, Drake thought. He was encouraged to feel that he was becoming part of normal human activity again.

Annie had kissed him when she arrived. Enough to acknowledge the connection he had felt from their first date and enough to encourage him to believe there might be a future to this relationship. Her blouse and trousers were a little less formal, but, like her make-up, they still made her look attractive, so attractive he found himself staring.

'I'm really sorry about last weekend,' Drake said.

'Don't worry. Your investigation must take priority. It must be so demanding having to be on call all the time.' She smiled.

Drake couldn't recall if Sian had ever said anything

like that in all the years of their marriage.

'I heard about that dreadful case in Deiniolen.' Annie lowered her voice. 'Are the deaths linked?'

Drake averted his gaze and gave their fellow diners a surreptitious scan, hoping nobody had heard her question. 'We don't know yet.'

Annie spared him any further embarrassment. 'I know you can't talk about it. I'm sorry.'

She took another sip of orange juice, studying the menu.

A waitress arrived and gave them a tepid smile. Drake ordered; Annie did likewise. The conversation flowed and soon Drake felt he had known Annie forever. It was like rekindling an old friendship, stepping back into a comfortable routine and familiar reminiscence. But he knew it was more than that; he could barely take his eyes off her. Her smile was warm and uncomplicated.

After the main course Annie ordered a tiramisu she described as her favourite. All Drake could think of was that it made a change from his former wife who would have turned her nose up at a fat- and sugar-laden sweet. He determined for the rest of the evening he wouldn't make any comparisons.

A waitress looked disappointed when they declined her offer of coffee. When Annie suggested she make coffee at home his pulse almost stalled. His lips dried, he hesitated. 'If it's not too much trouble, that'll be lovely.'

Too much trouble. How idiotic that sounds, Drake thought.

Annie lived in one of the terraces overlooking the Menai Strait in Felinheli. Drake followed her down into the marina development and parked behind her. He had assumed that many of the houses would be holiday homes but it was October and lights burned from the windows of a few of the properties. On the top floor she led him onto the balcony overlooking the Strait and they watched as two ribs made their way into the harbour. A Welsh Dragon flag flickered in the light evening breeze from a flagpole in the adjacent house.

'It's a fabulous location,' Drake said.

'I loved the place when I first saw it.'

Back inside Annie fiddled with a machine on the worktop. Eventually she produced two mugs of coffee. They sat down on a comfortable sofa. Drake wanted to kiss her. Feel his lips on hers, run his hand over them, pull her hair away from her face. Slowly unbutton her blouse.

An embarrassed stiffness invaded the space between them. They didn't say very much. Drake couldn't find the right words.

'How is your coffee?' Annie said.

'It's fine.'

Drake regretted his reluctance to move closer to her along the sofa. But he sensed he would have been welcome. He finished the coffee, thought about making excuses, thought how natural their relationship had become.

She reached over and kissed him firmly. Her lips tasted of sweet coffee. It sent a powerful bolt of emotion through him, reminding him what he had missed. Now he kissed her back, strongly, with a passion and fervour he thought he had lost.

When they broke off he gazed into her eyes. She smiled. He smiled back. He reached a hand to touch her face – it was a moment to treasure. One of many to come, Drake thought.

A sound filled the room and for a brief moment they both ignored the insistent ringing of a mobile telephone.

It had to be Drake's. He wanted to throw the damn thing into the Menai Strait.

He got up and found his jacket.

He recognised Winder's voice. 'We've found Carol, boss.'

'Where?

'She's in hospital. She's been assaulted tonight by Michael.'

Drake turned to look at Annie. He wanted it to wait until the morning. She gave him a nervous smile.

'You need to see her, boss. She's been telling the officers about Harry Jones.'

Drake sighed. 'I'll meet you at the hospital.'

Annie joined Drake, placing a hand on his arm.

'I understand. Really I do …'

Drake didn't allow her to finish. He kissed her intensely and then left.

Chapter 28

Drake parked in a disabled parking slot – he was on police business and he doubted many disabled patients would be attending hospital late in the evening. After a revolving door reduced his pace momentarily he hurried down the deserted main corridor but ignoring the lifts, he took the stairs to the ward. Winder stood waiting for him outside, a bottle of water in hand.

'Sorry to disturb you, boss,' Winder said.

Drake brushed away the apology although it did occur to him whether Winder knew where he had been.

'The uniformed lads in Bangor were called to an incident a couple of hours ago. Apparently, Michael arrived at the house where Carol had been staying. He was pissed up to the eyeballs and was in a fighting mood.'

'So, what happened?'

Two nurses and an orderly appeared from one ward pushing a patient on a trolley, ventilators strapped to his face. They ignored Drake and Winder and hurried towards the lifts.

'Michael broke into the house and assaulted Carol. The medics think she may have a cracked rib as well as a fractured cheek. Once the uniformed lads found out who she was they realised we wanted to speak to her.'

Drake nodded. 'You did the right thing, Gareth. Let's go and talk to her.'

Winder pushed open the door and they passed two small bays with half a dozen patients in each, mostly fast asleep. At the nurses' station in the middle of the ward Winder stopped and nodded towards a tall woman with tightly cropped blond hair.

'This is Detective Inspector Drake.' The nurse gave Drake a polite nod. Winder continued. 'We need to speak to Carol Parry.'

'Don't be too long. She really needs to get some sleep.'

Luckily Carol had a room to herself. Drake pushed the door closed. There was little sign sleep was imminent as Carol was playing on her mobile telephone. Drake recognised her face from the CCTV in Harry's office. Carol had large, seductive eyes, and a well-proportioned face with good bone structure. Even dressed in a hospital nightgown she looked attractive.

Winder pushed over a stiff plastic chair for Drake and both officers sat down, looking at her.

'We've been searching for you,' Drake said.

Carol gave an ineffective shrug. 'I want to make a complaint about Michael assaulting me. He should go down for what he did to me.'

'I want you to tell me what you know about Harry Jones.'

'Have you found who killed him?' Carol sounded too matter-of-fact.

'Were you having a relationship with him?'

'Yeh, suppose so.'

'Tell us about your relationship.' Drake moved forward slightly in his chair.

It flustered Carol. 'He'd take me out sometimes. We'd go to that fancy hotel.' She waved a hand in the air to some point in the distance. 'We would have a nice meal then … And you know what.'

'What?' Drake wasn't going to make it easy for Carol.

'Well …'

'You would have sex with him.'

She gave Drake a coquettish smile.

Drake lowered his voice. 'I'm only interested in knowing exactly what happened one particular day when you were with Harry in his office.'

Carol gave him a puzzled, almost disappointed look, as though she were expecting him to ask for more lurid details about their relationship.

Drake nodded at Winder who produced from a folder a set of still photographs of Carol and Harry. He handed the first to her.

'Is this you?'

Her eyes opened wide. 'Where the hell did you get this?'

'Harry Jones had a CCTV camera recording everything that happened.'

'The dirty bastard.'

'This particular day when you called to see him you were interrupted.'

Drake showed her various static images of Harry and her until it was clear she was inside the cupboard at the far end of Harry's office.

'Why did he tell you to go inside the cupboard?'

Colour drained rapidly from Carol's cheeks. 'He said he wouldn't be too long.'

The next pictures were of Richard Perdue and Harry Jones.

'Do you know this man?'

Carol shook her head.

'Have you seen him before?'

'No.'

'It's very important you tell us as much as you can remember about what happened that day.'

Her earlier bravado disappeared. She blinked away the tears, glancing over at Drake and Winder.

'They argued. They argued a lot. I don't remember everything that was said but I do remember this guy threatening to sort out Harry. He was going to get his friends and nobody would get the better of them. All sorts of stuff like that.'

Drake looked over at Winder, pleased he was busy noting everything down in his pocketbook.

'I want you to remember precisely what was said.'

Half an hour later after a lot of cajoling and repetition Drake was satisfied he had a clear record. Now Carol did look as though she should be sleeping. There had been explicit threats to Harry's life from Richard Perdue, a promise to bring his friends to sort him out in due course. Drake sensed the decision to arrest him would be a formality. Wolfgang and Penny Muller's lying could wait.

'How did Harry react afterwards?' Drake said.

'I don't know. But we were supposed to go out that day and he made excuses.'

'Did he seem frightened?'

Carol dipped her head. 'Yes, I suppose he did.'

'Why did Michael assault you?'

'Because … He thought we were an item … you know going out.'

'Do you have a regular boyfriend, Carol?'

She picked up her mobile and started playing on the screen again.

'I'll make arrangements for an officer to get you to sign a formal statement in due course.' Drake stood up; the plastic chair squeaked against the floor.

'Is Michael going to be charged?'

'It'll be up to the officer dealing with the case.'

'Bloody well should be.'

'You need to get some sleep, Carol.' Drake opened the door.

'What did you make of her, boss?' Winder said as they made their way out of the ward.

'I think she was telling the truth.'

'I wouldn't like to be her boyfriend. You'd have no idea what she was getting up to.'

Both officers took the stairs down to the ground floor then made their way back to the front entrance. The night air chilled Drake's face. Winder went off towards his car and Drake glanced at his watch, realising by now Annie would be safely tucked up in bed.

His eyes burned, his skin felt greasy, an ache twinged at the bottom of his back.

He needed a good few hours' uninterrupted sleep, so he went home.

Chapter 29

The following morning, Drake was parked near the newsagents, working on the Sudoku puzzle in the newspaper when his mobile rang. Feeling pleased with himself for managing three squares quickly he studied one particular line as he answered.

'Drake.'

'Operational control room, Inspector. We have the reports of a suspected homicide.'

'Send me all the usual ...' Drake then realised he had to pay the call more attention. 'Suspected murder? Is there a body?'

'Yes, Inspector. A Frank Smith.'

'Frank Smith,' Drake yelled. He threw the paper to one side. 'What are the details?'

A few seconds later he punched the postcode into the system. When the voice down the telephone gave him the address at the end of the call – the slate museum – he knew he needn't have bothered.

Drake's mouth dried, anticipation frantically developing in his mind. He crunched the car into first gear, checked his rear-view mirror and accelerated away.

He called Sara.

'I've just heard, boss. Is it the same Frank Smith as our witness?'

'I was thinking the same. I don't know yet. I'm on my way – check the status of CSIs and I'll see you there.'

Drake didn't wait to hear Sara's response.

He flashed his car headlights and blasted his horn at a car dawdling in front of him. The elderly woman driver pulled into the side of the road and he powered on to the junction he needed, ignoring an irate man who jerked his middle finger when Drake cut across him.

He reached the A55 and hammered the car into the outside lane. He sped through the tunnel under the Conwy estuary, thankful that the traffic lights at the roadworks in the mountain tunnels near Penmaenmawr were kind to him. By the time he approached the turning for Llanberis he had spoken to Superintendent Price, who confirmed their meeting would be postponed, and to Sara, again to confirm the CSI team were en route.

Tearing down the road towards the slate museum he almost mowed down three walkers who had strayed into the middle. More gesticulating and angry faces followed him.

A uniformed police officer stood by the entrance to the museum building. He ran over to Drake once he had parked. Drake recognised Chris Newland from the morning that Harry Jones's body had been discovered. 'It's over here, sir.'

Newland pointed towards a building some distance away.

Another uniformed officer stood by the door of the old structure, its windows grey and its roof sagging.

'Apparently this was a building they used up until a few years ago. A lot of the machinery is still there but the place is unsafe,' Newland said as he joined Drake heading towards it.

The second officer pushed open the doors. The smell of decaying wood, grease and oil filled Drake's nostrils. To his right was a rickety wooden staircase, several of the risers missing. The staircase led up to a platform supported by wooden posts that stretched out to the far end of the building.

Drake noticed two figures inside a makeshift office against the wall to his left. Movement stopped as they turned to peer out and gaze over at Drake.

Newland said. 'He's at the far end.'

The officer led Drake along a path marked out with faded yellow paint. On one side were crates of different-sized slates, some sitting on large slabs, others with shards of slate propped up against them. Ancient tools and hammers and sledgehammers littered an area to Drake's right. The place had an abandoned feel as though it expected to be busy but nobody knew what to do with it.

As they approached the office, Newland lowered his voice.

'These are the two members of staff who made the discovery.'

'I was told the victim is Frank Smith.'

'One of them recognised him.'

A man in his forties wearing a blue overall left the office ready to talk to Drake but Drake raised a hand. 'Please wait inside. I'll come and speak with you in a minute.'

The man kept his mouth open, and then retreated back to the office, a hurt look on his face. He sat down with the youngster inside.

Newland led Drake to the far end of the building. There were heavy machines that Drake guessed had been used to split and cut enormous pieces of slate. In an age before forklift trucks dozens of men would have been needed to lift and carry such items. In the middle of the floor was a piece of machinery with enormous wheels and a withered leather belt.

Newland stood and pointed down at the lifeless body.

It was a man in his early twenties, although Drake could only guess his age from his slim build and lack of facial hair. A blue Welsh slate had severed the man's neck. Drake's stomach churned at the sight of blood splattered over the scene.

'It looks like he fell from the platform above us, sir,' Newland said.

Drake looked up at the gaping hole in the platform, pieces of slate scattered on its surface. To his untrained eye Drake could see the rotten timbers.

'Who has access to this building?' Drake asked aloud, not expecting Newland to answer.

'Apparently it was part of the museum until a couple of years ago when they closed it down.'

Drake took a step back, away from the immediate prospect of being decapitated by a falling piece of loose slate. He gazed around the scene where the body lay. What was this young man doing in an old disused building?

He paused and looked up again – pushing him off the top would have been easy. His head smashed on the heavy machinery below and a loose slate dropped to finish him off. Forensics would have to comb the place, searching for evidence, fragments, anything that might suggest who else had been present.

On impulse, Drake retraced his steps to the entrance and staircase. Newland followed him. Drake snapped on a pair of latex gloves and ascended the staircase, grabbing one of the handrails as he did so. The whole thing shook with his weight.

'Are you sure this is a good idea, sir?'

'Tell me when the CSIs arrive.'

At the top Drake reached a section of platform that led across the building. He tried to picture what had made the victim walk along the rickety construction. At the end of the first section that balanced above the office area he heard the faint sounds of car engines stopping and raised voices outside. He turned right towards the fateful section of the rotten timber decking. It creaked in protest. He paused for a moment.

A few hours ago a man had likely stood where he was now. Why? He had fallen to his death but was it an accident? Or made to appear like one? He couldn't look down; it was too dangerous.

He heard Sara's voice from the entrance and gingerly retraced his steps, testing the occasional section of timber. She stood at the bottom of the staircase as he descended, Newland by her side.

'The place is a death trap,' Drake said. 'Come over here.' He nodded towards the far end of the building. He led Sara to the spot under the platform and she gasped. 'Christ Almighty. Looks like something out of a Schwarzenegger film.'

'Let's talk to the members of staff who found the body.'

Sara followed him back to the dilapidated office. The older man had the complexion of a dirty pavement slab and a developing paunch. A white T-shirt under his overall was translucent with age. The youngster alongside him looked completely lost.

'Who found the body?' Drake said.

'I'm Dan, Inspector,' The older man said. 'Luke made the discovery. We came in here this morning

269

looking for an old piece of equipment. The curator
wanted to use it as part of a demonstration for a
documentary being filmed about slate mining over the
centuries.'

'What is this place?' Sara asked.

'A lot of men worked in here years ago. But then
the place couldn't be repaired economically and it was
closed. Now it's used mostly for storage.'

'Was the building secure?' Drake said.

Luke nodded. 'I was the first one here. I opened
up.'

'And were you the first to see the body?' Sara said,
in a soft voice.

Luke choked back the nausea.

'It is important you remember everything you can
about what you first saw.'

'He was lying there. A piece of slate through his
fucking neck.'

'Don't swear, Luke,' Dan said.

Luke appeared hurt. 'There was nobody else here.
The place gives me the creeps. There's always a
disgusting smell.'

'Do either of you know when anybody was in this
building last?'

Dan and Luke shook their heads in unison.

'So, basically if you had a key there's nothing to
stop you getting access,' Drake said.

Both men gave Drake a blank, noncommittal look.

Drake noticed the pathologist scampering past the
window. There wasn't going to be much doubt that life
was extinct. An important vein had been severed in the
man's neck. Either it had been a ghoulish accident or a
carefully planned and executed murder.

Drake turned to Luke. 'The officer tells me you know the victim.'

Luke nodded slowly. His voice whispered. 'It's Frank … Frank Smith.'

Drake and Sara exchanged a glance.

'And do you know where Frank lived?'

Luke stammered an address. 'I've never seen a dead body.'

Drake looked over at Dan. 'Who has keys to this place?'

'There are keys in the slate museum building. But the place is hardly secure. Why would anyone want to come in here?'

'We'll need your full names, addresses and contact details,' Drake said.

Sara and Drake watched as both men left the building. The office behind him was grimy, paint peeling off the walls. He glimpsed the framed images on the wall. He recognised some of the councillors who he had seen earlier in the investigation at some function, one of them with a chain of office around his neck.

'So it could have been anyone,' Sara said.

'Assuming it wasn't an accident.'

Drake continued, scanning the faces in the images. 'And that someone would need to know about this place.'

'That could include a lot of people.'

Drake focused on one group in particular, thinking how many of the faces were familiar, when Foulds interrupted him.

'I thought you should know we found some identification.'

'Good.'

'There's a driving licence on the body belonging to Frank Smith.'

Sara called Winder, who confirmed that their eyewitness was the same man as the corpse. She turned to Drake. 'It's the same Frank Smith.'

'Then we have another grieving family to speak to.'

Chapter 30

The PVCu windows and fresh paint suggested that most of the properties in the cul-de-sac of former council houses were now privately owned. Number six was different; the Smiths obviously paid little attention to the niceties of a neat front garden judging by the density of the weeds and the moss-covered piece of lawn. Parked in the drive was a supercharged Mini, less than two years old, its paintwork gleaming. Behind it was a white Ford transit van, rust eating at the wheel arches.

The door was opened quickly once Drake got the bell to work.

'Mr Smith,' Drake said. 'My name is Detective Inspector Ian Drake and this is Detective Sergeant Sara Morgan of the Wales Police Service.'

It was difficult to make out the man's age. His head was clean-shaven but he had a thick beard. A thin T-shirt stretched over muscles toned by regular visits to a gym but his face didn't look healthy. He looked shrunken; little wonder, Drake thought – his son had been killed.

'Richie Smith.' The man gulped back the words, raising a hand to an eye, though the tear he wanted to wipe away never materialised. 'Come in.'

The hallway stank. Dog hairs covered the thin carpet, which made a crunching sound as Drake walked over it. Habit made Drake glance around for the existence of a vacuum cleaner.

Drake recognised the family liaison officer who was hauling two hardback chairs into the sitting room. A woman sobbed uncontrollably on a faux leather sofa pushed against the wall.

'This is Connie Smith, sir.'

Drake nodded.

Richie sat down next to his wife, placing a hand over hers.

'I need to ask you some questions about Frank.'

Richie and Connie shared uncompromising looks on their faces.

'Can you tell me where Frank was going last night?'

'I've got no idea,' Richie said. 'Shouldn't you be out there searching for who killed my Frankie?' The strong Scouse accent made Richie sound hostile.

'When did you see your son last?'

Connie Smith stared at him, stared through him really. Drake could see her mind struggling to comprehend that she would never see her son again. Frankie was gone.

'I can't remember,' Connie said.

'He comes and goes,' Richie added. 'He hasn't got a girlfriend at the moment. He was dead keen on that German girl until her mad father – Wolfgang fucking Muller – came to the house. I heard him at the door telling Frankie to steer clear of her or otherwise he'd break both his legs. That's the bloke you should be going after.'

Drake exchanged a knowing look with Sara.

'When was that exactly?' Sara said.

Richie shrugged. 'I can't remember – six months ago maybe.'

'What exactly happened?' Sara's tone was conversational. She jotted down in her pocketbook precisely what Richie Smith told them.

Drake turned back to Smith once Sara had finished. 'Did he have any other friends that came to the house regularly? What did he do in his spare time?'

'He was out all the time. Never at home.'

Connie Smith added in a croaky voice. 'He did some odd jobs, that van outside belongs to him.'

'He moved some furniture for that Harry Jones a while back. I told him to be careful.' Richie Smith sounded the paragon of virtue. Drake had his doubts.

Richie continued. 'One of Harry Jones's mates called here a couple of times. He called himself a business associate of Harry's.'

'Do you remember his name?'

'Perdue, like them guns.'

Another link to Richard Perdue. Sara used another version of her soft, let-me-be-your-friend tone. 'Mr Perdue might be able to help us; do you recall what he said?' She even smiled.

It did the trick and once Sara had finished gathering details about jobs Frankie had done moving furniture for Perdue, Drake turned to the Smiths.

'Can you give us an idea as to who your son was mixing with?'

'He was friends with Mal Owen,' Connie said. 'They went fishing together.'

Richie butted in. 'And he's done with all that poaching nonsense. I told him to keep his nose clean.'

'Where can we contact Mal Owen?'

Connie sounded vague as she gave them another address in the village.

Drake and Sara left after telling the Smiths to expect more police officers to take statements.

On the way to the car Sara turned to Drake. 'Do

you think Frank Smith's death is linked to the other two murders, sir?'

'It would suit Wolfgang Muller if Frank Smith were out of the way, and perhaps Richard Perdue had something to fear from Frank Smith. And let's not forget Fiona Jones. I learned last night that Harry was the father of Heulwen Beard's child. If that child had made contact, recently opening up old wounds, then it might be enough to tip her over the edge.'

Sara nodded.

A message bleeped on Drake's phone for him to call the Incident Room. Winder sounded breathless when he answered.

'I've been trying to contact you, boss.'

'Poor signal here. What's up, Gareth?'

'One of the guests of the outward bound centre sent us some video footage. And you'll never guess who is seen leaving Heulwen Beard's house.'

Winder paused.

'Get on with it, Gareth.'

'Fiona Jones.'

'Send me the video clip. We'll go and see her now.'

Drake fired the engine into life. He drove the short distance to Fiona's home and let out a long breath when he saw her car in the drive. 'At least she's in.'

Drake parked. Turning to Sara, he shared his theory that Harry was Matthew's father.

She nodded. 'It would explain the trust fund and Jean's suicide.'

'We need to ask Fiona. You take the lead,' Drake

said, before they reached the front door. 'She might be more forthcoming to a woman.'

Sara nodded. They reached the door and she rang the bell.

Eventually Fiona Jones appeared on the threshold, peering down at them, a puzzled look on her face. Drake barged in. 'We need to ask you some questions.'

In the sitting room two other women, a similar age to Fiona Jones, sat drinking tea from china cups and saucers, a plate of bara brith on the coffee table. Normal life continues for Fiona Jones, Sara thought. She kept an open mind about the possibility Harry Jones's widow was also his killer and if her answers to their questions that morning appeared evasive then she could be facing an interview under caution at the police station.

'Let's talk in the kitchen,' Sara said.

She sat by the kitchen table gesticulating at Fiona to do the same.

Sara fumbled with Drake's mobile telephone until she found the video clip. She pressed play and thrust the handset towards Fiona.

'This is your car leaving the house of Heulwen Beard on the morning she was killed.'

Fiona bit at her lower lip and cleared her throat. 'It's not what it seems.'

It never is, Sara thought. 'Why did you go and see her?'

Fiona cast a glance towards the door into the hallway. Then her gaze drifted around the room. She looked down at the table. 'I wanted to reason with her. She wanted to announce to the world she had a daughter: she and Harry had a daughter. Apparently, she's some famous celebrity who was tracing her roots for one of those television programmes. I told her I didn't want anything to do with it.'

'Was Harry aware of her plans?'

Fiona nodded but her chin trembled. 'He wanted to change his will. Make her a beneficiary.'

'How did that make you feel?'

'I wasn't happy. I told Harry not to do it.'

Sara contemplated the real possibility she was about hear a confession to both murders. She glanced at Drake who frowned but he nodded an encouragement.

She hadn't cautioned Fiona; the interviews weren't in a police station and not being recorded. The only other option was to arrest Fiona, formally caution her and record everything in her pocketbook.

Sara decided to carry on but Fiona continued. 'When I left Heulwen's place she was standing on the doorstep. She had her usual defiant, supercilious look in her eyes.'

'What did you talk about?'

Fiona shrugged.

Drake cut in. 'You must have talked about something?'

'I told her that with Harry gone there was nothing to be done with the … girl. I didn't want her to be contacting me, and Harry had died before changing his will.'

'Were you pleased Harry hadn't changed his will?'

Fiona gazed at Sara and then Drake, uncertain how to reply.

Sara continued. 'How long were you there?'

'I don't remember.'

'I want to ask you about your family.'

Fiona frowned. Sara could see her pallor greying.

'I understand your sister Jean was married to Glyn Talbot.'

Fiona pressed a fist to her lips, fighting to keep her emotions in check. Sara realised how deep the family hurt had become. She still needed confirmation.

'Jean and Glyn's son Matthew is named as a beneficiary in one of Harry's trusts.'

Fiona nodded, but made no eye contact.

Sara drew her chair nearer the table, and softened the tone of her voice. 'I need to know, Fiona; is Matthew Harry's son?'

Fiona let out a brief whimper; her eyes watered. There was no going back now, no hiding place any longer. She nodded. Sara struggled to imagine the raw emotion of knowing your husband had slept with your sister and that they had a child.

A son Fiona never had. Sara could only guess at the anguish that would have caused.

Somehow Fiona had managed to live with that, but had it all now proved too much?

'Glyn never knew. I suspected but didn't know for certain until I saw his will and the trust papers last year.'

'Did he admit it?' Drake said.

Tears fell now, streaking her make-up.

'He told me it was nothing to do with me.'

'You must have found that a cruel thing to have said.'

Fiona gulped for breath. 'I could have killed him the night he told me.'

Chapter 31

Drake took Sara back to her car near the slate museum and then navigated for the A55. Travelling back to headquarters alone gave Drake time to prepare for his meeting with Superintendent Price and the senior lawyer from the Crown Prosecution Service. Despite the emotion Fiona Jones had shown earlier that day she was still a suspect in his mind. And her final comments to Sara showed the depth of that emotion. He didn't really think it was an admission to actually killing Harry Jones. The evidence implicating Richard Perdue in direct physical threats against Harry Jones and Heulwen Beard made him a more compelling suspect. And one Drake looked forward to interviewing.

After parking, Drake left his car and his mobile rang. He didn't recognise the number.

'Detective Inspector Drake, it's Ralph Erdington, the Big Thrill Company. Can you tell me what's happening with the Heulwen Beard investigation?'

It puzzled Drake why the businessman would take an interest in the inquiry. 'What do you mean?'

'I just need to know about the property.'

'I have no idea what you're talking about.'

Erdington exhaled noisily down the telephone. 'Heulwen Beard was about to sign a contract to sell us a piece of land crucial to the development of the bomb storage facility.'

'What the hell do you mean?'

'I mean, Inspector, that unless the sale of land goes through, our development will not proceed.'

Drake reached the steps for the main entrance trying to work out the significance of what Erdington had told him. Did it mean someone wanted to stop the project? But killing Heulwen Beard wouldn't prevent the sale proceeding; her legal representatives could finalise any agreement.

'You'll have to speak to her executors.'

'It's not that easy, Inspector. The entire development depends on government grants. And unless the monies are drawn down in the next two weeks the project won't proceed.'

Drake stood in reception. 'Email me the details.'

Erdington's complaints faded as Drake finished the call abruptly. His mind was already focused on persuading Price and the prosecutor that Richard Perdue was worthy of a lengthy stay in the cells of Northern Division.

He took the lift to the senior management suite and visited the bathroom where he scrubbed his hands clean, and pulled a comb through his hair. Rituals complete, his mind settled, he arrived at Price's office to be greeted by a smile and a professional nod from his secretary. Drake could hear voices from behind Superintendent Price's door and guessed Andy Thorsen, the Crown Prosecution Service lawyer, had arrived before him.

The wait wasn't long – Price appeared at the door to his office and waved at Drake.

Andy Thorsen gave Drake a brief nod of acknowledgement from the other side of a highly polished table but made no attempt to stand up or offer a hand for a courtesy shake. He was the most characterless individual Drake knew but annoyingly he always got the interpretation of the law correct.

'I've seen the statement from Carol about what she

witnessed, or rather heard, from inside the cupboard. I daresay you want to arrest and interview Perdue.'

'Yes. He lied to us about when he saw Harry Jones last—'

'Everyone seems to have done that.' Price grinned.

Thorsen didn't react.

Drake continued. 'He threatened Harry Jones's life. And his links to the organised crime groups in the Midlands makes it clear Harry Jones was involved with some serious criminality. Perdue needs to be asked under caution about his connection to Patrick Lennon and account for his movement on the night Harry Jones was killed.'

'I wonder what Detective Chief Superintendent Overend will make of that?' Thorsen said.

Price threw a ballpoint he had been turning through his fingers onto the desk. 'That's my problem. And the deaths of Harry Jones and Heulwen Beard, and now Frank Smith this morning, is *our* inquiry. I'm not going to play second fiddle to the Midlands police force.'

Drake saw the opportunity to share the information he had learned from the Smith household. 'When I spoke to Mr and Mrs Smith they confirmed Frank had worked for Richard Perdue a few times – moving furniture – and that he had described himself as a business associate of Harry's.'

Price guffawed. 'These toe-rags really try and dress up what they do. Frank Smith was driving stolen goods around.'

Thorsen nodded. 'And you've got the evidence from Beard's secretary that Perdue threatened Heulwen Beard too. It all builds a picture. Juries like that sort of thing. And who found her body again?'

'Glyn Talbot. He is Harry Jones's brother-in-law. His wife, Jean, killed herself some time ago. But we believe her son, Matthew Talbot, was probably fathered by Harry Jones.'

'Is this Talbot a suspect?' Thorsen said.

Drake paused, picturing Glyn Talbot in his mind. 'He's certainly dysfunctional. A bit of a loner and an eccentric, but he had no motive to kill Harry Jones or Heulwen Beard. In fact, I think he quite liked her; he worked with her on the local newspaper.'

Thorsen moved some of his papers around. 'Let's talk about Mr Muller for a moment.'

'We know he has a violent temper. We have a statement from Emyr—'

'Do you really think Emyr will give evidence now Frank Smith is dead?' Thorsen said, acknowledging what was on everyone's mind.

Drake continued. 'And Penny Muller provided her husband with a specific alibi for the afternoon and evening that Harry Jones was killed.' Thorsen and Price stared at Drake intently. 'She came to the station with Nicholas Frobisher.'

'Frobisher?' Thorsen said. 'I thought he had stopped doing run-of-the-mill police station work. I couldn't abide the man myself.'

Drake pressed on. 'And we now know from CCTV coverage that Penny Muller was with Harry Jones that afternoon. And Wolfgang was parked in his Range Rover outside the supermarket watching them leave.'

'I am very unhappy about that, Inspector,' Thorsen said. 'It will need to be clarified in due course.'

'And we know Wolfgang Muller assaulted Frank Smith, breaking his arm.' Drake paused for a moment, allowing a thought to develop in his mind. 'Whatever Frank Smith knew cost him his life.'

'I daresay you're right, Inspector. If you can find out what he knew you'll find the killer.'

Price butted in. 'That's a useless piece of advice, Andy.'

Thorsen read the time on his watch and closed the folder on the table in front of him. 'I suggest you arrest Richard Perdue, get him into a cell first thing in the morning and interview him under caution. We'll request a search warrant and a team can take his place apart. Hopefully that'll produce some results.'

Drake didn't want the meeting to finish quite so quickly. 'We still have Fiona Jones as a person of interest.'

Thorsen rolled his eyes. Price nodded for Drake to continue.

'Harry Jones was going to change his will and benefit a child he fathered with Heulwen Beard. And Fiona Jones admits going to her property on the day she was killed supposedly to try and remonstrate with her about possible publicity over the identity of the child.'

'Is that a strong enough motive for murder?' Thorsen sounded tired.

'But Harry Jones was having an ongoing relationship with another woman who he kept in a house nearby.'

Price snorted. 'Christ Almighty, this man didn't know how to keep his trousers on.'

Thorsen stood up, papers in hand. 'That's all well and good. I suggest you focus on Richard Perdue for the time being.' He looked over at Drake. 'I think you have a long evening of work ahead of you.'

Chapter 32

By ten-thirty the following morning Drake sat drinking a double-strength instant coffee in the canteen of the police station in Caernarfon. Sara, opposite him, turned a spoon through her tea. A doughnut for each of them perched on a plate in the middle of the table. 'I thought you might need the sugar hit,' Sara said.

As soon as Drake and his team had arrived, Perdue had called his lawyers. Then he had made some complimentary comments about his lawyer from Liverpool making certain the case wouldn't get anywhere. Drake was unfazed. Lawyers could bitch and moan as much as they liked but when he interviewed a suspect he was in charge. And having taken a dislike to Richard Perdue, Drake's mind relished the prospect of the interview.

They had left a full search team, eagerly anticipating the task of taking apart Richard Perdue's immaculate property. It pleased Drake to see other officers enjoying their work. Perdue had whinged and complained and threatened all sorts of severe consequences but he had piped down by the time the paperwork at the custody centre had been completed and he was sitting in a cell cradling a thin watery tea.

Whatever happened with Richard Perdue, he would be held for the entirety of the twenty-four hours allowed by the law. More than enough for the search of his property to be completed.

Andy Thorsen's remarks about Frank Smith kept playing in Drake's thoughts that morning as he had driven to the police station. Did Smith know something that had cost him his life? Drake reminded himself about the comments Richie and Connie had made. He had missed something. Something important. Something relevant.

He trawled his memory. Dog hairs instantly came to his mind and the smell. He tugged at his nose. Connie had said Frank had done some 'odd jobs' and that one of his friends was called Mal.

'Do you have the address for that Mal Owen the Smiths mentioned yesterday?'

'Yes, boss. Gareth is tracking him down today. Why?'

'I've missed something from our chat with the Smiths.'

Drake gazed out through the canteen window. A light shower drenched the glass. And then Drake remembered what Richie had said. He drew himself nearer the table.

'Richie said that Frank was finished with that "poaching nonsense".' He tapped a finger on the papers in front of him. 'What if Frank arrived at Heulwen Beard's property to leave salmon he had poached and he witnessed the killer and Heulwen arguing?'

Improbability turned to possibility on Sara's face. 'But why would Smith have gone to the slate museum?'

Drake leaned over the table. 'The killer lures him there because ... ' Drake took a moment. 'Smith took the opportunity to blackmail the killer.'

'We don't have any evidence—'

'Why else go there?'

Drake continued. 'And he tries to blackmail the killer.'

Sara nodded. 'And the killer finishes him off with a slate through his neck.'

'Let's ask Perdue.'

A message reached Drake's mobile from the custody sergeant confirming the lawyer had arrived. Drake drained the last dregs of his coffee. 'She's made good time.'

Sara had finished her doughnut but Drake hadn't taken up her suggestion he needed a sugar hit, the prospect of grains of icing sugar all over his hands too much to contemplate. Sara gave the doughnut he left a brief wistful glance before they left.

Drake and Sara found Richard Perdue and his lawyer, Glenda Blake, sitting in one of the interview rooms.

'Good morning, Mrs Blake,' Drake said, smiling across the laminated table.

Perdue pulled a puzzled face as though he expected Drake to be rude.

'How was your journey?'

'The traffic was heavy.' She had a brittle, accentless voice. It matched the sharp, immaculate navy jacket. Sitting down, it was difficult to make out her height but Drake's surreptitious scan suggested she was tall but perhaps the high heels exaggerated the impression.

He completed the formalities and turned to Perdue as the tape machine hummed into life.

'I'm Detective Inspector Drake and with me is Detective Sergeant Sara Morgan. We are investigating the deaths of Harry Jones and Heulwen Beard.'

'I understand you have already spoken to my client.'

'Indeed, we have.'

'Do you have your pocketbooks recording your

notes to hand?'

'We certainly do.' Drake hadn't expected her to be quite so aggressive so soon.

'I'll need to see them.'

'All in good time.' Drake turned back to Perdue. 'Let's start with your relationship with Heulwen Beard.'

'Nothing to it really.'

'She was your lawyer.'

'Yeah.'

'She handled the planning transaction for you in relation to the piece of land you hoped to develop. Please tell us what happened.'

'The planning application failed. I took a punt: it didn't work.'

'Were you happy to lose a lot of money?'

'Would you be?'

'I'll ask the questions. How much did you lose?'

'I can't be certain.'

'I don't believe you, Richard. You're a businessman; you said that yourself when we first spoke. Would it be right to say that you lost £200,000?'

'Not that much.'

'But you sold the land at a loss and you had all the costs involved.'

Perdue squirmed in his seat. 'It was about hundred grand, all right.'

'You must have been annoyed losing such a large sum.'

Perdue didn't reply, giving a dismissive shrug.

'You weren't happy with Heulwen Beard. We have an eyewitness that says you threatened her after you discovered the land had been sold on to Harry Jones, who subsequently made a substantial profit.'

'She's lying.'

'Who?'

'Your witness ... whoever she is.'

'How do you know it's a woman?'

'I don't ... I mean, it could be a bloke.'

'It took place in Heulwen Beard's office. So, you assumed it was her secretary that had given us the evidence of what you said. Losing £100,000 would make you very angry indeed. Angry enough to kill Heulwen Beard and Harry Jones.'

'Don't be daft.'

'Did you know that Heulwen and Harry had been an item years before?' Drake searched Perdue's face for recognition, some glimmer.

Perdue averted his eye contact, glancing at Blake. It vindicated Drake. 'And you thought they were both in it together, didn't you? Planning to diddle you and make a substantial profit themselves. So you killed them.'

Blake interrupted. 'Stick to one question at a time, Inspector. Otherwise you're badgering Mr Perdue.'

Perdue could take a lot more badgering than this, Drake thought. 'What was the nature of your relationship with Harry?'

'Like I told you before, we did some business occasionally. I got to know Harry because I collect antiques. Sometimes my mates from the smoke had a juicy deal on some furniture they picked up. Sometimes he'd buy stuff off me.'

'What was the last piece of furniture you sold him?'

'Jesus, you can't expect me to remember.'

'Well, try. Was it a cupboard, or table, or maybe a set of chairs?'

'A cupboard, yeah. I remember now.'

Drake found the photograph of the table from where the fingerprints of Richard Perdue and Patrick Lennon had been recovered. He pushed it at Perdue.

'Do you recognise this piece of furniture?'

Drake searched Perdue's face for any tell-tale sign of recognition, a nervous twitch or an earlobe being pulled. Instead there was imperceptible stiffening in his body language. The casual approach soon disappeared.

'I don't know what you're talking about.'

'It was a simple question. Do you recognise this piece of furniture?'

Perdue folded his arms together and drew them tightly to his chest.

'Now is your chance to answer my question.'

Drake gazed over at him, pausing for a moment.

'The table was recovered from a lock-up Harry Jones used for storage. It had your fingerprints on it. The item was stolen from a stately home in Nottingham last year. Can you tell us anything about it?'

'You don't know nothing.'

'Richard, your fingerprints are all over this piece of stolen furniture. We've already spoken to the Midlands police who are anxious to talk to you about how that might be the case. I think you were using Harry Jones to fence stolen goods. He had a lot of rich clients and he was handy for getting rid of stuff like this.'

Perdue shook his head.

'When did you last see Harry Jones?'

'Come off it, Inspector; if you've asked him then I am entitled to see the notes.'

Drake produced a copy of Sara's notebook. 'When we spoke to you initially you stated …' He pushed the sheet over the table. '… you said it had been "a few months ago" when you met him.'

'Yeah, that's right.'

'Perhaps you could clarify exactly what you mean. Was it in the last month?'

'Nah.'

'The last two months?'

Perdue shook his head.

'You'll have to say something for the tape.'

'Nope.'

'So it would be over two months ago. Was it over three months ago?'

'Yeah, I think so.'

Drake reached for the laptop on the table and, opening the lid, tapped the keyboard to bring the screen to life. The first of Richard Perdue's visits to Harry Jones started playing silently. Perdue and Blake gazed on incredulously.

'Do you remember this meeting?'

Perdue glanced at Blake. Her face barely moved.

'Yes. I had some business to discuss.'

'It doesn't look like a discussion to me. You threatened him, didn't you?'

Perdue chortled dismissively. 'Don't be silly; we were having a good old chinwag.'

'So does this meeting take place over three months before Harry's death?'

'If you say so.'

'This was recorded three weeks before his death.'

'I'm not very good with dates.' Perdue spat out the reply.

'Let's come back to that particular visit in a minute because you were a regular visitor to Harry Jones, weren't you?'

Drake leaned over and found the recordings of the other meetings between Perdue and Harry Jones. He glanced over at Blake and dictated the dates that matched the images on the screen. She looked embarrassed, obviously realising Perdue was lying.

'So it was a lie to say it had been three months since you last saw Harry Jones. Why did you lie to us?'

Perdue's face contorted as though he were restraining himself from answering. 'Like I said, I'm not much good with dates.'

'Did you ever see Harry with anyone else?'

A person with half a brain cell could see what was coming. Perdue was cocky and arrogant but he wasn't stupid, Drake thought. Perdue narrowed his eyes at Drake. Made no reply.

Drake kept his eye contact direct with Perdue as he announced formally. 'Mr Perdue makes no reply for the purposes of the tape.'

Drake paused. He reached over to the laptop and clicked open the image of Perdue and Patrick Lennon. 'Can you identify the man with you when you visited Harry Jones?'

Perdue shook his head slowly, then he threaded the fingers of both hands together and rested them behind the back of his head. 'No comment.'

'Let's go back to your most recent visits to Harry Jones. It was three weeks before his death.' Drake turned to Blake. 'Have you made a note of the right date?' He smiled at her. She gave him a lifeless look. Drake began to enjoy this interview.

The previous evening the technical department of the Northern Division had blanked out the face of Carol from the coverage. Eagerness filled Drake's mind at the prospect of how Richard Perdue might explain away Carol's evidence.

'I'm going to show you the recording for the few minutes before you arrived to see Harry Jones and threaten him.'

'I did no such thing.'

Perdue couldn't resist the temptation of one more lie.

Drake clicked the footage and watched as Perdue's expression turned into a frown edged with despair as Carol disappeared into the cupboard. Only to be followed seconds later by his own presence on the screen. Once he had left Carol re-emerged.

'You described your meeting with Harry as a "good old chinwag". The witness heard everything and will testify that you threatened him. Is that true?'

Perdue let out a long, lazy sigh. He glanced at Blake who tilted her head. Drake couldn't read what she said to him and he didn't care.

'No comment.' Perdue said eventually.

'The evidence is clear. You threatened Heulwen Beard, threatened Harry Jones, took one of your associates to see him and you had a ready-made motive for killing both of them.'

Irritation filled Blake's voice. 'Is that a question?'

'Do you know Frank Smith?'

'He did a couple of jobs for me.'

'Frank Smith's body was found yesterday in a building at the slate museum in Llanberis.'

'What the fuck is this all about?' Perdue gave

Blake a bewildered look.

'Did Frank Smith try to blackmail you when he overheard you arguing with Heulwen Beard?'

Perdue raised his voice. 'I don't know what the hell you're talking about.'

'Frank Smith was almost decapitated when a piece of slate severed his neck. We found his body yesterday morning.' From a file Drake slowly placed the images of Frank's body on the table facing Perdue.

'You have got to be off your fucking trolley. I knew Frank but I never killed him and I never killed Harry Jones or Heulwen Beard.'

'Where were you on Tuesday evening – the night Frank Smith was killed?'

Perdue cast a glance high into the ceiling.

'No comment.'

'If you have an alibi, now is the time to give us the details.' Drake sensed that Perdue wanted to say something but he was holding back for some reason.

'If you must know I was in this fancy hotel on the Wirral. They've got this special two-for-one night. I was there Monday and Tuesday. I didn't get back until Wednesday lunchtime.'

'We'll need the name of the hotel.'

Sara jotted down Perdue's reply in her pocketbook. But until they could check the details and until the search of his property had been completed, Perdue wasn't going anywhere.

Once Perdue was safely back in his cell and Blake escorted out of the police station Drake and Sara returned to the canteen. Now he did feel like a sugar hit and finished off a doughnut, ignoring the insipid coffee. He used a napkin and then a hand gel to get his fingers clean before picking up his messages – the search team supervisor indicated they wouldn't be finished until the following morning.

'I'll call the hotel,' Sara said. 'Even if he has an alibi for Frank Smith's death he's still a suspect for the other two.'

Drake nodded. If Perdue did have an alibi his theory about all three deaths being connected didn't make sense. A nagging doubt wiggled its way into his mind. 'There's nothing more we can do today.'

He left the police station and walked out to his car. A message reached his mobile and he smiled when he recognised Annie's number. *Found something of interest about Llanberis x.*

Chapter 33

Hearing her voice on the other end of the line cheered Drake up.

'I've been doing interviews this afternoon with some of the old men in the villages near Llanberis. A couple of them can remember the old bomb storage facility and they had some stories about their families who worked there.'

'One of them said I should be talking to a man who can recall the German air force crews that were captured after an aircraft crashed in the mountains. Apparently, some of the locals took trophies from the crash site.'

It reminded him of the old handguns recovered from Harry Jones's lock-up.

And of the bullet that killed him.

'I thought you might like to talk to him?'

'When?' Drake looked at his watch.

'Can you make it tonight?'

Drake didn't need to think twice. He jotted down the address. 'And I've got some more research papers that you can read while I make dinner.'

He left Caernarfon and drove up towards Llanberis, following the instructions from the satnav until he reached a terrace of properties. He spotted Annie's car and parked nearby. She appeared at the door of the property, gave him a warm smile and ushered him inside.

'His name is Gerald Pugh. He's a real character. His daughter is Manon.'

She led him into a parlour and introduced Gerald.

Gerald Pugh had large ears and wispy hair floating

over his head. The rest of his skin had a blotched complexion. Manon fussed around him as he sat in the living room of his home. She explained that Gerald still lived at home despite being ninety-five. His mind was sharp, too sharp sometimes, and he was a night bird who never went to bed before two a.m. Gerald smiled and told Drake he enjoyed channel hopping on the television.

A plate of sandwiches wrapped in cling film sat on the table alongside his chair with a glass of beer.

'Annie tells me you remember when the bomb storage facility was an RAF base?'

This man wasn't a witness so Drake embarked with a conversational tone. He was interested in the possibility a handgun from a Luftwaffe serviceman had found its way into the hands of someone with a reason to kill Harry Jones. What troubled Drake was whether it was the same person who was responsible for killing Heulwen Beard and Frank Smith.

Gerald settled back into a comfortable routine of entertaining Drake and Annie with his vivid memories.

'I can remember the place when the trains used to come back and forth carrying the ordnance into the storage facility. You can't go near the place now.'

Gerald meandered off several times with anecdotes about men he recalled and accidents that had happened, before telling Drake and Annie about the quarry. Gerald had been no more than a youngster when it closed.

'The Germans tried to bomb the place. Did you know that?'

'I do remember someone telling me about it,' Annie said.

'Three planes crashed on the top of the mountains.

We reckoned they'd got lost in the clouds that swirl around Snowdonia. And if they tried to navigate by using some of the lakes and failed to realise which lake they were looking at – then it would be too late.'

'Do you remember seeing any German servicemen?' Drake said.

Gerald beamed. 'We marched them down with pitchforks.'

'What happened to them then?'

'We kept them in the old station building until the soldiers arrived to take them away. It was really exciting.'

'Who else was involved?' Annie sounded genuinely interested. 'There are so many of the old families still around.'

'Harry Jones's grandfather worked in the bomb storage facility. He was one of the officers. Nobody liked him much. I can remember my father saying he was stuck-up. Dad mentioned the name of Arthur Talbot quite often – he was killed down there.'

'Is that Glyn's father?' Drake said, his interest stimulated.

'No, it was his grandfather.'

'Are the Talbots a large family?'

Gerald shook his head. 'I knew his father, David. I remember him telling me when he realised Glyn was a bit odd. It was when he went to secondary school. He liked to play at being the funeral undertaker. All of the other children laughed at him. You know how cruel children can be.'

Drake tried to hide his interest in Glyn Talbot, a man he had dismissed as an eccentric living in his own little world. He probably never left Deiniolen, Drake thought. 'What did he mean by odd?'

Drake sensed Annie giving him a sharp look, the equivalent of a poke in the ribs.

'I like reading the articles he writes. It takes me back to when I was a lad. I don't read so much in Welsh any more. Everything is about the box these days, isn't it?' Gerald tipped his head towards the television in the corner.

'Did David Talbot have any more children?'

Gerald shook his head. 'They got to be a funny family. Kept themselves to themselves. I could never work out why Glyn kept his grandparents' house once they died.' Gerald lowered his voice. 'And you know what happened to his wife, don't you?'

Drake nodded, uncertain whether Annie was aware of the details. 'It must have been terrible for the family when she killed herself.'

'He keeps the place like a shrine. And his grandparents' house too.'

Gerald took a sip of his beer and chuckled. 'Did I tell you about the time when the bomb disposal squad arrived in the village? Somebody had kept a rifle and some shells and bullets from the planes that had crashed on the mountain. I never did find out who told them. They came here in their big vans. And they blew them up on the common. What do they call it?'

'A controlled explosion?'

Gerald chuckled. 'I can tell you a lot about the history of the bomb storage facility.'

Neither Drake nor Annie interrupted Gerald as he regaled them with more details about the servicemen stationed in Llanberis. Then he recounted how the RAF dumped the unused ordnance at the bottom of a lake in the quarry. It took the Royal Air Force years to make the place safe. Gerald sounded sceptical, almost resentful, about the latest plans. He was an old man now clinging to his memories and the value of nostalgia. Gerald's head began to sag.

'Thank you, Gerald,' Annie said getting to her feet. 'I'll come back and see you one morning.'

He jerked his head upwards. 'Don't go. I like the company. There is so much more I can tell you.'

Annie reached out a hand to touch Gerald's shoulder.

'I'll call to see you again.'

Gerald smiled; the top row of his false teeth sagged.

Drake followed Annie down to her home on the Strait. The handgun used to kill Harry Jones was a Second World War relic but did it arrive in Llanberis from Germany with Wolfgang Muller or through Perdue and his criminal connections? Or had it been passed down to Harry Jones, and his wife, sick and tired of his philandering, had decided it was a suitable weapon to bring her humiliation to an end?

He parked at Annie's home a few minutes later.

Inside he followed her upstairs to the top floor. The moonlight cast a pallid light over the Strait, its surface calm. They stood outside on the balcony each drinking from a bottle of lager. Drake caught sight of Annie's profile against the light from the next-door property and realised how beautiful she looked.

'It's getting chilly,' Annie said.

Drake sat by the dining table watching her as she warmed a beef sauce and then put the pasta to boil. She put a bowl of parmesan in the centre of the table, and opened a bottle of Chilean Malbec before finding two glasses.

He watched her move around the kitchen: staring at her as she did the smallest of tasks. He realised he was enjoying this shared domestic activity. He wanted to grab her around the waist and kiss her.

Annie shouted over her shoulder. 'What did you think of Gerald Pugh?' She didn't wait for a reply. 'I've got some documents on my laptop about the bomb storage facility. There was a big explosion there just after it was built. A lot of local men were killed. They never found the bodies.'

Drake glanced over at a nearby table that had a laptop open, its screen blank. Reading a report was the last thing on his mind.

Annie brushed passed him as she placed a bowl of spaghetti Bolognese in front of him. Then she glided into a chair by his side and smiled.

When he started eating he realised he couldn't remember when he last had a square meal. As they finished he topped up their glasses a second time. He couldn't recall the conversation that ebbed and flowed naturally. As he filled the glasses for a third time, his body relaxed. And when Annie placed a hand over his fingers his skin tingled. Even the lights in the kitchen glowed more brightly.

'Help me clear the dishes.'

Drake got to his feet and cleared the table. He was standing next to Annie now. She turned to look at him. He moved closer, drew his arm around her waist and, pulling her towards him, he kissed her. Her lips and her skin felt sensational. And when she kissed him back he knew he couldn't hide his desire. She must have seen what was in his eyes because she squeezed his hand tightly.

They kissed again and they pushed and pulled each other out of the kitchen, past the table, where she yanked at his shirt. They tumbled downstairs to the bedroom on the first floor. His shirt fell to the floor on the hallway, her blouse soon followed. He had dreamed about this moment, fantasised about her shoulders, her breasts. He pulled her close, loosened her bra and drew his fingers over her shoulder down the smoothness of the skin, cupping a breast in his hand. She reached over and threw the duvet off the bed.

Drake pushed the door shut tightly.

Chapter 34

A weak beam of light fell over the bedside table next to Drake from a crack in the folds of the curtains covering the windows. Annie slept beside him. Her regular breathing massaged the air. It was quiet, the room comfortable even if it was unfamiliar. He felt more alive than he had done for weeks, months.

Gently he rolled over and kissed the lobe of her right ear. She murmured. He slipped out of bed, shrugged on a dressing gown and closed the door silently. In the kitchen on the first floor, he organised coffee and as he stepped out onto the balcony the autumn breeze blew a salty wind into his face. A rib made steady progress south towards Caernarfon against the tide.

Two doors down a man pottered in his garden, a dog playing at his feet. At that moment Drake wanted to shout out a greeting, share his elation, but he smiled to himself, sipping the coffee before heading back inside. Sitting at the table, he pressed *enter* on Annie's computer and it opened with the initial page from a report about the history of the bomb storage facility – RAF Llanberis Reserve Depot its formal name.

Drake read the index. He noticed a section about the original Glyn Rhonwy quarry. Another section about the famous labour dispute at the beginning of the twentieth century at the Penrhyn Quarry in the nearby valley reminded Drake of the proud tradition of slate mining in North Wales. He could remember his history teacher at school becoming animated describing the hardships the men and their families had endured.

The section with a heading 'commissioning the

facility' was a reference to the construction work necessary to build it deep into the workings of the old quarry. It was the only way to protect the ordnance against the inevitable German bombing. The process of assembling the tunnels and building the entrance passageways had been rushed and Drake spotted the paragraph headed 'loss of life'. It sounded so matter-of-fact. Accepting death must have been commonplace during the Second World War, although Drake wondered if it was any easier when the deaths were close to home and not in the field of battle.

Blame for the collapses was squarely apportioned on inadequate planning and failure to strengthen and secure the access to the various levels where ordnance had been stored. A dozen men had been killed, but Drake got the impression the Royal Air Force simply dusted itself down, extended formal condolences and rebuilt.

None of the bodies were recovered. How did the bereaved families react knowing they could never bury their loved ones and yet still have to live next to the facility – a constant reminder of the loss of life? They wouldn't have had a gravestone to visit, a place to lay flowers, to reflect for a moment on the life of the person lost.

Drake examined a black-and-white photograph showing a gang of middle-aged men in heavy workmen's clothes gazing self-consciously at the camera. They all had local names, Williams and Jones, the sort Drake would have expected, although he also noticed the name of A.W. Talbot. Drake peered at the man's features, and as he did so guessed he must have been Glyn's grandfather.

Drake sat back and hauled from his memory Gerald's comment about Glyn keeping his grandparents' home after they had died. Probably A.W. Talbot's wife, Glyn's grandmother, Drake thought. And she must have lived to a grand old age.

There was something secretive, obsessive, about Glyn. Drake understood it. For it often meant hiding real emotions, wanting to control every situation. On occasions when Drake faced the obsessions that drove his rituals it had meant an impact on his work, on his life and on his marriage.

Trying to build a picture of this community was like prising open a clam shell only to have it snapped shut before the contents could be revealed. Drake mulled over what he knew. Jean, Glyn's wife, had committed suicide. He suspected a dark secret lay buried and as he stared at the image of Glyn Talbot's grandfather he reminded himself that Harry Jones had left Matthew Talbot a substantial inheritance.

But what if Glyn Talbot discovered Matthew wasn't his son. Drake reined in his enthusiasm to implicate Glyn Talbot. It wasn't enough to be a motive to murder, surely? He found his mobile and tapped out a message to Sara suggesting they meet in Llanberis, adding – *I've got something to discuss.*

Annie stirred when Drake returned to the bedroom. He placed a mug of tea on her bedside cabinet. She smiled and he beamed back. He pulled her hair away from her face and kissed her lightly.

'I've got to leave.'

'I'll call you later.' Annie reached out and gently squeezed his forearm.

Drake worried whether Sara would notice he was wearing the same shirt, the same tie and the same suit as he had yesterday when he slid into the bench seat at Pete's Eats. He smiled to himself at the activity that had caused the creases in his trousers and the dishevelled look to the white shirt. The same waitress who took his order at the counter arrived with mug of a two-shot Americano.

He was trying to complete a jigsaw when he had corner pieces and a piece from the centre only. Sara passed the window, and moments later she joined him.

'I sent the hotel manager in the Wirral the dates and Perdue's photograph. I'm still waiting to hear from them.'

Drake nodded. Talbot had taken all of his focus that morning. Perdue could wait. An extension of the custody time limits would be authorised, allowing them to hold him for another twenty-four hours.

'I've been reading some historical papers about the bomb storage facility,' Drake said.

He steeled himself for Sara's questions.

'Glyn Talbot's grandfather was killed in a collapse during building work at the RAF base. They never found his body. We know Glyn Talbot is an odd character. All he has in his life is writing obscure highbrow articles for *Papur Padarn* and living in a house that looks like a throwback to the Dickensian era.' Drake looked over at Sara, a dubious look on her face as though she was uncertain what Drake was thinking. 'All his recent articles are dead against the development. We know that killing Heulwen Beard has stopped the project in its tracks. It might never actually take place.'

Drake thumped the table with a fist as another fragment of recollection fell into place. 'When I met him in the museum he said the place should be left as a mausoleum. What if he is so obsessive he thinks of the bomb storage facility as some sort of shrine that should not be disturbed?'

Sara nodded her head. 'It might have been Talbot who shot at the photographer.'

'Because we couldn't see an immediate motive for him killing Heulwen Beard we treated him as an eccentric, someone to be pitied. He went to reason with her, make her see sense and not sell the land. She was the only person who could realistically stop it. She refuses: tells him he's mad and he loses his temper.'

Drake fumbled with his mobile and found Luned's report on Talbot. 'Luned said that when he worked at the slate museum there were complaints of inappropriate bullying behaviour. Then he was made redundant. We saw him intimidate Harry on the CCTV.'

'It's a possibility.' Sara used calm, measured tones, apparently unconvinced by Drake's argument. 'But what gave Glyn Talbot a motive to kill Harry Jones?'

'He discovered Harry was Matthew's father.'

'Is that enough to give him a motive to kill ... ?' Drake finished his coffee and peered out of the window. A light shower of rain forced a woman pushing a pram to scuttle into a doorway for shelter. He was looking for a trigger, something that tipped Glyn Talbot's obsession into murderous intent.

'Parish council meeting.' Drake declared. 'Erdington gave a presentation to the council. Harry

Jones supported the plan vociferously despite Glyn trying to persuade him that morning to speak up against it.'

'But so did all the other councillors.'

'But none of them had slept with Glyn's wife.'

Drake told Sara about his meeting the previous evening with Gerald Pugh.

'So it's possible Glyn Talbot has a gun from the Second World War passed down through the family. Like some favourite clock.'

Drake nodded. 'We've been to his house; the place looks like a museum. And there were clocks there. They looked ancient, like something from ... an aeroplane.'

After a moment, Sara added. 'And what about Frank Smith's murder?'

Drake slipped his fingers through the handle of his mug. He tried to focus; the sound in the café faded away.

'There's no connection between him and Glyn Talbot.' Sara continued.

'The salmon. Smith was outside the house when Talbot was there. He heard them arguing. And Smith is stupid enough to try and blackmail Talbot.'

'Glyn lures Smith to his death?'

He blanked out what Sara said. He was back in the office in the slate museum building immediately after the discovery of Smith's body. All he could see was the image of various photographs on the wall.

'Let's go,' Drake said.

It took them less than five minutes to reach the museum building. Crime scene investigators were still working inside. Drake barged his way towards the office and stood, Sara alongside him, staring at the photographs on the wall. Grabbing one, he pointed his finger at the image.

'Glyn Talbot. He knew all about this place.'

'We need to bring him in, boss.'

Every muscle in Drake's body tightened. He reached for his mobile but it rang first. He grabbed it from his pocket recognising Winder's name.

'Boss, I thought you should know. A Maldwyn Owen has been reported missing.'

Drake struggled to place the name – it sounded familiar.

Winder continued. 'He's on the system as a friend of Frank Smith.'

Chapter 35

Drake ran back to his car, and fired the engine into life. At the junction of the main road his tyres screeched and he raced towards the home of Maldwyn Owen. He pulled the car onto the pavement near the property. Sara, following, did the same.

Drake shouted a greeting as he crossed the threshold into the kitchen.

A man he took as Maldwyn Owen's father appeared in the doorway to the hall. A thickly wrinkled brow contrasted sharply with the warm, round lived-in face. 'Who are you?'

'Detective Inspector Ian Drake.'

The wrinkles abated a notch.

'I'm Andy Owen, Maldwyn's dad. Come through.'

A woman stood by the window of the sitting room, her posture stooped. She clawed at a nail.

'This is Inspector Drake, Liz,' Andy said.

Worry was chiselled into every part of her face.

'Do you have any idea where Maldwyn might be?' Drake said.

'He sent me a message telling me to expect him back last night. We both work nights.' Liz nodded her head towards her husband. 'So when I got back today I expected to see him.'

'We've called his friends, but no luck,' Andy said. 'After the business with Frank Smith we're really worried. They were good friends.'

Drake nodded.

'Does he have a girlfriend?' Sara said.

'We've tried to contact Sioned. But we haven't heard anything.'

Sioned was a common name but still it jolted Drake. 'What's her full name?'

Liz shrugged.

Andy replied. 'Jackson, I think. She works in the Fox and Hounds.'

Drake couldn't say anything for a moment. His right leg started to shake.

Liz nodded quickly. 'I've left a message for her.'

'And she hasn't called you back?' A heaviness gathered in Drake's mind. He could feel his lips drying. His immediate thought was to find his mobile, call Sioned and reassure himself she was safe.

Liz shook her head. 'I really like Sioned.' It sounded like a desperate hope she was safe. The cloud in his mind darkened.

'Have you tried Maldwyn's work?' Drake said.

'He didn't turn up this morning. The foreman has no idea where he might be.'

Liz's eyes took on a watery glaze. 'I told him not to get involved with Frank Smith. He was bad news. Maldwyn is a good boy.'

'Are there any friends he could be staying with or family? The urgency in Drake's tone resulted in a panicked, desperate sobbing from Liz Owen.

'I'll see if I can find Sioned at the Fox and Hounds.' Drake headed for the door. 'Please give Sergeant Morgan details of his friends.'

How could he have known Sioned was Mal's boyfriend? He slammed a hand against the steering wheel as he drove over to the car park of the public house. He fumbled for his mobile, dialling Sioned's number, praying she'd answer. A voice message cut in and the darkest possibilities swamped his mind. Did the killer assume Maldwyn was the only surviving eyewitness to the murder of Heulwen Beard?

Their only eyewitness to any of the killings?

Drake parked outside the Fox and Hounds, imagining Sioned busy at work, her telephone lying at the bottom of her handbag; perhaps its battery was flat. Drake bustled into the public house and demanded to see the manager. He didn't bother with his warrant card. 'Where's Sioned?'

'She called in sick last night.'

'What do you mean?'

'Sick, like unwell. What the hell is this about?'

'I need to speak to her. It's urgent.' Drake realised he didn't know where Sioned lived. He assumed she lived over the Fox and Hounds. It dawned on him that wasn't the case.

'What's her home address?'

'I thought she was staying in Liz-halfway's place ?'

Drake paused. 'What do you mean, *Liz-halfway*?'

'Didn't you know? Liz Owen runs the café halfway up Snowdon.'

'Is that Andy Owen's wife?'

A confirmatory nod curled a knot of anxiety tightly in Drake's mind. He hurried back to his car and then stood, before getting in, taking deep breaths. He had forgotten that morning that a decision had to be made about releasing Perdue. Having him locked up safe and sound in the police station suited Drake. He had to concentrate on Talbot and finding Maldwyn Owen and Sioned. So he called the search team at Perdue's property who confirmed they had a full day's work.

Perfect reason to deny him bail for another twenty-four hours.

He called Price and explained the position with Perdue before turning to Talbot. An ominous silence down the telephone told Drake the superintendent was unconvinced by his suspicions. 'So you think there's a risk of Maldwyn Owen's and Sioned Jackson's lives being threatened?'

'Yes, sir,'

More breathing down the telephone.

'I'm sticking my neck out, here, Ian. But I'll authorise the detention of Perdue for another twenty-four hours to preserve evidence. I hope you're right about Talbot.'

Relief washed over Drake. If Drake wasn't right, he would have to explain Perdue's continued custody. But he had other suspects too and he realised he had focused too much that morning on Glyn Talbot.

'Thanks, sir.'

Drake called Winder. 'I need to know the whereabouts of Wolfgang Muller, Fiona Jones and Glyn Talbot. Right now.'

'Yes, boss.'

'Once we know where they are I need officers to babysit them.'

'What, all day?'

'Yes, Gareth. The lives of Maldwyn Owen and Sioned Jackson depend on it.'

He finished the call. He didn't want to comprehend that Sioned's life might be threatened. He needed her safe and well.

Andy Owen stood in his kitchen gazing through the

window when Drake arrived back at the Owen house. Sara appeared from the living room and gave him a questioning look. He hoped that his brief nod made clear he'd bring her up to date shortly.

Drake turned to Andy. 'I need to speak to you and your wife.'

In the living room Liz Owen looked up at Drake; he didn't bother sitting down. He got straight to the point. 'Do you run the halfway café on the path up Snowdon?'

'In the summer.' Liz nodded.

'Jesus, you don't think that he's gone up there?' Andy turned on his heel and strode into the kitchen. Drake and Sara followed him and watched as he squirrelled through various cupboards. 'They're not here.' He turned to give Drake and Sara a desperate look. 'The fucking keys aren't here.'

Liz joined them. 'He would never go up there.'

Drake wasn't so certain. 'It would be safe. Nobody would suspect they'd gone halfway up the mountain.' Already he was making the assumption Sioned was with him.

'Does anyone else have a set of keys?'

'Only the local park ranger.'

'Call him,' Drake said before nodding at Sara to step outside with him.

He unlocked his car and they sat inside for a moment.

'They're in danger,' Drake said. 'Maldwyn's not in work and Sioned called in sick. Something's wrong.'

'Frank Smith and Maldwyn *must* have been outside Heulwen Beard's property the morning she was killed.' Drake tightened his jaw. 'They probably heard, may even saw, the killer.'

Sara baulked. 'So Smith tries to blackmail the killer?'

'And Maldwyn is the next target.' Drake turned to Sara. 'We need to get up to the Halfway café.'

'Why would he take Sioned with him?'

'Maybe he thinks she's a target too or maybe he's being overprotective. Whatever is happening, we need to find them both.'

Andy Owen appeared at the back door and jogged over to the car. He leaned down as Drake powered down the window. 'The park ranger has got his set of keys. He lives round the corner.'

'Show us.' Drake left the vehicle and followed Andy Owen into the next street. A Land Rover with a high wheelbase covered in the markings of the Snowdonia National Park stood in the drive of a semi-detached property. A tall man in the national park's uniform opened the door before Drake or Andy Owen had a chance to reach the doorbell. 'Llew' was sewn into the name badge.

'What's all this about?'

'It's a police matter,' Drake said. 'Is that your Land Rover?'

'Yes, why?'

If Maldwyn and Sioned had made their way up to the halfway house overnight Drake had to get there quickly. A mental calculation told him it was a hike of an hour and a half and about the same back down. He had no time to waste.

'We'll need you to take us up there.'

He snorted at first. But he stopped when he looked at Drake's face. 'You're joking, right?'

'Get your keys.'

'I've got things to do.'

Drake pushed his warrant card into the man's face. 'This is official police business; three people are dead. I've got two missing persons and unless you're prepared to help me I'll requisition your vehicle.'

Llew's jaw fell open. 'Give me a minute.'

In the two minutes he took to find his jacket and keys Drake had sent Sara back to his vehicle. She returned with two expandable batons and stab jackets – no substitute for a bulletproof vest but it was the best they could do in the circumstances.

The first part of the route after leaving Llanberis was a steep section of tarmac. Several startled walkers descending the mountain stared at them as the Land Rover heaved its way up the road. After a few minutes Llew pulled the vehicle to the left and stopped in front of a gate. The tarmac abruptly finished although a narrow track continued along into the moorland on the valley floor. Once the gate was open the Land Rover bumped its way over the rocky surface.

'Are there many gates?' Drake said as Llew got back into the vehicle after locking the gate.

'It's not the gates you need to be worried about,' Llew said, frowning as he gazed upwards towards the narrowing path.

He selected the low gear ratios for the vehicle, glancing at Drake and Sara. 'No turning back now until halfway.'

Drake nodded.

The engine roared. It bumped and meandered its way over the slabs of rock and the narrow path. Occasionally it felt like the vehicle was tipping itself over. Llew cursed and allowed the vehicle to drift backwards until he could find a firmer, safer route. When they reached some open sections Drake was tempted to urge him to accelerate. Llew peered through the windscreen, concentrating intently.

'I haven't been up this path with the Land Rover for a long time.'

It wasn't an invitation for small talk, so Drake kept his mouth shut.

He and Sara were thrown around their seats. He grabbed onto his safety belt watching Llew selecting the right gear, cursing when he didn't get it right. More walkers gave them startled looks. A thin woman in running kit descending the mountain paid them no attention.

Down to their right Drake could see the railway track as it began its journey up the mountain. The shallow valley reached out into the distance and ahead was a steep escarpment leading up to the summit of Snowdon, it's top curtained in thick cloud.

Llew told them the journey would take half an hour and within twenty minutes a building appeared ahead of them. A group of walkers sat in its lee drinking from water bottles. They turned to gaze at the Land Rover as it neared.

Drake peered through the windscreen. He would have to warn the hikers.

'The only area where I can turn is a small flat area after the café,' Llew said.

'Slow down near these people,' Drake said.

He wound down the window as the vehicle slowed. Drake perched on the side of the window, warrant card in hand. 'This is a police matter. Please leave this area immediately.'

Stunned faces gawped at him. It took them a few seconds to gather their equipment and scamper away.

The Land Rover parked.

Drake jumped out, his heart pounding, and Sara followed him over to the door.

Drake found the keys in his pocket while Sara peered in through one of the windows. She looked over at Drake, shaking her head.

The door squeaked as it opened; Drake and Sara entered. A damp, musty smell filled the air. A couple of old chairs were pushed underneath the table. In the middle of the floor was a small tent. Drake drew to one side the opening and looked inside. There were two sleeping bags but nothing else.

'They must have left in a hurry,' Drake said.

Sara was standing by the kitchen sink. Drake joined her and looked out through the window over the bleak, windswept moorland. A thin fog gathered in the air. A bird of prey drifted in the afternoon currents.

'Where the hell have they gone?' Drake said.

Chapter 36

When Drake returned to Llanberis, dusk was approaching. He gazed upwards and recalled from childhood the spectacular autumn sunsets over Anglesey: there wasn't anything spectacular about that evening. It was dark and dismal, with a hint of drizzle and rain.

He had been jolted and banged as the Land Rover eased its way down the mountain. The muscles in his hands were sore from grasping tightly anything that would prevent him from rolling around in his seat.

Descending the mountain had given him little time to think until the last section when the vehicle covered the steep road down into the village.

Maldwyn and Sioned were hiding from someone; he was certain now. And he had to find them.

Once the Land Rover had parked Drake jumped out and stretched his back, pleased to be standing straight and not thrown around like some rag doll. Sara joined him, deep in thought.

After the intermittent coverage on the mountain Drake was pleased that his mobile showed a full signal. He called Winder.

'I've been trying to get hold of you, boss.'

'Bring me up to date.'

'Wolfgang Muller is in his wellness centre with his wife and a class full of students doing yoga.'

It was good news – one suspect accounted for. 'Good, and Fiona Jones?'

'She's not at home.'

Drake's chest tightened. 'And Glyn Talbot?'

'An officer called at his home, but he wasn't there.'

'Find him, Gareth.'

'Where—'

'The army museum, the local library, the supermarket ... any bloody place you can think of. And tell the officer to wait outside his house.'

He called Sioned again – another voice message.

He had to call Huw, his brother and Sioned's father. He had dreaded making the call and had delayed as he travelled to and from the halfway café. There was no avoiding it now. Sioned, Huw's daughter and Drake's niece, was missing. If his assumption about Maldwyn and Frank Smith was correct then Maldwyn knew something, and he might even be an eyewitness to the murder of Heulwen Beard.

He hoped, he prayed, that Maldwyn was somewhere safe and that Sioned was with him.

He had to find them before the killer did.

'Hello, Ian,' Huw said.

Drake took a deep breath. 'Have you been in contact with Sioned today?'

'No, why? Has something happened?'

'Did you know about Maldwyn Owen, her boyfriend?'

'She mentioned his name. I didn't think it was anything serious. What's this about?'

Tension laced Huw's every word. Would Huw be satisfied if he reassured him that everything would be all right, and that they would find Sioned and Maldwyn alive?

'Has this got anything to do with the murders in Llanberis? For Christ's sake, Ian, I need to know. I'll call her now.'

Drake wanted to say he had tried Sioned's mobile

telephone number several times, but he doubted Huw would pay him any attention. Drake could hear the fumbling over the telephone. A moment later he heard Huw's voice again.

'All I get is her messaging service.'

'I'm sure everything will be fine. We're doing everything we can, Huw.'

'That sounds like a real fucking cliché. I'm coming over to Llanberis.'

'I really don't think you need to.' Huw didn't hear Drake. The line went dead.

Would he have reacted differently had it been one of his daughters? He turned to Sara. 'That was Huw Jackson – Sioned's father, He hasn't heard from her either.'

'Any news about Talbot?' Sara said.

'There's an officer outside his home. Let's go up there now.'

A marked police car had taken the parking slot Drake had used when he last parked near Talbot's home. He nudged his own car up into a grassy layby a few yards away. He glanced in the mirror; the street was quiet. He read the time from the dashboard clock – more valuable minutes were flying by. They left the Mondeo and spoke to the young officer in the police car.

'I've tried the door and nobody answered. And nobody has called.'

'Thanks,' Drake said.

He stood with Sara on the pavement.

'We'll need a search warrant.' Sara drew the collar of her jacket to her face.

'To hell with that. I'm going to arrest him for murder.'

Sara would know that a warrant wouldn't be needed in those circumstances and he broke into a jog as he made for the property, Sara in tow.

He pressed the bell but didn't hear any sound from inside so he tried again, pressing his face nearer the glass panel in the upper part of the door. Satisfied the bell wasn't working, he thumped with a fist.

He listened intently but he heard nothing. Sara frowned.

'Glyn Talbot,' Drake bellowed.

Nothing.

'Let's go round the back.'

At the end of the terrace Drake found a narrow path leading towards the rear of the gardens. He hoped another path would cross the rear garden of each house. He was disappointed – it ran out into a piece of scrub wasteland. Then he looked over and saw the fencing marking out the rear garden of Talbot's property. It meant scrambling over rough earth with thick weeds and knee-high gorse bushes. He set off, discarding his usual worries about damaging his brogues or dirtying his clothes. He had a killer to catch.

Sara kept up with him and eventually they reached the boundary fence of Talbot's garden. 'I can't see anybody inside.' Sara peered into the downstairs window.

In one corner Drake found a post rotten with age; he kicked it onto the ground and flattened the ineffective chicken wire stapled to it just enough to allow them to step over. He waved at Sara for her to go first and she manoeuvred carefully over the fence before he did likewise. They hurried for the back door.

Drake tried it: locked.

'It seems almost pointless locking the door when it's so difficult getting access to the rear,' Sara said, looking up at the upstairs windows. She turned to scan the garden and the makeshift slabs that surrounded a shed.

If Talbot was an obsessive he probably left a key outside, somewhere safe. Drake tipped over various flowerpots, mostly plastic, brittle with age. Sara rejoined him. 'The shed is full of crap – garden tools, a bike and some old chairs.'

'He might have left a key somewhere.' Among the rubbish littered around Drake noticed a wooden crate with slots for bottles; he had seen the same sort of thing in Harry Jones's antique shop with a fancy price tag attached to it. He moved it to one side and under one corner was a rusty key. 'Yes,' Drake shouted, picking up the key like a prized possession and waving it in the air at Sara.

Seconds later they were inside Glyn Talbot's decrepit kitchen. It had a putrid smell of stagnant water as well as the same mothballs from their first visit.

'Glyn,' Drake yelled, not expecting a reply.

'This place stinks. Where the hell could he be?' Sara said.

Both downstairs rooms had furniture fit only for a bonfire.

It didn't take Drake and Sara long to go through the various cabinets, completing a cursory examination for the firearm they hoped to unearth.

They climbed the stairs. The bathroom hadn't been changed since the 1940s.

The wardrobe and cupboards in the rear room were all empty so they turned their attention to the larger room at the front. Glyn Talbot's clothes hanging in the wardrobe were cheap and old. The large, ancient furniture made the rooms feel small. But there was no sign of any Second World War revolver and back in the sitting room downstairs Drake began to think this was all a foolish mistake. Perhaps Glyn was simply an eccentric loner. Perhaps it was absurd to think of him as a killer.

He wrote articles for a local newspaper few people ever read.

Then it struck Drake that he must have a computer, or at the very least a desk and paperwork. He turned to Sara. 'He's got another house. There's no evidence here of someone who writes historical articles. No computer, no printer, not even a shred of paper.'

'How do you know he's got another property?'

Drake stared at one of the clocks in the display cabinet he had seen on their first visit. Even his untrained eye could read the German lettering on its face.

'Gerald Pugh told me. That's where we're going next.'

Chapter 37

'Good morning, Inspector.' Manon wore an apron and struck a busy, domestic tone. She gave Sara a quizzical smile. 'Annie not with you this morning?'

'I need to speak to Gerald.'

'It sounds serious. You had better come in.'

Drake followed Manon through into the same room where he had spoken to Gerald the night before. The TV was blaring with a property relocation programme. Gerald seemed to be fast asleep, a full mug of tea on the table by his side.

'Dad, wake up. That policeman is here again.'

As Gerald stirred Drake composed exactly in his mind how to ask for the information he needed. The old man blinked a few times before fixing his gaze on Drake and then, frowning, on Sara.

'Someone different with you today,' Gerald said before raising his voice. 'Manon, put the kettle on.'

Drake shook his head. 'Gerald, I'm really sorry but I can't stay. I'm trying to contact Glyn Talbot and when we spoke last night you mentioned he had kept his grandparents' house. Do you have that address?'

'Have you tried Glyn at home?'

Drake's body tensed, his chest tightened. He could hear Superintendent Price's criticisms about wasting valuable police time and that it had been a wild goose chase to track Glyn Talbot when the killer was already safely in custody.

'He's not there.'

'He's probably in the library.'

Manon appeared in the doorway.

'Annie would love a cup of tea.' Gerald smiled at

Sara. 'And one for the inspector too.'

Drake turned to Manon, shaking his head in a kindly fashion before turning back to Gerald. 'I'll come back again, and you can tell me all about Llanberis from years ago. But today it's really important that I contact Glyn Talbot. Have you got that address?'

Gerald looked disappointed. Drake could imagine how he valued company. He reached over and held Gerald's bony arm. 'You might even remember my grandfather – he was a farmer nearby. I do hope you can help me with that address I need.'

Manon cajoled her father until eventually they were able to give Drake an address. He couldn't get out of the place soon enough and almost ran to his car, Sara following in his slipstream. They slammed the car doors; Drake accelerated away from Gerald Pugh's home and up the side of the valley.

Nant y Mynydd was a detached property a little way back from the road. The front garden was a collection of random slabs of stone. Curtains were drawn tightly over the upstairs windows. The first owners must have thought the place salubrious compared to the nearby run-of-the-mill terraces, Drake thought.

Sara looked up at the property after leaving the car. 'It looks empty, boss.'

A man pushed a woman in a wheelchair into the rear of a disabled access vehicle outside one of the nearest properties. They left the car and Drake joined Sara on the pavement as traffic passed him heading down into the village. Drake steeled himself for what was waiting for them inside.

'Who was Annie?' Sara said.

'She's a historian I met. She introduced me to Gerald Pugh.' Drake made it sound very formal.

'I see.' Sara's reply implied she read far more into Drake's response than he had intended.

This time the front doorbell worked; he heard its chimes echoing inside. But as at Glyn Talbot's other property, there was nobody home. He didn't bother with banging on the door; he made straight for the gate to the rear he had noticed earlier.

He tried the handle of the rear door. Locked.

Lifting the various pots and loose slabs nearby didn't turn up the key as they hoped. Sara and Drake peered into the window. 'It looks deserted, boss.'

'Let's hope Gerald Pugh gave us the right address.' Drake resumed his search for the back-door key. He imagined himself living in this close-knit community. Burglaries of properties like this wouldn't be commonplace. People knew each other, trusted each other. Drake could recall his grandparents leaving their front door open during the day even when they were working the fields or visiting a local shop. He surveyed the rear. At the far end there was an old black wheelie bin and a small brown composting caddie. He moved the black bin out of the way and upturned the smaller compost bin, which rewarded him with the sight of a key duct-taped to its base.

Moments later they were inside the kitchen.

'Glyn,' Drake shouted.

They stood for a moment. There was no reply nor the sound of any movement.

To his right an old Belfast sink stood on a plinth, and next to it was an ancient electric cooker rusty with age. Sara flicked open a tall larder cupboard. 'Nobody has used these cupboards for years.'

Drake was the first to push open the door into a reception room at the rear and he did a double-take as he saw two mannequins standing in one corner. One dressed in khaki like an actor from a British Second World War movie and the second his German equivalent.

'That's spooky,' Sara said, joining Drake.

On the table in front of them was a laptop and a printer attached to it.

Against one wall was a bank of shelving units converted into a makeshift library. Drake noticed books on Welsh history, the development of slate mining and several about military history. 'This is where he writes his articles,' Drake said.

In the front room a Bakelite radio stood on an oak veneered cabinet and on a side table alongside a wing chair was a black rotary telephone. A collection of newspapers laid out as a fan on the coffee table gave the room an authentic 1940s feel. Drake read the headline of the first about the progress of the Allied troops in Europe.

'Let's see what's upstairs,' Drake said, glancing at his watch, conscious time was marching on.

He called out Glyn's name: again, no reply.

The carpet on the risers had worn thin and the handrail was loose as Drake and Sara made their way upstairs. They glanced inside the bathroom: it was much the same as they had seen earlier in Talbot's property. Drake and Sara fumbled for their mobiles and found the torch function that illuminated the rear bedroom. Drake fingered a towel, dry and thin from countless washings, lying at the bottom of the bed as though it were ready for a visitor.

'Wardrobe's empty, boss.'

Drake heaved out the drawers from an ancient chest, each emptying a musty wooden smell into the room.

They entered the first of the rooms overlooking the front of the property. A corkboard covered the entirety of the wall to their right. Drake and Sara ran the light from their telephones along the contents.

'This is all stuff about the bomb storage facility,' Sara said.

'You'd better open the blinds.'

Morning sunshine poured into the room and Sara and Drake squinted until their eyes became accustomed. They turned back to the massive selection of clippings, newspaper articles, reports, and photographs that made the patchwork of paper testament to one man's obsession.

'He must be completely mad,' Sara said.

Drake nodded and snapped on a pair of latex gloves once he noticed a report from a company called DNA Direct stored carefully in a plastic pocket pinned to the far end of the corkboard. Drake suspected what the report was going to tell him but when he read formal confirmation that Glyn Talbot could not have been Matthew Talbot's father he knew he had been right.

'What is that, boss?'

'What I suspected all along. Matthew Talbot isn't Glyn Talbot's son.'

An old map cabinet was the only piece of furniture in the room. Drake struggled with the top drawer as it caught. Eventually he yanked it out and stared down at maps of Llanberis and details about the old workings at Glyn Rhonwy.

Sara stood by his side as he opened the second and third drawers, revealing much the same contents as the first.

The fourth slid open more easily than the rest.

Drake gazed down in amazement at its contents.

'Jesus Christ,' Sara said.

Two pistols had pride of place on individual clean muslin cloths. Both looked like museum pieces. A label was attached to both. Drake found a ballpoint in his pocket and gently moved one so that he could see the writing. It had the words *Dornier Do 17 Fliegender Bleistift* and a date, May 1943, written in a neat hand. The second had a similar label, but the number and date were different.

What immediately worried Drake was the fact that between both pistols there was a space, empty apart from another piece of yellow muslin cloth and a label laid on top of it with the same details as the others – there was a third pistol.

Behind the pistols were tin cases with German stencilling and various logbooks kept neatly as though they were exhibits in a museum.

'We need to arrest him, boss.'

'We need to find him.'

Drake reached for his mobile and called Price.

'Talbot has a firearm. Lives are at risk. We have evidence that Glyn Talbot is in possession of illegal firearms and that he had motive to kill Harry Jones and Heulwen Beard. I'm going to arrest him for murder.'

Price paused; Drake could hear his breathing.

'And one more thing, sir. I need authorisation for

an armed response unit.'

 'Of course. Ian, catch this madman.'

Chapter 38

'Where the hell would Maldwyn and Sioned have gone?' Drake leaned on his Mondeo and scrolled through his contacts for Winder's number.

Sara made no reply. He wasn't expecting her to.

She fumbled with something from the compartment in the passenger door. She offered Drake a can of soft drink and half a chocolate bar. He realised he hadn't eaten or drunk anything for hours. He took half in one hit and ate the snack quickly.

'If the halfway house café didn't offer the security Maldwyn needed they must be hiding somewhere else, somewhere more secure,' Drake said, feeling the beneficial effect of the sugar hit his system.

'I didn't get much out of the Owen family about his friends,' Sara said.

Drake called Winder. 'No change, boss. I'm in the army museum and they haven't seen Talbot since his last visit. Luned is down in the local library. He hasn't been seen there either. He mentioned visiting the library in the university so I'm off there now.'

'And Muller and Fiona Jones?' Drake held his breath.

'The Mullers haven't moved and Fiona arrived back in the house half an hour ago.'

Drake let out a long breath. 'Thanks, Gareth.'

Drake straightened. 'Fiona Jones is back home now. Assuming I am correct that Maldwyn is the only surviving eyewitness to Heulwen's murder by Talbot then Talbot will want Maldwyn dead. And if Talbot hasn't found him already Maldwyn must be hiding somewhere, keeping Sioned safe as well.'

'I'll try calling some of his friends,' Sara said.

Drake pulled open the car door. 'In the meantime we go back and see the Owen family.'

By the time Drake reached the main road leading to Llanberis Sara had spoken to three of Maldwyn's friends. She shook her head after finishing each call. 'No luck, boss.'

Drake found himself in a queue behind a minibus hauling a trolley full of kayaks. There was no way he could overtake. He slowed, allowing a reasonable distance between him and the next car.

'What does Maldwyn do for a living?'

'He's a joiner for a building company. There was no explanation for his absence this morning.'

Drake's mind ran through the alternatives for how Maldwyn might protect himself and Sioned. On the opposite side of the road a builder's merchant's lorry craned a palette of blocks into a nearby building site. The driver had a long ponytail and the operation took Drake's gaze as an idea formed in his mind.

'Get hold of one of his workmates. Find out where they were working this week.'

Sara did as she was told and moments later she was shouting into the mobile telephone. When he heard her ask 'where are you?', and repeated back the name Fox and Hounds, he changed down into third gear, tried to spot an opening to overtake but they were almost into the village so he didn't bother.

'I take it one of his pals is in the pub.'

Sara nodded. 'I'm not sure you'll get much sense from them. It's a Friday afternoon, after all.'

After parking Drake and Sara trotted over to the pub. 'Folsom Prison Blues' by Johnny Cash played a fraction too loudly and Drake wondered if Talbot had watched any of his victims die. Five men in their early twenties gathered around a small, round table packed with half-empty pint glasses.

Sara went up to them. 'Which one of you is Scott?'

'That's me, love.' He gave her lascivious wink after scanning her twice, very slowly.

Bad start, Drake thought.

'Outside, smartarse,' Sara said.

They stopped on the porch area.

Sara stood close enough to Scott for him to smell her breath. She pushed her warrant card into his face and poked him in the chest with a forefinger. 'Don't try and be clever. I need to know where Maldwyn was working this week.'

Scott stared at Sara. Drake could see the conflicting immature emotions in his face. He wanted to challenge Sara but in the end decided to cooperate.

'We were working on a new factory on the industrial estate. Clearing out old rubbish. Mal and me are both joiners – we shouldn't be doing crap like that.'

'And the week before,' Drake said.

'Dunno. I wasn't working with Mal.'

Sara continued. 'So who can tell us where he was working?'

'Try Jack, the foreman.' Scott made to push past Sara.

'Not so fast. We need a contact number for Jack.'

Scott gave an exaggerated sigh, plunged a hand into a pocket and scrolled through his mobile. Then he dictated a number. 'Can I go now? It's Friday night, I want to get pissed.'

Drake made the call.

'Detective Inspector Drake. One of your joiners Maldwyn Owen has disappeared and his life may be in danger. He could be holed up in one of the empty properties where he has been working. I need details of all the barely habitable properties where he has been working.'

'It might take me some time.'

'I need the details now.' Drake raised his voice.

'Okay, calm down.'

Calm down.

'This is a murder enquiry, you cretin. I need the information right now.'

The minute that elapsed felt like ten until he heard the foreman's voice again. Drake nodded at Sara.

'I've got an address.'

Sara tapped the postcode into the satnav. Drake almost collided with a car turning into the car park as he left. He reminded Sara to direct the armed response vehicle to the new location and he listened as she called operational control.

Drake blasted the horn at a car dawdling at twenty-five miles an hour. He shouted profanities at the driver.

The barn conversion was in an isolated spot near one of the villages close to Caernarfon.

Drake parked on the road outside. A length of fencing slotted together formed the outer perimeter of the building site. The place looked quiet; Drake started having doubts that his theory was correct. He got out of the car as a message reached his mobile explaining that the armed response vehicle was delayed by a four-car pile-up on the A55. Traffic police were removing the debris to make it safe for the vehicle to pass. For now Drake and Sara were on their own.

He unlocked the fencing sections and ran over to the building.

New windows and doors had already been fitted. He pushed open the door; bags of cement and plaster lined the wall to his right. At the far end of the passageway bits of plasterboard had been thrown into one corner alongside offcuts of timber.

A moment's hesitation crossed his mind that his stab vest was no protection against a bullet.

He should wait for the armed response vehicle where a bulletproof vest would be available. He dismissed his concerns. He had to prevent more loss of life. He owed it to Sioned and his brother. And for a second Drake thought about his father, what he might think knowing his granddaughter was in danger. He would do everything to protect his family. At the end of the hallway, Drake entered a corridor, a staircase ahead of him.

Sara was behind him. There was an odd aroma in the air. Sara rubbed her nose; Drake nodded. It smelled like day-old takeaway Chinese. Drake's pulse beat a little faster knowing someone had eaten food here. Two large double doors led into a tentative sitting room and Drake peered in. Bare wires hung out of square metal boxes in the walls and dangled down from holes in the ceiling.

Back in the corridor Drake reached the end and inspected the kitchen. It too was empty. Drake pressed on to complete the search. Maldwyn would have found somewhere safe for Sioned. Surely Glyn Talbot wouldn't discover them here?

At the bottom of the staircase Drake stopped; there was a scratching sound from upstairs.

He turned to look at Sara; she frowned, glancing at the stairs.

Luckily the risers didn't creak as Drake and Sara ventured slowly upstairs. Drake fingered his service baton. It reassured him, but not as much as having two armed officers behind him. He counted four doors on the top floor. He pushed open the first; the various units for a bathroom were propped up against a wall in their boxes. Water pipes protruded from the walls and a large stain covered the floor.

The second room was empty too. Electricians had been working on the third judging by the fitted switches and lights. At the end of the landing in the final room tall boxes of fitted wardrobes dominated the space but what took Drake's attention was the strong odour of stale food.

'What's that smell?' Sara said.

Before Drake could reply he heard movement from behind the unpacked furniture. A figure appeared, wielding a long piece of timber that she swung viciously towards Drake and Sara. They jumped out of the way as Sioned lost her balance and fell in a heap on the floor.

Chapter 39

Sioned sobbed with relief when she realised it was Drake and Sara. Drake kicked the piece of timber to one side. Sara fussed over Sioned, making certain she was unharmed.

'I need you to tell me what happened,' Drake said.

Sioned gathered her composure, taking large lungfuls of breath. 'Once Maldwyn learned about Frank he got completely spooked. He told us we were in danger. He said we had to find somewhere safe.'

'You should have called me.'

'Maldwyn wouldn't listen. He panicked.'

Drake knelt down. Sioned wasn't making any sense. He needed to get a clear picture, learn precisely what Maldwyn had witnessed.

'Sioned, tell me exactly what Maldwyn told you.' Gradually Sioned calmed down, her breathing evened out and she glanced at Sara who smiled, then at Drake who gave her an encouraging look.

'He was there.'

'What do you mean?'

'Heulwen Beard hadn't charged Mal for some legal advice. Mal and Frank had been fishing. So Frank agreed they'd leave her two salmon.'

'So Maldwyn was at Heulwen Beard's house the morning she was murdered.'

Sioned nodded. Then she caught her breath.

Drake continued but his mouth was dry. 'Did Mal see who killed her?'

Sioned started to shake. 'He heard them arguing.'

'Did he see the man, recognise him?'

Sioned drew hair from her face – she looked tired

and dirty. 'He said it was Glyn Talbot.'

A vice suddenly released the tension suffocating Drake. There had been two eyewitnesses – Frank Smith and Maldwyn. Now he had to find Maldwyn before Glyn Talbot did.

The sound of footsteps on concrete and then heavy boots on the staircase drifted into the room. Seconds later two heavily armed police officers appeared in the doorway. Drake and Sara held aloft their warrant cards.

'Constable Warren,' the older of the officers said, introducing himself. 'And this is Constable Jack Pike.'

Both men scanned the room, and then Sioned. 'Do you still need us, sir? We shall have to report to the SFC.'

Superintendent Price would be the strategic firearms commander. Any decision authorising the discharge of their weapons would have to be taken by him. They were a long way from any such decision.

'You can return to your vehicle for the time being.'

Warren and Pike nodded, relaxed a fraction and exited the building.

Drake turned back to Sioned who gradually composed herself. If the sight of two muscular, heavily armed police officers couldn't reassure her then nothing would.

'Why did Maldwyn leave?'

'Carwyn, his brother, texted him.'

Drake glanced at Sara. She shared the tightening knot of worry in his stomach.

Drake tried not to sound fearful. 'Do you know where he went?'

Sioned bit her lip nervously. 'He didn't say. He looked worried, I mean proper worried.'

Stephen Puleston

Sioned blinked away tears as she shook her head. Sara held her arms as they walked out and over to Drake's car. The armed response vehicle was parked immediately behind his Mondeo, both officers standing, wide-legged, nearby. The radio crackled.

Drake's mobile went off. He recognised Superintendent Price's number.

'Update,' Price said.

Deploying firearms officers happened so rarely in Northern Division of the WPS that it sharpened every officer's attention, made brevity an art form.

'We rescued Sioned Jackson. Negative on Maldwyn Owen. I'm taking her back to Llanberis.'

'Keep me informed.'

Drake rang off and immediately called Gareth Winder.

'Where are you, Gareth?'

'Outside Glyn Talbot's property. There's no sign of him anywhere, boss. The place looks deserted.'

'Do house-to-house. Somebody must have seen him; somebody must know where he is.'

'Yes, boss.'

'No sign of Glyn Talbot?' Sara said.

Drake shook his head. 'He can't simply disappear off the face of the earth.'

Sioned sat in the back seat of the car shivering when Drake reached for his mobile and dialled Huw Jackson's number. 'She's safe.'

'Thank Christ for that. She is all right? I mean … unharmed.'

Drake glanced at Sioned. 'You can talk to her yourself.' He gave Sioned his mobile and leaned

340

against the car while she reassured her father she was in one piece, and safe.

Drake knew how he'd feel if either of his daughters had been caught up in something like this. It would be like staring into some bottomless pit. He did not want to imagine it. He glanced inside; Sioned was crying now. He read the time; they had to get back to Llanberis. Something had lured Maldwyn away. Computing everything they now knew about Glyn Talbot gave him grounds to arrest him for murder: the argument with Harry Jones, his history of intimidation at work and his obsession with the bomb storage facility which led him to kill Heulwen Beard when she refused to agree not to sell the land. He cursed himself that he hadn't made the connection earlier. Talbot had been the first at the scene of her death. His demeanour that day had been dismissed as distress, anguish, but Drake saw it now as guilt.

He motioned for the armed response team to follow him and he got into his car as Sioned finished the call. She passed him the handset only for it to ring immediately. It was area control. 'There's an urgent message for you to contact the family of Maldwyn Owen.'

Drake dialled the number.

A man's voice answered, instantly drowned out by a woman crying hysterically in the background. Then she demanded to speak. There was a fumbling as the receiver was passed from one hand to the next.

'It's Carwyn.' Drake recognised Liz Owen's voice. She broke up. 'He's gone too. Both of my boys, gone.'

'What do you mean?'

Nobody listened to Drake's question; it sounded

like the handset had fallen on the floor and was being kicked around like a football. Seconds later Andy Owen continued.

'Carwyn, our youngest, has gone missing.'

'I'll be with you as quickly as I can.'

Chapter 40

Seeing Drake and Sara walking into the sitting room of
her home only exacerbated Liz Owen's hysteria. Her
eyes bulged, and she let out a morbid whimper.

Andy Owen turned to look at Drake. His voice
croaked. 'You've got to find them.'

'Tell me exactly what happened. How do you
know he's missing?'

'He's not answering his mobile and he *always*
answers it.' Andy blinked away some tears. 'Carwyn
told one of his friends Maldwyn was in trouble.'

Liz sobbed again. Andy sat down by her side and
wrapped his arm around her shoulder.

'Have you found Maldwyn?' Andy's voice broke.

Drake shook his head.

'We'll need to speak to Carwyn's friends. Where
can I contact them?'

'Two doors down,' Andy said. 'Ask for Arwel.'

As Drake left he turned to Sara. 'Get operational
support to find a family liaison officer.'

Sara fumbled for her mobile. Both officers from
the armed response vehicle straightened when Drake
left the house but relaxed when he waved at them to
stand easy.

Once Drake had persuaded an angry-looking man
in his early forties that his son wasn't implicated in any
illegality he showed him into a sitting room similar to
the one at the Owen family. Arwel lounged on a sofa,
trying and failing to appear a nonchalant fourteen-year-
old. His Adam's apple bobbed up and down as Drake
and Sara questioned him. 'I didn't see nobody.'

'You're not in any trouble, Arwel. I need you to

tell me what you saw.'

'I'm not going to grass on anybody.'

Drake wanted to shout. This was a youngster who watched far too much television.

'For Christ's sake grow up. Your mate Carwyn has disappeared. Tell me everything you know. Now.'

Arwel's nostrils flared; he stared at Drake and then at Sara. 'I was walking back with Carwyn. He got this text message. He said that Maldwyn was in trouble. Carwyn wanted to meet up with somebody who could help.'

'Did he say where he was going?'

Arwel looked away.

'Your friend's life depends on this. Did he say who this other person was?'

Arwel shook his head.

'Where the hell was he going?'

'I can't be certain.' Arwel looked at his father who gave him a stern, reproachful glare. 'Before he left he said something about Barracks Mon.'

Drake recalled the photographs of the two facing terraces of derelict properties on the mountainside above the village. In the nineteenth century, quarrymen from Ynys Mon, the Welsh name for the nearby island of Anglesey, used the houses as lodgings during the week.

Drake stood for a moment staring at this youngster. They had nothing else to go on.

If Talbot had taken Carwyn in order to entice Maldwyn to meet him, there was every possibility that both boys' lives were at risk. Arwel's father mentioned something about a footpath up to Barracks Mon.

'Show me.' Drake fumbled for his mobile; it took

him seconds to find the map of the village.

The path zigzagged its way up the side of the mountain over the disused inclines that led down to the site of the slate museum. Barracks Mon were shown as two rows of tiny squares on the map open on his screen. He turned to Sara, and nodded for the door.

They reached the armed response vehicle and gave both officers a summary. The boot was flipped open. Warren found torches and then handed Drake and Sara heavy bulletproof vests. As Drake tightened the Velcro straps around his waist his stomach felt granite-hard.

Five minutes later they were double-parked at the bottom of the walled footpath that led up to Barracks Mon and the inclines that would have taken men up to the top of the quarries for their morning shift.

A milky moon cast occasional blankets of light.

Both armed officers checked in with Superintendent Price. Earpieces were clipped into place, microphones discreetly pinned to their jackets. Drake hoped that nobody would be killed. But he wasn't ready to take any chances.

It had to be Glyn Talbot.

There might even be some historical link to Barracks Mon that fascinated this obsessed and sick individual. Something that would make him value being there when he killed Maldwyn Owen and his brother Carwyn. It would be the last link to an eyewitness to the death of Heulwen Beard. Without Maldwyn's evidence Talbot probably thought he would be in the clear. Drake didn't see Talbot happily confessing his guilt.

They started up the track, its surface covered with broken shards of slate of varying size. The sharp edges would ruin his shoes, but Drake decided to pay no attention to his petty worries. He led the way, Sara following behind him. By the time Drake, Sara and the two officers had reached the first 90-degree turn in the path Drake was breathing heavily; he could feel the sweat running down his neck. Sara stood for a moment gathering her breath, but she seemed unaffected, as did both officers.

'Let's get on, sir,' Warren said. It wasn't a criticism: simply a statement of fact.

Drake pressed on, the beam from the torch bouncing around the walls of the footpath that must have been four feet high, carefully constructed from slabs of slate. Thousands of men had tramped this route on their way to work every day blasting the slate, risking their lives to roof the world.

The path rose gently until it turned back on itself and the gradient increased. The width narrowed and Drake's heart pounded, his feet fumbling on the uneven surface. He missed a footfall and fell heavily against the wall, breaking his fall with a hand. He winced in pain, wanting to cry out but he muffled any shout. The torch crashed to the floor and illuminated the side wall. Sara picked it up. 'You all right, boss?'

'Just a scratch.'

Drake shone the torch over his right hand. There was blood all over his fingers. He ignored the pain and discomfort. 'Let's carry on.'

After the path double backed again it was a short distance until it began a severe ascent as a bridge crossed a section of the incline. For a moment Drake peered down and scanned the workings where large slabs of slate would have descended from the quarry. They pushed on upwards. The retaining walls of the pathway had now given way to a forest track.

After five minutes Drake noticed the faint outline of the chimney stacks of the Barracks Mon terraces. He slowed and raised a hand to his companions, signalling they had arrived. He listened, but all he could hear was the humming of the hydroelectric power station deep in the heart of the mountain. Something made a scratching noise off to his left, more scared of him than he was of it. He took a step nearer, still under the cover of trees, and he looked down the trackway that divided both terraces. Everything was quiet, no sound and no light. For a fraction of a second it struck him that he was too late: all he would find would be the bodies of two brothers and no evidence.

Warren and Pike silently scanned the derelict properties in front of them. A voice whispered in his earpiece. 'We need him out in the open. In the middle of that space between the terraces,' Warren said.

The night vision scopes they clipped onto the rifles made the task of shooting at night easier. Drake hoped it wouldn't happen. Warren ran through his standard procedure with the strategic firearms commander back at headquarters.

'I think we should find somewhere less conspicuous,' Sara whispered.

Drake moved into the shadows with her. They waited. He glanced at his watch, exchanging a frustrated look with Sara. If nothing happened in the next ten minutes, Drake thought, we will call the whole thing off, return to Llanberis.

Ten minutes passed. Drake stayed put.

Another ten minutes elapsed. The damp of the mountain seeped into his bones. He shivered.

Suddenly he spotted movement at the far end of the terrace. A man darted into the first house. Drake couldn't make out who it was or make out his age. He was agile though. Drake half got to his feet but Warren's gentle voice in his ear spoke. 'Be careful, Inspector.'

The man moved quickly to the second house along the same row. And then to the third. He paused in the oblong hole where the door must have hung.

A shout broke the silence. 'Maldwyn, over here.' It sounded like an older man. Drake strained to recognise if it was Talbot's voice.

Warren and Pike exchanged some garbled message Drake didn't follow but assumed it meant they were ready.

The first man stepped out onto the pathway that separated the two terraces and Drake's chest tightened as he recognised Maldwyn Owen. From the derelict house opposite another man appeared, jacket lapels pulled high up to his neck and face. Held in his outstretched hand was a pistol pointed straight at Maldwyn's chest.

He gesticulated for the young man to kneel.

Maldwyn did as he was told. The man with the gun moved closer, preparing to do his worst.

'I'm going in,' Drake said.

'Negative, sir. We have an imminent threat to life.'

Drake ignored him.

'Fire on my command. I'm in charge.' Drake got to his feet and jogged down towards both men.

'Glyn Talbot. Put the gun down.'

When the man holding a pistol turned sharply Drake could see his face. Even in the gloom he could tell Glyn Talbot had become obsessed to the point of madness, hatred.

'Go to hell.'

Drake paced over towards him and stopped a few metres from Talbot. 'Don't kill another man. We know it was you.'

Warren's voice was a murmur. 'Clear shot, sir. Don't move.'

'I know about your grandfather. It must have been terrible knowing he was buried in that quarry.'

Talbot took a half turn towards Drake. 'How dare you. It's contemptuous to suggest you know anything about me. You're just a policeman scratching around in your pathetic little world.'

'And I know about Matthew.'

Talbot's arm and hand pointing the gun at Maldwyn trembled.

'Don't bring him into any of this.'

'I've seen the DNA report.'

Talbot shouted now. 'What … you've been into … you had no right.'

'It's over, Glyn. I'm arresting you for murder. You don't have to say anything—'

Talbot laughed out hysterically. 'You haven't got any evidence. And I've got the gun. You haven't.' He turned to the man by his feet. 'Tell me, Maldwyn, what did you see? What did your friend see?' Talbot raised the hand holding the gun and brought it down on Maldwyn's forehead with a bone crunching sound.

Luckily it was a glancing blow and the young man got back to his knees.

Drake thought he heard a chuckle in Talbot's voice. Then he lowered his hand, pointing the gun directly at Maldwyn Owen's forehead.

The decision should have been the hardest of his career. But he took it in an instant. 'Take the shot.'

Chapter 41

A bullet hurtled past Drake and tore into Glyn Talbot's head, propelling him into the dirt and weeds. Drake bolted over towards him, fixing his eyes on the pistol that lay a few inches from Talbot's knees. He wasn't going to take any chances. He picked up the gun as both firearms officers joined him. Sara stood over Maldwyn, helping him to his feet.

Drake handed the weapon to Warren before kneeling over Glyn Talbot. Checking for life signs was pointless. A gaping wound replaced his right eye where the bullet had crashed through his brain.

'Where's Carwyn?' Maldwyn said.

'Call headquarters.' Drake shouted. A firearm had been discharged; it meant protocols to be followed. 'You know the drill – secure the scene.' He turned to Sara and Maldwyn. 'What did Talbot say about Carwyn?'

'He said … that he had Carwyn … and that I had to …' Maldwyn shared a glance with Drake and Sara. 'You don't think he's dead, do you?'

'Let's search all the buildings and if he isn't here then …'

Drake and Sara started searching each of the abandoned houses along the north side of Barracks Mon while Maldwyn did the opposite terrace. The armed officers reported back to headquarters and the flurry of conversation about their exact location, the status of Glyn Talbot and Maldwyn echoed around the derelict properties. Drake and Sara flicked on the torch function of their telephones and swept the light around the first property. Crisp packets and empty bottles of cheap cider probably left by youngsters partying littered the ground. At the rear, the mountain was beginning to encroach into the properties: gorse bushes and the occasional thorn tree pushing their way into what remained of the houses. They hurried into the second property, but it had more thick undergrowth and no evidence of activity. Retreating back onto the path they met Maldwyn as he emerged from the other terrace, light from their mobiles bouncing over each other's faces.

'Jesus, I hope he's all right,' Maldwyn said before resuming his search.

Drake and Sara did the same.

Two derelict properties from the end Drake stumbled on a small rucksack leaning against a wall. He shouted at Sara. 'In here.'

Moments later she joined him. They waved their mobile phones carefully hoping for some sign of movement or sound. Out of the back of the property Drake noticed a section of thick weeds and brambles had been disturbed. He pushed through, stepping over the remains of a low wall.

He almost lost his balance; a length of bramble caught his jacket. Drake swatted it away only for it to catch on the back of his hand and he winced again. A couple of metres away he spotted a figure lying on the ground huddled in the foetal position. Drake turned to Sara. 'He's over here.'

He stamped the gorse and weeds away with a foot and reached down. When the body twitched, Drake shouted with relief. 'He's alive, call an ambulance.'

He knelt down and seconds later Sara was with him and then Maldwyn who frantically clawed at the thick rope holding his brother's knees and ankles securely. Carwyn's hands were bound behind him. Drake yanked off a black cotton sack pulled over his head. Initially Carwyn recoiled but then his eyes realised it wasn't Glyn Talbot and he saw his brother. Once Drake removed the duct tape covering his mouth he wept with relief.

By the time they had been able to move Carwyn to the front of the terrace a team of crime scene investigators had arrived. The process of securing the scene had begun. Drake's work had finished. There would be an investigation; there always was when a firearm was discharged. There would be paperwork three feet deep and awkward questions. But when Drake looked over at Carwyn standing with Maldwyn he knew it was all worthwhile. Lives had been saved.

Two paramedics arrived, breathless and sweating. Blood pressures were taken, eyes examined and pulses measured. Nothing more could be done without proper equipment and they insisted Carwyn be taken to hospital. Maldwyn joined his brother as they left Barracks Mon. Drake suspected neither of them would want to come back to this place for a long time.

Sara and Drake said very little as they descended the footpath.

Drake took his time finding a secure route. Weariness made him more careful that he didn't topple over and crack his head against the slate walls. He was glad when they arrived on the tarmac at the bottom.

Apart from his Mondeo and the armed response vehicle there were a scientific support vehicle, and two more marked police cars, lights still flashing, officers establishing a perimeter. It occurred to Drake that perhaps he should tell them not to bother. The case was solved. The murderer had been identified but he wouldn't be put before a court. There'd be no publicity for the papers to report.

The death of Glyn Talbot would earn no more than a byline.

The Wales Police Service would announce they weren't looking for anyone else in relation to the murders of Harry Jones, Heulwen Beard and Frank Smith. The press release would expressly make clear Glyn Talbot was the killer and that an independent enquiry would in due course report how a police officer had come to kill him.

Drake was certain nobody would care what the report concluded.

In the distance Drake could see a crowd of locals gathering, raising arms, gesticulating. The whole saga would go down in local folklore, discussed over pints of beer in the village pubs, spoken of in hushed tones in the cafés.

'Let's go and see the Owen family,' Drake said.

Drake arrived at the Owen household as the two paramedics he had seen earlier were escorting Carwyn back to the vehicle. One of them turned to Drake. 'We've had a hell of a struggle getting him and his mother to agree that he needs to spend the night in hospital. He has to be checked over.'

Carwyn gave Drake a half-hearted smile. The second paramedic took one look at Drake's bloodstained clothes and hands. 'It looks like you should go to the hospital too. When did you last have a tetanus injection?'

Drake shrugged. 'It's only a scratch.'

'Let me clean it up for you.' The paramedic ushered Drake back into the kitchen. Drake could hear the sound of Sioned's voice and that of Huw Jackson from the sitting room. Drake's wound was swabbed and cleaned and a bandage wrapped around. 'I really think you need to get a tetanus booster injection.'

'Okay.'

The paramedic left Drake with a beaming Andy Owen unable to disguise the delight on his face. He thrust a mug of milky sweet coffee at Drake. 'I want to thank you for saving my boys' lives.' His eyes watered.

'I'm glad they're alive.' Drake surprised himself by enjoying the hot comforting drink that he took through into the sitting room. There wasn't a single place to sit. Various neighbours had congregated and were reliving the excitement of the events that evening minute by minute. Despite deep bags under her eyes Liz Owen looked elated.

Huw Jackson stood up abruptly when he saw Drake. 'Ian, I'm so glad to see you. What happened to your hand?'

The bandage the paramedics had applied exaggerated the wound to his hand. 'It's nothing.' Sioned joined her father and gave Drake an enormous hug, gripping him tightly.

Drake left soon after acknowledging their grateful thanks.

He stood on the doorstep with Sara feeling the chill of the autumn air. A marked police car swept up the road and parked outside the property. Superintendent Price got out, pulling on his peaked cap and overcoat. 'Good job, Ian.' He glanced at Sara. 'And that goes for you, too, Sara.'

His gaze moved to the house behind them. 'I assume this is the home of the Owen family?'

'Yes, sir,' Drake said.

Price nodded at Drake's bandage. 'Are you going to hospital for that to be seen to?'

'I'm on my way there now.'

'Good, excellent.' Price switched into senior officer public relations mode. 'I'll go and talk to the family.'

Drake found the keys to his Mondeo and drove away from Llanberis fully intending to make his way to the hospital but by the time he reached Felinheli his eyes burned and he knew he wasn't fit to drive. Instead, he drove down to Annie's house and parked behind her car. Getting out he rang the doorbell. She was surprised to see him and shocked to see his hand. He ignored her suggestions he go to accident and emergency. A few minutes later Drake was sitting on a sofa with a glass of whisky in the hand that wasn't bandaged. He heard Annie insisting that he promise to visit the nurse the following morning. He mumbled his agreement before resting his eyes and falling fast asleep.

Chapter 42

Mair Drake stood on the threshold of her back door as Drake left his car with Helen and Megan. His sister's Mercedes estate was parked next to his mother's Fiesta. It was less than a year old – George, her husband, must be doing well, Drake thought. He struggled to recall when he had seen his sister last and he knew it disappointed his mother they weren't closer.

Huw wasn't expected for another two hours, which would give him time to catch up with Susan and her sons. His mother hugged her granddaughters and kissed Drake lightly on the cheek.

'Susan's in the parlour.' Her voice didn't mask her apprehension. 'I'll make tea,' Mair announced as Drake took his daughters through to see their aunt.

Susan was on her feet when Drake entered and she gave him a warm smile. She had gained some weight, he thought, and there were more wrinkles around her eyes and a fatigued look in them. Whenever they spoke on the telephone she complained about her busy lifestyle, which evidently impacted on her health.

She turned to the two boys on the sofa. 'Say hello to your Uncle Ian.'

Rowland and Marc gave Drake unconvincing smiles.

It reminded Drake of the last time he'd seen them when they'd shouted at their mother that they hated her and demanded to go back to Cardiff. Mair Drake had said little when she had seen Drake after Susan had left that time but her silence spoke volumes.

'Hello Helen, Megan, how are you both?' Susan managed to sound intensely disinterested. 'You can tell me about school later. Why don't you go and watch some television with Rowland and Marc?'

His daughters scanned their cousins as though they were mute foreigners.

Susan lowered her voice once they were alone. 'Now tell me about Huw Jackson. You must brief me fully. What is he really like?'

Drake found a rhythm as he talked with his sister about their brother. He skirted over how they had met through Huw's involvement in another case. Susan had persuaded herself Huw was a fake somehow with an ulterior motive, making her uneasy and wary. Drake made certain she understood that by knowing Huw they would get to know their father better.

Mair brought tea and sat on the edge of a sofa, contributing occasionally to the conversation. Time passed until the sound of a car on the gravel of the drive interrupted them. Susan gave Drake an uncertain look he hadn't seen before. Huw, Sioned and her brother Wil arrived on the threshold of the kitchen, looking hesitant.

Introductions completed, they all sat in the parlour. Huw carried a small photograph album. 'I thought you might like to see these. I found it in my mother's things after she died.'

Tears welled up in Mair's eyes as she saw the faded images of Tom with Huw's mother when he was a young man. He looked cheerful, happy even. They smiled at the camera as they embraced.

'Do you see your American relations?' Susan said.

Drake thought she sounded genuine and her expression was open and interested.

'I've been over a few times and they've visited me too.'

What remained unsaid was the connection Huw's family had with Mair and Susan and Ian Drake. It could wait for another time.

It had occurred to Drake that perhaps he should have warned Sioned to be circumspect about what she had been through. But when they gathered in the kitchen Sioned immediately launched into a detailed recounting of the recent events in Llanberis, explaining to the wide-eyed family audience how Drake saved her life and that he was a hero. Drake tried to shrug off the attention. He sensed genuine concern from Susan. 'You could have been killed.'

'These police marksmen are amazing shots,' Huw said, sounding knowledgeable.

An enormous spread was laid out on the table. Sausage rolls, quiches, chicken legs and an indulgent trifle. The new extended Drake/Jackson family fell into a comfortable relaxed exchange of life stories and Drake smiled to himself as he thought about Susan's initial reluctance to meet her brother. He wasn't going to make any demands, was normal, balanced and valued family life. As they did.

Huw Jackson's offer to help with the washing up was politely declined. Huw, Sioned and Wil left soon after. Drake stood with Susan alongside their mother as they washed and dried the dishes. Mair Drake's contented air told Drake she was pleased that things had gone smoothly.

At the end of the afternoon Drake organised to take his daughters home and he kissed Susan and his mother and said goodbye to his nephews, pleased they had behaved.

Tiredness overwhelmed Drake when he returned to

Annie's home. He threw his jacket onto a chair and he slumped onto the sofa by her side. He had wanted her to be there, introduce her to his mother, Susan and to Helen and Megan but she had persuaded him it was too soon.

'How did it go?' Annie said.

'Better than I had expected.'

'Did your mother think it was a success?'

Drake smiled. 'Yes, I think so. And Susan actually managed to be friendly.'

'So you don't want anything else to eat?'

'No, thanks. I'm exhausted. I'm going to have a shower.'

Annie moved to sit alongside him on the sofa, and ran a finger over his cheek and around his jaw. 'Would you like some company?'

Chapter 43

The chairman of the magistrates was an old friend of Drake's father; he gave Drake a discreet nod as he entered the courtroom. The woman to his left had tight blonde curls and a severe set to her jaw. The magistrate to his right had a blue rinse and a row of expensive-looking pearls around her neck that made her look blingy.

Various reporters sat against one wall. It was about the only newsworthy thing from the killing of Harry Jones and Heulwen Beard and Frank Smith. There wasn't going to be a trial after all. A simple two-line statement from the Wales Police Service confirmed their investigation was closed. All it meant was that no one else was being sought but there was still a pile of paperwork to be completed. Drake could ill afford to take the morning off to listen to the case against Fiona Jones.

The Crown prosecution lawyers had been as generous as possible with the charges she faced. Usually the background and the extent of the damage should have meant the case being heard in the Crown Court, but Fiona Jones had paid several thousand pounds to Wolfgang Muller and his wife for the cost of the repairs that helped persuade the magistrates to deal with her locally.

Looking at Fiona sitting in the dock, Drake found it hard now to believe she could have been a realistic suspect. The pretend world of half-truths and nods and winks that passed for real life for her when Harry was alive, and which made her life a mixture of embarrassment and pent-up anger had all come to an end. Did she feel some catharsis, Drake wondered. Perhaps she could get on with the rest of her life without people gossiping behind her back, sympathising that she was a cuckolded wife. She could be her own person now.

After the charges were read to her and her guilty plea entered Drake listened to the Crown prosecutor who sketched out the facts in undemonstrative, straightforward terms. It would be the task of the defence lawyer to stand up and mitigate on her behalf.

Dafydd Upton impressed Drake. He began confidently. 'My client accepts all the facts outlined by the prosecution.'

Drake mentally ticked off each positive point Upton made in favour of the magistrates dealing with Fiona Jones leniently. She had paid the compensation for the damage to the cars, she was genuinely contrite, and would readily pay any further compensation to Penny Muller the court deemed appropriate. Was there any risk of reoffending? Of course not. It helped that the Mullers had moved away. They had found a property in the Scottish Highlands they hoped to convert into a wellness centre. Bryn Hyfryd had been sold to a local authority in the south of England who were going to turn it into an outward bound centre for youngsters.

And more than anything Fiona Jones had lost her husband. Dafydd Upton paused before explaining to the magistrates in a soft voice how Harry Jones had been lured to his death and shot in cold blood by Glyn Talbot. It had been a lonely, shocking death. Fiona Jones would have to live with the trauma for the rest of her life, Upton explained.

Both women magistrates must have been the same age as Fiona, Drake guessed. He looked at the first and then the second, realising Dafydd Upton's mitigation was pushing at an open door. The sympathetic looks and the occasional glance over at Fiona made clear they were going to be lenient.

Once Upton finished, the court clerk announced the magistrates would retire to consider their decision. Upton went over to Fiona and gave her some warm words of encouragement because she briefly smiled. He nodded at Drake. Drake nodded back; perhaps he had been too harsh thinking Upton might not make a decent criminal advocate.

They didn't have to wait long for the magistrates to return.

Fiona stood up.

'This is a very difficult case …' The chairman pronounced solemnly.

He proceeded to impose a suspended custodial sentence as well as a sum in compensation payable within seven days to Penny Muller. Nobody in the courtroom was surprised. The journalists scurried out and Drake followed them, watching as they recorded pieces to the evening news broadcast on television. As Drake left the building one of them came up to him. 'Do you have a statement for the press?'

Drake shook his head slowly and carried on walking.

Brian Featherstone, the investigator from the independent police authority, removed his spectacles for the fourth time in less than an hour and cleaned them vigorously.

Drake looked over at Featherstone. He was a mousey little man with an intense stare and a hair-splitting manner, who Drake had taken a dislike to after the first question. Now Drake faced a grilling from the authorities who investigated whenever a police officer discharged a firearm so the interview was standard procedure.

'Explain to me *again* exactly where you were with your investigation.'

'We were about to arrest Glyn Talbot on suspicion of three murders.'

'But at that stage you didn't actually have all the evidence.'

'We had evidence of him intimidating Harry Jones from the CCTV coverage we recovered and he recently discovered Harry was the father of Matthew, his son. And he was completely obsessed about the bomb storage facility and keeping the place exactly as it was. We have eyewitnesses—'

'Eyewitness.'

Drake wanted to shout at this pedantic idiot.

'*Eyewitness* that confirms Talbot was in Heulwen Beard's home the morning she was killed. And we found evidence of the DNA result to make a compelling case that—'

'But Talbot is dead, Inspector. And he's not in a position to answer your *compelling case*.'

Policing would be so much easier without this moron, Drake thought.

'Did you demand Talbot lay down his weapon?'

'Yes.'

Featherstone peered over his glasses at Drake.

'I'm sure you're aware that I need to examine in minutiae every aspect of the decision to discharge a deadly weapon.'

Drake narrowed his eyes. Would Featherstone have stood there and watched Talbot kill Maldwyn Owen?

'There was a clear and present danger to the life of an innocent man.'

'I appreciate that but—'

'And we found Carwyn Owen bound and gagged in one of the derelict houses in Barracks Mon, which suggests to me and probably to any other police officer and any right-thinking member of a jury that Talbot intended to kill Maldwyn Owen and then his brother.'

'I appreciate that, Inspector—'

'What I don't think you appreciate or even understand is when I saw Talbot preparing to take a shot at Maldwyn Owen's forehead I didn't have a choice. I didn't have a chance to consult the fucking manual.'

'Bad language is uncalled for—'

Drake ignored him. 'An innocent man's life was at stake. And Talbot had killed three people. It wasn't a multiple-choice scenario. My priority was the preservation of life.' Drake stood up. Featherstone gave him a surprised look. 'You have my written statement, the statements from Detective Sergeant Morgan and the two firearms officers. Do you think for one moment it will be easy living with the decision I made to authorise the death of another human being?'

Featherstone settled into a stony glare.

'You know it was the right decision.'

Drake turned on his heel and left the investigator.

Over three weeks had elapsed and one Friday morning Drake was working on intelligence reports about a series of burglaries, but his mind was thinking about the executive suite he had booked at a five-star hotel in the Peak District with a luxurious swimming pool, spa and a Michelin-star restaurant. Since Wednesday his exchange of texts with Annie had become more flirty and it surprised him that he managed to feel so excited about a weekend away with his girlfriend.

When Superintendent Price appeared at the door to his office, Drake made to get up. Price waved him back to his seat. The superintendent passed a report onto his desk.

Drake could guess what it was.

'Featherstone has completely exonerated you. In fact, the authority complements you on the way you handled both the investigation and the events at Barracks Mon.'

Drake wanted to punch the air, do a jig around his room. A weight had been lifted from his mind even though he knew he had done nothing wrong.

'Thank you, sir.'

'Your team did well. Despite what happened there's no doubt that had Talbot been apprehended he'd have been spending the rest of his life behind bars. And I've heard from Overend too. They interviewed Perdue and Lennon and both came up with some cock-and-bull story about visiting Harry Jones who showed them the furniture in the lock-up as potential buyers. I don't think he was too pleased that he couldn't make a case against either man.'

Once Price left curiosity got the better of Sara

because she announced herself by tapping two fingers against his door. 'Did the superintendent have the report from …?'

'Yes, the investigation has absolved us of any blame.'

Drake sensed Sara's relief and gestured for her to sit. 'Have you seen the local paper?' He pointed to the corner of his desk. 'Apparently the bomb storage facility development will go ahead after all. Although Erdington was worried the grants might fall through, he was able to rescue the deal.'

Sara continued. 'The case had quite an effect on Luned because she has a family links with Llanberis. I'm sure it must be dramatic when you've got connections like hers. She heard Fiona Jones has got to know Harry's daughter. Apparently once she learned what happened the whole tracing your roots programme fizzled out.'

'Good, I hate those programmes – they seem so contrived.'

Sara nodded. 'Luned called to see Nancy Brown earlier this week for her to sign her final statement. She and Richard Perdue are now officially a couple.' Drake recalled the details from the hotel on the Wirral confirming Perdue's alibi but also a description of his companion – Nancy Brown. Sara continued. 'She has the house on the market and she's going to move in with Perdue. In January they're going on a world cruise.'

Sara got up. 'Doing anything nice this weekend?'

Drake smiled. He was leaving before lunch in less than an hour.

'Yes, as it happens I'm going for a fancy weekend

in the Peak District.'

Printed in Great Britain
by Amazon

60660733R00210